D1711315

DIVORCE CAN BE DEADLY

DR. BENJAMIN BONES MYSTERIES #2

EMMA JAMESON

LYONNESSE BOOKS

DEDICATION

To everyone who read *Marriage Can Be Murder* and waited,
patiently or impatiently, for the next installment: Thank you
from the bottom of my heart.

1

HAUNTED CORNWALL

27 NOVEMBER 1939

Two ghosts troubled Dr. Benjamin Bones. One he feared would never release him. Another he worried might slip away, however much he tightened his grip.

He'd arrived in the tiny village of Birdswing by government order. A native Londoner, he'd been fresh out of medical school when England declared war on Germany. It was hardly shocking, given Herr Hitler's pattern of aggression, but that made the grim news no easier to bear. The specter of the Great War still haunted England. Gallipoli and the Somme had claimed too many young men, killing them, maiming them, or driving them mad. By war's end their nation, once the world's wealthiest power, had collapsed into its biggest debtor. At the start of the Great War, many Britons had declared confidently "this will all be over by Christmas." Now they faced a second world war, and no one was whistling past the graveyard.

But that didn't mean the national mood was fatalistic or fearful. There was still pride, there was still hope, there was still willingness to do right, no matter the personal cost, and Ben believed such virtue would sustain them to victory. Nothing less than resounding victory would do, because the

Fuhrer's vision for the world was terrifying. And so in the winter of 1939, Ben found himself serving his country not as an Army doctor, but a country doctor, in a part of England like none other: Cornwall.

With its granite backbone, golden beaches, and windswept moors, Cornwall felt like a country apart. Certainly, the Cornish folk were a people apart, self-reliant and independent. Long before the Anglo-Saxons or the Romans, the West Country had been home to a seafaring people. They possessed their own language, culture, and forms of worship, as evidenced by the standing stones which remained. Only after a failed sixteenth century uprising did they even consent to name themselves English. New threats of revolution still bubbled up from time to time, mostly in the pub. Generally, Cornishmen were proud Englishmen, but in sentimental moments, their fiercest loyalty lay with the West Country.

Such loyalty didn't surprise Ben. There was a pull to this land, to its abandoned tin mines and jutting clifftops. During his Sunday afternoon rambles, he explored a coastline where, not so long ago, the wreckers plied their grim trade. With false beacons they'd lured merchant ships to crash on the rocks, seizing the plunder that washed ashore. Most of those sailors drowned. But occasionally while searching the shallows, the wreckers came across a man clinging to a bit of floating debris, and Ben could imagine what came next. A knife flashed; the sailor's throat opened in a hot gush. The flotsam was torn from his grip, and the sea drew the man to its bosom. Then the wreckers moved on, picking the beach clean.

Cornwall's neighboring county, Devon, was green and perfect, a land of velvet hills and pristine woods. By contrast, much of Cornwall was coastal. The rest was harder and wilder, framed by bramble and peppered with stone. In Cornwall, the legacy of the wreckers lingered. Memories of murder, of yellow lanterns and icy steel, had seeped into its granite bones, and granite does not forget.

Or so says Madame Daragon, thought Ben. He was seated in his front room with the Victorian psychic's book, *Revelations of a Reluctant Medium*, in his lap.

His Monday morning had not been entirely successful. Or in the common parlance, a comedy of errors. He hadn't slept well, for a start. Around four o'clock in the morning, a curious knocking in the attic had awakened him. When one lived in a haunted cottage, phantom noises weren't shocking. This particular knocking might have been a spectral attempt at communication, or it might have been squirrels moving in for the winter. Like many householders, Ben found the prospect of a squirrel infestation more ominous. He had enough on his plate without adding amateur carpentry.

At some point after the knocking he'd dropped off again, only to be rudely awakened when his alarm clock rang at five minutes past five, almost a full hour early. He didn't know if the blasted thing had turned temperamental or if it was another signal from the spirit world, but it started his day on a sour note. It seemed too early for breakfast, so he'd decided to take a walk as part of his ongoing effort at self-rehabilitation.

In late September, he'd broken both legs. That meant he'd spent much of October either lying in bed or sitting in a wheelchair. Getting back on his feet had taken considerable effort, first with crutches, then with a cane. His ultimate hope was to ditch the cane altogether, but as the days grew shorter and colder, his limp became more pronounced. Sometimes his right leg ached after a long day with patients, but his left leg was trickier.

Shattered in the accident, his left leg had healed better than his doctor predicted, which wasn't saying much. His thigh ached where the femur had snapped; his knee was swollen upon waking, and buckled if he pushed himself too much. He'd probably progressed as far as youth and good fortune could take him, but he still resented relying on cane. So despite the fact he owned an Austin Ten-Four, and had been granted a special petrol dispensation by the Birdswing Council, he walked as often as possible, hoping exercise would yield further improvement.

That morning he'd gone up the high street, through the village green, and around to Mallow Street, which led to a maze of narrow streets and old cottages, many lopsided and eccentric, that made up the heart of Birdswing. On Pigmeadow Lane, he'd looked in on a patient, Mrs. Smith, who was currently bedridden with rheumatoid arthritis. She hadn't appreciated his early appearance.

"I've only just dropped off after a night of tossing and turning," she'd complained. "Bring me that bed jacket, will you? Cornwall is meant to be temperate. This year everything has gone to the devil. First the war, now the winter." Buttoning the woolen bed jacket up to her chin, she'd snuggled under her quilt. When Ben had asked if he might at least listen to her heart and check for bedsores, his only reply was a phony snore.

Suspecting his other homebound patients might respond in similar fashion, Ben had given up on house calls and chosen to walk toward Little Creek instead. The creek served as Birdswing's unofficial northern boundary, just as Pate's Field created a buffer between Birdswing and Barking. But as he passed Mrs. Archer's restaurant, a pebble had struck his back.

"Oi! Fritz!" A broad-shouldered boy of about nine sat in the branches of a nearby elm, slingshot in hand. A shock of black hair hung over one eye. "That bullet was dipped in poison from darkest Africa. You'll die an agonizing death in mere seconds!"

"Yes, well, if you put out someone's eye with one of those pebbles, an agonizing death is the best you'll get from me," he said, and instantly regretted it. He sounded old before his time, like a geezer who collected garden gnomes, forever shouting threats at the neighborhood kids.

The boy, an Archer twin, didn't take the threat to heart. Fitting another pebble to the slingshot's ammunition pocket, he cried, "More Jerries!" The pebble whizzed past Ben, striking someone behind him.

"*Nein! Nein!*" cried the other boy, identical to the one in the tree. "A flesh wound. *Ja*, only a flesh wound!"

"Yes, but my bullets are poisoned," the boy in the tree shouted. "You're dying. Fall down. Die!"

"I took the antidote," his brother growled. "You die!" He lobbed a boomerang at the tree, but it went wide.

"Caleb! Micah!" Mrs. Helen Archer stood in the doorway of her restaurant, hands on hips. As the boys' heads jerked in their mother's direction, Ben intercepted the boomerang as it whipped back around. The polished wood slapped against his palm instead of Caleb's or Micah's temple.

"What are you two up to? Harassing Dr. Bones?" Mrs. Archer asked.

"No," the twins chorused. With other children, like the sort who occupied short films and sentimental memoirs, the moment would have been charming. With Caleb and Micah, it felt like something Ben might someday recount to a jury of their peers.

"Come have your breakfast, then. Hurry up. Chop chop! You'll be wanted at school before long." In that same abrasive tone, Mrs. Archer told Ben, "The restaurant's open for business if you're hungry."

"No, thank you. Breakfast is waiting at home," he lied. Actually his housekeeper, Mrs. Cobblepot, was off visiting a sick friend, forcing him to fend for himself that day. Mrs. Archer was a fine cook, but her resentment colored the restaurant's atmosphere the way tobacco stained teeth.

He turned to go. One of the twins tugged at his coat. "My boomerang."

Ben raised his eyebrows.

"Sir," added Caleb or Micah.

"Please and thank you," his brother supplied from the tree.

"Please, sir," Caleb or Micah repeated. Ben had seen bowls of porridge emote more convincingly.

"This isn't a toy," Ben said, once again sounding older than dirt. "It can be a weapon, too, you know."

"Yeah," Caleb or Micah said.

"That's the point," his brother said.

"Yes, well, do as your mother says, do as your teacher says, then come see me on Friday afternoon, and we'll see," Ben had said, walking away with the boomerang in hand. The boys had seemed unaffected by the cold, their coats unbuttoned, their hands mittenless, but he was chilled, and his left knee throbbed. After limping home, he'd tucked away the confiscated boomerang, eaten breakfast—a piece of toast—and turned on the electric fire in the front room. As his joints warmed, his thoughts returned to the two ghosts in his life, prompting him to pull Madame Daragon's book from the shelf and read.

The book, published in 1899, was bound in faded green Moroccan leather. Its pages had been dog-eared, defaced with cryptic notes, and in some cases, ripped right out of the binding. Judging by the various signatures on the flyleaf, it had been passed from owner to owner before Ben's friend, Lady Juliet Linton, discovered it in a Plymouth bookshop. Written by "The Renowned and Authenticated Madame Daragon" (known on the mortal plane as Mrs. Petunia Smoot-Whorley), *Revelations of a Reluctant Medium* purported to explain many things: why ghosts existed, how they behaved, and under what circumstances human beings could make contact with spirits.

Ben had read it once already. That is to say, he'd read as

much as a university-trained physician could before feeling disloyal to his calling. Many of Madame Daragon's declarations struck him as absolute rot. Others made sense, at least with respect to the apparition he feared might slip away: the former owner of his cottage, Lucy McGregor. Unfortunately, he'd found nothing thus far that applied to the ghost he wanted vanquished: his late wife, Penny.

That's because she's a figment of my imagination.

He'd been telling himself that for weeks. Telling himself, but getting nowhere. By and large, the villagers believed that Lucy McGregor haunted his house. So why couldn't Penny?

There were certain similarities between the two women. Both had died young—Lucy at twenty-three, Penny at twenty-seven. Both had died suddenly. Both had been born in Cornwall. And both had died there, in what Madame Daragon called the most haunted county in Britain. In *Revelations* she wrote, "If one listens, one may hear wights, phantom animals, and even the stones of long-tumbled castles crying in the dead of night, begging remembrance."

According to Madame Daragon, most ghosts were female. She gave no reason for this, beyond her belief that unfulfilled people sometimes clung to their former life, trying to wring a drop of joy out of a generally unhappy existence. Perhaps the medium's conflation of "unfulfilled" and "female" had less to do with phantoms and more to do with her girlhood during Queen Victoria's reign. Whatever the reason, Madame Daragon claimed the ghosts of unfulfilled women tended to linger where they died, often believing themselves still alive as they attempted to contact mortals via thumps, knocks, or whispers.

Ben had no proof that Lucy McGregor had died unfulfilled, but it was easy to imagine. Though she'd passed peacefully in her sleep, killed by a gas line rupture, she'd sampled little of what life had on offer. She'd never traveled, married, had children, or embarked on a career. Penny Bones, by contrast, had left little untasted. Though born in Birdswing, she'd traded rural life for the glitz of London at the first opportunity. During her formative years she'd danced in jazz clubs, gambled in Monte Carlo, and sipped champagne in the *Jardin des Champs-Élysées*. She might never had looked at Ben, then a bookish and painfully naïve medical student, except for an accidental pregnancy. Abandoned by the child's father, she'd been determined to secure a husband while there was still time, which threw her into Ben's arms.

For a few glorious weeks, Ben had been wildly in love. Marrying Penny made him the happiest man alive. But when he realized his beautiful, stylish bride carried another man's child, the revelation crushed his trust—not only in Penny, but in his own good judgment.

Still, a child might have pulled them together. When it perished in the womb, their marriage perished, too. Before Ben could decide whether to divorce her for good and all, she'd been murdered. The loss left him with a bewildering rush of emotions: shock, anger, powerful relief, and still more powerful shame.

That's why she haunts me. It has to be.

He'd confided these fears about Penny to no one. Lucy was an easier topic, because she was indisputably real. Even before Ben came to Birdswing, Fenton House was called haunted. Doors slammed; windows seemed to open themselves; the scent of books lingered in Ben's medical office, which had once been Lucy's library.

In addition to these curious events, there had been manifestations. Lady Juliet had heard Lucy speak; Ben had witnessed an object falling out of thin air. As a man of science, he craved hard facts, and while he'd be the first to admit nothing about the haunting was reproducible, at least in the sense of a laboratory trial, seeing was believing. Now he wanted to see her, not in his imagination but right before his eyes: that lovely and ethereal young woman he'd glimpsed in a dream.

With Penny, the evidence for a true haunting was thinner. Sometimes when Ben said or did something foolish, he heard her laugh. Other times he caught a whiff of her signature perfume, *Sous le Vent*, in places it couldn't be. Above all, he felt like he was being watched, constantly and without mercy. If only someone else—Mrs. Cobblepot or Lady Juliet or the woman he walked out with, Rose Jenkins—would notice something. If one of them remarked on the smell of perfume or a woman's laugh, he'd dare to confide in them about Penny. Otherwise, no. Suppose they adopted that strict, patronizing look—the one he, as a physician, adopted every time a patient came to him bleating nonsense—and said living with Lucy had eroded his good sense?

Frowning, he returned his attention to *Revelations* and re-read the table of contents.

PAGE ONE of chapter five read:

Dearest reader, we have come to that unhappiest of places. Here I must confirm the dark truth you already perceive in your heart of hearts. Yes, hauntings are rare. Most can be classified as what in Chapter Two I call "mementos"—impressions stored in granite or other hard stones, just as music may be pressed into gramophone records. The remaining hauntings are what I call "specters"—ghosts that observe, learn, and above all, yearn to communicate. Make no mistake: many specters despise the living.

*They may be the ghosts of men and women who have led wicked lives. They may be peculiar, outlandish phantasms who have been trapped between life and death for so long, they've lost all humanity. Perhaps they were never human at all. In either case, they utterly and irredeemably **hate** all living things. Once such a specter attaches itself to a particular individual, it will not depart willingly. Without successful intervention, it will draw strength from the individual like a parasite, growing stronger through torment, until it hounds that tragic soul to death.*

Thus I beseech you, dear reader. Before you dare attempt a séance, the Tarot, or the talking board, also called a spirit board, you must first

BUT THERE MADAME DARAGON'S breathless counsel ended, midsentence. Someone had ripped out the rest of the chapter, leaving a ragged gap in the binding. Ben wondered if the pages had been destroyed or kept like a talisman, perhaps by some other poor sod preoccupied by ghosts. Until Lady Juliet located the revelations of another "renowned and authenticated" spiritualist, Ben had a choice: give up initiating contact with Lucy or proceed blindly, without benefit of Madame Daragon's wisdom.

"Used and abused, Dr. Bones. Used and abused!"

Ben's front door banged open. Lady Juliet surged over his threshold, six foot three in her riding boots. She had wide shoulders, powerful limbs, and a broad face that was more pleasant than pretty.

"What a day! I started between the driftwood and the hardwood," she said, sweeping past him with a large wicker hamper tucked under one arm. "Now I'm in a proper boil."

Placing *Revelations* on the coffee table, Ben rose unhurriedly. Lady Juliet frequently burst into Fenton House when she had something to say, and no greeting from him was required.

Her wicker hamper caught his eye. "Is that lunch?"

Lady Juliet ignored the question. Clearly, she was in a state. When she was in a state, the rules of polite discourse were suspended.

"Tea. I must have tea," she declared, filling his tiny kitchen vocally as well as physically. She was dressed in her usual manner: grass-stained jodhpurs, a button-down shirt, and her winter coat. It was a horrible woolly thing, blackish-gray with a sheen of purple where the fabric was wearing thin. She insisted it was marvelously warm and a great bargain, bought for sixpence at a church jumble. To Ben it looked like something nicked off a sleeping vagrant, but it was his policy not to critique the attire of others, particularly women.

Lady Juliet dropped her hamper on the table with a thud. "Tea, or I will not be responsible for what happens next," she said, yanking open a cupboard.

"I say, is that lunch?" Ben repeated, noting the hamper's promising odor. Until its appearance, he'd been looking down the barrel of especially unappetizing leftovers: braised oxtail and parsnip fritters.

"Open and see for yourself." Lady Juliet banged two saucers on the table, followed by two cups. Red-cheeked and bristling with energy, she was robust as ever, but her light brown hair fell limp. This seemed right to Ben. Lady Juliet was a force of nature; clinging doggedly to her scalp was the best her hair could do.

He opened the hamper. Rooting under the red-checked cloth, he came up with two squares wrapped in wax paper. "And these sandwiches are...?"

"Roast beef."

"Smashing. Yesterday's oxtail was on the turn. Another day

won't have improved it." He unwrapped a sandwich and stole a bite. It was delicious. Sometime between his second and third bites, he noticed a ringing silence.

He looked up. Lady Juliet stared at him with slitted eyes. "What?"

"Nothing. Nothing whatsoever." She lifted her chin, looking heavenward sadly. "Far be it from me to bore you with my ruminations... my deep frustrations... the abject misery of my existence in this wasteland."

"Fair play," he said lightly. From the hamper, he brought out scones, a jam jar, and a bowl of clotted cream. Exasperation radiated from Lady Juliet like gamma rays as he examined the store-bought jam. "Fig? How exotic."

"Why did I expect any different?" Lady Juliet demanded of the ceiling. "Why should I find pity anywhere on the face of the earth?"

"All right, I've pity to spare, no need to get cross," Ben said. Teasing Lady Juliet was one of his favorite pastimes. "Sit down. Have a tart. Unburden yourself while I brew the tea."

"See that you brew it correctly."

He let that pass. "What am I meant to pity you for?" he asked, filling the kettle at the tap.

"Not a single blessed thing." She removed the horrible wooly coat, hung it on a peg, and sat down. "I am completely untroubled, Dr. Bones. Apart from the vexation of my plans and the assassination of my character."

"And it's not even noon. What plans?"

"I intended a lengthy *tête-à-tête* with our vicar. Most years we in Birdswing allow the Christmas festivities to coalesce in the ether, so to speak. Teachers plan the pageants, Mrs. Parry organizes the high street caroling, and Blind Bill chops down a tree that doesn't belong to him and drags it into the village green, at which point, Mother and I arrange for the decorating and lighting of said tree on Christmas Eve." She sighed. "Alas, because of the blackout, there will be no caroling by candlelight, no pageant on the Saturday night before Christmas, and certainly no tree-beacon to signal German bombers."

"I hadn't thought of that."

"Of course not. You're a man. All your life, the women around you have managed to pull off these beloved festivals by hook or by crook, for the betterment of society, while you presumed they occurred via spontaneous generation."

"Some might call that 'assassination of one's character,'" he said.

"Is it true?"

"Yes, of course."

"Our beloved Father Cotterill is much the same. He is responsible for our spiritual health, so he believes that so long as he preaches well on Christmas morning, his part of the bargain is done. This year I want to coax a bit more participation from him, so I asked Cook to pack a hamper. At the very bottom"—Lady Juliet reached into the hamper and pulled out a miniature pie—"are treacle tarts, his favorite. Alas, I've been branded *persona non grata*. Driven from the vicarage in disgrace."

"You're exaggerating."

"I'm not. Well, a bit. But not much."

"What was the dustup about? Not Gaston again?"

Clarence Gaston was Birdswing's ever-officious, often-meddling ARP Warden and special constable. He'd recently petitioned the village council, which was chaired by Lady Juliet's mother, Lady Victoria, to implement a new wartime prepared-ness scheme. According to Gaston, many of the great houses of England had resolved to no longer waste acres of cultivated soil on ornamental plants. From 1940 until the war's end, they would plow under their pleasure gardens to create additional farmland.

"Belsham Manor must do the same," he'd declared at the monthly meeting in St. Mark's hall. Virtually every villager who could walk attended those meetings. The folding chairs were always filled, forcing latecomers to lurk outside. Some came to air grievances or make suggestions. The rest came to eat biscuits, sip punch, and hope for a row. Usually there was an undercurrent of chatter, but when Gaston made his announcement, everyone fell silent but Lady Juliet.

"What do you mean?" she'd demanded.

"Your flower gardens do not serve the war effort. They must be torn out and replaced with winter veg," Gaston had said.

Mrs. Parry had gasped. Mr. Cranford choked on his biscuit and had to be thumped between the shoulder blades. Belsham Manor's lovingly-tended gardens were a point of residential pride.

Amidst all the ominous murmuring, Lady Victoria had urged calm, asking Gaston to name the great estates which had made this sacrifice. He'd hemmed and hawed, unable to produce even one. Further cross-examination revealed his information had been obtained over a pint in the Sheared Sheep, from someone he called a "disinterested patriot."

"You mean Angus Foss," Lady Juliet had accused, referring to the publican. "I agree. When it comes to patriotism, no one's less interested."

This had produced laughter, which Gaston never handled well, particularly since his elevation to Special Constable.

"Lady Juliet," he'd said solemnly, "I call upon you to lead this effort, so in the dark days to come, the people of Birdswing may eat. Tear out your heirloom roses and plant foodstuffs like onions. Or cabbage."

"Cabbage?" Lady Juliet had surged up like an aggrieved crocodile. "You first. Plow under the cricket pitch and replace it with turnips."

The ladies cheered. The men howled. Someone knocked over the punchbowl, which might have been an accident, or might have been anarchy taking hold. Lady Victoria banged her gavel and called for order, but a spontaneous adjournment followed as the villagers chased each other out of St. Mark's, taking their individual arguments into the street.

The next morning, sanity returned. The villagers decided, not by vote or discussion but through that strange telepathy that often arises in tightknit communities, to carry on as if nothing happened. The notion of demolishing any local landmark in favor of veg was tabled indefinitely, but Lady Juliet and the ARP warden had yet to mend the breach.

"Gaston?" Lady Juliet scoffed. "Of course not. I can obliterate him with a glance. And not Father Cotterill. He was away from the vicarage, ministering to someone or other. When I arrived, who did I find? None other than Lady Maggart of Fitchley Park, lying in wait like a cardinal spider on its web. She'd come to the vicarage to complain to Father Cotterill about me, if you can believe that. So when I appeared in the flesh, she took it as some sort of sign. Denounced me to my face as an agent of the occult."

"A what?"

"An agent of the occult. Among other things. As condemnations go, it was fairly comprehensive," Lady Juliet said. "She began with a jab at my hair and ended by calling me a necromancer."

"Who called you what?" Ben was doubly confused. He'd never heard of Lady Maggart or Fitchley Park.

"Odette Maggart, wife of Baron Maggart, called me a necromancer. Because—"

CREEEEEEEACK

Ben jumped. The noise had come from somewhere above his head—the master bedroom or the attic.

"Because of her." Lady Juliet pointed at the ceiling. "Lucy."

2

"MAYBE IT'S MURDER"

"That wasn't necessarily Lucy." Ben paused in case another volley of spectral knocking proved him wrong. None followed, but the teakettle whistled. "It might have been a branch scraping against the roof. The big oak in the back garden wants pruning." He spooned tea leaves into his brown betty teapot, then poured in hot water. "Mind you, I did have a rather rude awakening this morning. But I feel like I've lost the plot. I've never heard of Lady Maggart."

"She's the empress of Barking," Lady Juliet said. "Look upon her works, ye mighty, and despair. Her husband's ancestral home, Fitchley Park, is called the crown jewel of our little patch, don't you know?" She gave a dry chuckle. "Charmless and ossified, in my opinion. I'd sooner live in a mausoleum. Wait—perhaps I do."

Ben smiled. Belsham Manor did bear some resemblance to fictitious houses of horror. "I suppose you've known her since the day you were born, as you knew Penny. Familiarity breeds contretemps."

"Actually, the correct expression is—oh. Never mind," Lady Juliet said. "So unusual to find intelligent conversation in this village, much less mildly witty banter. And don't accuse me of being familiar with that woman," she added, tasting one of the tarts. "Odette Maggart isn't Cornish. She married poor Dudley and came to live in Fitchley Park around 1917, if I have it right. Making her an interloper."

"Like me," Ben said lightly. It would take a while for the tea to steep properly, so he helped himself to a tart. "But she accused you of witchcraft because...?"

"The story about Lucy speaking to me on Bonfire Night reached her ears. Odette's always been a Nosy Parker, but in the last year or two, she's become a sort of religious crusader. Pouncing on those she considers not morally up to snuff." Taking a scone and halving it, Lady Juliet stabbed her knife into the jam jar, giving its contents a violent churn. "You know the sort. Repeating gossip, spying, and so on. Whenever she digs up something to disapprove of, she trots about telling everyone how shocked and mortified she is." She spread jam on the scone's crumbly inside, topping it with clotted cream. "If that's the conduct of a good parishioner, I hope never to meet a bad one."

"So on the basis of Lucy speaking to you once," Ben said, "telling you something not only benign, but helpful, Lady Maggart decided you were a necromancer threatening Father Cotterill's flock?" He chuckled.

"Yes, and I'll thank you not to laugh at my pain. I'll admit she didn't actually employ the term necromancer. It has four sylla-bles. But she did want Father Cotterill to rebuke me on the dangers of consorting with spirits. According to Odette, there are only two everlasting locales, and I must renounce the Evil One if I wish to luxuriate, post-mortem, in the more felicitous destination."

"I thought Cornwall embraced the supernatural," Ben said. "Standing stones, bowls of cream left out for the fairies, that sort of thing. But if Lady Maggart is so distressed, why didn't she complain directly to me? I'm the one living in a haunted house."

"Yes, but you're an unknown quantity. She's had a grudge against me for years. Something about my deportment reflecting poorly on the gentry." Lady Juliet gave an unladylike snort. "I don't care if the tea is steeped or not. I can't wait another moment." Pouring them each a cup, she continued, "Fear not, Dr. Bones. Odious Odette will come round to you in her own good time, though perhaps in a different manner. You're precisely her sort."

Finished with his tart, Ben cut a scone in half. "What's that supposed to mean?"

"Oh, I don't know." Lady Juliet drummed her fingers against the tabletop. "But if you come across one of those flat reflective discs that hang on walls, do pause to take a look."

"She's a widow, then?"

"Not quite. Her husband is alive, though in poor health. The Dudley she knew was lost on the battlefield. He went off to fight the Krauts in 1915 and came back a broken man." She shook her head. "On that score, I almost—*almost*—feel sorry for Odette. It's twisted her personality. Turned her into a compulsive giver of advice who—" Lady Juliet broke off in horror. "Dr. Bones! For shame. How many times must I tell you? This is Cornwall. The clotted cream goes on top."

Ben, who was nonchalantly spreading his jam over the clotted cream, savored a bite of his scone before asking, "Where were we? Compulsive giver of advice?"

She rolled her eyes.

"This fig makes a nice change, but I prefer strawberry. Did you run out of homemade?"

"Yes. We mismanaged our harvest. A sorry state of affairs, with sugar soon to be as dear as diamonds, and bought jam as dear as rubies. Next year I shall supervise every aspect of canning at Belsham Manor. Perhaps even invite the WI to help. Assuming Odette doesn't drum me out. She controls the Women's Institute, just as she tries to control Barking." Pushing back her chair, Lady Juliet cast her gaze about like a woman in need of a mission.

"Enough about that wretched woman. What are you up to, Dr. Bones? When I arrived, you had Madame Daragon's book in hand."

"I was thinking of how we might contact Lucy. She was so active before, and now—"

"That's when there was a killer on the loose," Lady Juliet cut across him. "Of course she's silent now. As far as I'm concerned, it's all rather obvious. Lucy witnessed Penny's murder and wanted justice done. Now that our village is back to normal, she has no reason to intervene. Perhaps she's no longer even here. Perhaps she's crossed over to the other side."

"I don't accept that," Ben said.

Lady Juliet looked nonplussed. "Why? Because your house creaks and moans like every other house that's passed its centennial?"

"Because—" He broke off, unable to put his feelings into words. "Because she's still here. I'm certain of it."

"Oh. Well. I'm sorry to hear that. I barely knew Lucy, but that was my fault, not hers. How terrible for her, trapped on this plane. I wouldn't enjoy it." Lady Juliet laughed. "As a matter of fact, I don't enjoy it half the time. Perhaps you're right. Shall we screw our courage to the sticking place and attempt a séance?"

"A séance requires three or more," Ben said. "I thought Rose would be back by now, but it seems she's extended her visit to Plymouth for another week. But—"

"Rose. Of course. First-rate choice," Lady Juliet interrupted unconvincingly. "I wonder how she's getting on? The Barbican is so romantic. All those vermillion sunsets over the harbor. And isn't it good of her to visit a former sweetheart during his leave? I understand the young man in question is training to be an RAF pilot. Dangerous work. Very heroic. If they hadn't gone their separate ways over the summer, I suppose she'd be marrying him right about now."

"Rose is visiting a maiden aunt for whom she cares a great deal," Ben corrected, refilling his teacup. The cavalcade of insinuations Lady Juliet had packed into a mere seven sentences didn't trouble him. A young woman with Rose Jenkins's face and demeanor was bound to have a few old boyfriends knocking about. Besides, Rose had been perfectly honest about her intention to have lunch with her flyboy ex. She'd seemed almost disappointed when Ben didn't object, but he'd pretended not to notice, just as he overlooked Lady Juliet's tendency to carp about Rose.

He cleared his throat. "As I was trying to say a moment ago, what about Lucy's talking board? According to Madame Daragon, having only two people is ideal. In fact, a male and female are the perfect combination."

"The talking board." Lady Juliet sighed. "I'm willing, I suppose. But my initial concern remains. Though our intentions may be to contact Lucy, and only Lucy, what if the board opens a channel for other spirits?" She thought for a moment. "I don't suppose it's become less hideous since I saw it last?"

Ben had that inimitable sensation of eyes boring into the back of his head. He didn't turn around but braced himself for the scent of *Sous le Vent*. It didn't come.

"Let's find out," he said a touch louder than intended, in case Penny was listening. After repacking the hamper and putting it aside, he brought the talking board, also called a spirit or Ouija board, into the kitchen, placing it where the hamper had been.

"Good heavens. It's uglier," Lady Juliet said.

Made of walnut, it appeared hand-carved, with a sun on the

left, a moon on the right. A-Z and 0-9 stretched across the middle, with HELLO at the top and GOOD-BYE at the bottom. Across its surface were vaguely sinister scratches and gouges.

"I wish we had Madame Daragon's chapter on rancorous ghosts," Ben said. "When I was a boy, my grandmother had one of these and used it from time to time. She held séances, too. I wasn't allowed anywhere near them, but I eavesdropped when I could. In either case, Grandmother told her clients to bring something the deceased held dear—a piece of jewelry, a favorite book, that sort of thing. The personal item was meant to ensure the correct spirit answered, but with Lucy, the only item we have that belonged to her is the board itself, and I'm not sure that counts."

"Yes, well, don't be too hard on Mrs. Cobblepot," Lady Juliet said. "No one campaigns more tirelessly against filth. Of course she scoured the attic like Hercules scouring King Augeas's stables."

"What are you on about?"

"Your attic. Have you never been up there? Do you even know the history of Fenton House?" Lady Juliet shook her head. "Really, for an amateur detective, you have an appalling lack of curiosity. Next you'll tell me you never enter Morton's Emporium except to purchase goods." She *tsk*ed at him, brown eyes lighting up. "As for Lucy, it may interest you to know she lived in this house every day of her life. She inherited it, lock, stock, and barrel, when she was only thirteen."

"What happened to her parents?"

"She lost them in a car crash. No relation ever surfaced to take her in or lay claim to the property. Lucy lived here quite alone after their deaths, the brave little thing."

"At thirteen?"

"She was a country girl," Lady Juliet reminded him. "She could cook, clean, sew, do the wash, and keep her garden neat.

All she needed was a little help managing her pocketbook, and Father Cotterill saw to that. We always thought some long-lost uncle or cousin would turn up, but none did. By the time she was sixteen, she was markedly independent."

"Sounds a lonely life," Ben said. As a boy, he'd spent half his time trying to escape his parents, grandparents, and his little sister, Cathleen. They'd lived together in one small house in a row of twenty, on a street with so many other children, a bookish young man had to climb the fire escape to the roof for uninterrupted study time. During his medical training, he'd slept in twelve-bed dorm rooms and eaten most meals cafeteria-style at tables which seated twenty. Lucy's solitary girlhood was hard for him to fathom.

"I daresay it *was* lonely," Lady Juliet said. "Pity I didn't befriend her. At any rate, after Lucy died, Mother and I took charge of Fenton House. While I chose what to sell and what to give away on the ground floor, Mother went up to the attic. She came down and said it was jammed from stem to stern, positively crammed with personal effects, and we didn't dare disperse it until we were certain none of Lucy's relations would come and claim them."

"What sort of things?"

"I don't know. Clothing, furniture, and the like, I suppose. When Mother called it a problem for another day, that was good enough for me."

"Well. Today's another day." Ben drained his teacup. "Let's have a look."

———

"ARE you quite certain you're up to this?" Lady Juliet looked on critically as Ben ascended Fenton House's stairs, which were both steep and narrow.

"Which one of us is the doctor?"

"A question I frequently ask myself. Are you still using that gymnasium equipment I provided? Sloth is one of the seven deadly sins."

"Then you'll be pleased to know I'm so busy with patients, any mucking about with parallel bars would count as sloth. And yes, my right leg's as sound as ever," Ben said, gaining the landing at last. "There it is."

He pointed at the end of the hall, where a cul-de-sac had been papered in the same floral pattern as the walls, making it almost invisible. Inside, four steps led to a small door, two-thirds the usual height, squatting beneath a low lintel.

"Good Lord," Lady Juliet said. "Methinks this passage was constructed by knockers."

"Who?"

"Knockers. Beastly little creatures that lived in the tin mines, down in the darkest depths. They used to play tricks on the miners. Stealing their pickaxes or luring them into old corridors verging on collapse. I do hope the ceiling inside the attic is a bit higher, or I suppose you'll wish someone petite, like Rose, was accompanying you."

Ben tried the tarnished brass knob. It didn't turn.

"I don't see a key hole." He handed her the battery-operated torch he carried and tried again with both hands. "Must be stuck."

"Now that I think on it, perhaps you should wait until Rose returns," Lady Juliet said in a tone of brave suffering. "No doubt you've included me out of kindness...."

"I have no idea"—Ben pushed against the door—"what you're nattering about. Or how Rose's size"—he pushed harder, putting his shoulder into it—"has anything to do with any of this. Blimey! Won't budge. Something on the other side must have fallen and blocked the door. I've a crowbar in the garden shed. I'll just pop down and—"

"Step aside, Dr. Bones."

"It's stuck fast."

"Step aside. And look, so you may learn."

"Right. Very well. Don't hurt yourself. And don't say I didn't warn you." Taking a step back, he folded his arms across his chest and waited.

Lady Juliet jiggled the doorknob. It didn't move. She examined the doorframe, running her fingers around it as if such delicate tracery might reveal a point of weakness. When she put her ear to the door and listened, like a Wild West tracker listening for buffalo, Ben readied a sardonic remark. Just as he was about to deploy it, Lady Juliet hurled herself against the door. It gave way with a crack, frame splintering.

"Ha! I'd like to see Rose Jenkins do *that*." She shot him a look of triumph.

"Er. Well done. No doubt I softened it up for you," Ben muttered.

"No doubt." She rubbed her shoulder. "Well, what are we waiting for? Once more unto the breach, dear friends!" Lady Juliet ducked her head and plunged into the pitch-black attic.

Ben switched on his torch, but nothing happened. It took a few thumps against Ben's thigh to jar the battery and produce a feeble glow. Eyes unadapted, he aimed the dim beam straight ahead and followed it into the dark.

"Ow!" Ben banged an elbow into something unyielding.

"Mind how you go," Lady Juliet called. "You must feel your way. There isn't a path."

"Blast!" This time it was his shin. Ben had a glimpse of tall, dark shapes rising around him, and then the torch went out. "I haven't any other batteries. I should have brought the paraffin lamp."

"Yes, that would have been wise indeed. The light of a rampaging fire throws things into stark relief." Lady Juliet laughed. "A bit of illumination from the hall is coming in behind you, through the doorway. There's also a vent, just there, letting a bit of daylight through. Proceed with care toward my voice until your eyes—oh!"

"What is it?"

It took her a moment to answer. "I tripped."

"Are you hurt?"

"No. Only—I thought I saw something. A face."

"It's only nerves," Ben said, but the attic felt oppressive, like a jailer's embrace. As his eyes adjusted, one of those tall, dark shapes solidified into a cheval mirror. Another resolved itself into a coat rack.

"Stay where you are," he said, working his way past what he now saw were bits of furniture wrapped in sheets.

Scrape, scrape.

Ben stopped. It had come from a dark corner.

Scrape, scrape.

Lady Juliet sucked in her breath. "Dr. Bones. Is your home beset by vermin?"

"Squirrels, possibly."

"In Cornwall, we have red squirrels, and they're no trouble at all." Lady Juliet sounded more confident as she slipped into lecture mode. "Unless you brought some of those wretched gray ones from your part of the country."

CREEEEEEEEACK

Heart hammering, Ben squinted at the roof's exposed timbers. Was this it? Would he see Lucy again?

BANG

Lady Juliet gasped. Ben spun around. The attic door had slammed shut behind him.

"Who did that?" he shouted. "Who's there?"

His torch chose that moment to revive. S͟ the attic, Ben found Lady Juliet on the floor a toys. She appeared to have tripped over a tric͟ frame. Behind her, a popped-up jack-in-the-͟ spring, grinning maniacally.

"I seem to have found the face you mentioned," Ben said. "It's only—hang on."

Behind the jack-in-the-box sat an object he recognized: the antique lamp with the blue glass shade that had figured so prominently in his dream about Lucy.

"That's it. That's precisely what we need."

"Dr. Bones," Lady Juliet said. "I remain on the floor, awaiting a hand up."

"Sorry." He hurried to help her rise. "It's cold up here. There's probably a crack letting in a draft. Let me prop open the door with something so it doesn't slam again and frighten us out of our skins. Then together we can carry the lamp downstairs."

"I see just the thing. A stout crate," Lady Juliet said, taking charge again. "Let me test its weight." As Ben followed, sweeping the torch's beam in her path, it flashed across a woman in a white gown. Behind her lacy bridal veil was no face.

"Lucy!" Lady Juliet cried.

He didn't think it was Lucy. Truth be told, he didn't think at all. Lady Juliet's terror was so palpable, he threw himself between her and the spectral figure, moving faster than he'd thought possible. When it jumped, he did, too, tackling it midair.

CRACK

The woman's head flew off its shoulders. Veil still attached, it struck a rafter, exploding into powdery shards as Ben and the decapitated "bride" crashed into a heap of clothes.

"Dr. Bones!"

Ben flailed. The thing beneath him was only a plaster

_equin, that was now obvious, but the wedding gown's volu-
nous skirts were tangled about his legs. His left knee
throbbed. One of the mannequin's broken arms jabbed him in
the ribs. God only knew how ridiculous he looked.

Mercifully, his torch had gone out when it struck the floor.
Ben groped for it, but Lady Juliet found it first. The beam didn't
seem so feeble when flashed directly in his eyes.

"Let me help," she said, kicking away rubbish. Seizing the
headless mannequin by its lacy bodice, she chucked it aside.
Then, before he could protest, she gripped him under each arm
to haul him upright. That would have been fine, if slightly detri-
mental to his masculine pride, but the long white train was
wrapped around one of his ankles, anchoring a foot to the floor.
The moment Lady Juliet released him, the tangled fabric yanked
him back again.

Afterward, Ben would have had difficulty explaining what
happened next, assuming someone ever tied him to a chair and
forced him to try. Perhaps she overbalanced. Perhaps he overcor-
rected. Either way, they went down together. Ben fell on his
back. Lady Juliet landed on top of him but facing the wrong way,
the toes of her riding boots poking him under the chin.

"Get off!"

"I'm trying. Oh! Squirrel!"

A good deal of undignified scrabbling followed. Ben kicked
his way free of the dress. Lady Juliet twisted and turned, giving
little shrieks as the squirrel hopped, skipped, and jumped its
way from her to Ben to the nearest crate. From that vantage
point, it chittered angrily at them, tail twitching, before disappearing into the attic's depths.

When they were back on their feet, Lady Juliet shone the
torch full in his face. "Dr. Bones. Did you do that on purpose?"

Ben's patience, which had been steadily thinning since his
rude awakenings that morning, snapped.

"On purpose?" he all but shouted. "Yes, of course. You're on to me, I won't deny it. I set up that dress form to look like an apparition. I lured you up here under false pretenses. I rigged the door to slam *itself* through means Houdini himself couldn't divine, and I trained an obliging squirrel to knock over the dress form at *precisely* the right moment. Then like a fool I attacked my own prank ghost, falling on my arse and taking you with me. All to produce five seconds' indecency!"

"You needn't raise your voice." Lady Juliet shifted the torch beam around the attic. "Ruddy squirrels. And I wasn't being ridiculous. One hears of these things. Men maneuvering women into tricky positions."

"I'm sure." He massaged his aching knee.

"You sound unconvinced."

"Nonsense." He rubbed his eyes, blinking as vision returned.

"I can certainly be forgiven for a momentary suspicion. It did seem a touch convenient...."

"Juliet." Snatching the torch away, he flashed it in her eyes for revenge. "I've been alone with you many times, and I've always been the perfect gentleman. Believe me, if I'd planned that, I would've bloody well landed on top."

At that point, communications broke down entirely. Lady Juliet stomped downstairs, leaving Ben to wrestle the blue lamp down from the attic on his own. It was heavier than it looked. The claw-footed base was made of solid brass. Four panes of leaded blue glass made up the shade. Altogether, it was in good condition but coated with dust, triggering sneezes from Ben on the way downstairs. That was slow going, gripping the railing with one hand and the lamp with the other. His biceps were burning when he reached the front room, where Lady Juliet had retired to the sofa.

"Ah. There you are," she said airily. "I thought before we use the talking board, I ought to consult Madame Daragon's book to be certain I have her advice in mind and not some folderol from childhood. Did I ever tell you we used to play at channeling spirits? A certain insufferable little girl named Penny was always in charge."

"What?"

"Oh, yes. It was only a rainy day pastime, to be sure," Lady Juliet said. "Nothing serious. She would dress up in her mum's scarves, speak a bunch of gibberish, and claim to be possessed by the shade of Guinevere or some such. You may be surprised to learn that Guinevere made various unkind observations about the schoolgirl population of Birdswing. It's always remarkable, don't you think, when a famous spirit takes sides in the petty squabbling of—my goodness, Dr. Bones. I *was* having a go at Penny, but I thought we were past 'nothing but good of the dead' when it comes to her."

"It's not that." He placed the lamp on the coffee table. "Only —I didn't realize Penny ever tried making contact with the spirit world. You don't suppose she ever succeeded?"

Lady Juliet laughed. "Never. It was only an excuse for her to dress up and be the center of attention. How can you even ask?"

This was the perfect opening for Ben to reveal his fear that Penny was haunting him, but he couldn't bring himself to say the words.

"Now. According to Madame Daragon, it's imperative we attempt the talking board in a 'pitch-black' room," Lady Juliet said. "As I intend never to set foot in your attic again, perhaps we should darken this room by doing the blackout early."

"My thoughts exactly," Ben said. He glanced out the window, which afforded a fine view of the high street. In Birdswing, scrutiny was never one-sided; often when he looked out, he saw his across-the-way neighbor, Mrs. Parry, staring back. "Mind you, the birds will sing if I do the blackout in the afternoon with your Crossley parked out front."

"They will indeed." Lady Juliet sounded more pleased than scandalized. Rising, she joined him at the window, peering over his shoulder. "See Mr. Bunting? He's spent every afternoon in his window seat for the last twenty years. I assure you, my presence has been noted. If—botheration!"

A well-maintained, lovingly polished sedan slid up to the curb behind her Crossley. From it emerged Air Raids Protocol Warden and Special Constable Clarence Gaston, as puffed-up as a robin on a snowy day.

"There he is," she said. "The dirigible that walks like a man. If he weighs twelve stone, I reckon half of it's wind. I do hope he hasn't decided to apologize here, now, in the presence of a witness. If he does, I'll have no choice but to forgive him."

"He's carrying his 'Official Business' notebook. Perhaps I'm about to be cited for some infraction."

Like the rest of Birdswing, Ben was learning all the ways one could fall below expectations. To aid the war effort and enhance public safety, the government had passed dozens of new laws, which Gaston enforced with unflagging zeal. No one was exempt from his critical eye. Once he'd threatened to cite his own sister, Mrs. Cobblepot, for wasting food because he caught her scattering bread crumbs to the sparrows.

"I doubt he's here to correct you. He isn't smiling," Lady Juliet said.

"Fair point." Ben went to let him in.

Gaston always looked ready for action. Slim and spare, with thick spectacles, white hair, a white mustache, and meticulously pressed tan trousers, he was in his sixties but often displayed the energy of a younger man. His black helmet with the white letter *W* hung by its chin strap from a canvas bag that contained his gas mask; a silver badge with the crowned letters ARP was pinned over his heart.

"To what do we owe the pleasure?" Ben asked. "No one hurt, I hope."

"Hurt? No. Dead. At the manor," Gaston said, pretending not to notice Lady Juliet three feet to his left. "You know the law, Doctor. I need you to inspect the body and write up the death certificate."

"The manor?" Lady Juliet cried. "Dear Lord. Is it old Robbie? He never does well in winter. He's been laid up with chilblains all week."

"I never said *Belsham* Manor." Gaston employed the sort of meticulous civility Ben found synonymous with deep dislike. "If you look carefully, your ladyship, you'll notice I'm addressing someone else. Now. Dr. Bones. This morning, a dead man was discovered at Fitchley Park. That's in Barking. The home of—"

"Clarence Gaston," Lady Juliet interrupted. "That was inexcusable. You nearly frightened me to death. Robbie isn't the only one who's ill. Mother isn't a well woman, and you knew, *knew* I'd assume—" She stopped, probably because Gaston, though not precisely smiling, already wore a look of smug satisfaction that proved her right.

"Let's table the hostilities long enough to sort this, shall we?" Ben took control for Gaston's safety; he thought if he didn't, she might slap that look off the special constable's face. "Who died at Fitchley Park? Staff or family?"

"Neither, but someone of your acquaintance, all the same." Gaston's eyes gleamed behind his thick specs. "Bobby Archer. Death by suicide, as I see it, but you'll have the final word, of course."

"Bobby Archer took his own life? In *Barking*?" Lady Juliet clearly refused to silence herself in the face of Gaston's disapproval. Rather, she seemed determined to insert herself in the discussion all the more. "What was he doing in Barking? He lived in Plymouth, with his mother."

"Aye, but he was known to roam," Gaston said, still pointedly addressing Ben. "From door to door like that orange tomcat of yours, Dr. Bones. And for the same reason. The staff has clammed up, but it seems clear Bobby was fraternizing with one of Lady Maggart's maids. I suppose the affair soured, and he took the coward's way out."

Ben turned that over in his mind. While investigating Penny's demise, he'd briefly considered Bobby Archer a suspect; Penny had been the great unrequited love of his life. Even so, her murder hadn't driven him to suicide. To Ben, Bobby's grief had seemed like self-pity, a sense that fate had cheated him. Had a fling with a maid tapped a deeper despair?

"Poor Helen," Lady Juliet said. "I know they've lived apart for years. I know she despised the man. But it still won't be easy for her or the boys. Have they been told?"

"No, and I'm not looking forward to it," Gaston said. "I'd like Dr. Bones to weigh in first. Can't be hasty. Nothing good ever came from being hasty. And it's always tricky, naming a death a suicide...."

THUMP

In the attic, something crashed. Ben and Lady Juliet only exchanged glances, but Gaston's hair nearly stood on end.

"I, er, reckon something tipped over upstairs, Doc." He looked slightly abashed to be the only one visibly startled.

"Shows what you know, Special Constable," Lady Juliet sniffed. "Today, Lucy bestirred herself after a long absence. Begging the question: when did Bobby die?"

"That's for Dr. Bones to say."

"Then when was his body discovered?"

Gaston, who'd slipped back into the habit of addressing her normally, seemed to remember their feud. "I can only discuss the matter with Dr. Bones."

Ben sighed. "When was his body discovered?"

"First thing this morning. A maid came upon him, bloodless, white as milk. Her screams alerted the household."

"Ah." Lady Juliet turned to Ben. "Didn't you mention a rude awakening this morning?"

"Two of them."

"Lucy was quite active after Penny died. Now that poor Bobby's committed suicide, she's active again. Perhaps death is what impels her to reach out."

"I don't know. When Mr. Laviolette died at St. Barnabas, we heard nothing from Lucy," Ben said. "When pneumonia took Mrs. Kerrin, she was silent then, too. Maybe it isn't death that bridges the gap. Maybe it's murder."

3

BLOODY BARKING

That morning, Juliet Linton had awakened with a longer-than-usual list of goals. Some of them were perpetual, like "organize the potting shed" or "write a book of kind but firm advice for ladies who find themselves married to worthless men." Unless the winter of 1939-1940 dumped fifteen feet of snow on Cornwall (which hadn't happened since the blizzard of 1891), and she found herself trapped inside Belsham Manor for days on end, those perpetual items would never be crossed off the list.

Certain other goals, like "discuss events in the *Western Evening Herald* with Mother" or "monitor cleanliness and morale among the staff," were checked off on a daily basis. But one goal, deceptive in its simplicity and confounding in its depth, sat on her list untouched. Untouched, and mocking her. It was simple: "Give up on Ben."

Aloud, she never called him that. "Dr. Bones" sounded better; it was cool, distant, safe. Feeling safe was imperative, because the truth was all too clear: he had no idea how she felt about him, and should he ever learn, he'd be mortified.

He probably thinks of me as one of the blokes, she'd told herself over breakfast that morning, nodding and smiling absently as her mother ruminated aloud on hemlines. *I made a wretched first impression in those jodhpurs.*

She knew the problem ran deeper than an unflattering pair of trousers, but it was nice to have something simple to blame. When she'd gone to meet Ben on that fateful day, she'd given no thought to her tattered garden clothes because she hadn't expected to like him. In fact, she'd expected to hate him, because Penny had married him, and Penny was vile.

By the same token, while Juliet had expected Ben to be handsome (Penny was far too shallow to accept a less-than-handsome husband), she'd been unprepared for his masculine beauty. Piercing blue eyes, reddish-brown hair, strong chin, infectious smile—all those things attracted her to him, but there was something more. A high-minded literary type, like Dr. Carl Jung, whom she very much admired, might cite Ben's quiet strength; his steadiness; his willingness to do the right thing, no matter what. A low-minded literary type might employ the term "animal magnetism," especially if she was feeling shameless.

She'd heard about such physical chemistry but never experienced it, not even during her honeymoon with Ethan Bolivar. She'd loved that man, loved him with all the pink candy-floss foolishness of someone placing her heart under the hammer. Certainly she'd loved the idea of Ethan. Good-looking, well spoken, and taller than her, which in itself was a dream come true. But looking back now, even at their happiest moments, she saw that what she'd called love was mostly fantasy. Certainly Ethan had never inspired the sort of intense feelings that Ben did. Perhaps the chief difference lay with her? Maybe the candy-floss had to melt, and one or two deep truths had to be recognized, before a woman could respond to a man that way.

"Juliet, darling, are you listening?" Lady Victoria had asked, breaking into her musings. "I wanted to start a conversation, not deliver a monologue."

"Of course. Sorry," Juliet had said, trying to focus on what her mother was saying. Clothes rationing, that was it. Like food rationing, it was sure to be part of the war effort, and many dreaded it. Lady Victoria, still remarkably lovely at forty-nine, could weather any sartorial storm, but rationing's potential effect on the poor troubled her. The less fortunate, and particularly the children of the less fortunate, relied heavily on second-hand shops, where outdated or damaged clothes could be bought on the cheap and made over. But when ordinary folks began feeling the pinch, they might decide to make over their old clothes or wear them till they fell apart. If the racks in secondhand shops emptied, how would the poor get on?

"I suppose rag and bone men still exist," Juliet had replied, hoping she was more or less on point. "Though I haven't seen one in Birdswing for a dog's age."

"Good. Only think of it! Picking through pushcarts for a girl's pinafore or a boy's jumper."

"Perhaps sewing one's own clothes will come back in vogue."

"Yes, but where will women find the material, darling? Will mothers be forced to steal what they cannot buy?"

Before Juliet had formulated a response, her mother had added, "And whatever shall we do about you?"

"Me? I've a wardrobe stuffed with togs, thank you very much."

"Of course you do. And very well made they are. A treasure trove of top-drawer material," Lady Victoria said stoutly. "But who knows how long the war will last? If you decide you'd like a change next year, or the year after, it may be too late."

"I never give a thought to what I wear," Juliet had replied, and while her mother said nothing, a cruel voice inside her head said, *Which is why Ben will marry someone who does, like Rose Jenkins.*

The idea of Ben standing up with Rose always gave her a physical pang. Not so much in the heart as the stomach—the place where all her troubles resided. According to certain romantic novels, heartbreak cut like a dagger between the ribs. It stole a woman's vitality, destroying her strength as well as her hopes.

But Juliet was as hale and hearty as ever. Her main symptom of heartbreak was a stomachache. That, and a desire to kick someone in the shins.

Before he came to Birdswing, I was content, she'd thought, glaring around the solarium where she and Lady Victoria ate breakfast each morning. All the little sights and sounds Juliet knew so well, like china cups clinking against saucers or the mantel clock ticking loudly, assaulted her, infuriating her with their familiarity.

This is what comes of wanting what one cannot have. Contempt for one's blessings, great and small.

That realization had crystallized Juliet's desire to make a start, at least, on her goal to give up on Ben. Step one: plan her day so as to avoid Fenton House altogether. First, she'd call on the vicarage to discuss Christmas. Next, she'd visit the Birdswing lending library and borrow every weighty Russian novel she could find, to occupy her on the long winter nights to come. Finally, she'd saddle her favorite mare, Epona, and head to the moor for a long, bracing ride.

This scheme would have worked brilliantly had the rest of the world stuck to the bloody script. The confrontation with Lady Maggart had left Juliet too upset to drive to the library or even home. She'd been accused of many things in her life, but never out-and-out service to the Fiend. If Lady Victoria asked what was wrong, Juliet feared a crying jag would follow. Instead, she'd motored around Birdswing four or five times, belatedly coming up with all the things she should have said and practicing them aloud. Heaven knew what the villagers thought of her careening around, shaking her fist and speaking sternly to her windshield.

This exercise could have gone on for hours if she'd lived in a large city like Plymouth, but there was only so many times Birdswing could be circumnavigated. When she'd passed the chemist shop for the umpteenth time and its proprietor, Mr. Dwerryhouse, offered a timid wave, her joyless joyride was done. The sight of him watching nervously made her want to laugh, and nothing defused her wrath like laughter.

She parked, closed her eyes, and sat in the Crossley for a time, shoring up her composure.

I can do this. I can face Mother without bursting into tears. As Dr. Jung said, 'Real liberation comes not from glossing over or repressing painful states of feeling but only from experiencing them to the full.'

Refreshed, she'd taken a deep breath. Stepping out of the car with chin held high, she'd found herself facing Fenton House instead of Belsham Manor. It seemed that in publishing his psychological papers, Dr. Jung had once again written advice specifically meant for her. That left her little choice but to go inside.

"Murder? I suppose it's possible." Gaston's ponderous tone snapped Juliet back to the present. "'Twas a strange death, to be sure."

"What was the method? You mentioned exsanguination," Juliet said.

"Come now. No need to go so far." Gaston cleared his throat. "Bobby wasn't a member of the C of E in good standing, I reckon, but Father Cotterill never—"

"Not excommunication. Exsanguination. You said he was bloodless. White as milk."

Gaston chose to respond by not responding. "Can we get on, Dr. Bones?"

"Yes, of course. Just let me get my bag," Ben said.

"You'll need the stretcher, too. I'll fetch it." As Juliet hurried to Ben's medical storage room, a delicious possibility occurred to her, one that might permit her to get a little of her own back, should the opportunity arise. To that end, she diverted to the kitchen before sweeping back into the front room carrying the dissembled stretcher, which consisted of two long wooden poles and a length of canvas. It might be difficult, managing all this in addition to her oversized handbag, but she felt sure she could do it, if she wore the bag cross-body like a bicycle messenger.

"Him with his bag and you with your stretcher," Gaston said, throwing his hands up. "When will you cotton on? Bobby Archer's as dead as a doornail, *your ladyship*."

"Indeed," she replied coolly. "When will you cotton on? Baronesses don't play hostess to corpses, *your air wardenship*."

As Gaston manufactured a cough to hide his irritation, Ben entered, black doctor's bag in hand. Ever since what Juliet called the Jane Daley Affair, he carried it everywhere, whether he anticipated a patient in need or not.

"All right. Lady Juliet, we're off," he told her. "Don't lock up. Mrs. Cobblepot will be back soon."

"Not so fast. Did Dante negotiate the horrors of the Inferno alone? No. He had Virgil as his guide. You deserve no less, Dr. Bones. Therefore, I shall accompany you to Fitchley Park."

She expected gratitude. Instead, she got wariness. "I don't know. You don't plan on attacking Lady Maggart with a stretcher pole, do you?"

Juliet shifted her grip so she held the poles in a less threatening manner. "Violence is unnecessary. To upset her, I need only turn up on her doorstep. If only I could manage something more terrifying. Appear in a puff of smoke, perhaps, or fly in on a broom."

Gaston muttered something under his breath.

"How dare you!" Juliet bellowed, with no idea what he'd said.

"I only mentioned my car is a two-seater," he said mildly. "There's room for naught but me and the doctor."

"Then I'll drive myself."

"Aha! Waste!" Gaston said eagerly. "Employing two vehicles for one purpose. The kind of excess a country at war must avoid."

"I manage my petrol ration quite prudently, I assure you," Juliet lied, knowing he would soon hear of her rage-induced circuit around Birdswing. "What's more, my car will accommodate all three of us. Thus, as a patriot," she said, smiling, "I invite you, Special Constable, to ride with us. Unless you'd sooner waste petrol than accept my offer?"

She had him. He twisted in the wind for a moment, and then Ben came to his rescue.

"As lovely as that sounds, let's not forget about Bobby. His body will probably be in full rigor, so we'll need two vehicles. I'll ride with Lady Juliet; Special Constable, you can follow. Let's be off."

THE HALF-HOUR DRIVE to Barking was pleasant enough. Even in winter, Juliet considered the beauty of Cornwall second to none. When she rode Epona to Bodmin, she frequently galloped along this route, taking in the frost-limned fields and towering hedges.

"I can barely see Gaston," Ben said, looking over his shoulder. "He drives slower than he speaks. Sheep pass him at a trot."

"Good. That's how I prefer him. In my rearview mirror and

receding," Juliet said. "He read in a government pamphlet that fast driving wastes petrol."

"He brought me a stack of those pamphlets." Ben sighed. "They're on my desk, along with everything else. The Ministry of Labor and National Service sent a letter that wants a reply. I'm to provide statistics on the number of patients I've seen so far. If I don't hit the magic number, which wasn't revealed, I'll be seconded to a Plymouth hospital two days a week."

"Well, now you'll be able to say you've expanded your services to Barking. Just don't mention that the livestock outnumbers the villagers."

"I was told a thousand people lived there."

"Hah! Five hundred at most, but each and every inhabitant has an inflated sense of importance, so perhaps it will feel like a thousand." As she spoke, Juliet topped a rise, giving Ben his first look at Barking's chief landmark. He gave a low whistle.

"What a magnificent church. All those spires. Must be Gothic."

"Naturally. It's called St. Gwinnodock's. Fear not, Dr. Bones. I shan't take offense if you rhapsodize over its stained-glass windows or enthuse over its flying buttresses. I do happen to prefer our own St. Mark's, which has good plumbing and reliable heat. Yes, it's a touch utilitarian, like all contemporary structures, but that's a modest price to pay for moving with the times."

"Slow down," Ben said, "I feel as if I've traveled back in time. It's so...."

"Picturesque," she supplied, reducing speed so he could admire a knot of pretty cottages. "That's the term everyone uses. Picturesque."

"Precisely. Look at those thatched roofs. You'll find nothing like that in London."

"Yes, well, after the Great Fire of 1666, I should hope not. Our roofs in Birdswing represent the current thinking about human dwellings, in that they are less likely to roast the inhabitants alive."

She thought that was rather clever, but Ben ignored it. "Look. The only car parked on the street is a dogcart—twelve horsepower at best."

"You'll find few motorists in Barking. The horse and wagon were never really displaced." Juliet enjoyed acting as guide. It played to two of her strengths: telling others what they were seeing, and telling others what to think about what they were seeing.

"Peaceful, isn't it?"

"Apart from the murder."

"Are there shops? Or a petrol station?"

"The few who need petrol purchase it in Birdswing. As for shops, we passed a general store, but as it possessed no charm or appeal, you can be forgiven for missing it," Juliet said. "Discerning folk soon realize Barking is bereft of common comforts. Whereas Birdswing is resplendently modern. Founded in 1840. Think of all the conveniences we enjoy as a result. Various shops. The Palais. The cinema. Two perfectly lovely restaurants and one ghastly one...."

Ben looked backward at Barking's receding high street. "Was there even a post office?"

"Yes. Young Mrs. Trentham operates it out of her front room."

"What about a pub? Can't have a village without a pub."

"That's operated by Old Mrs. Trentham, out of the very same front room, on days the post office is shut." Juliet took the roundabout's first exit, which sent them down a narrow dirt lane.

"Don't get me wrong. I prefer Birdswing," Ben said. "But there's something alluring about an escape from twentieth-century distractions. Amateur artists and photographers must flock here."

"They do. It's a sore point with me. Birdswing attracts no sightseers," Juliet admitted. "Day-trippers keep our three restaurants in business, but that's as far as it goes. Whereas Barking is invaded by would-be *artistes* each weekend. Often there's a line of easels just there," she said, pointing to a ridge. "And behind them, a line of time-wasters, committing atrocities in watercolor."

Ben laughed. "Come now. Surely at least one day-tripper has painted Belsham Manor."

"No, but a man who claimed to be a novelist was caught peeking in our window. He said he was writing a book about a madwoman trapped in a derelict house. I sent him packing but said he could try back in ten years." Juliet pointed west. "Squint and you might see Fitchley Park from afar. We'll be there before you know it."

"Good. I'm still trying to puzzle out the news about Bobby. He was born in Birdswing and spent the last few years in Plymouth. Why was he at Fitchley Park?"

"Don't tell our intrepid air warden, but I'm inclined to agree with his tomcat hypothesis."

"Gaston called it suicide. If it was, why did Bobby end his life in Barking?"

"Because it's bloody Barking." She chuckled. "Sorry. I shouldn't make light of such things. But a Londoner like you can scarcely conceive of the unutterable boredom. There's nothing to do but the three *S*'s: snobbery, sheep, and single-malt scotch."

"Throw in another *S,* and you're back at the tomcat theory."

"Dr. Bones! How saucy of you," Juliet said. "However, that unmentionable *S* was already covered. I said sheep."

His wicked laugh pleased her no end. Usually he was teasing, and she was arch. This was altogether new.

"I owe that to Ethan. He came up with the three *S*'s," she admitted. "The wretched man can be witty, when he isn't pretending to be sincere."

"Oh, yes. Ethan," Ben said with the studied blandness of someone trying to sound offhanded. "I've told you a good deal about Penny, but you've scarcely said a thing about your husband."

"Ex-husband."

"Right. The divorce is final, then?"

"Final in my head. Final in my heart," Juliet said as Fitchley Park came into view. The tall wrought-iron gates stood open, as they usually did in daylight hours. "But not final in the eyes of the law. I still have to collect Ethan's signature on the decree, but I took back my family name to let the world know that despite one wearisome technicality, the union is dissolved."

"I see." Clearing his throat, Ben pointed to the great house, which was constructed of pale Syreford stone. "Three columns and a pediment. That's Palladian, yes?"

"Indeed. The façade was added in the eighteenth century. The Maggarts claim the main part of the house is far older, built around the time of the Protectorate, I think. But in Barking, truth and myth commingle. They also claim Fitchley Park was raised upon the foundation of King Mark and Queen Isolde's castle. A broken stone wall in Odette's formal garden is offered as the only proof, and it's clearly the skeleton of an ancient longhouse, not a fortress. But I cast no aspersions. No doubt it kept some ancient pig-herder warm and dry, and all his porkers, too."

"Queen Isolde," Ben said. "Didn't she run off with Sir Tristan?"

"Yes, so whether you view Fitchley Park as an adulteress's ancestral home, or a place where men lie down with swine, you'll get no argument from me." As the Crossley bounced and rattled down the long gravel drive, she added, "Don't be surprised if Lady Maggart insists on calling me 'Mrs. Bolivar.' She does it merely to aggravate me."

"Charming. But can she really refuse to call you 'Lady'? There's never a copy of *Debrett's* when I need it."

"'Mrs. Bolivar' is all I'm entitled to. 'Lady' is merely a courtesy title. My goodness, didn't you know?"

He shook his head.

Parking adjacent to the great house's wide marble steps, Juliet tooted the horn to signal their arrival. "Mother is an earl's daughter. From the day Father carried her over the threshold, all of Birdswing was in awe of her. They insisted upon calling her Lady Victoria. When I came along, the same consideration was extended to me, for her sake."

"Is that so? All this time, I assumed your title came from Ethan. That he was a knight or a baronet."

"Why?"

"Because you married him."

Juliet bristled reflexively. "Meaning *what*?"

"Meaning Ethan's a bounder," Ben said patiently. "I thought perhaps your parents made the match. If he possessed a title, that would have helped them persuade you to marry him against your own good judgment."

Juliet sighed. If only Ben's scenario were true. Alas, her parents were not to blame; in fact, the precise opposite was true. Fortunately for her, Lady Maggart's butler, Mr. Collins, chose that moment to appear in the doorway, postponing her duty to correct the record.

"Time to sally forth, Dr. Bones," she said. "I give you my solemn oath, I shall strive for decorum and a spirit of harmony. Unless...."

"Unless what?"

"Unless Odette puts a toe over the line. If she does... I apologize in advance."

4
___

THE BROKEN MAN

Ben took one look at Mr. Collins—proud bearing, stern features, a mountain of luxuriant brown hair—and formed immediate expectations. In London, he'd observed this type of smartly-dressed, patrician-faced manservant many times. They managed vast households with ease, often with no more than snapped fingers or a look. When no underservant was available for a task, they performed it themselves, often faster and more skillfully than footmen half their age. Thus when Mr. Collins appeared, exuding manservantliness like the sun exudes rays, Ben expected the butler to head straight for Lady Juliet's door and help her alight.

He did not. Instead, Mr. Collins closed the black-lacquered doors behind him and merely stood there, gaze fixed on some distant point.

"What's he doing?" Ben asked Lady Juliet. While there was perhaps no woman in Cornwall less in need of such old-fashioned cosseting, the attention suited her station. To omit it was a deliberate slight.

"He's gathering the courage to order us round to the tradesman's entrance, most likely. On his mistress's orders, of course."

"Right." Ben exited the car with his black bag while Lady Juliet brought out the stretcher canvas and those six-foot wooden poles. He tried to take charge of the canvas, but she seemed unduly invested in carrying it, as well as the poles, up the great house's marble steps without assistance. Why? Because his limp had compelled him to take the stairs in Fenton House rather slowly?

Stung by the thought, Ben did his best to stride confidently up the stairs. It would have gone better if sitting in the Crossley hadn't stiffened his knee, making his limp more pronounced, or if Lady Juliet hadn't dropped a stretcher pole halfway up. It rolled all the way down to the gravel, forcing her to go after it with one pole in the air and the canvas clutched to her bosom. Through it all, Mr. Collins remained at his post, offering no assistance, only an expression of genteel disgust.

"Good afternoon," the butler said coldly. Up close, his hair was flawless. "It would appear there's been some mistake. I'm afraid I must ask you to—"

"Excuse your lack of decorum? Of course. I'm Dr. Bones. Special Constable Gaston sent me. Please show me and Lady Juliet Linton"— as represented by poles rattling somewhere behind him—"to the deceased."

Mr. Collins's impenetrable blankness could have shamed a cardsharp. "This is a misunderstanding. You're in the wrong place. I'm afraid I must insist—"

"On apologizing to Lady Juliet? You're quite right." Ben glanced over his shoulder to be sure the lady in question really was behind him and not chasing a pole down the hill. "Allowing her to alight without offering assistance, or even a proper greeting, is inexcusable."

"Sir." Mr. Collins lifted his chin. "As a courtesy, I came to explain how things are done. You must go round to the tradesman's entrance, and your associate must depart or wait out-of-doors, as she pleases. Good day."

"Very well. Give my regards to the special constable when he arrives," Ben said. "A physician from St. Barnabas's Hospital may agree to come by in a day or two. Until then, preserve the corpse as best you can. If it's ruled a murder and Fitchley House is seen as obstructive to the normal course of inquiry, I suppose Scotland Yard might appear on your doorstep. Resist the temptation to send them around back."

He returned to the car with Lady Juliet in tow, poles rattling. They got back inside unhurriedly. As Lady Juliet started the engine, Ben saw Mr. Collins descending the stairs at speed.

"Shall we continue?" Lady Juliet asked.

"Absolutely."

As she started down the long gravel drive, Ben watched the butler try to wave them down, shouting "Dr. Bones" all the while. Only when she picked up speed, forcing Mr. Collins to break into a run, did Ben suggest showing mercy.

The trio ascended the grand marble steps a second time. Ben carried his doctor's bag, Lady Juliet carried the canvas bundle, and Mr. Collins brought up the rear, a stretcher pole in each hand. His hair had fallen in his eyes.

Fitchley Park's double doors opened. Out swept Lady Maggart, who seemed to have been lurking nearby all along.

She smiled upon them graciously, as if the spectacle of her butler chasing a moving vehicle had never happened. Ben thought she resembled a middle-aged version of Penny. Slim and artfully made up, with red lips and arched brows, her blonde hair was styled in smooth, swept-back rolls. A silver fox stole was draped across her shoulders, boneless legs dangling horribly, mouth wide.

It looks surprised. And not without reason, Ben thought. Thanks to Lady Juliet's tale of woe, he'd already worked out some of

Lady Maggart's movements. She would have left Fitchley Park by nine o'clock, if not earlier, and returned home around eleven, unless she made additional stops. Presumably she had left Fitchley Park before the body was found, rowed with Lady Juliet, then returned to find a corpse at home. Many ladies would be shaken, if not distressed. Yet here she was, not only receiving guests, but looking like a Paris fashion plate as she did so.

"Dr. Benjamin Bones," she said warmly. "You're younger than I expected. More commanding, too. I respect that, even if you were a touch unkind to poor Collins." She extended her hand limply.

Ben chose to shake the proffered hand rather than kiss the ring. "There was a mix-up about which door I'd use. I'm a physician, not a ratcatcher. I've come to see about the dead man. My friend Lady Juliet has kindly agreed to assist me."

"Yes. Very well." Lady Maggart's long-lashed eyes narrowed. "I confess, Mrs. Bolivar, I'm surprised you'd show your face here. This morning, I thought I made my opinion of you and your occultist activities perfectly plain."

"Oh, really?" Lady Juliet huffed. "Well. Speaking of this morning, I thought I plainly made my opinion of you, and your opinion on my activities, which you call occultist, perfectly plain. This morning," she concluded senselessly.

Lady Maggart smirked. Lady Juliet cleared her throat and tried again.

"Nevertheless, the situation which brings us to Fitchley Park takes precedence over a clash of personalities," she said loftily. "Poor Bobby Archer's death is deeply shocking. I would brave any unpleasantness to be of swift service in this time of need."

"Swift? Yes, I can see that. You must have been scouring dust bins when the news came. What a remarkable coat you're wearing. I pity the tramp who misplaced it."

"Aren't you clever? And brave, to be so unaffected by another human's demise that you still glue on false eyelashes and wrap yourself in a murdered fox."

"This is fashion." Lady Maggart's tone could have etched glass. "Something you cannot comprehend."

"It's rather cold," Ben announced, though both women were probably too hot under the collar to notice. "Daylight's at a premium. Can we get on?"

"Of course. The body is in the servants' wing. Collins and I will be pleased to escort you," Lady Maggart said, resuming a semblance of her former warmth. "But first, a word. As you declined to use the less obtrusive entrance, I have no choice but to bring you through the great room, where my husband takes his ease."

"Ah, Lord Maggart," Lady Juliet said. "How is he?"

"Unchanged," Lady Maggart said coolly.

"Given the bizarre nature of this event, I feared perhaps—"

Lady Maggart cleared her throat. To Ben, she said, "My dear husband Dudley fought in the Great War. Bravely, as English patriots do. Over the top at the Battle of the Somme. Alas, he was injured, and though he underwent treatment at Craiglockhart, there was no cure. Here at home, he's found a measure of peace. Therefore, I must ask you not to disturb him. No questions, not even pleasantries. And you absolutely mustn't identify yourself as a physician. When it comes to your profession, Lord Maggart has a rather a low opinion."

This didn't surprise Ben. Craiglockhart, sometimes referred to as "Dottyville," had been a psychiatric hospital for officers suffering from war neurosis—the affliction more commonly known as shell shock. At the time, most doctors had been ignorant of war neurosis, refusing to believe soldiers could be wounded mentally as well as physically. Thus many such patients, at Craiglockhart and elsewhere, were labeled cowards, malingerers, or emotional weaklings. They returned home to a country that regarded them not only as failed soldiers but inadequate men. Psychiatry had learned much in the intervening years, and Ben believed the Second World War's casualties would receive better treatment. But nothing could erase the sins of the past.

"Thank you for explaining, Lady Maggart," Ben said. "I'll do my best not to disturb him."

"I have no doubt you'll behave, Dr. Bones." She shot Lady Juliet a warning glance. "But remember Dudley is in continual pain. It's caused him to become terribly frank."

"I wouldn't dream of accosting the poor man," Lady Juliet sniffed.

"Good." Lady Maggart turned to her butler, who was trying to repair his coiffure with a minimum of pole-rattling. "Lead on."

THE CEILING in Fitchley Park's great room brooded over its lone occupant like an ominous sky. The tiered golden chandelier held no candles and didn't seem to be fitted with gas or electric, but torchiere lamps burned here and there. Casting their light up, they revealed what looked to Ben like a half-hearted effort to scrub away layer upon layer of black soot. Perhaps the ladder had been too short, or the servant unequal to the back-breaking task, especially if armed with only soap, water, and a long-handed brush. The result: the ceiling's plaster design, an endless procession of garlands, ribbons, and urns, stood out in bone-white glints amid the black background. What had been intended as cheerful now looked funereal, like a shallow grave giving up its secrets.

A coal fire burned low beneath the elaborate mantel. Positioned before it sat Lord Dudley Maggart, one leg propped on a leather hassock. Without turning his head, he called in a rasping voice, "Who was at the door, Odette?"

"No one of consequence, darling." Lady Maggart sounded unconcerned, but her heels clicked rapidly on the marble floor as she made a beeline for the room's far door. Ben tried to step softly as he kept pace, but his footfalls seemed absurdly loud, as did Lady Juliet's.

"Good Lord, woman. Hannibal's elephants crossed the Alps more quietly than you." Lord Maggart turned in his chair, probably to upbraid his wife, only to behold two strangers accompanying her and Mr. Collins.

"Great Scott!" Lord Maggart pointed a trembling finger at Lady Juliet. "That's a rough sort of man to admit through the front door. Was the tradesman's entrance nailed shut?"

"Lovely to see you again, Lord Maggart," Lady Juliet called in her sweetest tone. "I'm not a tradesman or indeed a man at all. I'm Juliet Linton. Lady Victoria's daughter from Belsham Manor."

"Yes, don't let the dirty trousers and mannish boots deceive you. It's Lady Juliet, come to take tea." Lady Maggart maintained her carefree tone. Had she become adept at lying to soothe her husband, Ben wondered. Or could she lie smoothly on a variety of topics?

"Lady Juliet. Yes, of course. Misplaced my specs. Useless things," Lord Maggart said. His raspy inhalations made each sentence painful. "Well, now you're here, don't run away like thieves in the night. Come closer. I have a right to look over who's traipsing through my house."

Lady Maggart grimaced, but in a light voice, she said, "Naturally, darling," and led them over.

At close range, Ben was struck by the baron's frailty. If he'd gone over the top at the Somme, he was probably around Lady Maggart's age, the middle forties. However, he looked sixty—a weak and wasted sixty. His cheeks were hollow, his forehead stacked with creases; his hair and mustache were pale gray. Bizarrely, given the time of day, he wore evening dress. White tie, no less, with a red carnation in his buttonhole.

"Collins," Lady Maggart said, her pleasantness becoming strained. "Why in heaven's name is the baron attired for dinner? Dudley, you know we don't stand on ceremony these days."

"Don't berate the man," Lord Maggart said. "I'll wear what I please. Besides, the earl has always been one for the old observances. We'll have a drink together in the library before Collins rings the bell."

Lady Maggart shot Ben a glance that communicated two things. Her husband had dressed for a visitor who wasn't coming, and this wasn't the first time he'd muddled his dates or perhaps even his years.

Lord Maggart squinted at Lady Juliet. "Still unnecessarily tall, I see."

"I fear so, my lord. Should I ever discover a remedy for excessive female stature, I'll be sure to disseminate it far and wide."

"What? Hm. See that you do." Lord Maggart looked Ben up and down. In the pervasive gloom, he couldn't be sure, but the whites of Lord Maggart's eyes appeared yellow.

"Well? Out with it. Who the hell are you?"

"Benjamin Bones, Lord Maggart. Forgive my intrusion. I'll try to be brief."

"Brief? You'll be brief, will you?" Lord Maggart *harrumphed* as only a blueblood could. "Damn generous, keeping your intrusion brief. What is your business, sir?"

Ben involuntarily glanced at his black leather bag, and Lord Maggart cried out as if struck.

"White coat! A white coat. Come to poke and prod me!"

"Dudley, calm yourself," Lady Maggart cried.

"No bloody white coats in my house." Lord Maggart shifted

his elevated leg off the hassock with surprising speed. Fumbling beside his chair, he seized on a hardwood cane with a pewter grip, leaning on it as he got to his feet.

"I'll teach you to go where you're not wanted," he roared, swiping wildly at the air with his cane. Lady Maggart gasped, but Ben easily stepped aside. He didn't think the baron meant to land a blow so much as to frighten him. Handing his bag to Lady Juliet, he lifted his hands to prove they were empty.

"I'm not a physician, Lord Maggart." A plausible fiction occurred to him. "I'm an undertaker."

"An undertaker?" The baron stumped closer, leaning on his cane instead of brandishing it. His scleras were indeed yellow. So was his skin.

"I'm not dead yet, young man, however much these jackals may wish it," Lord Maggart said. "Come to stake out your territory? What abominable cheek. Even if my wife invited you to measure me for my coffin."

"Dudley. Please don't be cruel in front of our guests."

"In front of our guests," he repeated to Ben. "That's forbidden. Cruelty when guests are absent? Compulsory. I shall inform the earl. He knows the king. David, he calls him. David."

King Edward the VIII, who'd abdicated the throne in 1936, had been called "David" by friends and family. It seemed Lord Maggart did indeed have his years muddled. Ben knew better than to argue with a delusion, especially in someone whose medical history was unknown. Redirection was better.

"The king, eh? Extraordinary," he said briskly. "Me, I've come to clear up this business of a dead man where he doesn't belong. I'll remove the corpse and be on my way."

"Corpse? There's no corpse here. I know about them. Why do you imagine I wear this poppy?" he asked, pointing at the red carnation.

"I understand you fought in the Great War," Ben said, because the baron seemed to expect it.

"Yes, and be glad you're not a white coat, young man." Lord Maggart waved the cane alarmingly, forcing Ben to sidestep again. The pewter grip looked weighty enough to crack a skull or knock out teeth. "I've had the misfortune to know many, but MacHardy was the worst. Infamous quack! I told him I took a bayonet to the calf." He slapped his leg. "Then a bayonet to the belly." He slapped his midsection. "Two devilish wounds. Pain from dawn to dusk. And do you know what that charlatan MacHardy said?"

Ben shook his head.

"That it was all up here." Lord Maggart jabbed his temple. "Can you believe it? There's a bayonet of the cruelest steel, I tell you. To be called a liar by the very blackguards meant to help me.

"But MacHardy wasn't finished, no sir," he continued. "He turned the other white coats against me. Convinced them not to help. I needed surgery, injections, pills—something. But MacHardy wrote down two words on a piece of paper. Know what they were? Combat hysteria. As if war had turned me into a woman." Lord Maggart waved his cane again, more feebly this time. "All because I told him I dreamed of men with the heads of elephants. Glassy-eyed elephants, walking toward me, coming to make me join their ranks. MacHardy put my name on a list. Doctors do that, you know. Once your name's on a list, there's no getting off." He shook his head. "Smug, condescending white coats. Accusing *me* of cowardice. What do you say to that?"

"Bastards."

A smile broke across Lord Maggart's face. "Yes. Yes, precisely. You see, Odette? Even an undertaker knows the truth when he hears it. Bastards, he calls them. Yes, indeed. What did you say your name was, young man?"

"Bones."

"Ah. Well. Good luck to you, Mr. Bones. Keep an eye on the tall one in trousers," the baron said. "Do you know why women wear trousers?"

Ben shook his head politely as Lady Juliet leaned closer, presumably to hear some essential truth about herself.

"Women wear trousers so they may run faster, climb higher, and kick harder. So they may subvert the natural order, set down by God Almighty. A woman in trousers is a woman who's up to no good."

With that, Lord Maggart limped back to his chair by the fire. As he sank into it with a raspy sigh, Lady Maggart took the opportunity to hustle them out the door at last.

"Sorry about that," Ben whispered to Lady Juliet as they exited the great room. "It's best to humor the deluded."

"It's not as if he offended me." She grinned. "As a matter of fact, he's spot-on. I may have new calling cards printed. 'Juliet Linton: in trousers and up to no good.'"

"Ordinarily, I disapprove of profanity, Dr. Bones," Lady Maggart said, taking Ben's arm as Mr. Collins led them down to what he called "below stairs," the servants' domain under the house's ground level. "But how can I reproach you when you defused my husband's agitation with a single coarse word?"

"He isn't the first old soldier I've met, Lady Maggart," Ben said. "And I can certainly understand why he distrusts physicians. But surely a doctor oversees his care?"

"No. He truly believes he's on some sort of list, and they're all in league against him."

"Then I must tell you he appears jaundiced, my lady. Too much bilirubin in the blood. It's a sign that may indicate any number of disorders." He didn't mention the first that came to mind, pancreatic cancer. "Some, such as gallstones, can be resolved with surgery."

"Dudley says he'll go to his grave before he goes to another hospital. You've seen what he's like," Lady Maggart said. "Dressed to the nines for a dinner that happened years ago. My husband may not look like a threat, but when his ire is roused, he fights like a cornered rat. I've resigned myself to early widowhood." She tightened her hold on Ben's arm. "For some of us, the first blush of youth brings melancholy, but true joy comes in the prime of life."

Lady Juliet coughed violently.

"Are you quite all right back there?" Lady Maggart asked, not deigning to look over her shoulder.

"Yes. Sickened by a touch of fatuity."

"By what?"

"She's fine," Ben interjected before Lady Juliet could define what ailed her. At the bottom of the stairs, the basement spread out before them, cheerless, cold, and reeking of the same kind of disinfectant used on hospital floors.

Mr. Collins nodded to his left. "The kitchen, scullery, laundry, and game room are that way." He nodded to his right. "The staff dormitory is that way. The dead man was discovered in an unassigned room. Third door down."

Ben had seen morgues with more charm. Places like this, designed by the rich for the working class, constituted his idea of purgatory. He could imagine existing among these gray-green walls, feeble lighting, and cold linoleum floors, but not living here. Or, for that matter, dying here. Particularly by choice.

"I don't know why Special Constable Gaston hasn't arrived yet," he said, wondering if he should make a start without him. "Let's give him another moment. In the meantime, I'd like to know why Bobby Archer was here in the first place."

"We have no idea." Lady Maggart released his arm.

"Did he have some connection, however distant, with your husband or Fitchley Park?"

"None whatsoever."

"You said this is the staff dormitory," Lady Juliet said, clearly champing at the bit to investigate, Gaston or no Gaston. "For males or females?"

Mr. Collins ignored the question. Lady Maggart extended the silence by smoothing all four of her fox-fur's dangling paws. Then she said, "Dr. Bones, I accept your insistence that this woman's presence assists you. However, I will not be interrogated by her, and neither will Collins."

Ben glanced at Lady Juliet. Heaving a great sigh, she pressed her lips together and studied the ceiling.

"Speaking of this staff dormitory," Ben said mildly, "is it for males or females?"

"Our staff is entirely female," Mr. Collins replied, "but for me and the boot boy. He's an innocent sort and likely to remain so, if you take my meaning. There is no question of fraternization."

Except maybe with you, Ben thought, wondering if a man who exuded such vanity could be trusted not to abuse his employees.

"No fraternization among the staff, perhaps," Ben said, "but what about from outside?

"No."

"Where's the tradesman's entrance?"

"Between the game room and the laundry," Mr. Collins said.

"So if Bobby slipped inside, whatever his reason, he would have passed several common areas," Ben said. "It seems far more likely someone let him in. If Bobby was walking out with a kitchen maid or a cook's helper...."

"Impossible," Lady Maggart said.

"Our housekeeper, Mrs. Grundy, does not permit our female employees to have followers," Mr. Collins agreed. "Any girl breaking that rule would be discharged on the spot. Moreover, I retain veto power over every maid hired. Only good girls serve at Fitchley Park," he said proudly. "They are blameless in this sordid escapade, and unable to peacefully resume their duties with a corpse in the house. May we hope, Dr. Bones, you're ready to inspect the dead man and see to his removal?"

"Of course. Please send the special constable to me the moment he arrives," Ben said, wondering how a man who leapt to such rapid conclusions could drive so slowly.

"One moment, Dr. Bones," Lady Juliet called. She'd drifted back to the stairs, standing on the bottom step as she examined the carpet runner. "Is this blood?"

5

CADAVERIC SPASM

The suspicious red spot had stood out to Juliet not because she was a preternaturally gifted detective, but because she'd been searching high and low for something to complain about. Lady Maggart was unbearably smug about her beauty, her style, her country estate, and apparently even her future second husband, if that nauseating remark about attaining "true joy" was any indication. It infuriated Juliet, who yearned for beauty, style, a more attractive country estate, and—most especially—a second husband. Relegated to observe silently, she'd cast about for some imperfection in the servants' domain. The walls were spotless and the lino betrayed no flaw. Just as Juliet had been ready to concede even the bowels of Fitchley Park were exemplary, she spied a spot no bigger than a sixpence.

It was on the stairs, a splotch on the pale blue carpet runner. At first glance, she took it for a bit of jam, too trivial to mortify the baroness or her butler. Only when Ben raised a perfectly reasonable supposition—that a maid had sneaked Bobby Archer into the servants' dormitory for a rendezvous—and Mr. Collins started tutting about good girls and sordid escapades, did Juliet decide the man was definitely lying. And that gave the round red stain an entirely different meaning.

Ben looked the spot over. "Could it be blood?" he asked Mr. Collins.

The butler folded his arms. "Certainly not. It's a bit of wine from last night's supper."

"You can tell without looking?" Juliet raised her eyebrows.

Mr. Collins advanced on her with measured steps. She wasn't easily cowed, but he came so close, glaring at her with such intensity, her heart sped up. This wasn't the sort of polite contempt that well-bred servants routinely visited on dishonored guests. This was genuine menace.

"I can tell," Mr. Collins said, "because Gertie dropped a tray while bringing up last night's supper. Surely you make no accusations?"

"*Lady* Juliet merely asked a question. There's no reason so take offense over so small a thing," Ben said firmly.

Mr. Collins took a step back. Unclenching his hands, he folded them together, perhaps to keep from balling them into fists again.

"Did you pack the phenolphthalin?" Juliet asked Ben. He nodded.

The chemical reagent called phenolphthalin was a key part of the detective's armamentarium, as Juliet had recently learned. Ever since she'd helped Ben catch his wife's killer, she'd been eagerly studying the art of private detection. Finding crime fiction thick on the ground, but manuals for aspiring detectives almost nonexistent, she'd enrolled in an American correspondence course called Private Dick Academy.

The course promised to transform an ordinary citizen into a steely-eyed gumshoe in just thirty-six monthly lessons. That amounted to three years, or the time Ben had spent in medical school, but Juliet was undaunted. She'd inhaled lesson one, The

Kastle-Meyers Scientific Test for Confirming the Presence of Blood, successfully performing it in Ben's office while his back was turned. Now she longed to try it "in the lawbreaking arena," as Private Dick Academy's founder, retired American police sergeant Dirk Diamond, called a crime scene.

"Odette, with your permission, I'd like to test the stain," she said.

"Milady, with your permission, I'd like to set about rubbing it out," Mr. Collins countered.

"It's midafternoon," Ben reminded them, pointedly checking his watch. "We'll be lucky to get Bobby sorted, and only if we crack on."

"I agree," Lady Maggart said. "Show them the room, Collins."

The unassigned servant's room was cramped and unadorned, lit by a naked light bulb hanging from the ceiling. The only furniture was a chest of drawers, an empty wash basin, and an iron-framed bed. A corpse in this bleak limbo seemed fitting, even inevitable.

Bobby Archer lay on the blue-ticked mattress, naked except for a pair of black silk underpants. They were the latest kind, with wide leg openings and an elasticized waist, similar to what boxers wore in the ring. In life, he'd been uncommonly handsome, with curling black hair and sculpted features. In death, he'd lost not only his dignity but his good looks.

A jagged wound across his throat gaped wide, exposing the trachea. His flesh had gone milk-white with deep blue undertones. His eyes were open, the corneas frosted. As for his position, it was peculiar to the brink of black comedy. He was flat on his back, knees drawn up, heels perpendicular to the bed. His left arm hovered above his chest; his right arm extended toward the ceiling, palm up. He didn't look like a man who'd died in bed. He looked like a statue, knocked off its plinth and carelessly dumped in an empty room.

"I've never encountered a dead body frozen that way," Juliet said. Like most women in Birdswing, she'd seen a few corpses over the years, though most had died of natural causes. "Where's the blood?"

"Wherever he died, I should think." Ben turned to confront Lady Maggart and her butler. "Why was the body moved?"

Lady Maggart tried an open-mouthed routine similar to the poor fox around her shoulders. Mr. Collins frowned as if his ears deceived him.

"Right. Let's start at the top," Ben said. "I'll ask the questions. Lady Juliet will act as scribe."

Startled by this, Juliet set down her canvas bundle atop the chest of drawers. She'd been so focused on the possibility of revenge on Lady Maggart, she'd neglected to bring the obvious accoutrements, such as paper, a clipboard, and a fountain pen.

She dug in her handbag. Uncharitable types called it the saddlebag, because it was big, brown, and patched with contrasting leather, but it held everything Juliet required to get through her day, plus a little additional firepower. She came up with a pocket notebook and a pencil stub.

"Proceed."

"You mentioned no member of staff is assigned to this room," Ben said. "Is it used for anything at all?"

"No," Mr. Collins said.

"Who has access to the room?"

"No one. It's kept locked."

"Who has access to the key?" Ben asked.

"Only myself. That is to say, it hangs on a peg near the house phone for convenience. But everyone knows they're not to touch it," Mr. Collins said.

"So the body was discovered when one of you unlocked the door?"

"No," the butler said, his face assuming that impenetrable blankness. "One of the maids, Betsy, passed the room shortly after getting up and noticed the door was open. She looked inside, saw the dead man, and alerted Mrs. Grundy."

"So the housekeeper was the first person in authority to see him," Ben said. "Why isn't she here?"

"She's in her room, composing herself," Lady Maggart said. "Mrs. Grundy is a sturdy woman, but it was a ghastly shock."

"Were you here at the time?" Ben asked her.

"No, I breakfasted early and set out for Birdswing before half-eight."

"When were you alerted?" Ben asked Mr. Collins.

"Around nine. Perhaps half-nine."

"I see. Lady Juliet, do you have all that?"

Juliet's penmanship, which tended toward the hieroglyphic, looked worse than usual as she struggled to get everything down. "I believe so," she said, scribbling faster.

"Stop," Ben said sharply. "Now. Take this down. Maid, Betsy, noticed door open after getting up. Housekeeper alerted. Butler alerted. Time approximately nine or thereabouts." As Juliet's pencil scraped, Ben continued, "I've never lived in a stately home, but given what you've just told me, it seems one of your maids got up between half-eight and nine. That's rather slug-a-bed, is it not?"

"She was under the weather," Mr. Collins said.

Juliet glanced at his face. It betrayed nothing, but the tops of his ears had turned pink.

"And Lady Maggart, you breakfasted early and set out for Birdswing," Ben said. "I just made that journey. It isn't long. Lady Juliet, when did you arrive at the vicarage?"

"Eleven o'clock."

"And Lady Maggart was already there?"

"Yes. The better to accuse me."

"I see." Ben looked from the baroness to the butler. "Thus far, I've been told no one here has the slightest connection to Bobby Archer. That he must have slipped into Fitchley Park without help, entered a room that's kept locked, cut his own throat, and bloodlessly bled to death."

"Without a knife," Juliet put in.

"Fair point. So let me see if I have this right," Ben said. "No servant noticed the open door but the one who rose the latest, pushing the discovery into midmorning. Lord Maggart never cottoned on, which I can accept, at least for now. But Lady Maggart missed the commotion because—why? She was making the half-hour drive to Birdswing over the course of approximately two hours?"

Juliet wanted to cheer. Mr. Collins's ears were now bright red. With any luck Lady Maggart would follow suit and spontaneously combust.

"Dr. Bones," Lady Maggart said sweetly. "Benjamin. May I call you Benjamin?"

"Ben," he said, looking as uncertain as Juliet felt.

"Ben, yes, thank you. Your eye for detail is remarkable. I fear Birdswing's special constable is not quite so exacting. Then again, perhaps as a lifelong resident, he understands that all great houses have their share of skeletons, not all of them figurative. I expect Lady Juliet has told you that I repudiate the occult and reject those who practice it. What is perhaps less well known is my struggle to cleanse and purify Fitchley Park."

Juliet stopped writing and looked up, wondering what Lady Maggart was getting at.

"No doubt you saw St. Gwinnodock's on your way to the park," the baroness continued. "The rector, Father Rummage, is a frequent guest. We've prayed together, blessed the house both as a whole and room by room. We've reconsecrated the chapel and compelled all staff members to attend Sunday service, either here or St. Gwinnodock's. Nevertheless, strange doings still plague this house. The mystery of my long drive to Birdswing is easily solved. I stopped along the way to drop in on a friend. But the mystery of how this poor man's blood disappeared may never be solved. Or, indeed, what lured him here in the first place."

"Are you telling me a ghost did this?" Ben asked.

"You needn't pretend disbelief," Lady Maggart said in a tone of sweet reason that made Juliet want to throttle her. "You reputedly live in a haunted cottage. Your associate boasts of hearing otherworldly voices. Have you the arrogance to tell me that your experiences are genuine, and mine are mere superstition? Look at that poor man's contortions. Tell me he didn't behold something unbearable just before he died."

Juliet was scribbling so rapidly, she feared not even she would be capable of deciphering the result.

"Those contortions aren't supernatural, your ladyship," Ben said. "They're the result of cadaveric spasm. You've heard of rigor mortis, yes? Cadaveric spasm is akin to that, with one key difference—it doesn't require hours to develop. It happens instantly, at the moment of death, as the result of severe shock and trauma. In this case, we're fortunate it occurred."

"Fortunate?" Lady Maggart said.

"Yes. It's frozen his limbs into a position that gives us some incontrovertible evidence about his death," Ben said. "Look, I'll demonstrate.

"Suppose I'm Bobby. I've come here to, er, romance a maid. When I get out of bed, probably to get dressed, someone attacks me from behind." He lifted his chin, drawing his finger across his throat. "Blood spurts everywhere. About a gallon, if you didn't know. I go to my knees"—he eased down—"and catch myself against a wall with one hand"—he demonstrated—"but shock has already killed me. The resulting cadaveric spasm freezes me like this, in the last position I ever took.

"Now," Ben continued, rising and massaging his knee. "Imagine the scene. Blood everywhere. It's clear to me the killer decided—"

"Why must there be a killer?" Mr. Collins interrupted belligerently. "I once knew of a man who cut his own throat. Why not this man?"

Juliet snorted. "Did that corpse hide the knife and relocate to a clean room, too?"

"Lady Juliet," Lady Maggart said coolly, "perhaps it's escaped your notice, but you are unfeminine, uncouth, and altogether unwelcome."

"Insults aside," Ben said firmly before Juliet responded in kind, "my associate, as you call her, is correct. Whether Bobby was murdered or committed suicide, his body has been moved. That would take at least two people. He weighed about twelve stone, I think, and he's stiff as marble. Getting him in here would have been difficult. Doing it without being seen beggars the imagination."

"That is quite enough," Mr. Collins burst out, once again displaying the irascibility Juliet had glimpsed by the stairs. "Milady, I find this insupportable. What he suggests is nothing less than a conspiracy. He would have you believe one of our girls is a strumpet and a murderess. That others aided and abetted her crime. Worse, that I am either incompetent or complicit."

"I'm sure Dr. Bones doesn't mean to accuse you," Lady Maggart said. "I can see he's an earnest, capable man, despite the company he keeps. We shouldn't take offense or hinder his efforts in any way. There is no murderer. Not in the human sense," she declared. "Something lured Mr. Archer here. Look into the history of Cornwall, of ghost lights and moving sign-posts, and perhaps you'll see why I consider the occult so dangerous. I know nothing of this man, but something condemned and tormented him, and stole his blood away. Such things can only be fought with prayer and piety." She shot a glance at Juliet. "And the repudiation of those who commune with spirits."

"I disagree," Juliet said, realizing the moment had arrived. Putting aside her pencil and notebook, she seized the bundle of stretcher canvas, unwrapping it to expose the talking board within. "Communing with spirits shall reveal the truth. Let us call upon the dead."

Raising the sinister-looking board like Circe lifting her bowl of poison, Juliet said in ringing tones, "My HOUR is almost come! When I to SULFUROUS and TORMENTING flames must RENDER up myself...."

"Stop!" Lady Maggart shrieked.

"I could a TALE unfold whose lightest word would HARROW up thy SOUL—"

"The Fiend. You speak his tongue!"

"Shakespeare's tongue," Ben corrected, snatching away the board before Juliet's big finish. "From *Hamlet*, if memory serves. With such a hammy delivery, it's hard to tell."

"Hammy? Nonsense. I'm a natural actress," Juliet said, taken aback. Her mother adored her impromptu recitations. So did her mare, Epona, and her heirloom rose bushes.

Lady Maggart either didn't believe she'd been fooled by the Bard, or the realization made her angrier still. "Witch!" she flung at Juliet.

"Beef-witted canker-blossom!" Juliet flung back.

"*Enough*," Ben snapped, stepping between them. "Milady, I'd like a word with you. Alone."

"Yes, of course," Juliet said.

"Not you." He pressed the board back in her hands. "Take this and wait in the hall."

"You, too, Collins." Lady Maggart sounded genuinely shaken.

The butler obeyed. Juliet didn't want to. Her natural tendency was to answer back, to argue until he changed his mind or relented in exhaustion. But as American gumshoe Dirk Diamond said, "The case must come first."

With a sigh, she followed the butler out.

6

SOUS LE VENT

"Lady Maggart," Ben began. "Forgive me if I overstep, but may I take your pulse?"

She extended her wrist. As Ben expected, given her dilated pupils and quick breaths, he found tachycardia: an elevated heart rate, impossible to manufacture for sympathy.

"Shall I live?" She forced a smile. Once again, she reminded him of Penny in her kinder moments, when he'd loved her almost against his will.

"Yes, of course." He released her wrist. "I wanted to check because I've been astonished by how you've managed this situation, until moments ago, so coolly. The discovery of a dead man in your house, your proximity to a fresh corpse...."

He trailed off as she looked sidelong at Bobby, unflinching.

"The sight doesn't trouble you. The smell doesn't trouble you. All those questions I raised, which upset your butler no end, didn't trouble you. Nor did the implications about a conspiracy among your staff. You've behaved very much like a hostess addressing some minor unpleasantness, which can be seen as admirable," he put in, so as not to goad her without reason. "But then Lady Juliet pulled an admittedly tasteless prank, which was perhaps to be expected, given your run-in at the vicarage this morning, and you fell apart. Why?"

"Because that sort of thing, whether playful or in earnest, is ruining my life," she said, voice breaking into a sob. She turned away, took a moment to compose herself, and then resumed speaking with her previous strength. Only the tears standing in her eyes signaled distress.

"This year has been beastly. Absolutely beastly." She hugged herself, pressing the fox fur against her chin. "Noises. Voices. Objects disappearing. Threatening signs, impossible to ignore. Father Rummage agreed there was some spiritual deficit in Fitchley House and directed me to do several things. I followed through, and the occurrences stopped. Then in September, it returned, no doubt because of occult devotion in your village."

She believes it, Ben thought. Then again, his truth-detecting instincts weren't foolproof. Penny had tricked him by lying to his face more than once.

"I've experienced most of what you describe," Ben said. "But in my case, it's the talk of the village. People I barely know stop me to ask about the ghost of Fenton House. How is it none of them ever mentioned you having similar troubles?"

"Because Barking is not Birdswing, thank heavens. Here, people retain some semblance of discretion," Lady Maggart said. "My staff is sworn to secrecy. The only person outside Fitchley Park who knows is Father Rummage, and he's silent as the grave." She sighed. "We've worked so hard, he and I, to remove whatever curse has fallen upon this house. To rectify whatever sins," she added softly, "left an opening for evil. But this morning over breakfast, when I learned that absurd woman was *boasting* about communing with spirits—"

"Don't speak ill of Lady Juliet in my presence," Ben cut in. "Please."

She accepted the rebuke with a nod. "You're a good man, Dr.

Bones. I can see that about you. As for the matter of my composure, let me remind you, this house is accustomed to strife. The Dudley I married vanished in the war, and a stranger returned in his place. So this"—she glanced at Bobby—"is not the first changeling to appear in my life. If this haunting continues, I fear he won't be the last."

"Lady Juliet heard a voice. I saw an object fall from thin air. But you mentioned threatening signs. Like what?"

"Don't force me to dredge it up just now. Probably nothing you'd regard as evidence. Except that I'm going mad."

"I understand. I've had a scientific bent as long as I can remember," Ben said. "At home, I've managed to accept what I've witnessed as something beyond the norm. Maybe beyond the scientific method itself. But here," he continued, careful not to sound as if he were lecturing, "I've yet to witness anything that can't be understood with further investigation. Which you might find comforting, in a way. A human killer would be preferable to a spectral one, surely?"

"Yes, of course."

"Will you allow me—and Special Constable Gaston, when he arrives—to search the house?"

"For what?" she asked.

"The place where Bobby died. And the murder weapon."

"Very well. As long as you maintain your discretion around my husband and cause him no distress. And," Lady Maggart added, "if you promise to remove this body, and your friend Lady Juliet, as soon as possible."

"Agreed," Ben said quickly before she could change her mind. "But before we take Bobby away, I think we should preserve certain details for future reference. Have you a camera, my lady?"

"No."

"Does Barking have a photographer?"

"Father Rummage," Lady Maggart said. "An amateur, naturally, but very accomplished. His prints are sold around the village as day-tripper souvenirs. I could send a maid to the rectory to ask—"

"Stop," cried Lady Juliet from the hall. "Stop, or I'll make a citizens' arrest!"

"Excuse me," Ben told Lady Maggart. Fighting to keep his temper, he threw open the door, expecting something on par with Lady Juliet's pseudo-spiritualism. Instead, he saw something alarming.

"Collins! Good God, man. Let her go."

The butler's face had gone as red as a pomegranate. At Ben's command, he released his grip on Lady Juliet's shoulders just as she kicked him in the kneecap—at least, Ben hoped that's where she was aiming. When he let go, she overbalanced, staggering backward, and fell over a uniformed maid. The maid, who'd been bent over the stairs, scrubbing something as if her life depended on it, yelped.

"See what you've done!" Mr. Collins roared at Lady Juliet.

"You're under arrest!"

"That's enough," Ben shouted. No one paid him any mind. He pushed between the combatants. "What happened?"

"Evidence! They're destroying evidence," Lady Juliet said.

"I have authority below stairs," Mr. Collins said.

"I only did as I was told," wailed the uniformed maid, a pretty girl with an elaborate lace cap. She clutched a bottle of solvent in one hand and a flannel in the other.

"No one's blaming you." Sighing, Ben helped the trembling girl up as he checked on Lady Juliet's alleged blood spot, or rather, the place where it had been. The chemical had acted so aggressively, not only the spot was gone. Even the carpet fibers were blanched.

"It was only a drop of wine," Mr. Collins said. "As I explained the moment you pointed it out."

"Yes, well, perhaps I'd trust you better if I hadn't found you manhandling Lady Juliet," Ben retorted. "While your girl was using enough Borax to bleach coal."

"Sir, I swear, I was only doing as I was told," the maid said.

Ben pinched the bridge of his nose. *Where* was Special Constable Gaston? In this situation, the man's high-handed, sternly authoritative manner would have been a help rather than a hindrance.

"What's your name?" he asked the maid.

"Kitty," she sniffed.

"Chin up, Kitty. You've done your duty, and no one's cross with you," he said. "But Mr. Collins knew we intended to test that stain for the chemical properties of human blood. Should Bobby Archer's death become a CID manner, I will inform the authorities he deliberately destroyed evidence."

"Very well," the butler said. "No doubt you'll also explain to Scotland Yard that the dead man lost a gallon of blood, yet you went to pieces over a single drop. A purported single drop. Come, Kitty." He marched upstairs with her in tow, slamming the door behind him.

"I would apologize for Collins's behavior," said Lady Maggart dryly from behind Ben. "But it seems even the most reliable servant can be pushed too far."

Ben saw no reason to argue. He wasn't concerned about the butler's rudeness. The depth of his anger, however, was intriguing, and would need to be revisited later.

"Lady Juliet, are you recovered?"

"Yes, of course." She squared her shoulders. "Thank heavens no member of Belsham Manor's staff would ever treat a woman in such an ungallant fashion."

"My dear husband mistook you for a man," Lady Maggart said. "Perhaps Mr. Collins did the same?"

Before this back-and-forth could devolve into a second altercation, Ben interrupted with a direct appeal to Lady Juliet. "I need to conclude my examination of Bobby. May I trouble you to fetch the rector from St. Gwinnodock's? He's an experienced photographer. I'd like him to document the body's position before we remove it."

"Since when am I an errand girl?"

"You aren't. But I trust you impress the urgency of the matter upon him," Ben said, holding her gaze steadily.

"Just go," Lady Maggart snapped. Lady Juliet obeyed, but as she ascended, the staircase's acoustics proved too tempting to resist.

"By the PRICKING of my THUMBS, something WICKED this way COMES...."

AFTER LADY JULIET'S DEPARTURE, Lady Maggart cited a headache to excuse herself to her bedroom. Alone with Bobby, Ben rechecked the gloomy little room. For what, he didn't know. Outside of phenolphthalin, his knowledge of modern detective methods began and ended with fingerprints. In the cinema, there was also the option of hauling a suspect into a small room, shining a bright light in his face, and haranguing him for an indefinite period. The idea of putting Mr. Collins through that particular wringer struck Ben as a good start.

Despite Ben's careful inspection, the room gave up nothing: no fallen objects, no blood smears, no signs of conspicuous scrubbing. He checked his watch; seven minutes had elapsed. It would probably be another quarter-hour before Lady Juliet returned with the rector. He decided to have another look at Bobby's corpse.

Lady Maggart's belief that Bobby had taken his life due to some form of phantasmagorical interference was bizarre, but suicide wasn't impossible, even if it was statistically unlikely. As a medical student, Ben had learned that toxic gas inhalation was far more common, since it was painless, bloodless, and didn't require some outside force, like a bridge or a tall building. In a poorly ventilated sitting room, for example, one could shut the door and windows, turn on the unlit gas jets, fall asleep on the settee, and never wake up. Sticking one's head in a gas oven would also do the trick. But around 1900, self-inflicted throat wounds like Bobby's had been a prevalent method of suicide, especially among men.

Except there are no practice cuts, Ben thought, reexamining the dead man's throat. Even for a person in the grip of despair, overcoming the human survival instinct required desensitization; thus, the fatal wound was usually surrounded by shallower "practice" cuts. Bobby had died because of one deep slash. Judging by the architecture of the wound, Ben guessed the blade had been pulled from right to left. The slash rose from the collarbone to behind the ear, suggesting a left-handed killer. Had Bobby been left-handed? What about Fitchley Park's staff?

The girl on the stairs. Kitty. She had the bottle in her right hand and the flannel in her left.

A familiar fragrance, the sensuous entwining of bergamot and lavender, tickled his nostrils, bringing with it a tangle of competing emotions: tenderness and hurt, desire and repulsion. The combination—a paper-white corpse and the scent of his dead wife—lifted the hairs on the back of Ben's neck.

"Penny?"

Turning in a slow circle, he reexamined every inch of the

room with far greater dread than he'd ever felt in Fenton House. Nothing had moved.

Checking the corridor, he found it empty. The room next door was unlocked and also empty. From the direction of the kitchen and scullery, he heard chatter and pots clanging. No woman wearing *Sous le Vent* was near.

He returned to the room where Bobby lay. The scent was stronger now.

The first time Bobby strayed from his wife, Helen, it was with Penny. No one was sure if they were actually lovers, but they stepped out together, and he carried a torch long after she moved on.

He'd gone through *Revelations of a Reluctant Medium* thoroughly enough to guess Madame Daragon's take: Malice sometimes survived death and extracted vengeance on the living. But Ben couldn't fully embrace that, at least not yet. He decided to go over the room a third time, this time looking for the simplest explanation: something soaked in French perfume.

The nightstand was empty except for a liner of yellowed newspaper. It smelled like mildew. The blue-ticked mattress, which clearly hadn't been aired in recent memory, reeked of compounded body odor. The only thing left was Bobby's fashionable silk underpants. Unfortunately, Ben was submitting them to the sniff test as St. Gwinnodock's rector arrived.

"Oh my." Schoolgirlish tittering followed. "Aren't you the thorough one?"

Backing away, Ben saw a portly man dressed entirely in black, apart from the dog collar round his throat. Perhaps five feet tall, he appeared even shorter with Lady Juliet looming beside him. "Father Rummage?"

"Yes, indeed. What an unusual way to test that region." Beaming as if the corpse was a basket of daisies, he tittered again.

"Dr. Bones is a cunning investigator. He leaves no stone

unturned," Lady Juliet said loyally, though she, too, looked mystified. "Odor may provide a clue."

"Precisely," Ben said, clearing his throat. "Thank you for coming, Rector."

"Such a blessing to be of use," the little man agreed. Pink-cheeked, with a fringe of white hair, he was perhaps fifty, with circular specs and a sunny grin. His camera, which resembled the sort used by reporters, hung around his neck.

"I've brought rolls of film, my tripod, and all my flashbulbs. Seventeen," he said proudly, placing a heavy-looking leather bag on the floor. "I do hope that will be sufficient. I order them special by catalog, you see. They take two weeks to arrive." He laughed again, for no reason Ben could divine. "Lovely to meet you. Dreadful shame about this poor soul. Dreadful, dreadful. But lovely to meet you. Hah!"

Ben didn't know if the rector was still amused at having caught him doing something apparently unwholesome or if his laughter was a nervous tic. Either way, he was relieved when Father Rummage stopped chortling and started taking pictures.

"Dr. Bones," Lady Juliet whispered in his ear. "May I presume something smelled amiss?"

"What do you think?" he snapped and instantly regretted it. "Sorry. I'm on edge. Do you smell anything?"

Pleased to be consulted, Lady Juliet wandered about the room, sniffing theatrically.

"Nothing but a corpse and a mattress that ought to be burned."

He wasn't surprised. The odor of *Sous le Vent* was gone, if it had ever existed.

When the rector finished taking pictures, Ben checked his watch and saw there was time to tour at least part of the house, but since Gaston still hadn't arrived, someone would need to remain with Bobby's corpse to forestall tampering.

"Me?" Lady Juliet asked. "Why? I didn't even manage to save the blood stain. Shouldn't I accompany you and take dictation? Surely the rector would be kind enough to stay."

"The rector is also a photographer," Ben said. "If I find anything, documentation will be invaluable."

"The rector is the best choice of companion, if I may be so bold," said Mr. Collins, joining them once more. He'd regained his composure during the short break. "Father Rummage's presence in the family rooms is both familiar and welcome, should Lord Maggart notice us going about.

"And I do hope, Dr. Bones," he continued stiffly, like a man reading a statement prepared by his captors, "you'll forgive my earlier rudeness. Lady Maggart asked me to express my sincere apologies. I extend them wholeheartedly. These strange and disturbing events have taken their toll."

Ben nodded. There was no polite alternative, even though he didn't want to accept the false apology any more than the butler had wanted to issue it.

"Where, pray tell, are my sincere apologies?" Lady Juliet asked. Father Rummage giggled.

"I'm sorry, but we haven't time for this," Ben told her, turning to Mr. Collins. "Let's begin with the rest of the servants' area."

"I demand an apology," Lady Juliet shouted as the three of them departed. "I was manhandled in an egregious fashion!"

Neither Ben nor the others looked back.

7

UNDER ARREST

Mr. Collins began by showing Ben what he clearly considered the epicenter of the below-stairs world, his personal sitting room and adjoining bedroom. It didn't make for compelling viewing. Ben saw no spilled blood or signs of a struggle, just evidence of an abstemious life. Mr. Collins's bed was as bare as a prisoner's. His bookshelf contained only the Bible and the *Book of Common Prayer*, and his hearth was cold. A hip bath and a chamber pot sat in the corner.

No running water in here, Ben thought. Even if Bobby's throat had been cut from behind, which was almost certain, the killer would surely have ended up with bloody hands and blood-stained clothes. A private spot to wash up would have been essential.

"Where is the servants' W.C.?"

"We haven't one," Mr. Collins said. "There's plenty of hot water in the kitchen and a privy outside."

"Don't look so surprised, Dr. Bones," said Father Rummage. "Luxuries are rare in Barking. I, for one, think our community's the better for it." He punctuated this last with another meaning-less laugh.

Nervous tic, Ben decided.

The rest of the basement was cold, drab, and virtually deserted. The staff dining room was deserted; even the assigned bedrooms were empty. Nowhere did he see anything worth troubling Father Rummage to expend another flashbulb, much less a murder weapon or a bucket of spilled blood.

"Where is everyone?"

"Most of the women are upstairs, consoling one another," Mr. Collins said. "The boot boy—have I mentioned him?"

"You called him an innocent."

"Yes. In other words, an imbecile. At any rate, the boot boy took this very hard and has gone out-of-doors. In times of stress, he burrows into a haystack and remains there till his belly forces him in for a meal."

Ben winced. "You don't mean to say he'll be out all night?"

The butler shrugged.

"But it may snow."

"If it does, I imagine he'll come back inside," Mr. Collins said. "He's fortunate that we provide employment, as he's fit for very little. Coddling him would render him fit for nothing. Wouldn't you agree, Rector?"

Father Rummage looked unhappy. "You know my feelings perfectly well," he muttered, fiddling with his camera.

The true below-stairs nexus, the kitchen, contained only two workers: a skinny girl basting a joint, and a middle-aged woman at the butcher block, reading a book. She was plain, apart from her extravagant brown hair, which was shot through with white.

"Jasper," she said, looking up and scowling. "What's this? I see you brought the God-botherer and his camera."

"Good afternoon, Mrs. Tippett," Father Rummage said, nodding and beaming.

The woman ignored that. Gimlet gaze on Mr. Collins, she said, "I asked you a question, Jasper."

"And I've asked you to remember that whilst on duty, you'll address me as Mr. Collins. And treat the rector with all due respect."

"That little, eh? Fine. Please forgive me, your great and powerful butlership. I mistook you for my little brother," Mrs. Tippett said.

Ben saw a faint resemblance between the cook and the butler, mostly in their hair. Hers, less lovingly coiffed, was gathered in a single thick braid, piled atop her head. Her features were coarser than her brother's, her teeth yellowed by tobacco, her hands red and cracked. By contrast, Mr. Collins's hands were beautifully manicured.

"Who's this bright young thing?" Mrs. Tippett asked, grinning at Ben.

"Dr. Bones of Birdswing," Mr. Collins replied. "He is assisting Special Constable Gaston with his inquiries regarding the, er...."

"Dead bloke? Lovely. The sooner sorted and forgotten, the better." Her eyes roamed over Ben, up and down and up again, lingering on him like he was a choice bit of beef. He was accustomed to a certain amount of female attention, and generally enjoyed it, but her sort of outright leering made him uncomfortable.

"Not that you aren't welcome," Mrs. Tippett said, "but why are you looking in here? If a man had been butchered like a hog in my kitchen, I think I would have noticed."

"Lady Maggart has given me leave to search every room," Ben said.

The girl basting the joint dropped her brush. It clattered to the floor, splattering grease everywhere.

"Oh! Sorry," she cried. Ben received only a flash of wide eyes, high cheekbones, and blonde strands sticking out from under a white mobcap. Then she was on her hands and knees, cleaning up the mess.

"That's Betsy," Mrs. Tippett told Ben. "Sixteen years old and daft as a donkey in a drainpipe. Maybe she killed the poor sod while I was rolling out this morning's scones."

"Betsy?" Ben repeated, noting that she scrubbed with her right hand. "You're the maid who got up late and found the door unlocked?"

"Hey?" The girl shot him an uncomprehending look.

Ben turned to Mr. Collins. "Is there more than one Betsy?"

"No. But if you think back carefully, you'll find I said it was Kitty who made the discovery," the butler said.

"*No*," Ben said, wondering if the real conspiracy in Fitchley Park was to make him think he was losing his wits. "You said Betsy."

"I said no such thing. However...." Mr. Collins seemed to recall Lady Maggart's directive. "I beg your pardon if I misspoke or was somehow unclear. I meant Kitty."

Ben decided to accept that, at least until he could check Lady Juliet's notes. He turned to Mrs. Tippett. "Did you know Bobby Archer?"

"Aye."

"I've been given to understand he had no connection to this household."

"He didn't," Mrs. Tippett agreed, with a teasing lilt in her tone. "Doesn't mean I didn't know him. Fine looking specimen. Particularly when he was your age."

"This sort of talk is unacceptable in front of Betsy," Mr. Collins said. "And while Lady Maggart gave you leave to inspect the house, Dr. Bones, I'd advise you not to waste too much time questioning the staff. It's clear the poor man wandered into Fitchley Park for reasons we can never understand and took his life for reasons we can never know. Mysteries abound in life."

"Oh, aye, 'mysteries abound,'" the cook mimicked, winking at Ben. "Taught himself to talk that way as a footman and was

soon made valet. Now he's butler, and all he does is talk. That's
where a clever tongue gets you. Hard work and knowing your
place gets you here." She waved a raw red hand, indicating the
kitchen.

"As for who did it," Mrs. Tippett continued, "there's a crime-
solving ghost in Birdswing, is there not? I told her ladyship
about it just this morning. She got her back up, yes she did. Her
ladyship on a mission is a fearsome thing." The cook laughed, as
if she knew exactly the degree of strife her shared gossip had
created. "If your Birdswing ghost can solve crimes, I reckon our
Barking ghost can commit them."

Chuckling, she returned her attention to her book, Mrs.
Beeton's *Household Management*. "Carry on, Doctor. Search my
kingdom. Let the God-botherer pray over it a second time. Or
would it be a third?"

"Third," Father Rummage said. He appeared so intimidated
by Mrs. Tippett, all he could manage was a *heh-heh* under his
breath.

"Whichever. I have no secrets. Neither does Betsy, even if she
thinks she has."

The brush clattered to the floor.

"Sorry, ma'am," Betsy whispered.

"Donkey in a drainpipe," Mrs. Tippett said, turning the page
with her left hand.

Ben was surprised, given Fitchley Park's splendor, by the
antediluvian conditions Mrs. Tippett and her underlings
endured. Instead of an evenly-cooking gas stove, there was an
open range—a massive coal fire surrounded by hanging
cookpots and an iron oven. The wall racks held plain white
dishes, some with chipped edges. The shelves overflowed with
pots, pans, molds, and platters, all of them tin. Ben's mum had a
kitchen the size of a postage stamp, but it possessed the twentieth-century basics: copper cookware, a pop-up toaster, and an

electric tea kettle. Mrs. Tippett's culinary arsenal dated back to the days when turnspit dogs were mod cons.

The kitchen knives were stored in a stained old woodblock. All of the slots were filled but one, large enough for an eight-inch blade.

"Has a knife gone missing?" he asked.

"Last week," Mrs. Tippett replied, eyes still on her book. "I asked you about it, Jasper. Don't you remember?"

"Rubbish. First I've heard of it."

She tutted. "Memory, Jasper. It's the first thing to go. I reported it to you Monday last. You told me you'd look into it. I suppose I should have taken the matter to Mrs. Grundy. Perhaps she's the one who took it in the first place."

"Mrs. Grundy might have taken a large kitchen knife without your leave, then forgotten to return it?" Ben asked.

"Maybe, if she wanted to kill an especially large rat," Mrs. Tippett said, that teasing lilt returning. "Great houses attract vermin of all sorts. And all sizes."

After Father Rummage took a photograph of the knife rack, Mr. Collins continued the below-stairs tour, leading them through the storehouse, larder, and game room. The first two were unremarkable; the third had worn floorboards stained brown-black with decades of bloodletting. But no carcasses hung from the ceiling's iron hooks, and Ben found no evidence that anything had been butchered there lately, not even a pheasant or hare.

"Lady Maggart dislikes the taste of game?" he asked.

Mr. Collins made a noncommittal sound.

"It's Lord Maggart," Father Rummage volunteered. "He no longer shoots. Can't abide hunting dogs. The sound of a bark or a gun sets him off." He chuckled. "A blessing, really. A man so quick to anger shouldn't mix with guns."

"Father Rummage," Mr. Collins said sternly.

"Oh. My. I spoke out of turn, didn't I?" The rector looked abashed for half a beat before dissolving into giggles.

"Lord Maggart is not quick to anger. Merely irritable," Mr. Collins told Ben. "Daylight is a more germane concern. Shall we continue above stairs?"

They did, skirting the great room where Lord Maggart still sat before the fire. The rest of the ground floor was large enough to serve as a casualty ward, and for the most part was equally charmless.

This heap could use a splash of paint, Ben thought, taking in the bare walls and dustless, ornament-free shelves. *Is this austerity deliberate? Or an indication of financial troubles?*

The first floor was more of the same: gloomy, with over half the rooms closed, the furniture shrouded in snowy sheets.

"Well! No bloodstains thus far, least of all here," Father Rummage announced cheerfully as Mr. Collins led them into a small ballroom filled with white shapes. "Lady Maggart and I prayed together here not a fortnight ago. Lovely. But I still half-expect a sheet to bestir itself."

"Do you?" Mr. Collins asked dryly. "Small wonder your prayers failed to ease the baroness's fears."

"That's unkind, and unfair besides," the rector said. "A bit of levity doesn't negate the power of my spiritual guidance. 'For God hath not given us the spirit of fear; but of power, and of love, and of a sound—*oh!*" Shrieking, he fell into Ben, who reflexively shoved him away.

"R-rustling. Just there," Father Rummage quavered, pointing at a cluster of white blobs in the far corner. "I saw it move!"

It fell to Ben and Mr. Collins to investigate as the rector, now embracing the spirit of fear, withdrew to the hall, where he could wait in comparative safety. As they drew closer to the wall, Ben heard the rustling and saw small black pellets on the carpet.

"Rats," Mr. Collins said. "I'll bait the traps tonight. Mrs. Tippett is right about one thing: this house draws vermin."

"There's nothing here but rats," Ben called to Father Rummage and then he smelled it, faint but unmistakable: *Sous le Vent*.

"Ah! There you are, Dr. Bones," said Special Constable Gaston, red-cheeked and bright-eyed, from the hall. He'd donned his white helmet with its black *W*. His truncheon was clutched in both hands. "Why are you poking about in a ballroom?"

Father Rummage emitted his heartiest laugh yet. "Searching for clues and finding rat droppings."

"For shame." Gaston tutted. "When I got no answer at the front door, I went round back and shouted for the cook to let me in. Then I went and sorted Bobby. He's wrapped decently in a blanket and loaded in Lady Juliet's car."

"Rat droppings aside, I've found plenty of indications of foul play," Ben said. "Did Lady Juliet put you in the picture?"

"Her?" Gaston bristled. "The day that woman can tell me something I don't know is the day I take up knitting."

"Yes, well, we'd nearly given you up for dead. Is that where you've been? Knitting?"

"Far from it." He smacked the truncheon against his palm. "While you were swanning about, playing detective, I was placing the murderer under arrest."

8

A VOICE FROM BEYOND

"Preposterous," Juliet heard herself say for the fourth time. "Simply preposterous." Repeating this to Ben was preaching to the choir, but she couldn't seem to stop.

After spending a quarter hour unsuccessfully trying to convince Gaston that his actions were premature at best and grossly unwarranted at worst, they'd had no choice but to set out for Birdswing. As they passed St. Gwinnodock's, the sun dissolved into red-orange streaks across the horizon; as they exited Barking, the woods went dark, the pastures sinking into gloom. Now they were in near-total blackness, apart from two narrow beams from her car's shielded headlamps. If she meant to reach Fenton House without sideswiping a hedgerow or rendering some poor animal airborne, her focus had to be equally narrow, yet her thoughts stubbornly returned to the person Gaston had arrested for the murder of Bobby Archer: his estranged wife, Helen.

It wasn't because they were friends. Just as Bobby's twin sons, Caleb and Micah, were arguably the most dangerous children in Cornwall, Helen was arguably the least pleasant person in

Birdswing. "Arguably" was, in fact, the perfect word to attach to Helen. She balked at authority, ignored most of the rules of polite society, and collected feuds the way entomologists collect bugs. But that didn't make her a murderer.

Besides, Juliet suspected if Helen did kill someone, she would stand up and admit it, boldly and without shame. But Helen had not confessed, nor had she exhibited her trademark belligerence. Silent and pale with shock, she'd allowed Gaston to put her in Barking's tiny lockup.

"Consigned to the Cow Hole. Such an indignity!" Juliet squeezed the steering wheel the way she wanted to squeeze Gaston's thick neck. It had to be thick, to hold up his impenetrable skull.

Ben, seemingly miles away, perked up at the mention of the local jail. "I wondered what Gaston was talking about. Why is it called the Cow Hole?"

"It's actually the *kowel*," Juliet said, pronouncing it "cowl," which she hoped was correct. Precious few native speakers remained, so she'd only seen the Cornish word in print. "The majority of Barking began life as a feudal lord's courtyard, you know. St. Gwinnodock's was the priory. Some houses along the high street were the soldiers' barracks. The stocks and gibbet were located on the village green, and the Cow Hole stood nearby. A stone roundhouse where the condemned awaited judgment."

"I saw one on the drive from London, when we stopped for lunch. A local man said it was still in use as a lockup for drunks and poachers."

"Yes. Mostly drunks. Cornish poachers are famously hard to catch." No matter how dire the situation, Juliet never missed a chance to brag about her county. "Ethan spent the night there once, when he tried to drink as much as he gambled. No less than he deserved. But poor Helen, cast into an oubliette!"

Ben made a surprised noise. "The Cow Hole is a coffin-sized dungeon?"

"What? No, of course not. It was redone ages ago. That's hardly the point," she said, waving away his tendency to let specifics bog him down. "What matters is Helen has been falsely imprisoned. Heaven knows she's a difficult woman, and I never thought I'd take her part, but I must, because it's preposterous— listen to me, I'm so discombobulated, the only word I can come up with is *preposterous*—to think she murdered Bobby."

Juliet waited for Ben to agree with her. He did not.

"Dr. Bones. When you spoke to that nincompoop Gaston, you argued for Helen quite passionately. Don't tell me you're having second thoughts."

"Second ones. Third and fourth ones, too." She could hear the smile in his voice, even if she couldn't see it. "Gaston arrested her on the strength of two facts. She hated Bobby, she's never denied that, and Gaston saw her walking along Barking's high street in the middle of the day. I may not be a student of Private Dick Academy," he said lightly, "but that seems like insufficient grounds to toss the mother of two young children into the clink. That's what I was arguing—that Gaston should let Mrs. Archer go home to her sons and take up the matter in the morning. Still...." He trailed off.

As they passed it on the left, Juliet recognized the shape of Birdswing's easterly landmark, the Barrow Stone. That meant Fenton House was mere minutes away. "Still what?" she prompted.

"Why was Mrs. Archer window-shopping in Barking, of all places, at one o'clock in the afternoon? Isn't that her restaurant's busiest stretch? Doesn't the noonday crowd make up the bulk of her business?"

"It does."

"Then closing up between noon and two o'clock only makes

sense if there's an emergency," Ben said. "Gaston asked why she did it. She said she felt like a change. But closing up and cycling all the way to Barking to wander along the high street is—"

"A lie," Juliet interrupted. "Yes, of course. She's never closed her restaurant during peak hours for anything I know of. Obviously, she came to Barking to pray."

"Obviously?"

"Helen has been feuding with Father Cotterill for years. Consequently, she boycotts St. Mark's. Which you would have noticed," she couldn't resist adding, "if you weren't apparently boycotting St. Mark's yourself."

Ben let out one of his harassed noises.

"But we shall address your churchgoing delinquency another day," she said, slowing as they entered Birdswing proper, where running down a pedestrian or a pet was a real danger. "At any rate, Helen prefers Father Rummage at St. Gwinnodock's. She cycles to Barking a few times a year."

"Even on a cold day in December?"

"If she was desperate enough for spiritual solace, I suppose she might."

"Gaston's lived in Birdswing all his life. Why didn't he know that?"

"Because he has the intellectual capacity of a mollusk. A mollusk that has fallen behind in its studies and is looked down upon by other mollusks."

"Fair point. But why didn't Mrs. Archer tell him?"

"Because she's a shrew. Well, perhaps that's harsh." Juliet felt guilty for speaking unkindly about the newly widowed. "But her instinct is always to lash out, even when she's the only person who suffers. Metaphorically speaking, she cut off her nose and shot off both her feet ages ago."

"I know how prickly she is, but an innocent person would explain themselves," Ben said. "It doesn't matter if she dislikes

Gaston, or even if she hates him. Why allow herself to be jailed on suspicion of murder when she could simply tell the truth?"

"I don't know," Juliet admitted. The waning moon had yet to appear, but the stars were bright, revealing Fenton House's welcome shape. "All I can say for certain is she looked gutted. Like it took all her strength not to weep."

"Over Bobby? He let her down in every possible way," Ben said. "When I interviewed her about Penny's death, I came away with the firm impression she loathed him."

"Of course she did. But a woman can't hate a man with such intensity without loving him. At least in some respect," Juliet said wisely. She wondered if Dr. Carl Jung would be impressed with her insight. Ben was, judging by his contemplative silence.

Juliet parked in what had become her familiar spot by the curb. Poor Mrs. Parry, Ben's inquisitive across-the-way neighbor, was missing a great deal, thanks to the blackout. With her cardboard and curtains blocking the windows, she couldn't spy on their late return, which in itself would raise eyebrows, much less marvel at the six foot, man-shaped parcel they would soon carry inside. At least it *was* man-shaped now. Bobby's atypical rigor had eased as afternoon became evening, relaxing his position.

As Juliet opened the Crossley's back door, a gust of wind swept through the bare trees. "Manfred Pate predicts the coldest winter on record. That would be festive, wouldn't it? A bit of snow for the traditional Christmas afternoon walk?"

Ben nodded absently.

"Dr. Bones, I have the distinct impression you're not listening. Are you working out some alternate theory of the case?"

"Hm? No," he said. "Working out how to get Bobby into my office. I suppose I'll use the stretcher as a litter. Why don't you go inside and let Mrs. Cobblepot get you a cuppa? Then you can ring Belsham Manor and let Lady Victoria know you'll be taking my guest room for the night."

Juliet nodded. Of course he'd offer; that was only common decency. And of course she'd accept; that was only common sense. To read anything special into the invitation would be to behave like a ninny.

"The cuppa can wait. What is this nonsense about a litter? If you take the head and I take the feet, we'll have him inside straightaway," Juliet said. "We'll ring the special bell till Mrs. Cobblepot opens the door."

The expression "dead man's weight" had been coined with good reason. Carrying a stiff, twelve-stone body was difficult, even for a short distance. Ben rang the office bell with his elbow three times, but his housekeeper didn't respond. Leaning against the door handle, he managed to push it open and walk backward to his examination table in the dark. Together, they hefted their burden into place.

"You left the door unlocked?" Juliet asked, trying not to pant.

"I'm losing my London ways," Ben said, closing the door and switching on the light. "They're being replaced with a zealous observation of blackout rules, as you just saw. But it seems Mrs. Cobblepot made other arrangements for the night. No matter, I'll put the kettle on. Thank you for helping."

"But of course. Why do men resist my help? I'm as fit as anyone."

"Fitter," Ben said with a smile. "From now on, I promise to think of you as one of the lads."

Juliet did her best not to grimace. It was the second time she'd fallen into a trap entirely of her own making, and the evening had barely begun.

A NOTE from Mrs. Cobblepot awaited them atop the kitchen table. Juliet picked it up and read it aloud.

Dr. B,

Sorry to abandon my post. My brother rang with the news about Bobby and Helen. I must go to the Archer house and take charge of the twins. You'll find conger pie in the baker and half a sultana loaf in the blue tin.

AC

"THAT'S GOOD OF HER," Ben said. "I hope the boys bear up under the news."

"Father murdered and Mother arrested?" Juliet shook her head. "I wouldn't. And this is Caleb and Micah we're talking about. More bad news may be yet to come."

"At least there's dinner. I feared we'd dine on bread and butter," Ben said. "Let's wash up and tuck in."

They ate in silence, apart from Humphrey the orange tabby. Usually he was out all night, but the cat had a sixth sense for fish in all its incarnations, including leftover conger pie. After he'd finished noisily eating, he sat in a kitchen corner, grooming his whiskers. There was a certain elegance to a cat's every action, even the most mundane. Juliet tried to distract herself from thoughts of Helen and her sons by watching Humphrey, but the twins posed a new issue.

Suppose Helen was sent to prison for twenty years? Caleb and Micah would be effectively orphaned. Suppose she was hanged? Women got the noose far less than men, but it still happened, especially for capital crimes. The boys were exasperating, and probably budding anarchists, but they were her fellow villagers, and in Birdswing, that counted for something.

She shifted her attention to Ben. He'd finished his slice of lukewarm pie and was staring into space, brow furrowed, lower lip compressed. Probably it was too soon for him to feel the sort of responsibility to Helen and the twins she did, but he was clearly ensnared by the puzzle.

"You know, Dr. Bones," she said, striving for a coolly disinterested tone. "My recent unpleasantness with our acting constable aside, I fear he is unsuited to discover the truth about who killed Bobby. Whereas you...." She paused, hoping he would take up the dangling thread.

He kept right on staring into space.

"Dr. Bones!"

"Sorry," he said, sitting up straight. "I was thinking about Mrs. Archer and the boys. I know Gaston does his best, but what if he's in over his head? I had a bit of luck before—with your help, and Lucy's, obviously. Maybe tomorrow I should go back to Barking? See what I can dig up?"

"I think that's a wonderful idea. Now. Pudding?"

"Please."

They both had a sweet tooth, but Ben in particular never seemed to miss a dessert. If not for her presence, Juliet suspected he would have skipped the conger pie, polished off the sultana loaf, and called it a night. It seemed like fair game for a joke—certainly he brought her foibles up often enough—but she'd never mastered the art of teasing, especially when it came to men she fancied. True, others frequently found her observations humorous. But that usually happened when she was dead serious.

"Here you are," she said, placing a generous slice of sultana loaf before him. "Shall I tell you my theory about Bobby?"

"Absolutely."

"One of Odette's maids is the killer. Probably that pretty bit of stuff who blotted out the stain."

"Was she left-handed?"

"I don't know," Juliet said. "Why? Could you deduce the killer was left-handed from something about the wound?"

"I can surmise it. Nothing definitive," Ben warned. "But it strikes me as more likely than not, and I'd testify under oath to that. But if Bobby was romancing a maid, how did she keep everyone else in the dark?"

"She didn't," Juliet said triumphantly. "Everyone knows. Among the staff, I mean. Not Lord Maggart; he's far too ill to be part of a conspiracy. Not Odette either. Much as I dislike the woman, I just don't think she has it in her. Mind you, I've said something like that before," she added, remembering. "And I'll be called to give evidence about that misjudgment myself, in a week or so."

"Everyone on staff," Ben repeated, as if turning the idea over in his mind. Or perhaps he only wanted to keep her chattering while he polished off his pudding.

"You noticed how the housekeeper was off having the vapors, and the girls were consoling themselves out of sight. Mr. Collins kept underfoot, disputing your conclusions and destroying evidence. Otherwise, you might have shot off a cannon without hitting a servant."

"There were two in the kitchen," Ben said. "Mrs. Tippett is Mr. Collins's sister. There doesn't seem to be much love lost between them. And a girl named Betsy. She did seem rattled."

"Is this the Betsy who noticed the unlocked door?"

"Mr. Collins told me I misheard him or he misspoke," Ben replied. "That it was actually Kitty, the girl with the Borax. And she *is* left-handed, I think."

"That's wonderful," Juliet exclaimed. "I mean, it's terrible about the murder, and terrible for the girl who let Bobby's predilections drive her to such depths, but if I'm correct, I shall write to Detective Diamond. How pleased he'll be to discover a prodigy among his international students."

"I don't know," Ben said. "Mr. Collins wasn't just obstructive. He was downright brutish to you. A uniformed servant taking hold of an earl's granddaughter?"

"Oh!" Something about the phrase thrilled her. "Dr. Bones. I think you may be a bit of a traditionalist at heart. I had no idea you felt so strongly about those who get above their station."

"I don't. I feel strongly about men who handle women like furniture."

"Tried to handle a woman like furniture, at least in this case," Juliet corrected. "You'll notice he didn't succeed. Don't misunderstand me. The only combat I enjoy is verbal. But Mr. Collins didn't intend serious harm. He's just one of those men."

"Which men?"

"The ones who haven't a clue how to respond when a female disagrees, or talks back, or laughs at him, God forbid."

"Do you think he killed Bobby?"

"I don't know. The sort of man I mean might kill a woman behind closed doors," Juliet said thoughtfully. "And afterwards feel very powerful indeed. But he'd crumble under arrest, weep in the dock, and beg on the scaffold." She finished her smaller portion of the sultana loaf. "Killing another man takes courage. Probably more courage than one of those men could ever muster. Then again, the idea that *the butler did it* is too good to be true. Imagine! We'd dine out on that story for the rest of our lives."

"True. As for my returning to Fitchley Park tomorrow... I suppose I can say I want to finish what I began, as far as interviewing the staff," Ben said. "They may not object if they believe I'm gathering information that will go against Mrs. Archer. It will give me another chance to look for the place Bobby died. But I'll need to be careful. Only Gaston has the authority to officially question suspects, though I suppose he might deputize me if I managed to convince him it was his idea."

"Then you agree with my hypothesis? One of the maids, probably Kitty, killed him in a fit of jealous passion?"

Ben frowned. "I can't imagine a chambermaid slicing a man's throat from ear to ear."

"Hell hath no fury, Dr. Bones. It was true in Shakespeare's day and perhaps even more true today."

"I don't doubt that, but there's the question of physical strength. Bobby was standing up when he was killed. If he'd been quick enough, he could have caught her wrist and had her at his mercy. Doesn't it seem more likely a woman would attack him while he was lying down?"

"I see what you mean. Perhaps I'm wrong to exclude Odette, but her behavior was nothing short of bizarre," Juliet said. "If a dead stranger was discovered in Belsham Manor, you wouldn't find me wafting about in a fox fur, as if a murder investigation was all so jejune."

"I have some insight there," Ben said, rising and stacking their plates in the sink. "If I tell you, you must promise not to use it against her. Or share it with anyone."

"Dr. Bones, you wound me."

He lifted an eyebrow. "Promise."

"Oh, very well."

"She believes Fitchley Park is haunted," Ben said, returning to the table to pick up their cups and cutlery. "That some sort of evil spirit killed Bobby by luring him into the house and tormenting him, as she put it, till he topped himself."

"Hah! The woman who motored all the way to Birdswing to complain of *my* occult ways blames a murder on a ghost?"

A nearby thump and clatter made them both jump. It was Humphrey, who'd leapt into the sink to inspect their plates.

"He makes a good point," Ben said, glancing wryly at the big cat. "We jumped, because we thought of Lucy. Do we owe Lady Maggart's views closer consideration?"

"What are they, precisely?"

"That Fitchley Park has been haunted for some time. She claims she and Father Rummage have been trying to exorcise the spirit. That's why she was so upset with your activities," Ben said. "She said something to the effect that she and the rector kept trying to close the door on supernatural interference, while you and I kept prying it open."

"Codswallop. Bobby was killed by a human, not a ghost."

"I thought the veil between worlds was supposed to be thinner in Cornwall."

"Oh, it is," Juliet agreed. "But people presume evil has far greater latitude than it does. Evil is quite real, of course, but it isn't alone, and it certainly isn't in charge," she said, articulating a view that had been coalescing in her for some time. "Moreover, from what I've seen, evil seems to work entirely through human hands. It's not that I don't believe in the occasional supernatural intervention. Unlike *one* of us," she couldn't resist adding, "I attend St. Mark's on a weekly basis. I believe the supernatural occasionally intervenes in our lives, but I think it does so only to help, never to harm."

"I like that," Ben said. "We're alone in the house and will be till morning. Should we take the next step?"

"What?" Juliet stared at him.

"The talking board." He sounded surprised that she needed explication. "We were all set to try it before Gaston interrupted. The house is dark and quiet. It might be a long time before we find such perfect conditions again."

"Oh. Yes. Yes, of course," she babbled, embarrassed by where her mind had gone.

"You're sure? Our attic expedition gave us a couple of scares," he reminded her. "Blackout or no, if you scream, Mrs. Parry may burst in to see what she's missing."

"Scream?" Juliet scoffed. "What do you take me for, a ninny?

No matter what happens, you won't hear a peep from me. Not if a voice from beyond speaks my name. Not even if we conjure Anne Boleyn in search of her missing head."

———

To Juliet's way of thinking, it seemed vital to prepare their surroundings. As Ben focused on the blue lamp, filling its reservoir with paraffin oil and fashioning a wick out of medical gauze, she raided Mrs. Cobblepot's cache of emergency candle stubs. There weren't enough candlestick holders for all the stubs, so Juliet popped them into kitchen jars of various shapes and colors. The result was eclectic and surprisingly pleasing: a flickering green glow on the bookshelf, a red one beside the clock, and a line of yellow ones on the mantel.

"Here we are," Ben said, lighting the makeshift wick. "It will burn fast, but I reckon it'll last for a half-hour, perhaps more."

"It's perfect. Conducive to phantasmagorical communion," Juliet said as the lamp's cool blue light fell upon the talking board, highlighting HELLO, GOOD-BYE, and the long, deep scratches.

As per *Revelations of a Reluctant Medium*, the rest of the preparations were simple: two straight-backed chairs arranged face-to-face for "Petitioners to the Spirit Realm," preferably male and female. "This universal dichotomy," wrote Madame Daragon, "yields the most interesting results, particularly when the door is locked and the Petitioners are undisturbed."

Juliet was inclined to agree. A man, a woman, candlelight, and a locked door? Interesting results indeed.

She sat down. Ben took his place opposite her, roughly four feet away, and said, "This won't do." He dragged his chair toward her till their knees touched. "That's better. We're meant to make a table with our legs and balance the board on it."

"I feel a bit ridiculous," Juliet said, though perhaps that wasn't the most appropriate word.

"So do I, but the book was written in 1899. I suppose if Madame Daragon wanted to sell books, she had to throw in a thrill or two. Here we are," Ben said, placing the planchette, a miniature table with a hole in the center, on the board. "Ready?"

She nodded.

He rested the fingertips of both hands on the planchette. Juliet did the same. On the mantel, the flame inside a pink jar flickered and danced, as if bedeviled by a curious draft.

Ben's eyes were closed. By candlelight, he looked more beautiful than perhaps she'd ever seen him, the planes of his face perfectly delineated by shadow. She meditated on that for a time, enjoying herself, before suddenly realizing a few minutes had passed without any movement of the planchette.

"Is one of us meant to say something?" she whispered.

He opened his eyes. "Have you forgotten Madame Daragon's advice?" he asked, chuckling. "'Empty your brain and become a vessel for the beyond.'"

"Oh. Right."

He closed his eyes again. Rather than gaze at his face, which was probably keeping her grounded in the tangible plane, Juliet closed hers as well. *I shall think of nothing. Nothing whatsoever. My brain is empty, which is hardly the sort of thing one should strive for, but there it is.*

Something creaked.

Juliet resolutely kept her eyes closed. After a moment, Ben said, "It's only Humphrey."

She heard a pattering of feline feet. It was very hard to achieve thoughtlessness when the slightest stimuli triggered an avalanche.

It's not my fault I have an unusually overstocked brain. I've spent years expanding my intellectual arsenal.

"Do you hear it?" Ben whispered.

Juliet's eyes popped open. "What? Did it move?" she asked, looking at the planchette.

"No. Footsteps."

She listened. Nothing. Reflexively, she drummed her fingers lightly on the planchette, which shot toward the word HELLO.

Fenton House's floorboards creaked. One heavy footfall, then another. As Juliet's heart hammered wildly, a voice spoke.

"Ju.... It's your husband, Ethan. I've come back to you, my love."

Juliet screamed.

9

THE BOUNDER

Ben leapt to his feet, sending the board and planchette flying. "How did you get in?"

"Why, your patient entrance, of course." Ethan Bolivar's booming voice was good-humored and boundlessly confident. To Ben he sounded like the star of a boys' wireless program: a fearless adventurer who laughed in the face of death, dug up buried treasure, and rescued damsels between adverts for tinned soup.

"I braved the blackout in search of my wife," Ethan said. "What a shock to find her alone with another man, in the throes of seduction."

"*Seduction?*" Ben spluttered.

"For heaven's sake." Lady Juliet switched on the front room's twin electric lights. The glare swiftly transformed Ethan from a shadow to a man.

"Seduction," Ethan repeated gravely. At least six foot four, he was broad-shouldered and barrel-chested, with jet-black hair and a mustache like Clark Gable's. "When I arrived in the village, I went first to the Sheared Sheep, which received me very kindly. There I was told my beloved Juliet was under the spell of a vagabond quack."

"Quack?" Lady Juliet balled up her fists. "You'll quack like a duck when I'm done with you. It's been months! Not a letter. Not a phone call. Now you return like a thief in the night to accuse *me* of infidelity?"

"Darling—"

"I'm not your darling. Not after the way you carried on with Lenora. With Helen. And heaven knows how many more?"

"I deserve your recriminations," Ethan said smoothly. His heroic chin was cleft by a dimple; his Savile Row suit was set off by all the right accoutrements, including a silk necktie and a bowler hat. "If only I'd known you craved a letter, I would have posted a thousand. I would have sent cables daily and phoned weekly. My neglect has driven you into the arms of a lesser man."

Lady Juliet gave a strangled cry, lunging for him.

"Stop!" Interposing himself, Ben squared his shoulders, standing as tall as he could in the midst of such titans. "Listen, Bolivar. I'm prepared to overlook your trespassing, but the rest is out of bounds. Lady Juliet is my friend. No more, no less. We spent the afternoon in Barking. By the time we got back, it was too dark for her to drive to Belsham Manor, so I offered her my guest room."

"A likely story," Ethan said.

"Yes, it is," Ben shot back. "If we were carrying on, why on earth would she park her car outside my house for the entire village to see?"

Ethan stared at Ben for several seconds, then he pointedly turned to Lady Juliet. "Who is this Bones character?"

She tried again to lunge at Ethan. Ben blocked her.

"I mean it," Ethan said. "What sort of man entertains a

married woman in a pitch black house and shamelessly calls it innocent?"

"*You*," Lady Juliet barked. "And I'll have you know it was innocent. See the spirit board? See the planchette?" Scooping it off the floor, she waved the planchette under his nose. "Fenton House is haunted. You'd know that if you hadn't spent the last year gallivanting across the Continent."

"Spiritualism?" Ethan frowned. "You're cleverer than that. Spiritualism is a shell game. A way to milk cash out of dotty old bats."

"Just because you see an angle to everything under the sun doesn't—" She broke off. "It doesn't matter," she said, visibly straining for composure. "You're here. I'm even glad to see you. Tomorrow, first thing after breakfast, we'll get those divorce papers signed, and you can start your life anew."

"Divorce?" Ethan's dark eyes widened. "Ju, sweetheart, I've just said it. I've returned for one reason—to win you back."

Ben, who was still between them, decided it was time to step aside. He would have preferred to order Ethan out of his house, but Lady Juliet's earlier explanation of Helen Archer's behavior —that a woman couldn't hate a man so much without also loving him—had shaken his assumptions about her feelings. Did she still love her estranged husband? If so, Ben's duty was clear. He couldn't stand in the way of a potential reconciliation, literally or figuratively.

With the way cleared, Ethan smiled at Lady Juliet. He opened his arms wide, which left his chest unguarded. She shoved him with both hands.

"Ju," Ethan gasped, arms windmilling.

Ben didn't move a muscle. He enjoyed watching Ethan sit down hard. The wall sconces rattled, a book fell off the shelf, and Humphrey galloped out of the room.

"Ethan." Lady Juliet took a deep breath. "I lost my head. Are you injured?"

"No," he said weakly.

She kicked him. "How about now?"

"I adore you," he moaned, shielding his face with his hands.

Ben wanted to applaud, but it was probably inappropriate for the village physician to cheer on bodily harm.

"All right. That's enough." Dragging Lady Juliet to one side, Ben gave Ethan a hand up. "On your feet."

It took most of his strength to haul the big man off the floor. As Ethan stood, panting and gazing mournfully at Lady Juliet, Ben retrieved the man's bowler, which had been knocked off.

"You saw yourself in. Now see yourself out. Switch on the office light as you go," he added, hoping the sight of Bobby's corpse would administer a well-deserved shock on the way out.

"But, Doctor, I'm hurt. I need treatment," Ethan said.

"You fell on your arse. Here's your treatment: take that arse out of my house before something worse befalls it." He pressed the hat into Ethan's hands.

"I can take a hint," Ethan said. "Juliet, you heard him. Gather your things."

"You're not giving orders. You're leaving." Ben went to the front door and put his hand on the knob. "Now."

Ethan glared at him. Ben returned the look stonily, wondering if he'd be forced to dust off his right hook. If memory served, he hadn't used it since age fourteen, but he hadn't turned pacifist in the intervening years, either.

That must have shone in his eyes, because Ethan's demeanor changed. He smiled at Ben as if he'd always intended to go quietly.

He's a good judge of character, Ben thought. *I suppose a con man must be.*

"My love, I understand how very cross you are," Ethan told

Lady Juliet. "Therefore I'll return to my room at the Sheared Sheep and ponder my crimes. Can't I persuade you to join me for a nightcap?"

Lady Juliet trembled like a rocket prior to launch, so Ben flung the front door wide. Light spilled into his garden, prompting an ARP officer to blow his whistle from several yards away.

"Douse that light!"

"You heard the man," Ben told Ethan. "Go, and I'll close the door. Stay, and I'll keep it open till the officer arrives to issue a citation. Then I'll turn you in for trespassing."

Ethan sighed. "Goodbye, Ju, darling. I'll call upon you at the manor tomorrow."

"You'll be received with tea and cake—*if* you sign the papers."

Ethan stepped onto the porch, then turned. Straightening his back, he put on his hat, which added three inches, and looked down at Ben. "You haven't seen the last of me."

Ben couldn't think of a retort that wouldn't be unimaginatively profane, so he slammed the door in Ethan's face.

"I'll lock it," he told Lady Juliet. "I'll lock the patient entrance, too. Perhaps I'll check the windows for good measure," he added, mostly as a joke, but she made no response. She wasn't crying, but she had the stiff posture and blank face of someone who would soon break down. When he finished securing the ground floor, he found her where he'd left her, standing in the middle of his front room, staring into space.

"Right." Ben spoke sharply enough to cut through her daze. "Follow me."

"Please, Dr. Bones. Don't force me to talk about it," she quavered. "I couldn't possibly—"

"No discussion." Taking her by the hand, he steered her

toward the guest room, which Mrs. Cobblepot kept in a state of perfect readiness. "Have a seat. I'll be back momentarily."

When he returned, Lady Juliet wasn't sitting. She paced like a caged tiger.

"You're very kind to offer me this room," she said. "But I can't allow Ethan to run rampant. I can walk to the Sheared Sheep easily enough. You needn't worry, I know this village blind-folded. Someone has to tell him what an insufferable, boorish, egomaniacal—"

"No. Sorry. Doctor's orders." He pressed a glass into her hands. "Drink it. All of it, no waffling. Down in one."

"I don't want a drink."

"Yes, you do. It's medicinal." He'd poured her the same amount of scotch he would pour himself after a terrible shock. A woman of her stature and unstinting good health would prob-ably require every drop.

Lady Juliet sniffed the glass. Shrugging, she knocked back the whiskey like it was water.

No dainty cordials for her. And no tears either, at least while I'm in the room. That's grit, he thought with some pleasure.

"Well done," he said, collecting the glass. "I'm off to bed. I suggest you turn in as well. I realize Ethan's reappearance may cause a strain, but I'm counting on you to help me tomorrow. We can't forget about Mrs. Archer. She may be innocent, and we can't rely on Gaston to work that out."

Something flared in her eyes. He'd hit upon a nerve, and precisely the right one. Not daring to risk this positive result by pushing any harder, Ben exited, closing the door behind him.

————

HE SHOULD HAVE BEEN asleep on his feet, given the day's events, but relaxation eluded him. He tried to read a bit of the new du

Maurier novel, *Rebecca*, but found himself reading the same paragraph twice without comprehension. His unread issues of *The Lancet* and the *New England Journal of Medicine* proved even less engaging. Lady Juliet's relationship with Ethan Bolivar, whether it ended in divorce, reconciliation, or a longer separation, was none of his affair. But that didn't stop him from thinking about it.

At least now I know why she married him. Well-dressed. Well-spoken. Physique like a circus strongman. All he needed was a cheetah skin and some mustache wax.

He went downstairs, had a dose of his own medicine—scotch—and went back up, resolved to get in bed and hope sleep followed.

He'd fallen into a ritual for undressing, now that Mrs. Cobblepot had taken charge of his laundry. His jacket went on its peg, as did his tie, since neither could be washed, only aired or spot-cleaned. Shrugging out of his braces, he stepped out of his trousers and draped them over a chair, braces still attached. They would be worn again tomorrow. He had three pairs of trousers, one for best and two for everything else. They would last another five years if he treated them well, and that meant putting them through Mrs. Cobblepot's mangle as rarely as possible.

His shirt, vest, socks, and sock garters went in the basket; his shoes went under the bed. Mrs. Cobblepot had designated the top drawer of the highboy for his pajamas. They were starched and ironed according to her high standards, which left them stiff and scratchy. His preference was to sleep nude, but Gaston had promised air raid drills during the night, as well as the day. Ignoring them wasn't an option; every villager was obligated to vacate their beds and take cover in the nearest approved building or Anderson shelter. Exiting Fenton House *au naturel* during a drill was unlikely to be well received.

Wasn't there a story about Ethan leaving town naked? Something about Juliet locking him out of Belsham Manor without his clothes?

Chuckling, he got into bed, switched off the lamp, and closed his eyes.

THWACK

He sat up. Why had the nurse let him nap so long?

After a few seconds, Ben realized he wasn't in a cot at London's St. Thomas Hospital. His sleep-addled brain had mistaken the *thwack* for the sound of a patient's chart slapping against his chest. One of the senior physicians had delighted in waking exhausted junior doctors that way.

Turning on the light, he immediately saw the source of the noise: his cane, which had fallen on the floor. Had he left it against the nightstand again?

He was too sleepy to care. The bedside clock read five minutes past four, which gave him plenty of time before that infernal hammer beat the double brass bells. He was about to switch off the lamp when it hit him.

I haven't used my cane all week.

The hairs on the back of his neck prickled. He'd tucked the cane in the back of his wardrobe, hoping he could delay its use a bit longer.

The wardrobe door was slightly ajar.

"Lucy?"

No answer. His heart thudded in his ears.

He sniffed. No French perfume. Only the faint odors of laundry soap, drawer sachets, and floor wax.

He sat up for a long time, pondering the cane. When he finally switched off the light and closed his eyes, sleep was slow to return.

10

SILK PURSE AND SOW'S EAR

28 NOVEMBER 1939

T he infernal hammer never hit those double bells. Maybe Ben had turned off the alarm while half-asleep; maybe Lucy decided he needed extra rest. Either way, when he awoke, it was ten o'clock. Mortified, he shaved and dressed as fast as possible, then hurried downstairs.

Lady Juliet and Mrs. Cobblepot were in the kitchen. Lady Juliet sat at the table, disconsolately chewing a piece of toast. Dark circles lurked under her eyes; her hair was still damp. Clearly she, too, had woken late and performed her morning ablutions in a rush.

On the other hand, Mrs. Cobblepot was wide awake. She bustled about, opening cabinets, shutting cabinets, pulling out drawers and pushing them in again, apparently searching for something wrong to set right. Sixtyish and heavyset, with white hair and round spectacles, she usually managed her kitchen with calm mastery. Today she seemed on the verge of mania.

"Good morning," Ben said, or tried to.

Mrs. Cobblepot pounced before he could get out the second word. "Doctor! Thank goodness you found the clean shirt I put out for you. If I let you go out wearing yesterday's, people will tut." She plucked what he suspected was an imaginary bit of lint off his jacket, straightened his already straight collar, and examined his immaculate tie for stains. He felt nine years old again.

"How are the Archer twins?"

"Still in the dark," Mrs. Cobblepot replied. "I told them their mum was delayed in Barking, and it might have something to do with their dad. That gave them one last night of peaceful sleep, I reckon. But of course I daren't send them to school. The baby birds sing in Birdswing! I said they could spend the day helping Father Cotterill bring Christmas decorations down from the church attic, then clean and polish them. With any luck, they'll be in the dark till they've had their supper. Then—I don't know. I may bring them back to church, to pray."

"Sounds like you have it very much under control," Ben said, taking a seat.

"I don't know about that. And I do hope you aren't cross because I didn't wake you. When you didn't come down at your usual time, I looked in on you but didn't have the heart to wake you. It was the same with Lady Juliet." Without pause for breath, Mrs. Cobblepot flitted to the next subject. "So lovely to have a guest! With you two still abed, I *did* take advantage of the extra time to pop round to Morton's. Just to pick up some necessaries, mind you. In and out! No dilly-dallying. No time-wasting or tongue-wagging."

Lady Juliet met Ben's gaze. He hoped she could see the humor in Mrs. Cobblepot's position. Gossip was an essential part of village life; when there was nothing new to discuss, the collective mood turned grim. But in the space of a single day, a year's worth of news had happened: Bobby was murdered, Helen was arrested, and Ethan had returned. This last was especially juicy, but out of respect for her guest and friend, Mrs. Cobblepot couldn't broach the topic. Small wonder she was compulsively wiping down everything in sight.

Lady Juliet looked away. Clearly, the humor eluded her.

"Right." Ben stood up. "Mrs. Cobblepot, if you'd be so kind as to pour our tea into a thermos, we'll be on our way. Please don't think us ungrateful. But I'm expected back at Fitchley Park, and I'm sure Lady Juliet would like to get home."

"Of course. Let me at least pack breakfast to go with your tea."

"THANK YOU FOR RESCUING ME," Lady Juliet said as they exited the cottage through Ben's front garden. The day was chilly but bright, the sky a soft cloudless blue. "I know Agatha means well, but if I'd sat in that kitchen much longer, I don't know what might have happened. As for last night...." Her eyes shone with gratitude. "It was very kind of you not to ask questions."

"You know you're welcome to talk to me, but I won't force a confidence," Ben said.

"Speaking of talk, you should know I used your telephone again this morning. Do send me the bill," Lady Juliet said. "Poor Mother. Because she eschews vulgar language as a general rule, Ethan's behavior renders her speechless. I mentioned his threat to turn up at the manor. He never sets about any activity before half-eleven, so she has sufficient warning. If she doesn't answer the door, she may find him creeping through the garden or trying to pry open a window."

"He did strike me as persistent."

"Like a dog with a bone. He's run out of money," she replied. "Depend upon it. When Ethan starts bleating about love and reconciliation, his debts have barred him from the best casinos. At any rate, after I called Mother, I rang up Angus Foss and told him I ought to shear his sheep."

"Why?"

"For renting Ethan a room. When he does a runner, as he must, that Scottish skinflint will expect me to cover the bill. Last but not least, I rang my solicitor. He urged me not to take matters into my own hands, as the Crown takes a dim view of dismemberment. Even the kind male farm animals routinely survive," she added darkly.

Ben winced. It was time to change the subject. He checked his watch. "I'd better be off. Gaston agreed to meet me at the Cow Hole at eleven o'clock, so I'm already late. I hope he didn't ring Plymouth CID to collect Mrs. Archer yet. I want another crack at convincing him it's premature. Give my regards to Lady Victoria."

"What? I'm not going home," Lady Juliet said. "You can't imagine I'd desert you in your time of need."

"But—"

"If I go home, Ethan will take that as a sign of weakening. He'll think he's getting through to me. No," she said firmly, lifting her chin. "The best way to handle him is to remain elusive. If he needs the money badly enough, he'll meet my terms and sign the papers. I'll gladly give him a farewell gift."

"We English do have a long and storied history of paying people we don't like to stay away," Ben said. "And yes, your insight on the Archer case would be helpful. But are you sure you're up to another run-in with Lady Maggart?"

"Of course. I know I must look like the dog's breakfast," she said, buttoning her horrid woolly coat to hide the previous day's ensemble, which had been bad enough the first time around. "But I'm not vain enough to let that stop me."

THIS TIME BEN DROVE, since the Council had been kind enough to give him a petrol allowance. Suspecting Lady Maggart might decline to offer them refreshments, and aware that Barking had no restaurants, they ate along the way. Mrs. Cobblepot had transformed their breakfast—toast, fried eggs, and bacon—into two soggy but surprisingly delicious sandwiches. Despite the thermos, their tea had gone tepid, but they drank it anyway.

"Oh!" Lady Juliet cried as a bump in the road caused her to splash her trousers. "This is entirely uncivilized."

"Sorry. The Austin has developed something of a bounce," Ben said. "I blame Cornwall. All these uneven country lanes."

"Do you miss London?"

"Sometimes." He thought about that. "Not really. I took it for granted, growing up. I suppose I still take it for granted, that it will always be there when I'm ready to go back."

"Every time the *Home Service* mentions projected bombing targets in London, I turn off the wireless," Lady Juliet said. "Otherwise I get nightmares. Once I dreamed St. Paul's Cathedral took a direct hit and burned to the ground. All that lovely wood. I fear it's indefensible, and I'll never walk through it again."

"You've been to London?" Ben asked.

"Once. Which reminds me. You said something remarkably chivalrous yesterday. About how I must have been persuaded to marry Ethan against my own good judgment." She sighed. "I apologize for not correcting you at once. Ethan is a misery I brought entirely upon myself."

"What happened?"

"Perhaps I should start with why it happened. No doubt it hasn't escaped your trained eye that I am the sole heir to Belsham Manor. I had three elder brothers, but all died shortly after birth. Mother had a very difficult time with me. She consulted a Harley Street specialist, who told her there would be no more babies. Thereafter, the hopes of both sides of the family —the Lintons and Mother's people, the Ellissons—were pinned on me."

"When you say 'pinned,' I see a moth on a specimen card," Ben said.

"Not without reason," Lady Juliet said with a smile. "They were seriously discussing marriage before I knew what the word meant. When I was sixteen, I said I couldn't bear the idea of the debutante's ball. Grandmother Ellisson knew that would probably be a disaster, so instead she proposed taking me abroad for a year. Showing me around to all the younger sons and impoverished viscounts—anyone willing to trade connections for a wealthy wife. I didn't want to go. I had a grudge against my grandmother over something childish."

"I had a grudge against my Uncle Billy, growing up," Ben said. "Whenever he saw me, he always said something like, 'Reading will ruin your eyes,' or 'Put down the book and pick up a ball.'" He laughed. "If Uncle Billy turned up tomorrow with hat in hand, I'm not sure I'd receive him. We never forget the slights of childhood."

"No. Even when I was sixteen, and too old for such things, I was still quite the outdoorswoman. Mother allowed me to wear practical clothes as much as possible, which Grandmother Ellisson found appalling. One day I overheard her tell Mother no man would ever have me. She said I needed a wardrobe heavy on lace, ribbons, and soft colors. I heard her say, 'You can't make a silk purse from a sow's ear, but you can make a sow's ear *look* like a silk purse, at least in a certain light.'

"No young girl wants to hear herself described as a sow's ear," Lady Juliet continued. "Especially one who already feels gawkish and overgrown. I was mortified. Mother, bless her, told me she saw nothing wrong with my mode of dress."

"Lady Victoria has a kind heart," he said.

"And an eye for fashion. She pays close heed to the seasonal edicts from Paris but never presses me to follow her lead."

"Don't be offended, but given your intellect, I'm surprised

she didn't consider sending you to university. Even if it's a touch unorthodox."

"I wanted to," Lady Juliet said. "In fact, I assumed I would. But then my parents took ill—first Father, then Mother. It was a dreadful time. Old Doc Egan actually lived at Belsham Manor for ten days, never leaving them except to sleep. In the end, Father died, and Mother was never the same."

"Heart failure."

"Yes. For months it was touch and go. She would rally, relapse, and rally again," Lady Juliet said. "Wild horses couldn't have dragged me away, not even to university. By the time Mother recovered, at least as much as she ever will, Grandmother Ellisson insisted I attend Clarion Academy in Switzerland."

"Penny was at one of those places," Ben said, meaning a finishing school. "She made it sound like prison. Uniforms. Lights out at nine o'clock. Locked in her dorm at night."

"That's exactly what I used to imagine. Prison."

"She did say the food was good. Apparently they held a mock dinner party twice a week. Authentic down to the oysters and the bubbly. The teachers acted the part of distinguished guests, like Leslie Howard or the Prince of Wales. If a student was rude or clumsy, she got a demerit."

Lady Juliet shuddered. "Positively hair-raising. I would have been sent down inside a week."

"Penny told me when she flubbed a title—called someone 'Duchess' instead of 'Dowager Duchess'—they made her copy modes of address out of *Debrett's* for three hours."

"Sounds as if Abandon All Hope, Ye Who Enter Here should have been written above the door. A phrase I learned by studying Dante myself, thank you very much," she added proudly. "While nursing Mother, I devised my own syllabus.

Literature on Mondays. History on Tuesdays. Art on Wednesdays, geography on Thursdays, and philosophy on Fridays."

Ben stopped to allow a sheep to amble halfway across the
road, stare at the Austin, and slowly amble back. "What about
science? Or maths?"

"Science is always reversing its opinion on this and that. If
one has a question, it's best to consult the experts," she said
airily. "As for numbers, I mastered arithmetic at an early age."

"What about algebra?"

"I'm of the opinion you men made all that nonsense up. At
any rate, I was pleased with my personal course of study and
violently opposed to being packed off to Switzerland. I asked
Mother to let me spend the tuition money on a holiday in
London.

"Think of it," she continued. "Me, alone in London, when I'd
never even been alone in Plymouth. I was terrified she would
say no, and even more terrified when she said yes. But fear can
be invigorating. I viewed the Magna Carta in the British Library.
I spent a morning in the National Portrait Gallery, gazing at
faces long dead. I roamed the Victoria and Albert Museum from
end to end. It was glorious. There was more than I could learn in
a lifetime." She stopped. "But instead of staying the course, I
steered my life off a cliff."

"How did you meet Ethan?"

"Our eyes locked across a crowded ballroom."

Ben glanced at her, surprised.

"Of course not," she laughed. "It was at the V & A. Mind you,
I fancied myself worldly and sophisticated, so I was already on
guard against tricksters. I thought if I dressed modestly and kept
my head down, no one would pay the slightest attention. I didn't
realize my choice of hotel, my habit of dining alone, and ability
to haunt historic spots in the middle of the day marked me as a
tourist with means. Ethan's never admitted it, but I think he

picked me out in the hotel, asked the concierge for details, and watched me for a time. His opening gambit was nothing I'd expected."

"Oh, really?" Ben thought about it. "If you were in the V & A, I expect he asked you to help him make sense of some exhibit."

"My goodness." Lady Juliet stared at him. "How on earth did you guess?"

"If I wanted to chat you up, that's how I'd start."

"Because I'm an insufferable know-it-all?"

"Because you can never say no to a person who needs help." Ben glanced over a second time and was pleased to see her smile.

The Austin jostled along the lane. Hedgerows stood tall on either side, gray stone peeking through a lattice of bare vines. Pastureland stretched for miles, the grass brittle but still alive. Copses of oaks and mulberry trees dotted the fields, leafless but cloaked in English ivy, which was green year-round. On a hillside, black-and-white milk cows reclined, and in the distance, St. Gwinnodock's Gothic spires appeared.

"You've put your finger on Ethan's strategy," Juliet said. "He asked me questions, and he listened to my answers, starting with my extemporaneous lecture in the Egyptian room, explaining the pre-Ptolemaic dynasties he pretended not to know about. The truth is he's too clever by half."

"He did strike me as decently educated," Ben said grudgingly.

"He turned up the next day, and the next, and soon we were meeting in the evenings as well," Juliet said. "I should have wondered why he never expressed curiosity about the Linton name or asked about my family home. This was because he already knew he had an heiress on the line. So he played the besotted suitor, bringing me sweets, reciting sonnets, showing me the Elfin Oak at Kensington Gardens. One afternoon in

Greenwich Park, we climbed a hill and watched the sky change from pink to purple. It was the happiest moment of my life. That night, he took me to dinner at the Connaught and asked me to marry him. I said yes before he finished speaking."

"Did he ask for money right away?"

"Only a little. Otherwise, everything was perfect until I turned up in Birdswing with a surprise fiancé. Mother was charmed, but Grandmother Ellisson prophesied doom. She urged me not to marry in haste, to give her a few weeks to dig up the truth with the help of a private detective. I wasn't an idiot. The wedding bells started sounding like alarm bells," Lady Juliet said. "But I couldn't hear the truth from Grandmother Ellisson. Perhaps if she hadn't called me a sow's ear, I could've swallowed my pride and taken her advice. Instead, I ran crying to Ethan and said they were all against us."

"I'll bet he said you should elope."

"Yes, of course, just like Lydia and Wickham in *Pride and Prejudice*. I should have thought harder about the analogy. Oh, there's the Cow Hole—just there." She pointed. "Three weeks later, when I returned home a married woman, Mother forgave me at once but insisted Ethan wait outside. Then she handed me the report from Grandmother Ellisson's detective.

"There it was in black and white," Lady Juliet continued. "The man I married wasn't the heir to an industrialist's fortune. He was the second son of a haberdasher. He had nothing but a little schooling, some natural charm, and fifty thousand pounds of debt. His story of serving in the Army was false. And his claim of being related to T.E. Lawrence? More 'Lawrence of Stoke-on-Trent' than Arabia."

Ben drove onto the verge, trundling toward the Cow Hole, a heap of ancient stone with a cap-like roof.

"Well. Aren't you going to laugh at me?" Lady Juliet demanded. "I spent an hour last night rehearsing my confession.

Every time I imagined it, you laughed at me for being foolish enough to believe the lie about Lawrence of Arabia."

"Will anyone object to me parking here?"

"Park up a tree for all anyone cares. Why aren't you laughing?"

The Cow Hole's door opened, and Special Constable Gaston emerged. It wouldn't take him long to close the distance.

Ben knew what he wanted to say. He needed to do it swiftly, in a minimum of words. "Penny didn't marry me because she loved me. She needed a husband because she was in trouble," he said, looking Lady Juliet in the eye. "The baby's father did a legger. Penny reckoned I was too thick and lovesick to do the math when she started to show, but I was a physician. When I confronted her, and she told me the truth, part of me died." He cleared his throat. "Just died."

Lady Juliet looked stricken. "Oh, Ben. You didn't have to tell me that."

"Yes, I did." He opened the car door. "Let's see what the Great Detective has to say for himself."

11

FIRE WITH FIRE

"Good morning, Dr. Bones," Special Constable Gaston said. For a man who'd spent the night away from home and been forced to wear yesterday's garb, he looked remarkably sharp. Portentous as his pronouncements were, and unfounded as his conclusions could be, he was always the dignified old soldier, suited up and ready for action. "Good morning, your ladyship," he added stiffly. "Why are you here?"

Ben pretended not to hear the question. "I still have several questions about Bobby's death, so I'll be returning to Fitchley Park next. How is Mrs. Archer?"

"As hardened as Pharaoh."

"Has she confessed?" Lady Juliet asked.

"No. She hasn't even got out of bed. Still has the covers pulled up over her head." Gaston shook his head. "Didn't stop her from banging on about her boys, saying Agatha won't be able to handle them because they're so wild. I said if they're wee rapscallions, it's down to how she raised them, isn't it? Should've put the fear of God into those boys when she had the chance."

"In bed?" Ben repeated. "I don't understand. Has her shingles flared up?"

"You're the one carrying the black bag. You tell me." Gaston eyed him suspiciously. "But that's not the only reason you've come, is it? You're here to second-guess my detective work."

"I have no intention of second-guessing you," Ben lied. "I only want to help. If Mrs. Archer claims to be unwell, I should examine her. You said she hasn't confessed. It's worth noting that people confide all sorts of things to their physician."

"Examine her, interview her, it's all the same to me," Gaston said. "I reckon you'll have a quarter hour or so before Plymouth CID arrives to take her into custody."

"But how can they involve themselves so soon?" Lady Juliet asked.

"What did you give them?" Ben asked. "Physical evidence? A witness?"

Gaston widened his eyes and pursed his lips.

"Don't try to look knowing," Lady Juliet snapped. "To look knowing, one must, in fact, know something. You look like a netted fish trying to work out where the water went."

"I detected," Gaston said with dignity. "When questioned as to why she came to Barking in the middle of the day, Mrs. Archer said she'd been round to see the rector and spent the better part of the morning with him. I checked with Father Rummage, and he said, on the contrary, he hadn't seen her in several days. Moreover, during that visit, she made shocking remarks. In light of her husband's murder, those statements, which I cannot repeat, indicate premeditation. Therefore, I rang Plymouth CID. They agreed I'd sewn up the case," he said, chest puffing, "and Mrs. Archer should be transferred to Plymouth for remand."

"If speaking ill of an estranged spouse is enough to put one behind bars, I shan't be at large much longer," Lady Juliet said.

"Helen's outspoken and irascible, everyone knows that. Let me speak to her, woman to woman. Perhaps I can—"

"Certainly not," Gaston cut in. "Professionals with a clear duty to the accused must never be refused. Meddling civilians, on the other hand, threaten an investigation's integrity."

"Thus sayeth Dirk Diamond!" Lady Juliet cried, pointing a finger in his face. "You're enrolled in Private Dick Academy."

"Loose lips sink ships," Gaston said, again attempting to look knowing. "Speaking of that, milady, I hear Mr. Bolivar's returned. Take it from a man who was happily married for twenty years—don't nag him. Nothing good ever came from nagging."

"We're wasting time," Ben said. "I propose a division of labor. I'll examine Mrs. Archer, then drive up to Fitchley Park and interview the staff. Lady Juliet, would you be so kind as to call on Father Rummage at the rectory? I'd like to see those crime scene photos, if he's developed them." He felt like a phony, bandying about law enforcement terms like "crime scene," but neither of Dirk Diamond's mail-order students looked amused.

"Certainly, Dr. Bones," Lady Juliet said crisply. "If the pictures are ready, I'll bring them with me to Fitchley Park," she continued, setting out toward St. Gwinnodock's. "Please let Helen know that she's in my prayers, Dr. Bones."

"I will." Starting toward the roundhouse, he was surprised to find Gaston dogging his heels. "I do plan to medically examine her, Special Constable."

"Oh, aye. I'll take notes."

"She won't fancy disrobing with you present."

Gaston coughed. "Will that be necessary?"

"Perhaps. Shingles is a serious disease."

"Is it?" Gaston asked. "Just a bit of redness, really. I thought she was an attention-seeker. You know what they say: 'Always ill and sickly, more likely to live than die quickly.' But have it your way, Doc. I'll be out here, taking the air."

Like a child impatient for the ice cream trolley, Gaston positioned himself at the top of a hill, giving himself an excellent view of the lane by which Plymouth CID would arrive.

The roundhouse doorway was low enough to make Ben duck his head. The occurrence was both a pleasant novelty and a testament to the building's medieval origins. After Lady Juliet's "oubliette" remark, he expected bare stone walls and arrow slits, but it seemed that postcard-ready Barking was incapable of ugliness, even in the local lockup. The floor was inlaid with black and white marble. The walls, lemon-yellow, bore photographs celebrating the village. Ben recognized Fitchley Park with its staff assembled out front; St. Gwinnodock's on a snowy day; a village fête, complete with maypole.

Father Rummage's work, Ben thought.

He studied the image of Fitchley Park. Lord Maggart wasn't in evidence. The staff was lined up in two rows, with Lady Maggart off to one side. She stood beside a handsome younger man in a tartan coat, a hand on his forearm. It was an odd pose for mistress and servant. Was this the gamekeeper who'd been discharged after Lord Maggart's outburst?

Otherwise, the photo was typical of its sort. The staff looked straight at the lens, unsmiling, except for a tall woman in a black dress who looked at her feet.

That must be the housekeeper, Mrs. Grundy.

Surely she'd recovered enough to speak to him. Would she choose to be helpful if he asked her about a possible liaison between Bobby and one of the maids? In the photo, they were all young and attractive, which was typical. In great houses, pretty faces were often considered part of the décor.

"If you fancy a print, we sell them in the gift shop," someone said cheerfully. Ben jumped.

The speaker was a wizened little woman with a mound of snow-white hair on her head. Her dress, scarf, and shoes were lavender; her earrings were chips of jet. Seventy-five years ago, when lifelong mourning for women was common, widows of long standing sometimes shifted from unrelieved black to pale purple. If not for her twentieth century hemline, this tiny woman could have been transplanted whole from 1860.

"I'm Mrs. Richwine," she said, smiling. "Chair of the Round-house Society. Are you here to see our guest?"

"I'm sorry. Did you say gift shop?"

She indicated a row of wall shelves. "The Cow Hole, as the roundhouse is known, is popular with day-trippers and locals alike. Today, we have on offer pastels, framed and unframed. We also have canvas, brushes, and boxes of watercolors, ideal for capturing the English countryside. I would offer the usual complimentary tour, but at the moment, we have a guest." She indicated the back third of the roundhouse, which was hidden behind a red velvet curtain.

"I've actually come to see Mrs. Archer," Ben said. "Is she, er, behind the curtain?"

"Yes. We've never had a female guest," Mrs. Richwine whispered. "Modesty must be preserved."

She led Ben around the curtain, where he discovered two things. First, Helen Archer really was still in her cot with the covers pulled over her head. Second, the red velvet curtain was the only thing standing between Helen and an escape attempt.

"We consider Barking a welcoming place," Mrs. Richwine said happily. "As you see, this cell has no window. It used to be enclosed by a great studded door with a slot in the middle." She shook her head. "This is much lighter and airier."

"The Cow Hole operates on the, er, honor system?" Ben asked.

"Oh, no, dear. I lock the front door at night, and when I pop home for tea."

"Who's there?" Helen asked from under the blanket.

"It's Dr. Bones, Mrs. Archer. I heard you were unwell." He approached the cot. At second glance, he saw it wasn't precisely a blanket Helen had taken refuge under. It was a pink counterpane, edged in red ribbon. Ben would have bet five pounds it came from Mrs. Richwine's linen closet.

"Go away," Helen said.

"I understand Plymouth CID will be here soon," Ben said. "Please allow me to examine you before they arrive. Even if you're charged with murder, you still deserve the best of care."

Under the counterpane, Helen rolled toward the wall. Had she uncovered her face, she might have been cheered by a framed rendition of Fitchley Park, painted in watercolors and signed by the artist.

"I still have that plate of scones, Helen, dear," Mrs. Richwine said. "Won't you reconsider? It will be a long ride to Plymouth."

"May I have a moment alone with my patient?" Ben asked.

"Of course. I'll take a turn in the garden. The roundhouse roses took honorable mention in the spring fête, you know," Mrs. Richwine said. "Have a look before you go."

"Bloody Barking," Helen muttered under the counterpane, as the click of Mrs. Richwine's heels signaled her departure. "*Some* people think highly of themselves."

"Oh, yes. A proper stay in Birdswing's constabulary, locked behind bars with a moth-eaten blanket and a bucket," Ben said archly, noting the porcelain chamber pot under Helen's bed, "would be far preferable to allowing Mrs. Richwine to kill you with kindness. Unfortunately, Caleb and Micah blew up the constabulary on Bonfire Night, if you'll remember. I shudder to think what they'll get up to now, with their father dead and their mum fitted up for murder."

"Maybe I weren't fitted up," Helen said dully. "I hated Bobby. I told you so myself, when you thought maybe I done in Penny. You looked at me and saw a murderer. Maybe you were right."

"I didn't see a murderer," Ben said truthfully. "I saw a devoted mother with a restaurant to run, a missing husband, and two, er, *spirited* lads. I hope Mrs. Cobblepot is up to the challenge. Even so, I imagine they'll be Borstal boys by this time next year."

That did the trick. Borstal schools, managed by officials from His Majesty's Prison Service, had been established to reeducate juvenile offenders and quickly gained a sinister reputation. The notion of keeping wayward boys away from adult convicts made perfect sense, but inside such "schools," proper oversight was rare or nonexistent. Inmates were hard-pressed to survive the merciless hierarchy, with nascent psychopaths on top, hardened young malcontents in the middle, and first-time offenders at the very bottom.

"Borstal boys!" Helen threw off the covers and sat up. "What a terrible thing to say."

Ben stared at her lacerated, blood-stained face. "Good God. Who did this to you?"

Helen crossed her arms, equally lacerated, and looked at the floor. "You wouldn't understand."

Ben knew a bit of Helen's history. By all accounts, when she married Bobby, she'd been a lovely girl. They'd enjoyed a brief honeymoon, but then the twins came. Bobby had resumed his tomcat ways, which led to living apart. In the midst of her personal misery, or perhaps because of it, Helen had developed shingles. As a result, her nose was scarred, her right eye was blind and shrunken, and the right half of her face was afflicted with persistent neuralgia. It extended across her scalp, which meant that years after the initial flareup, even brushing her hair on that side remained excruciating. Ben had expected all that.

But now her cheeks, forehead, and throat were marked with at least two dozen red, ragged cuts and scratches. Some were scabbed over; others were open and oozing. There was no pattern to the shallow wounds, but all were the approximate width of a fingernail.

"May I see your hands?" he asked, striving for a neutral tone.

She extended them reluctantly. Most of the fingernails were torn to the quick. There was dried blood under the rest.

Ben opened his black bag. His hands worked without input from his brain, gathering treatment materials: antiseptic, cotton wool, aspirin, forceps, and a packet of Mersutures, in case the lacerations proved deeper than they looked. As a medical student, he'd been urged to develop an iron-clad routine, an order in which he acted, inflexibly, no matter how trivial or grievous the complaint.

Perhaps because he was silent and methodical, Helen allowed him to clean and disinfect her self-inflicted wounds. Stitches proved unnecessary, and bandages would have been impractical, so Ben decided all he could do was hope she healed without too much scarring.

"You didn't have these wounds yesterday," Ben said, "and Gaston doesn't know about them. If he did, he would have told me. This happened last night."

"Yes."

"Why did you do this to yourself?"

"Because I'm haunted."

"What?"

Unbuttoning her sweater and pushing up her dress sleeve, Helen revealed a mass of scars above the elbow. Some were a few weeks old; others were puckered and faint, dating from childhood.

"In my family I was the only girl," she said in a low, unin-flected voice. "Me against six brothers and my old dad, who never worked a day if he could help it. Maybe if I'd had a sister, we could have looked after one another. But I didn't."

Rolling down a stocking, she revealed more self-inflicted scars on her thigh. "One day, I cut myself by accident, and the pain cleared my head. Like magic. Such a pure sensation. Cleansing." She pulled the stocking back into place. "I loved watching the blood well up. When my thoughts turned black, when I felt like throwing myself off a cliff, I made a cut and let the pain out.

"My mum noticed," she continued, shrugging her sweater back into place. "It took the best part of a year, but one day she looked my way and saw me, if you know what I mean. I couldn't tell her the truth, so I said I was haunted. Mum was superstitious. Believed in ghosts that slap and scrape folks in their beds." She laughed bitterly. "She could believe a ghost would punish me, but she couldn't believe anything else I said went on in our house. To her it was like stigmata—but from the other place, and for the other reason. Marks to signify wickedness."

Ben bit his lip. He almost wished she had another fresh wound or glaring symptom for him to treat. Anything to occupy his hands while he cast about for something to say.

"I did stop for a time," Helen said. "When Bobby was courting me. Best year of my life. Then we married, and it all went to the devil, and I needed that pain again."

"Neuralgia isn't enough?"

"Who are you to judge me?"

"I'm not judging you. I only want to understand. Most people are terrified of pain," Ben said. "They'll do anything to make it stop. Even die."

"My shingles is a different kind of pain. Forced upon me. So much is forced upon me. Father Rummage says when our souls are heavy, we need cleansing, exculpatory pain. That's how he sees it. How I see it is, I fight fire with fire. When the world hurts me, I can take control. All I need is a razor or a fingernail."

Something from Ben's medical school training returned to him: a paper about Eastern European women who stabbed themselves with needles. He also remembered the true story of a Roman citizen who'd been pilloried for mutilating himself, yet refused to stop, even under threat of additional public shaming.

This is compulsive behavior. Trying to convince her it's illogical misses the point, he thought. *Helen's clever enough to run a business and provide for herself and the boys, but this is beyond logic. It's a drive inside that tells her she* must *do it.*

He took Helen's hand. She started to pull away, then took a deep breath and endured his touch.

Ben said, "All I want is to help, no matter what the truth is. Did you kill Bobby?"

"No. I told you once before," Helen said. "Thinking and doing are different things. If I had the raw nerve to take a life, I'd have done in your Penny, wouldn't I? Maybe that would have saved my marriage."

"All right. When did you see Bobby last?"

"Friday. He turned up at the restaurant while I was doing the books. Humming to himself, the bloody mongrel. Told me he needed a divorce."

Ben recalled their first meeting, when Helen had said emphatically that no one in her family had ever been divorced, and she refused to be the first. "How did you answer?"

"I said, never."

"I understand," he said gently. "I really do. But you and Bobby lived apart for years. What practical difference would it make?"

"None." She pulled away. "I always knew one day he'd ask and mean it. I thought I was prepared, that I'd been prepared for years, but when he said the words, it felt like death."

"How did he take your refusal?"

"He offered me money. Then he tried to be tough. Said he'd paint me as an adulteress. That got my dander up, you can ask my neighbors. They heard me call him everything but an Englishman. Cheeky beggar just laughed. Said he'd come back when I had a chance to think it through and went off whistling."

Ben studied Helen's brutally scratched face and the equally brutal set of her mouth. Something in her tale reminded him of Lady Juliet and Ethan, and that reminded him of how he'd driven the bounder out of his house.

"Helen, where were you Sunday night?"

"At home abed, like decent folk."

"Did you know Bobby would be in Barking?"

She sighed. "Yes."

"How?"

"His new woman lives there, don't she?"

"What's her name?"

"He wouldn't say. Maybe he thought I'd scratch her eyes out." She emitted a humorless laugh. "Should have known I'd scratch mine out first."

"This new woman of his. Could it be a maid at Fitchley Park?"

"I don't think so," Helen said. "He claimed she was a real lady, like Penny."

"Why did you close your restaurant during its peak hour and go to Barking?"

"I needed advice from Father Rummage."

"Can you see how a jury might not believe that? They might think it too much of a coincidence. I don't suppose someone got word to you about Bobby's death?"

"No." She returned his gaze unblinking, the good eye and the dead one.

Ben studied her for several seconds. "I think you did know

about it," he said at last. "Gaston agrees. He talked to Father Rummage, who denied speaking to you yesterday. So I'll ask again: Why were you in Barking?"

"I was in a state!" Helen cried. "Trying to scrape up the courage to ask the rector if he'd still minister to a divorced woman. I was walking up the high street when that old windbag pulled up, and the next thing I knew, I was under arrest. They brought me here and locked me in for the night. If not for my fingernails, I would've gone mad." She traced the marks on her cheeks as if caressing a talisman.

"All right. Thank you, Mrs. Archer. I'll speak to Gaston," Ben said, rising.

"I'll be here, won't I? Wasting away under a silk coverlet till Mrs. Richwine forces a scone on me. Probably force a cuppa on me, too," Helen grumbled. "Bloody Barking."

"WELL?" Gaston asked as Ben joined him on the hill over-looking the lane. "Is Helen fit for transport?"

"Broadly speaking, yes. You'll have a bit of a shock when you see her, though." Ben realized he had to make some explanation for Helen's face, but he couldn't tell Gaston the absolute truth. If he did, it would be discussed in Morton's Emporium the next morning and spread across Birdswing thereafter. Besides, who knew how a jury might receive such information? They might assume a compulsion for self-harm indicated the capacity for harming others.

"A shock? What do you mean?" Gaston's eyes glinted curiously. He was as committed a gossip as any of the ladies in Morton's. "Did she rend her garments? Heaven knows she loved the man."

"She had a nightmare and clawed at her face," Ben said.

"Now she's ashamed to show herself, which is why she hid under the covers."

"Oh." Gaston frowned. "Peculiar woman. I suppose murderesses always are."

"As to that... I have a question for you in your capacity as ARP Warden."

Gaston's thick neck swelled. "Of course."

"Who patrolled Birdswing last night?"

"Corporal Briggs and Corporal Jones."

"Do you trust them?" Ben asked needlessly, just to watch Gaston's nostrils flare.

"Aye. Trained by me and trusted by me. They'd die for Birdswing, and so would I."

"Let's hope it doesn't come to that. Now. The quickest route from Birdswing to Barking is Clodgey Lane. If Mrs. Archer took that road, presumably on her bicycle, during the blackout, which of your men failed to report it?"

"Corporal Briggs has that zone. He would never fail in his duty."

"Very well. It's possible Mrs. Archer reached Barking by cutting through Pate's Field and going through the woods on foot. Is that Corporal Jones's patch?"

"Yes."

"Did he miss a woman carrying a torch or a lantern?"

"Impossible!"

"I agree. Last night, I let a bit of light out my front door, and either Briggs or Jones shouted at me straightaway," Ben said. "So if Mrs. Archer killed Bobby sometime in the predawn hours, how did she get to Barking?"

Gaston's mouth worked.

Ben was tempted to let him twist in the wind indefinitely, but Plymouth CID would arrive any minute. They needed to present a united front.

"If your men are blameless," Ben said, "I suppose there's only one answer. Mrs. Archer left while the sun was up and returned after sunrise the next day. The twins were alone for hours, and her restaurant didn't open on time."

"But it did," Gaston said, still transparently dragging Ben's contention through the narrow avenues of his mind. "When I passed, I caught her scraping a pan into the dustbin. I reminded her that leftover food must go to the pig barrel, and she scowled at me."

"Right. So it's down to this. One of your officers fell asleep on the job, or Mrs. Archer couldn't have done it."

"No man of mine sleeps on the job!" Gaston slapped a fist against his palm. "I must get back to the village and look into this. In the meantime, Helen shouldn't go to Plymouth."

As if on cue, a sleek gray automobile appeared on the lane, running so smoothly, it seemed to glide on a bed of air. Enthusiasm squelched, Gaston walked out to meet the Plymouth CID men as they disembarked. One was middle-aged, in a blue suit with a fedora; the other was younger and taller, with a pronounced limp. Both seemed markedly serious and professional next to Gaston, who suddenly looked like an old man in a borrowed kit. To his surprise, Ben found himself resenting the flashy policemen and hoping they treated Gaston with respect. Was that proof he was becoming a true Birdswinger?

The exchange was brief. From his position, Ben couldn't hear every word but he caught most of Gaston saying, "There are new developments." Predictably, the policemen did not look overjoyed at what may have been an unnecessary pilgrimage into postcard country. The younger man remained outside with Gaston, taking notes, as the man in the fedora entered the roundhouse, apparently to question Helen himself.

Satisfied that Helen would be freed at best, or allowed to remain in Barking's cozy lockup at worst, Ben started toward his car. Just as he got behind the wheel, the older policeman exited the Cow Hole, leading Helen by the arm.

"I say! What's happening?" Ben called.

Neither policeman paid him any mind.

"Don't be hasty," Gaston shouted at their backs. "No good ever came from being hasty!"

"Mrs. Archer," Ben called to Helen before they loaded her into the gleaming silver car. "What happened? What did you say?"

"The truth." In direct sunlight, the scratches on her face looked all the more vicious. "I did it. I followed Bobby into Fitchley Park, cut his throat, and threw the knife in the river."

12

"ON ACCOUNT OF HER LADYSHIP"

"I don't understand," Gaston said, deflated.

"Neither do I. She told me she was innocent, and I believed her. How did she know his throat was cut? How did she know we hadn't found the knife?" Even as Ben asked, suspicion flared. "Gaston. You didn't discuss the case with her, did you?"

"No," the special constable cried. "I tried picking her up on the high street, but you know how she is. She wouldn't get in the car. So I told her Bobby was dead, and she was under suspicion of murder. She got in, shrieking all the while, and then she wanted to know how he died. I had to say something, didn't I?" He sounded unconvinced by his own narrative but continued nonetheless.

"I told her his throat had been cut. Then she wanted to know where he died. I said below stairs at Fitchley Park. Then she wanted to know who did it. That brought me to the end of my tether. I said, 'Good Lord, woman, it must have been you! Where did you stash the knife?' But otherwise, Doctor, I give you my oath," Gaston concluded solemnly, "I kept mum and let her do all the talking, just as Dirk Diamond recommends."

Ben counted to ten, reached it, and started again.

"Perhaps it doesn't add up yet," Gaston said. "But she confessed, Dr. Bones. Case closed. You raised good questions about Corporal Briggs and Corporal Jones, but don't forget, Helen knows these parts as well as I do. Maybe she didn't need a lantern. Maybe it's possible to make it through Pate's Field, the woods, and across Little Creek—"

"The *river*?"

"A narrow point," Gaston said. "Easy enough in daylight. In darkness, what with mossy stones and perhaps some ice...." His eyes widened. "Maybe she an accomplice. Someone skilled and underhanded. Professional enough to do the impossible," he said, clearly warming to his own theory.

"Leaving aside how she met this assassin," Ben said, "and how she paid him, since I've never heard of hired killers accepting payment in pies, why would she claim to have done it herself?"

"If I knew that, I'd be poncing around Plymouth, flashing my CID credentials, now wouldn't I?" Gaston snapped. "All I know is an innocent woman wouldn't confess."

He had a point. Ben had read about accused men recanting their confessions in the dock, of course, but it always sounded like mere desperation.

"Well. Right. Whether Helen is guilty or not, there are still unanswered questions at Fitchley Park," he told Gaston. "I'd better be off to interview the staff."

"Aye. I'll head back to the village. Can't put off breaking the news to the Archer twins much longer. As for Briggs and Jones —just because I have faith in them doesn't mean I won't investigate. If either man failed in his duty, you should arrive in time to perform the post-mortems."

"Oh. That reminds me," Ben said. "I overslept this morning, then rushed back here to continue the investigation, but Bobby's still in my examining room, awaiting post-mortem. I don't suppose Plymouth CID will want me to muck about with their evidence."

"I can ring them. Tell them to collect the body," Gaston offered. "Agatha's tough as hobnail boots, but I bet she'll be glad to get Bobby out of Fenton House. Poor bugger," he added, shaking his head. "I never liked him, but this was a sorry end. His old mum will be destroyed. Do you suppose those Plymouth dandies will take the trouble to inform her?"

"I doubt it," Ben said.

"I was afraid you'd say that."

They shook hands. Then Ben, still pondering Helen's confession, got back in his car and drove to Fitchley Park.

———

"Good afternoon, Dr. Bones," Mr. Collins said with passable civility, stepping aside to permit Ben entry. He'd made peace, it seemed, with the notion of Ben coming and going through the front door. "Lady Maggart is not at home. However, she welcomes your assistance and bid me provide anything you might require. Within reason, of course."

"Of course. I'd like to start by walking through the house. All of the house, including the family rooms."

"I see. As it happens, I am engaged with various responsibilities, but if you can perhaps wait an hour or two...."

"No need," Ben said cheerfully. "I prefer to wander at liberty. Easier for me, and no interruption for you."

The butler's eyes narrowed. "Most of the family rooms are locked."

"Then I'll go where I can, while you procure the keys."

Mr. Collins stared at Ben as if weighing the consequences of refusal. "Very well."

As before, Ben passed through the great hall on his way to the grand staircase. And as before, Lord Maggart was ensconced in front of the fire, leg propped on a hassock. Last time it had been the right leg. Now it was the left.

"Who's that?" the baron called, squinting.

"Ben Bones. We met yesterday, my lord."

"Oh! The undertaker." Lord Maggart coughed, groping for his pewter-tipped cane. Finding it, he coughed harder, rising with a groan. "Didn't I tell you I'm not dead yet?" Grinning, he thumped toward Ben. "Bones! Fine name for an undertaker. Why are you back?"

"The special constable enlisted my help," Ben said. "He asked me to check on a few details. Lady Maggart graciously gave her assent."

"Oh, well, if Odette gives you leave, who am I to argue?" Lord Maggart said sourly. "Anyone would think she's a widow. Always gallivanting around the West Country or finding an excuse to visit the rectory. I'd think she was having an affair with Father Rummage, but for one thing."

You've seen him? Ben thought unkindly but chose a more traditional response. "What's that?"

"I'll kill any man who makes me a cuckold, and she damn well knows it!" Lord Maggart banged his cane against the marble floor. The yellowed skin of his face pulled tight, making his cheeks and jaw startlingly prominent, as if his skull was fighting to emerge.

"Your wife is faithful and only wants the best for you," Ben said soothingly. "Let's get you back to the fire."

Without asking permission, he took Lord Maggart's arm. After a moment's resistance, the sick man allowed himself to be led back to his chair.

"Good chap," he said as Ben draped a blanket over his gaunt frame. "What a world. Doctors are ghouls and undertakers are kindly. Before I went to war, I never thought of violence. When I was there, in the thick of it, all I wanted was to run away. Any soldier who tells you he isn't afraid from time to time is a liar."

"Any person who claims they aren't afraid from time to time is a liar," Ben corrected, wondering if Lord Maggart would ever forgive him, should he reveal his true vocation. Surely this was late-stage cancer; if not of the pancreas, perhaps the liver. Either way, medicine could offer the baron nothing in the way of a cure. But his remaining days could be made far more comfortable, if he could be persuaded to accept help from a "white coat."

"Did I tell you how I was wounded, boy?" Lord Maggart held up his hand. The palm was deeply scarred, and the little finger was missing. "Hardly seems worth talking about. Sometimes I say I was bayonetted in the leg or the gut. Better that, than to admit I cut myself on barbed wire, and it was gangrene that put me in Dottyville."

"Gangrene can kill." The fire had guttered, so Ben stirred up the coals, exposing the red which pulsed beneath the grayish white.

"Of course it can kill. Perhaps that's why I let it go so far." Lord Maggart pulled the blanket up to his chin. "God and country, my boy, God and country. I was expected to kill the enemy, but the only person I wanted to die was me." He closed his eyes, speaking slowly, as if already dozing. "Now my side aches, night and day. Perhaps I *was* bayonetted and only forgot. Take that, Dr. MacHardy, you bloody nightmare."

Ben glanced at his black doctor's bag. Lord Maggart had failed to note it, even though it sat on the floor not far away. The bag contained a pocket medicine case of twenty-four bottled drugs, including phenobarbital and morphine. Either one would afford the baron deeper, more restful sleep than a day spent propped before the fire.

"Is it possible, your lordship, that young doctors—recent graduates trained to modern standards—are more trustworthy than MacHardy and his ilk?"

The baron's eyes opened, glittering with sudden acuity. "Are you trying to trick me?"

"What?"

"She tries to trick me. I know her game. I recognize her agents," he said, staring hard at Ben. His eyes, shadowed by the fire, seemed to recede in their sockets, the skull once again straining for preeminence. It would win before long, Ben thought. Maybe in six months. Maybe in six weeks.

"Do you mean Lady Maggart's tried to trick you? How?"

"Sleep." Lord Maggart coughed. "Rest. All I want is rest. You wouldn't understand."

"Oh, but I would. I've been jarred out of a sound sleep for two nights running."

"Is that so?" The baron's voice dropped to a whisper. "Who wakes you? Do you believe what they tell you? They kicked up such a ruddy fuss about the evening dress, but she told me the earl was coming, I swear it. Now I wonder. When I saw Charlie upstairs, bold as brass, Collins told me it must have been a dream. She came to me later and said it was true. I've always trusted her. Why would she lie?"

"She wouldn't. Lady Maggart has no reason to lie to you."

This time his soothing reply made Lord Maggart cast his blanket onto the floor. "You're not listening!" he cried, as loud as his limited breath allowed. "Go bury someone else. I'm not dead yet, damn you, and I'll show MacHardy I'm no coward before the end, I swear it."

BEN SPENT the next hour working his way through most of

Fitchley House's ground floor, checking rugs, walls, and upholstery for splattered blood. Of course, after roughly forty-eight hours, anyone determined to conceal blood could have taken action, but Ben was betting the undertaking was too massive to pull off flawlessly. He'd never seen a man's throat cut, but he'd witnessed the immediate aftermath in St. Thomas Hospital's lobby, when an assailant from the notorious Elephant & Castle Mob turned up to finish a fight.

Sauntering into the lobby, the killer had spied his rival, a member of some lesser gang, waiting to have a wound stitched. Pulling a knife, the killer had plunged it into the man's neck. By the time Ben got there, the victim was dead, the killer had fled, and blood was everywhere. It soaked the rug, stained the seat cushions, and seeped into the mortar between the floor tiles. A relatively small spurt had discolored the blue wainscoting and ruined the wallpaper. Even days later, after the floor had been scoured, the seat cushions replaced, and everything repainted, those red-brown flecks kept turning up. Ben had spotted them on the doorjamb, on the ceiling, and even baked on the surface of a lightbulb.

The search for blood in the solarium and conservatory—two areas easily cleaned, since they had bare floors instead of fitted carpets—turned up nothing. A glance out the solarium window, however, revealed more than an overcast afternoon vista. Ben saw a young man in a cap and overalls pushing a wheelbarrow loaded with smoking debris.

He hurried out the French doors, undaunted by the blast of cold air that greeted him. "Hello there!"

The boy's head jerked up guiltily. He looked about fifteen, with greasy hair, red cheeks, and prominent front teeth. "Sir?"

"You're the boot boy?"

He nodded, eyes wide, as Ben reached him. "I'm Dr. Bones," he said, sticking out his hand. The boot boy stared at it.

"Shake?" Ben prompted, smiling.

The boy put forth a gloved hand. The rawhide was caked with ash, but Ben shook it anyway.

"What's your name?" he asked in a friendly tone.

"John."

"Do you know why I'm here, John?"

The boy shook his head.

"Do you know a dead man was found below stairs?"

"Yes, sir." His voice shook.

Ben put a hand on John's shoulder. "Don't be frightened. I'm not here to hurt anyone. I'm just sweeping up some loose ends." He looked at the smoking heap in the wheelbarrow. "What's all this then?"

"I found it over there," John said, pointing at a cluster of trees. "I think Mr. Collins made a mistake. When he burned the rug."

There was no rug in the wheelbarrow—no recognizable remnants of one, anyway. Instead, Ben saw a pile of scorched clothes and a handful of blackened metal objects. "May I have a look?"

John didn't answer. He probably wasn't used to people asking his permission.

"Why don't I just check?" Ben poked gently at the first object, a metal cylinder. It was cool to the touch. The scorched clothes were damp. "Did you douse them with water?"

"Yes, sir. When I came out of the privy, I saw smoke," John said. "From where he burned the rug."

Ben removed the cylinder's cap and studied the blackened residue inside. After a moment he pegged it as a tube of lipstick. "Where did the rug come from? Below stairs?"

"No. Her ladyship's room. I think," John said without conviction.

He'd make a dreadful witness, Ben thought. *Let a barrister speak sharply, or tell him he's got it wrong, and he'll recant immediately, or say what he thinks they want him to say.*

"What about these other things?" There was a scorched compact, a pot of face cream with the label burned off, a broken hand mirror, and the remains of a brush, its bristles gone. Both the mirror and the brush were partly melted, which meant they were silver-plated rather than steel.

"I reckon they were Mr. Archer's. Like the clothes."

Ben poked gently at the wet, half-burned fabric. One large remnant had five buttons along a seam, and could be called men's trousers. The rest were, objectively, nothing but rags. If they'd once smelled of blood, they now reeked of paraffin.

"You knew Mr. Archer."

"Yeah." John smiled. "Lemon sherbets."

"I like those. Did he?"

"Yeah. He shared them when he came round. I used to open the gates for his lorry. He would say, 'Thanks, mate.' Like we was friends. Then he'd give me a lemon sherbet."

"Was this day or night?"

"Night."

"How often?" Ben asked.

John shrugged, again seeming markedly diffident. Ben had the impression if he pressed too hard, John would agree with anything he said. He had to be careful not to telegraph the expected answer.

"I wonder what happened to Mr. Archer."

The boot boy looked at the ground.

"It's all right. I don't want any trouble. I'm just curious. Some say he was killed."

John nodded emphatically.

"I wonder if the person who killed him is someone important."

Another nod.

"If you whisper the name to me, I promise not to tell anyone," Ben said truthfully. It would be cruel and pointless to drag John into the investigation; a conviction would require something more substantial than the boot boy's word. He leaned close to the boy, who smelled of sweat and worse. His clothes were stiff with grime, as if they hadn't been washed in weeks.

"Mrs. Tippett said...."

"Yes?"

"She said Father Rummage did it. On account of him being a right villain and likely to do anything."

"Dr. Bones! What do you think you're doing?"

Ben looked back at the house. In his haste to intercept John, he'd left the conservatory's French doors ajar, signaling his egress to Mr. Collins. The butler ran toward them, just as he'd run after Ben's car.

John made a frightened noise. He probably wasn't used to seeing the butler moving at such speed.

"Never fear. He's cross with me, not you." Ben leaned over the wheelbarrow to pat John's shoulder. At the same time, he seized the scorched compact, slipping it into his jacket pocket. "Chin up, John. I'm game for his worst."

"Dr. Bones," Mr. Collins gasped. Running apparently wasn't his forte, not even downhill. "Lady Maggart," he puffed, "only gave you leave," he gasped, "to search the house...."

Ankle turning, he slipped on the grass and lost his footing altogether. Ben darted right, John darted left, and Mr. Collins collided with the wheelbarrow. It flipped over as he hit the ground, its wet, blackened contents slithering out. He crawled aside before they could make contact with his suit's fine fabric.

"You're quite right, Mr. Collins," Ben agreed cheerfully. "I'm out of bounds. Entirely my fault. May I give you a hand up?"

No doubt desperate to preserve his suit, Mr. Collins accepted that hand. But once upright, he rounded on John. "Idiot! What the devil are you up to?"

"He was at work clearing up rubbish," Ben declared firmly. "Once again, the fault is mine. I interrupted to ask a few questions. But John said he doesn't know anything. Isn't that right, John?"

"Yes, sir," the boy said fervently.

"As a matter of fact, he referred me back to you," Ben said. "Wasn't that what you said, John? That only Mr. Collins could answer?"

"Yes, sir."

The butler still looked faintly suspicious, so Ben pretended to discover the blackened mess at their feet. "What *is* this?" He poked at it with the toe of his shoe.

"Heaven knows. John will dispose of it." Mr. Collins snapped his fingers at the boot boy. "As for you, Dr. Bones, it's too cold to linger out here, wouldn't you agree?"

They returned to the house. Once inside the solarium, the butler withdrew his keyring, locked the French doors, and drew the curtains. His bearing suggested he'd regained his confidence, and felt certain he'd blocked a devastating discovery.

"Now that you've completed your examination of the house, may I show you out?"

"I've finished this floor," Ben said. "Now I'm heading upstairs."

"I see. I would never insinuate that you're using these circumstances as an excuse to pry," Mr. Collins insinuated, "but are you quite sure further intrusion is necessary, Dr. Bones? I took the liberty of making inquiries and discovered you report to Dr. Kidd at Plymouth City Hospital. No doubt he'll want an account of how you use your time, just as Birdswing's council will expect justification for how you use your petrol."

"That's true," Ben said, as if such considerations had never occurred to him. "But as the physician for Barking, as well as Birdswing, I feel a responsibility to Fitchley Park. Mrs. Archer has confessed, but she may yet implicate others in this household," he added, watching the butler's face. "Probably just out of malice. But suppose she claims, for example, that poor John opened the gate for her? Or that someone—even you—abetted her in another way, such as turning a blind eye or disposing of evidence?"

Mr. Collins's chin dropped a notch. He seemed to be trying to decide if Ben had accidentally hit two key points or if he'd issued a deliberate warning.

"So far I've found nothing," Ben said, deciding not to reveal the scorched compact in his pocket just yet. "When I'm called to give evidence, as I surely will be, I can swear that Fitchley House's ground floor is clear. If I could only double-check upstairs...."

"As you wish," Mr. Collins said politely, but the fear didn't leave his eyes.

13

ABOVE STAIRS

L*ady Juliet may be right about a conspiracy*, Ben thought as he climbed the stairs. *Mr. Collins is in up to his eyebrows. How could he have failed to notice that the body was moved? Then there's the spot on the stairs. It might have been blood, or it might have been wine, but thanks to him, we'll never know. He burned a rug, according to John. He burned clothes, probably Bobby's, and a handful of women's things. Did he do it for himself, or on Lady Maggart's orders?*

Halfway up the stairs, Ben stopped to rest his knee, which had predictably started to throb after his brief time in the cold. Lucy, never far from his thoughts, returned to the forefront again, as she frequently did when he was in pain. He didn't know why. Perhaps because he'd arrived at Fenton House in a wheelchair, unable to walk or stand without assistance, the ache in his bones had somehow become associated with Lucy.

Or can she sense pain? Is that why she put out my cane for me?

At the top of the stairs, he paused again, feeling in his jacket's inner pocket for a pencil stub and his leather-bound notebook. Flipping to a blank page, he wrote:

MR. COLLINS—*no motive yet to kill Bobby, but might move heaven and earth for the sake of Fitchley P.*

Rev. Rummage—*often here, staff seems to dislike him; per John, Mrs. Tippet said he killed Bobby on account of her ladyship*

Kitty—*pretty, apparently left-handed, might have been Bobby's future wife*

Lady Maggart—*seems genuinely afraid of supernatural killer but could be an act*

Lord Maggart—*physically weak but volatile, muddled*

HE STARTED to tuck the notebook away, then reopened it and added after Lord Maggart's name:

CARRIES a cane

HE'D COME to the oldest section of the house, which contained the family rooms. Judging by the arrangement, all of them offered Fitchley Park's best view: Lady Maggart's garden, with its remnant of an ancient wall and the dark, thick woods beyond. From left to right, there were four doors. He tried the first. Locked.

Bobby and Helen have been separated for years. Now, suddenly, he asks for a divorce. Helen said he called his new love a proper lady, like Penny.

Ben tried the next door. Also locked.

I took "proper lady" to mean she didn't earn her living in her knickers. But what if he literally meant lady? As in Odette Maggart?

Annoyed by his limp, which was growing more pronounced, Ben stumped to the third door. As expected, it was locked.

That photograph he'd glimpsed in the Cow Hole returned to

him: Fitchley Park's staff assembled solemnly in front of the house as Lady Maggart smiled beside the handsome game-keeper. Father Rummage had access to the house and a clear monopoly on her attention, but Ben found it difficult to imagine them carrying on. The rector seemed at least reasonably dedicated to his higher calling, and because Lady Maggart resembled an older version of Penny, Ben was inclined to view her as such. Thus it was far easier for him to picture her having an affair with fit, handsome Bobby than a plump little man who might burst into giggles after every kiss.

Conducting an affair in a house her husband rarely left would be incredibly bold, but given Lady Maggart's position as a local celebrity, meeting Bobby in Barking or Birdswing would have been nearly impossible. Before the war, they might have had rendezvouses in Plymouth, but the blackout and the petrol ration made that problematic. By contrast, Lord Maggart's diminished faculties meant his wife might get away with slipping Bobby into the house, as long as her servants were loyal.

But there are flaws to the theory, Ben thought, reaching the last door in the hall. *Starting with Mrs. Archer's confession.*

He gave the brass handle a perfunctory twist. To his surprise, the door opened, revealing a gold-and-peach suite.

The suite's outer room looked like something out of a Hollywood film. The sofa of crushed velvet was unabashedly feminine, as was the delicate glass coffee table and matching drinks trolley. Near the door, two umbrellas and a Baroque brass cane stood inside a cloisonné urn. In pride of place sat a giltwood vanity, its mirror framed in round white lightbulbs.

"Is that you, Mrs. Grundy?" Odette called from the suite's inner room. "I didn't ring the bell."

Ben cleared his throat. "Er, no, Lady Maggart, it's me. Dr. Bones. Forgive the intrusion, I was told you weren't at home."

He expected her to order him out, but instead she issued a tinkling laugh, the sort Penny had learned at finishing school.

"You're quite right, Ben. I'm not at home, in the social sense. Do come through." She laughed again. "Said the spider to the fly."

He hesitated, searching for an excuse that would give no offense. He'd heard of scenarios like this. They emanated almost exclusively from blokes in the pub, usually half in the bag. They claimed to have been innocently going about their business when they stumbled into a boudoir like this, inhabited by a welcoming female. The voluptuous interludes that followed had always struck Ben as outright lies. Now, after years of scoffing at such tales of opportunistic lust, he seemed to have wandered into one.

"I wouldn't want to disturb you," he called. "I'm only doing as we discussed—checking the house for blood or anything pertinent to my written account of Bobby Archer's demise."

"Why, Dr. Bones. Should I take your reluctance to inspect my bedroom as proof you consider me above suspicion?"

He coughed, which was his standard way of acknowledging a question he had no intention of answering. He couldn't turn down her invitation. Not after forming a plausible scenario in which Lady Maggart and Bobby had been lovers.

The suite's inner room proved just as conspicuously feminine, all giltwood and flowing lines. The changing screen was upholstered in peach satin; the bedclothes were made from the same fabric. No man would accept such an arrangement, so it was clear that the baroness and her husband maintained to the old fashioned tradition of separate bedrooms.

"My husband's poor health makes it difficult for him to climb the stairs. His room is on the ground floor," Lady Maggart said, as if reading his mind. She sat beside the hearth, which was fitted with a three-bar electric fire. Dressed in a peach silk robe, her blonde hair loose around her shoulders, she looked relaxed and happy. A book with a familiar dust jacket lay in her lap.

"*Rebecca*," he said. "I'm reading it, too, on my housekeeper's recommendation."

"What do you think of the second Mrs. De Winter? Such a nonentity," Lady Maggart said. Though not yet dressed, she was fully made up, including those fanlike black lashes Lady Juliet had called glued-on. Her high-heeled mules were accented by puffs of white rabbit fur.

"I do envy Rebecca, though," she continued, putting the book aside and rising. "She had life arranged to her satisfaction. And Maxim—oh, Maxim. If only I had such a man in my life." She slipped her fingers under his lapels, fondling the material as she stared into his eyes.

"My wife," Ben said, letting those words hang in the air as he gently disengaged her hands, "died not long ago. Your husband is still alive, and may even rally for a time, if we can convince him to accept treatment." He took a step back, smiling to lessen the sting of his rejection.

"My husband. Yes. Of course." Lady Maggart sighed. "But as I told you, his experience at Craiglockhart makes it impossible for me to do anything but give him his head. He hasn't been a husband to me in twenty years. I owe him nothing but kindness and a calming influence."

"Calming? Is he violent?"

"Oh, for heaven's sake. He was branded a coward in the war. Do you think he's grown courageous in his waning days?" Turning away, Lady Maggart crossed to the window and pulled back the curtains. As she stared down at her garden, the sunlight highlighted a downward slash along the side of her mouth. "Dudley didn't kill that wretched man. I already gave you my opinion on what did."

"You said Fitchley Park was haunted. I know my ghost's history. What about yours?"

"Not mine. Though I freely admit it was almost certainly my own sins that opened the door to this torment. Dudley told me he grew up hearing stories about a lady in black. She wears a heavy mantle, like a Victorian lady, with a hood falling over her face. From midnight till dawn, she walks the halls of Fitchley Park, listening to whispers and punishing evildoers."

"Especially naughty children, I'll bet," Ben said. "It seems very human to me, this belief that something all-seeing and malevolent lies in wait. I'm certainly not immune to it. But I've heard it said that humans also create their own strife and wickedness. Perhaps when it's too painful to accuse ourselves, we like to imagine something else at work. A cruel person who won't die, instead of a cruel truth."

"I've seen her," Lady Maggart said, turning away from the window and looking him in the eye.

"What? When?"

"In the summer. A crash woke me in the middle of the night," she said. "I sat straight up in bed. My vanity used to sit just there." She pointed at a space occupied by a chest of drawers. "The crash was the mirror, shattering into a thousand pieces."

"The vanity in the outer room?"

"Yes. With the replacement mirror I ordered from New York City to cheer myself up. Bit of glamor, you know. Dudley wasn't too happy. I thought, given the funds the barony conserved by sacking poor Charlie...." She broke off.

"This lady in black," Ben prompted. It was clear to him that Lady Maggart could hardly bring herself to finish the story. Her distress made him inclined to believe her, or at least to believe *she* believed.

"I didn't see her at first." Lady Maggart said. "But this was before the blackout, so the room wasn't completely dark. There was another crash, a little one, then another. She was flinging my cosmetics about, smashing them on the floor and hurling them against the wall. Perfume, pots of rouge. A tin of talc broke open and powder went everywhere. Then I saw her—a woman in a mantle."

"What happened next?"

"I screamed. Screamed like a madwoman. Then...." She shrugged. "I suppose I fainted. When I came round, all the lights were burning. Collins, Kitty, and half the maids were clustered around the bed. Even poor Dudley climbed the stairs to see what had happened. Collins tried to say I'd been sleepwalking and done it myself. Mrs. Grundy sent for Dr. Egan, in Birdswing, but he never came. We learned the next day he was dead." She stared hard into Ben's eyes, as if gauging his trustworthiness, just as he'd gauged her truthfulness. "I still wonder if it's connected, just as I wonder if our two hauntings are connected."

"I understand that, too," he said sincerely. "Once we factor in the supernatural, even innocuous facts can look like signs. But that doesn't mean they *are* connected. In the interest of seeing justice done, would you permit me to ask a personal question, Lady Maggart?"

"Am I being interrogated? Should I seek counsel?" she asked suspiciously. "Collins said a woman from Birdswing was arrested. Isn't that an end to it, at least from your point of view?"

"Not necessarily. Were you having a love affair with Bobby Archer?"

"How can you ask? I've told you, I didn't even know him!"

"What about Father Rummage?"

"Now you're just being insulting."

She didn't seem particularly outraged by either question. That might mean he was far off the mark—or that her finishing school had prepared her for difficult questions, as Clarion Academy had prepared Penny.

"Forgive me, my lady. I've intruded unnecessarily on your peace." As Ben turned to go, he noticed something: a circular mark on the inner room's fitted carpet.

"Hang on." Eagerly, he knelt beside the blemish, but it wasn't a bloodstain. It was a deep depression—one of four.

Rising, he checked the bed's placement. It was off-center compared to the wall sconces, giving the impression the room was crowded with furniture. "I see you've recently moved things."

"Yes."

"Why? If you'll forgive me for asking, Lady Maggart."

"To conceal a huge blood stain, of course," she snapped. "You'd like that, wouldn't you? No doubt that woman you associate with has painted me as a monster, but the truth is rather more mundane. Even after the new mirror was mounted, the mere sight of my vanity reminded me of that terrible night. So I banished it. Now my boudoir is out of balance, no matter how Mrs. Grundy and I shift the furniture about."

Ben nodded, but his gaze roved the room, searching for anything—a cut-out section of carpet, a curiously hung painting —that might indeed conceal a blood stain.

"That chest of drawers is quite heavy," Lady Maggart said coolly, returning to her seat by the fireplace and pointedly reopening her book. "Perhaps you should look behind it?"

He did. It wasn't snug against the wall; there was about half an inch of daylight between the chest and the gold-and-peach wallpaper. It was unblemished, either by blood or the sort of powerful chemical, like Borax, needed to blot it away.

"I meant that as a cutting rebuke, not an invitation," Lady Maggart said. "But if you're going to behave like a Keystone Kop, by all means, inspect the carpet under the bed, too."

The indignity of being caught sniffing around Bobby's corpse for *Sous le Vent* returned to Ben, but he couldn't let it deter him. Not when Lady Maggart's bed could so easily hide the bloodstain he sought.

He was down on all fours, running his fingertips over carpet fibers he couldn't thoroughly examine without a torch, when he heard footsteps.

"Milady, what's all this?" a woman asked. "Should I ring for Collins?"

"Oh dear, Mrs. Grundy, we thought you were my husband." Lady Maggart sounded overjoyed. "My lover is hiding under the bed."

That got Ben to his feet in a hurry. "I've no idea how you got your reputation as a moral crusader."

"Don't be ashamed, darling," Lady Maggart said, flashing a predatory smile. "I won't tell anyone you propositioned me. You aren't the first man to corner me and make a fool of himself."

There was nothing he could say to that which wouldn't scorch the earth and get him barred from Fitchley Park forever, so Ben didn't reply. Instead, he turned to Mrs. Grundy and literally jumped. If scrambling up from the floor hadn't set his knee on fire, that sudden jarring action would have done it, but for the moment, he felt nothing but mortification.

In the photograph he'd glimpsed in the Cow Hole, Mrs. Grundy had been looking down. Her face had appeared somewhat distorted, which Ben automatically dismissed as a lens artifact or trick of the light. Now he saw her face was indeed misshapen—not her lips or her eyes, but the bones of her skull. Her forehead bulged like the top of an hourglass, and her cheekbones were unusually prominent, connected to her nose by a thick ridge.

"Hello, Dr. Bones," she said.

"In case no one's ever told you, it's rude to stare," Lady

Maggart said, clearly reveling in his discomfiture. "Unless gawping is your idea of what's commonly called a bedside manner."

"Please excuse me, Mrs. Grundy, if I seem to have misplaced my manners. The bones of my legs are tetchy after an accident." He was looking at someone with a severe case of *osteitis deformans*, also known as Paget's disease of bone, or simply Paget's disease.

"If your bones ache, we share a common burden," Mrs. Grundy replied with a slight smile. Something about her measured tone, her quiet dignity under scrutiny, allowed Ben to forget his own kneejerk rudeness. He admired anyone who could meet surprise and distaste with such forbearance, and even offer a second chance for him to redeem himself.

Lady Maggart, however, clearly had no interest in allowing that second chance to play out on her patch. "Mrs. Grundy, my guest has exhausted every possibility to humiliate himself above stairs. However, I said he could speak to you and the maid, and I'm a woman of my word. Take this young man down to the kitchen. Give him some biscuits and a glass of milk, and let him ask his questions. Nothing will come of it, I promise."

14

THE GOD-BOTHERER

Juliet's loyalty to Birdswing was well-known, in no small part because she declared it aloud at every opportunity. A corollary to this loyalty was her disdain for Barking, which she also advertised without fail. But despite all this, she nurtured a secret passion for something in Barking, and that something was St. Gwinnodock's church.

It was about the same size as St. Mark's but felt larger due to the soaring vertical space and colorful rose window. Juliet loved to sit and contemplate the complex tracery, which reminded her of a mandala. She'd never learned to meditate, or at least never found serenity in the practice, because the chatter of her thoughts was too insistent. The worries, questions, and hopes never seemed to stop, and in fact increased whenever she tried to clear her mind. But in St. Gwinnodock's cool interior, she gave herself permission to relax and enjoy the beauty. It seemed to chase out of her head those worries and questions, and even the hopes, which were sometimes more vexing than fears. No effort was required. Only to sit down, breathe in that "churchy" odor comprised of old wood, older stone, and stale incense, and fix her eyes on the window's central rosette of Madonna and child.

In the interest of justice (a phrase Dirk Diamond employed frequently), Juliet began by visiting the rectory, a two-story stone cottage situated beside the cloister garth. Father Rummage's private residence was upstairs; the ground floor contained his office, the church secretary's office, and his darkroom.

"Hallo!" she called as she opened the door. Like the previous day, she found an exasperated-looking young woman behind the secretary's desk, which seemed to have vomited its contents on the surrounding floor. "Still at it, Mrs. Lobb?"

"It doesn't end," Mrs. Lobb replied. "When Thomas was called up, he told me he had a 'highly individual' system of tracking the church's expenditures and contributions. I assumed that meant a system involving bits of paper with numbers written on them. I'm beginning to think the system exists only in his mind." She pushed her spectacles onto the top of her head. "He used to come home every night complaining of exhaustion. I was worried sick about taking over for him. I thought perhaps I couldn't measure up." She laughed. "Now I have no idea what he did all day. But when he comes back, he'll find this office shipshape and Bristol fashion."

Juliet smiled. If Mrs. Lobb kept up this habit of greeting her with a series of complaints, she'd be in danger of making a friend. "I, for one, think this country could use a greater influx of female influence. The men have been mucking about unsupervised for too long."

"You'll get no argument from me," Mrs. Lobb said. She couldn't have been much older than Juliet—twenty-six—but exhibited the self-possession of a more seasoned woman. "Do you know Father Rummage keeps no diary? His time is completely unaccounted for, except for services, of course, and when the Council pins him down for its weekly meeting. Since I took over for Thomas, I've had to go on numerous fishing expeditions. I usually find him at Fitchley Park or out taking pictures."

"Dare I ask where he is now?"

"In the sacristy, I think. Unless he slipped out again."

Juliet thanked Mrs. Lobb and crossed the churchyard. No Anderson shelter would be needed here; St. Gwinnodock's crypt would serve as the shelter for Father Rummage and ten or more neighboring families. Not for the first time, Juliet was grateful that Belsham Manor had a wine cellar and was situated just far enough from the village proper that ARP Warden Gaston couldn't critique the minutiae of their responses to air-raid drills. Waiting out an actual bombing in the wine cellar would be distressing, but at least she and her mother and the staff would all be together on familiar territory. She didn't envy anyone obligated to dash out of their home into the night, coats buttoned over their pajamas or nightgowns, to squat for an undetermined time in some mass shelter like a church basement.

Entering St. Gwinnodock's, she passed a row of candles, two of them burning. Using a taper, she lit another four—for Helen, Bobby, Caleb, and Micah. She pinched out the flame, then changed her mind and lit one more candle, for Lucy MacGregor. For many, the Fenton House ghost was a bit of fun or an agreeably spooky story. But she was real, and quite possibly suffering, trapped between this world and the next. Juliet thought it important not to let herself forget that.

Roughly in the center of the nave, a side chapel had been renovated into a sacristy. Juliet rapped on the door.

"I'm quite busy, sorry!"

"I do apologize. It's Juliet Linton. If I could have just a moment of your—"

"Lady Juliet? Come in."

She entered to find the portly little man surrounded by C of

E essentials: vestments, hangings, altar linens, anointing oils, and white wax candles, bought in bulk. He sat on a stool, reading a magazine about photography. When her gaze lingered on the cover, he rolled up the magazine, hid it behind a box of candles, and gave her a sheepish smile.

"Forgive my little untruth," he said. "But that Mrs. Lobb is always after me to do this or that. I haven't had a moment's peace since Thomas left. There's a reason why married women don't fit in the workforce."

She must not have looked happy with his pronouncement, despite its near-universality, because he followed it up with, "Except of course when they work alongside other women, in a laundry or a kitchen." He giggled.

"Yes, well, you'll soon show Mrs. Lobb who's boss," Juliet said. "By retreating to your ecclesiastical foxhole while she takes charge of St. Gwinnodock's records, finances, and other essentials, you've sent a clear message. But never mind all that. I don't suppose you've found the time to develop those crime scene photographs?"

"I was just about to," he said. "I was only waiting for Mrs. Lobb to go home for tea, so she wouldn't pester me while I worked."

Another caustic remark came to Juliet, but she chose not to deploy it. A new possibility had occurred to her. "I don't suppose you'd let me watch? I haven't the faintest idea how photos are printed." This wasn't true, but she'd only read about it, never seen it demonstrated, and as she expected, Father Rummage seized the chance to expound on his hobby.

"But of course!" he cried, giggling again.

Juliet willed her face into what she hoped was an amiable expression. She was genuinely interested in the process, and listening to his nervous laughter was the inescapable price of admission.

THE TWO HOURS spent in Father Rummage's darkroom proved worthwhile. Juliet learned the four stations, or metal pans filled with liquid, which were visited in the same order: developer, stop bath, fixer, and water rinse. She learned the process had to occur in a "light-tight" room, with no illumination except for the glow of a red bulb, or the film would be overexposed, and therefore ruined. She also learned that merely pointing the camera at the correct subject and safely getting the film out of the camera was only the beginning. In creating prints from negatives, timing was everything. Too much time could result in a washed-out image with no subtle details; too little time, a dark, confusing image.

"I do hope Dr. Bones hasn't given up on me," she said as they waited for the last group of photos to dry. They hung behind Father Rummage, clipped to the same kind of retractable indoor clothesline ladies used to dry their unmentionables. "And I never thought darkroom photography would smell so much like making chutney."

"That's because I use common kitchen vinegar for fixer," Father Rummage said. "You can buy an official preparation, of course, but there's no real difference, so I save a few pence."

"I see you also found a creative use for old news, too," Juliet said, indicating the wads of paper the rector had used to block out light from under the door.

"It's difficult to find a door hung so perfectly, or a floor so level, that light doesn't penetrate," Father Rummage said crisply. His habit of laughing nervously had disappeared. His mastery in the darkroom was obvious, and his enthusiasm proved contagious.

"My father gave me a Brownie when I was nine years old. That was forty years ago, when it cost five quid. It was a hand-

some gift, one I did my best to live up to," he said. "It changed
the way I see the world. Taught me to appreciate the subtleties
of light and shadow. Not only how they commingle, but how my
choices in the darkroom—exposing more, exposing less—trans-
forms not only the print but a viewer's perception of the
original."

"I've been guilty of saying the camera doesn't lie," Juliet
admitted.

"A common refrain. The archdeacon said it once at a fête. I
made the mistake of imagining he had some interest in photography and might like to hear more on the topic." Father
Rummage's laugh sounded genuine for once. "I'd forgotten the
archdeacon never likes to hear from me, on any topic. I
mentioned the commingling of light and shadow, and how the
photographer's choices can change the objective to subjective.
He said he hoped I understood our Christian faith better than I
understood optics, which are 'mathematically immutable,' in his
words."

"In my opinion, some people are immune to art," Juliet said.
"I don't mean they dislike it or consider it inconsequential. I
think they're simply insensible to its existence, just as humans
are insensible to certain whistles any dog can hear. To them, a
photo is just a picture of something or someone. A book is either
full of information, if non-fiction, or full of lies, if fiction. They
can see prettiness, I think, and ugliness. But art offers a portal to
transcendence, and I don't think they perceive the door. Perhaps
your archdeacon may be numbered among such individuals."

"Interesting point, Lady Juliet," Father Rummage said. "I
wonder...." There was a plaintive note to this last, and he did not
continue.

Once the final batch of photos was ready, they exited the
darkroom to review them. Mrs. Lobb was still unearthing, examining, and re-filing papers, a process that caused Father

Rummage's nervous laugh to rematerialize. Therefore, Juliet suggested they look over the pictures in the church, where he could focus on the matter without cringing every time Mrs. Lobb tutted.

"It's so disappointing," Juliet sighed after they'd gone over every picture twice. "They look exactly like I remember."

"Well, yes. Dr. Bones did ask us to document the scene for posterity," Father Rummage said. "We've done that quite well, I think."

"Not we. You."

"You created the last batch of prints," the rector said generously. In truth, he had coached her every step of the way, mostly on the timing. "I suspect you've uncovered a hidden talent."

Juliet liked the sound of that. It was another skill she could cultivate for future investigations, along with her correspondence lessons from Private Dick Academy. Perhaps, given the manipulation of light and shadow Father Rummage had mentioned, she could even find a way to make Belsham Manor look pretty. If not pretty—acceptable.

"The credit goes entirely to you. You're a fine instructor. Do you ever...." She stopped, surprised at herself. The question she'd been poised to ask was completely inappropriate. "Well, I suppose I ought to gather these up and take them to Fitchley Park. I just hope Dr. Bones is having better luck."

"Yes," Father Rummage said, gazing up at the rose window. "I do."

"What?"

"You were going to ask me if I wished I'd pursued photography as a vocation, rather than the priesthood," he replied, not looking at her. "The answer is yes."

She took that in. Perhaps Father Rummage's earlier comment about the archdeacon had been less about art and more about his disinclination to listen.

"What drew you to the church in the first place?"

"Security." He sighed. "And Mother. If she couldn't have an MP in the family, she set her sights on a bishop." He emitted that nervous laugh, which now sounded entirely appropriate: unhappy and counterfeit, like the man himself, at times.

"I imagine ministering to Barking isn't all fêtes and awarding the prize for the biggest pumpkin," she said. "I had the impression you're expected to be at Lady Maggart's beck and call. Which could have its advantages," she added, striving to sound neutral, so as not to negatively influence his answer.

"Oh, it does. She's been a great benefactress to St. Gwinnodock's," Father Rummage said. "Her work in the WI is unimpeachable."

Juliet waited, but no additional praise followed. To keep from filling the silence, she studied the shafts of colored light that fell upon the lady chapel's small altar.

"Of course...." Father Rummage began.

She stifled the urge to press him, which proved wise. After half a minute, the silence prodded him far more effectively than anything she might have said.

"Her fear of the supernatural is exhausting. Not to mention contagious. Even I feel watched in Fitchley Park, and I've never been the superstitious type," he said. "I thought agreeing to lead her in prayer, in her bedroom, would ease her mind and put the matter to rest. Instead, it created all sorts of problems."

Juliet decided if she was ever wanted to apply a gentle push, this was the moment. "I never repeat gossip, but it's long been said Lady Maggart had an affair with that handsome gamekeeper, what's-his-name, the one who was dismissed under a dark cloud. Were you not concerned that spending so much time with her, including in her bedroom, of all places, might expose you to the same speculation?"

"No," Father Rummage said. "He was called Charlie. Did you

ever see him? We're cut from very different cloth. Her ladyship would never look at me." He didn't sound regretful. "Only one woman ever did, and she despises me now. I don't know why. I expect I would have made a dreadful husband. When parishioners come to me for marital advice, I feel such a fraud. Poor Mrs. Archer. I wish she'd stuck with George Cotterill. His marriage is the model of amicability."

Juliet nodded. She felt a little guilty, tacitly encouraging the man to discuss matters on which he ought to keep mum, but Helen's freedom was at stake, and possibly her life. "Special Constable Gaston said Helen named you as an alibi, but you couldn't confirm her claim."

"No. She may have closed the restaurant and come to Barking with the expectation of seeking my counsel, but it never came to pass. I tried to be fair, and scrupulously honest, when I relayed the information to the constable, but I think he took it as a virtual confession."

"Having known Helen all my life, I imagine she wished the plagues of Egypt on Bobby. She's always said he deserved death, and if not that, an everlasting case of piles."

He nodded. "I told the constable that in my opinion, she was merely expressing pain and frustration. He said my perception made no difference, only her words, and the precise meaning of those words."

"Literalism, thy name is Gaston. What happened to Bobby was hideous. I don't believe Helen committed such a terrible act, not for one moment. Nor do I believe she paid someone else to do it for her. I think our special constable would do better looking into Mr. Collins."

Father Rummage squeaked as if she'd given him an especially hard pinch. "Jasper?"

"I realize you weren't present for some of his strange behavior, but I assure you, he was as opaque as a man can be, when he wasn't being openly hostile."

"I've been a witness to his hostility for some time," the rector said. "I'll say this: he'd do anything for Fitchley Park, because he conflates the house's image with his own. If he knows who killed Mr. Archer, and he thinks that news would bring scandal on his employers, he'll move heaven and earth to conceal it. But I don't think he'd kill someone. The act might adversely affect his hair."

Juliet laughed. He beamed at her.

"You have a lovely laugh. Musical."

"In a tête-à-tête you're a very different man, Father Rummage. As for Fitchley Park's housekeeper, I didn't meet her, but I've heard about her. Poor thing. I wonder who has more control below stairs: her or the cook?"

"Mrs. Grundy," Father Rummage said. "She has grit. Inner beauty, if that doesn't sound ridiculously condescending. She never raises her voice, and the staff respects her all the more. Whereas Crystal is all bark and no bite."

"Crystal?"

"The cook. Mrs. Tippett." He emitted that wretched *heh-heh-heh* that Juliet now recognized as a sign of deep unhappiness. "She calls me 'the God-botherer.'"

"I expect many do. Preaching has never enjoyed universal popularity, as I'm sure you knew before undertaking your vocation. Some people flinch at the sight of the dog collar."

"It's not the dog collar. It's my neck inside it."

"Crystal and Jasper," Juliet said, again nudging the rector obliquely. "Lovely names. Did the three of you grow up together?"

Father Rummage nodded. "Mother said they weren't our sort. Conscious of the distinctions, as it were, was Mother. That only made us more devoted. Later, Jasper focused on polishing his self-presentation while Crystal and I...."

"Formed an attachment?" With the rector, a bolder phrase, like "walked out together" or "fell in love," seemed indelicate.

"Yes. I asked her to marry me. Then I chose the church over photography and withdrew my offer." He folded his arms.

"Why?"

He didn't answer.

"Parental disapproval, perhaps?"

"No. I loved Crystal, and no one spoke against her directly. Only...." He sighed. "As a curate, I knew I would mix with a different circle. Religious scholars. Missionaries. Deacons, bishops, and their wives. Crystal would have been expected to play hostess to all of them. Any, er, tension between her and those various entities would have, well, reflected poorly on me, which would in turn have created misery for her. So you see, for her benefit, which was always paramount in my thoughts, so as not to place her in a situation for which life had not prepared her...." He stopped. "Bother. No. I can't lie here, in sight of the altar. I loved her, Lady Juliet. But I was ashamed of her and certain her manner was too coarse for such refined company."

There was nothing Juliet could say to that. Her heart went out to Mrs. Tippett, who she knew mostly by reputation as a woman whose tongue was as sharp as her knives. But she pitied Father Rummage, too, who had never married, though his situation had surely afforded ample opportunities to do so. In the two biggest decisions of his life, he'd chosen wrong both times, and probably no one had suffered more than he had.

"Crystal never forgave me. In her mother's day, a man couldn't withdraw an offer of marriage without being sued for breach of contract. It was such a stain on the lady's honor, you see. All that has changed, but I think if she could have accused me in court, she would have. Certainly she never called me 'Stephen' again. I became the God-botherer. That pestering fly who circles, buzzing about theosophy and eschatology to people who fret about crops, wages, and keeping food on the table."

"Surely that isn't true."

"I don't know. I've grown into my responsibilities, but I can't claim to have ever had a true calling. As for Crystal, she married an intemperate man who didn't believe in sparing the rod. Not with children, and not with wives. Even after he died, his sons and daughters never returned to Cornwall. And neither did my Crystal, the girl with a warm laugh very much like yours."

Tears stood in the rector's eyes. Seeing them, Juliet decided it was time to go off in search of an envelope to carry the crime scene photos in. Naturally, Mrs. Lobb produced one, and they spent a pleasant five minutes discussing the time of day. Juliet was pleased to see that, despite the opportunity to gossip about her fellow villagers, Mrs. Lobb loyally refrained. She was bright, witty, a touch outspoken, and determined to make herself useful, a vital mix of traits, particularly in uncertain times.

I really am in danger of making a friend, Juliet thought, surprised at herself. *From Barking, of all places.*

"Your temporary church secretary is marvelous," she said to Father Rummage as she reentered St. Gwinnodock's sanctuary. "Pleased to be here and excited to be part of the church's mission, even if her part amounts to mostly paperwork."

"I know. Very commendable." The rector's composure had returned, along with an aura of resignation. She saw it in his slumped shoulders, heard it in the false cheer he injected into the word commendable. Soon he'd be forcing that laugh again.

"I'd better be off to Fitchley Park. Thank you for allowing me to help in the darkroom, Father."

"Hm? Oh, yes, of course," he said, rising at last. "Thank you for listening to me. No doubt I said things I shouldn't. I don't know why. This year—the war, Mr. Lobb being called up, now the murder. It's dredged up questions I thought I'd put to rest."

Fixing a smile on his face, he emitted that desperate little *heh-heh-heh*. "May I beg your discretion?"

"Naturally. I wonder—may I ask a question of a religious nature?"

He looked surprised. "Please."

"Do deathbed conversions count?"

"What?"

"Deathbed conversions," she repeated. "When someone spends their life doing the wrong thing, choosing the wrong path over and over. Then at the very end they repudiate it all, choosing the path they should have taken at the outset. Is such a thing possible?"

"I believe so, if the conversion is sincere," Father Rummage said. "To wholeheartedly reject what is wrong and unequivocally embrace what is right always counts, even when the hour is late."

"I'm glad to hear it. St. Gwinnodock's is a treasure," Juliet said. "Should you ever depart to pursue your photography, your successor here is sure to be overjoyed. And Mrs. Tippett may even call you Stephen again, if she believes your conversion sincere."

15

BELOW STAIRS

As Ben followed Mrs. Grundy through the green baize door and into the servants' domain, the housekeeper asked over her shoulder, "Would you like tea, Dr. Bones? Or would you prefer to sit down and question me without a sham ritual beforehand?"

He smiled at the term "sham ritual." If Mrs. Grundy and Lady Juliet hadn't met, perhaps they should.

"'Question' is too strong a term. This is an interview. And tea would be marvelous, thank you."

"Her ladyship said to take you to the kitchen, but I detected a certain amount of, let us say, whimsy in her words." Withdrawing a key from her pocket, she steered him to the room across from Mr. Collins's.

"Come through to my sitting room, if you please," she said, leading him to a wingback chair across from a worn sofa. "Make yourself at home. I'll be back directly with tea." Ben tried to thank her, but the housekeeper turned swiftly on her heel, leaving him talking to empty air.

Her avoidance of engagement was understandable. Paget's disease was typically mild, and usually afflicted older folks, many of whom mistook their symptoms for arthritis. Even when Paget's affected the skull, as it often did, the remolding of the bone tended to be subtle. Mrs. Grundy had been unlucky enough to develop the disease early in life and as severely as he'd ever seen, outside of a medical textbook. Given the tendency of human beings to mock, bully, and shun those who looked different, she was remarkably fortunate to have found any employment, much less a position of authority in a baron's ancestral home.

While she was gone, he couldn't resist a quick look around. Unlike the Spartan surroundings Mr. Collins apparently favored, Mrs. Grundy's living space revealed a bit about its occupant. Two pieces of highly detailed embroidery hung on the wall; a third lay atop her sewing basket, half-finished. On the coffee table was a stack of the cinema magazine *Picturegoer*, which featured glowing profiles of stars like Polly Ward and Douglas Fairbanks, Jr. Ben wasn't surprised when he found nothing out of the ordinary, much less a gigantic blood stain.

"Here we are, Dr. Bones," Mrs. Grundy said, returning with a tray bearing tea, cucumber sandwiches, and a slice of cake. She served him with smooth efficiency, eyes directed to her task. When finished, she seated herself, folded her hands in her lap, and lowered her chin as she had in the photo, as if shielding him from the necessity of looking directly at her face.

"Won't you join me?" he asked.

"I'd prefer to resume my afternoon routine as soon as possible. Is the tea to your liking?"

"Very much so." He had to restrain himself from asking about her disease. Though he considered his motives benign— to see if he could help and to increase his clinical knowledge— the fact was, she was under no obligation to satisfy his curiosity about that aspect of her life. Best to crack on with his questions.

"How long have you been at Fitchley Park, Mrs. Grundy?"

"I was born here. My father, Edmund Grundy, was butler to old Lord Maggart. My mother, Sarah, was housekeeper before me. Because my parents were reliable employees, and because the old baron had a kind heart, I was educated alongside the Maggart children until I was twelve. Then I joined the staff as undermaid, in the days when it took an army to maintain a house this size, and I've been employed at Fitchley Park ever since."

That explained her manner of speaking, which resembled that of the upper classes. The chief difference being, the true upper crust cultivated a jovial, aggressively chummy style. Ben considered it a sort of manufactured commonality, made up of slang, catch phrases, and a superficial friendliness that both charmed and repelled. Mrs. Grundy had been brought up to speak the King's English but not to use upper class shibboleths, like calling her father "pater" or expressing thanks with phrases like, "Awfully good of you, old bean."

"And your husband is...." He trailed off so she could confirm that her title, "Mrs.," was a courtesy bestowed on unmarried female servants of rank, but she did not. Instead, she lifted her chin, looking him in the eye for the first time.

"There are only two possible answers to that question, Dr. Bones. Either my husband is called Grundy because I plucked him from the branches of my own family tree. Or that I have no husband, only the pretense of one."

"You don't suffer fools gladly, do you, Mrs. Grundy?"

"Not gladly. But I do suffer them with regularity, for which I'm paid, thank goodness."

Smiling, he thought, *She absolutely must meet Lady Juliet.*

"I wish you'd been available yesterday," he said truthfully. "There was an abundance of foolishness, if you'll forgive me for being blunt, and very little sense to be found. But I understand the discovery of Mr. Archer's body shocked you greatly."

"Yes."

She seemed completely unemotional now, he noted. "How was it discovered?"

"One of my girls found it. Kitty. She missed breakfast and was late to her duties. At some point she crept downstairs, probably to beg a morsel from Betsy in the kitchen. She noticed the open door, looked inside, and screamed. Betsy dashed up to find me while Mr. Collins took charge of the matter."

"What time was that?" he asked, draining his teacup.

"Quarter past nine."

"I don't pretend to know much about the management of a house like this, but I imagine the workday starts before dawn, at least for Mrs. Tippett. Why did it take three or four hours for someone to find a corpse so close to the kitchen?"

"I wouldn't know. I was overseeing the turning of mattresses upstairs."

"The odor would've been offensive. Blood and bowels."

"I no longer possess a sense of smell, Doctor. Compression of the olfactory nerve, according to Dr. Egan. He wanted me to see a specialist in London, but I declined. They could have done nothing for me. Except photograph my face, document my symptoms, and publish papers on the topic of *osteitis deformans* to enhance their own reputations."

"And educate young doctors like me, who have little experience with severe cases. However, in your shoes, I don't think I'd want to be paraded through the Royal College of Physicians."

"It's not as if there's any preventative," Mrs. Grundy said as Ben refilled his teacup. "Dr. Egan was delighted by my case, positively gleeful, and told me everything he knew. Even hauled out a dusty old book and read to me from it. He said I should be grateful it didn't cripple me, or take my hearing, or my sight." She gave Ben a distorted smile. "So much to be grateful for."

"If I may ask—at what age did your condition develop?"

"Seventeen," she said matter-of-factly, but Ben could almost feel the bitterness behind her calm gaze, like waves crashing against a seawall. "I used to be pretty enough. Father Rummage took a picture of me and gave me the print. For years, I held onto it, as if it proved something. Then one day, I turned a corner, and burned it.

"Dr. Egan assured me I wasn't alone," she went on. "He mentioned a certain gallery containing a portrait of medical interest called *The Ugly Duchess*. It depicts a noblewoman with the same condition, or so he believed."

Ben, who'd seen it, nodded.

"I suppose if I ever go to London, I can visit the gallery and commune with that portrait. Reminding myself how lucky I am not to be alone."

"I suspect Dr. Egan meant well," Ben said. "But if his, er, excessive enthusiasm for the disease, without regard for how that disease affects you, engendered a distrust of physicians, I wouldn't blame you. Still, I'd be happy to make inquiries with my London mentors. Perhaps there's a new therapy...."

"That's kind of you." She sounded cautious but not openly suspicious. Maybe she would call on him and let him investigate on her behalf, if he didn't spoil things by pressing too hard.

"Getting back to your question about the body and the smell," she said. "I don't know why Mrs. Tippett or Betsy didn't notice. Perhaps because of the game room. After years of working beside it, perhaps they learned to blot it out."

"I understand the gamekeeper was discharged, and shooting parties canceled, as Lord Maggart can no longer tolerate the noise."

"Is that what Mr. Collins said?"

"Yes."

"He told me someone was arrested for the murder. The dead man's wife. Is that true?"

Ben nodded.

"Ah. I hoped it was not."

"I almost get the impression," Ben said carefully, "that Mr. Collins frequently circulates information that isn't entirely true."

Mrs. Grundy did not contradict him.

"I've said clearly, time and again, that Bobby Archer couldn't have died where his body was found," Ben said, trying the cake. The sponge was dry and the icing, too sweet. He wasn't surprised that Mrs. Tippett couldn't equal Mrs. Cobblepot's results; few could.

"Of course not." The door behind Mrs. Grundy stood open, theoretically allowing anyone passing to overhear, but she maintained the same level tone. Like any housekeeper, she exercised discretion, but her willingness to answer his questions without retreating behind closed doors impressed him.

"It may have happened in the game room. Even someone who's lived here as long as I would find it hard to tell. Its floor and walls are so deeply stained, you see. Or the kitchen. After— well. My point is, the floor could be cleared of blood in record time."

"You sound certain of that."

"I am. I expect that if I tell you something later judged essential, you will be obligated to take it to the authorities," she said. "Otherwise, may I trust it will never leave this room?"

He nodded.

"Did Lady Maggart tell you about our troubles over the summer?"

"She said there's a ghost in this house. She woke one night and saw her."

Mrs. Grundy looked down at her hands, folded in her lap.

"Have you heard the story? About a woman in black?"

"I did say I grew up in Fitchley Park." She flashed a smile. "There's been rumors of strange doings here since the days of

Cromwell. Cavaliers, priests, and smugglers. It's all part of the lore."

"Do you believe the house is haunted?"

"No. Not by ghosts. His lordship can't forget the war. Her ladyship... it's not for me to say what she feels guilty about. But I think if she had a bit of a breakdown, and smashed a mirror and some of her toiletries, she wouldn't want to explain it to the staff. So an insistence that a woman in black did it papered over the disturbance, however imperfectly."

He took that in. "How does that connect to clearing blood from the kitchen floor?"

"It was a fraught time," Mrs. Grundy replied. "The game-keeper, Charlie, had recently been discharged. Her ladyship was unhappy. Lord Maggart was ill. Then Lady Maggart's dog, a Pomeranian called Phoebe, died in the middle of the night. I heard a terrible howl. I raced into the kitchen, thinking Mrs. Tippett was being murdered. Instead, I found Phoebe, dead on the butcher block."

"How was she killed?"

"Her throat was cut." In the hall, two maids passed carrying an enormous basket of laundry between them, but Mrs. Grundy didn't let that deter her from answering. "Her ladyship blamed the ghost."

"And you?"

"Mrs. Tippett always hated that dog. Especially when it followed her ladyship into the kitchen. Her temper is always uncertain. Or perhaps Charlie slipped back inside and killed poor Phoebe for revenge. He took his discharge very hard."

"Do you think Lady Maggart might have done it herself?"

"I don't know. Sometimes she surprises me."

"What about Lord Maggart?"

The housekeeper twisted her hands. "I won't consider it."

"Because of his illness?"

"Because I've known him all my life. We played together. We had lessons together. We even took meals together, when old Lord Maggart and his wife were in London for the season. For years I thought of him as my own brother. Until I put on my apron and starched cap."

Ben finished his cake, choosing his next questions carefully. Then he asked, "Did Lord Maggart care for the dog?"

"No. He'd asked her ladyship to get rid of it."

"Was he shocked by what happened?"

She shook her head. Ben had the impression she could have said more but declined. It wasn't surprising. The Maggarts provided her home and livelihood. Should that situation come to an end, she was unlikely to find anything but factory work.

He took another tack. "With regard to the dead man, Bobby Archer—did you know him?"

"We never spoke. I'd seen him, of course, many times."

"What was his business at Fitchley Park?"

"Only her ladyship can say."

The implication was unmistakable. Would Mrs. Grundy reveal more if she understood what was at stake?

"Policemen are meant to be entirely disinterested," Ben said. "I, on the other hand, make no such claim. I came here to write a death certificate. But fundamental questions remain unanswered, and I'm nothing like convinced Mrs. Archer killed her husband."

"No," Mrs. Grundy agreed with surprising strength. "The blackout would make it almost impossible for a woman to slip into the house through the window. It's true the tradesman's entrance is never locked—permitting access to the privy, you see —but she'd still need to find her husband without waking the staff." She shook her head. "Once these thoughts overtook me, I felt quite ill."

"What do you mean?"

"I mean the killer must've had help from within. Three people at minimum, I should think, to carry, clean, and conceal. And when that was accomplished, they lied to the special constable, to you, to me, and anyone else who would listen. When it became clear that I live among those who have aided and abetted a murderer, I hid away for a few hours. Until I could face the world without weeping, or screaming, or both."

He thought about that. He'd finished his tea, so Mrs. Grundy rose and began transferring the dirty dishes and cutlery back onto the serving tray. As she lifted the pot with her right hand, something occurred to him.

"I wonder, Mrs. Grundy—who on the staff is left-handed?"

She set the pot down with a clatter. "Why?"

"It's impossible to be certain, but from the angle of the wound, I think Bobby's killer was left-handed."

"Oh. Well. As to the gamekeeper, I can't say I ever noticed. For the indoor staff, most of us are right-handed. Except for Kitty, of course."

"The maid who discovered the body?"

"Yes."

"Would you mind if I spoke with her?"

"Of course not. I'll fetch her, and you may interview her here, in my sitting room."

"Thank you. If you don't mind, may I ask you one more question?"

Mrs. Grundy turned back. The bulging brow made her look angry, even faintly menacing, when she probably only meant to seem polite.

"You mentioned living among people who aided and abetted a murderer," Ben said, watching her eyes. "Does that mean the murderer resides upstairs?"

She blinked. "I hope not. I owe Lord Maggart everything, Dr. Bones. So with all my heart—I hope not."

16

WORRY STONE

K itty Ryan was one of those young women for whom "pleasingly plump" had been coined. She had a round face, dimpled cheeks, a dimpled chin, and the ivory-pink coloring of a porcelain doll. A single yellow curl escaped from beneath her mobcap, right in the middle of her forehead, where it just so happened to accentuate her prettiness. Without being asked, she closed Mrs. Grundy's door before sitting down across from him.

"I'm glad to see you again, Doctor. Thank you for being kind to me over the spot," she said in a high, chirpy voice. Ben might have found it acceptable in a Punch and Judy character, but it was altogether grating in a human being.

"You should know," she continued, pausing for dramatic emphasis, "the drop on the carpet really was red wine. That's why I drain the glasses before I fetch them back to the kitchen. Waste not, want not."

"How long have you been at Fitchley Park, Kitty?"

"A year."

"How old are you?"

"Fifteen." She fluttered her lashes.

"No, really."

"Twenty," she admitted, giggling behind her hand.

"Why lie?"

"Why ask?" She giggled again, blue eyes bright with what was probably perpetual mirth. "I like a bit of fun."

"You were late getting out of bed yesterday. Why?"

"Forgot to wind my alarm clock."

"Is Mrs. Grundy cross when you're late to your duties?"

"Yes, but she forgives me," Kitty chirruped. Reaching into her skirt pocket, she withdrew a smooth red stone the size of a sixpence, shifting it from palm to palm like a worry stone.

Ben took her through the morning, asking the logical questions and receiving the same answers Mr. Collins and Lady Maggart had supplied the day before. Either all three were telling the truth, or they'd done a good job getting their stories straight.

Ben decided to toss a stick of dynamite into the mix. "Did Lady Maggart have a love affair with Charlie the gamekeeper?"

Kitty's eyes popped.

"I'll take that as a yes. I'm not interested in circulating gossip," Ben said. "Nothing unrelated to the murder will leave this room, and I'm convinced it was a murder. Plymouth CID will come to Fitchley Park soon, with Scotland Yard sure to follow," he said, wondering if Dirk Diamond offered any lessons on outright lying. "They'll arrest the murderer. Then they'll arrest everyone on staff who helped conceal the crime."

Kitty began passing her worry stone along the gaps between her fingers, an operation that required some dexterity.

"Those who help the cause of justice will surely be treated better than those who continue to lie," Ben continued, watching the stone travel back and forth. "We know Bobby Archer was carrying on with someone in this house. I have reason to believe it was you."

"What?"

"You're the sort he'd pursue," Ben said, making another stab in the dark. "You're left-handed. His killer was left-handed. Did Bobby break your heart? Change his mind about divorcing his wife for you?"

"No. *No!*" Kitty cried, fingers closing over the stone. "I didn't kill him. I didn't even know him!"

"You contrived some way to lure him into the game room. Crept up behind him and cut his throat," Ben said, not believing the scenario for a moment, at least not with Kitty wielding the knife. "All you needed was another conspirator, perhaps two, to help drag the body away and mop up the blood. I don't know how you opened the room—lifted the key, perhaps—but once the body was in there, you went to bed and waited for someone to find it. You hoped it would be like Phoebe the Pomeranian, something ugly and bizarre that would be ultimately blamed on the ghost."

"I didn't know him," Kitty insisted, blinking back tears. "I was never out of bed."

"Which of the girls do you share a room with?"

"Betsy. But—b-but she sleeps like the dead. She'll say she doesn't know, that I might have slipped out and how can she be sure... I mean, of course, she shouldn't assume I'd go out, except to the privy, but if she were asked under oath...." Kitty trailed off helplessly.

Ben folded his arms. Sitting back in his chair, he continued to regard her without saying a word. It was a trick that had always worked with his younger sister, Cathleen. He wasn't surprised when Kitty cracked in under a minute.

"I didn't kill him," she pleaded, beginning to sob. "I didn't do anything but see the door was open. It wasn't supposed to be open. I looked at him lying on the bed, naked as the day he was made, and ran out screaming."

"Naked?"

She nodded.

"When I saw Bobby, he was wearing black silk underpants. The new sort," Ben said.

Once again, Kitty looked stricken.

"Who put underpants on the body?"

"I don't know. I swear it. I don't know."

It occurred to him she might be telling the truth on that point. He couldn't be sure, and he was feeling his way in the dark with this line of questioning anyway.

"Did they come from Mr. Collins's wardrobe?"

She shook her head.

"Lord Maggart's?"

"Yes, but...."

"But what?"

"They aren't truly his lordship's. Her ladyship bought them in Plymouth. She put them in his chest of drawers, and sometimes Polly launders them special," Kitty said, back to rubbing the worry stone with her thumb. "But I think they were meant for Charlie. Or...."

"Bobby?"

"I don't know," Kitty said, voice breaking.

He didn't think he could push her much further. It was probably time to stop throwing sticks of dynamite and try to forge a connection.

"I'm sorry if I seem hard on you. I only want to find out what happened to Bobby Archer. That stone you carry—it's rather pretty."

"It's from my sweetheart. A promise of better days to come."

"When the war is over?"

"Sooner than that, I hope," she said, sniffling miserably. He offered her his handkerchief, which she accepted, dabbing at her eyes. Red glinted in her palm.

"What sort of stone is that?"

"Jasper. May I go, sir?"

"Not just yet. Are you sure there's nothing more you can tell me? Because if Mr. Collins is involved," Ben said slowly, "he should go to the police rather than wait to be arrested. And so should you. Claiming loyalty to a husband makes a difference in court, but not a sweetheart."

Once again, Kitty's eyes popped. "Cor! How do you know these things?"

"I have a knack for getting at the truth." It was a shabby trick, implying great powers of perception. In actuality, Ben had heard Mrs. Tippett call her brother "Jasper." It seemed a sure bet that a man so evidently vain would give Kitty a gift that bore his Christian name.

"I couldn't help noticing how bare Mr. Collins's room was. Above stairs, there's not much furniture and plenty of space. Does he keep a second bedroom—an actual bedroom—up there? To be close to Lord Maggart, should he require something?"

Kitty nodded. The poor girl clearly regarded him as a magician who couldn't be lied to.

"Were you there with him early Sunday morning?"

She nodded again.

"This liaison is an open secret among the staff? Meaning, if you're late for your morning duties, it's overlooked because Mr. Collins is the butler."

"They know we have an understanding. And when we're married, I'll...." She stopped.

"Be better liked among the staff than Mrs. Grundy?" Again, Ben made a guess based on what little he knew of domestic

servants. "She's been with Lord Maggart since they were children. Why would he—" He stopped as it became clear. When
Lord Maggart died, his wife would be obligated to leave Fitchley
Park. After she turned it over to her late husband's heir, probably
a cousin or nephew, that person could reconstitute the staff as he
saw fit. It was quite likely that a new master, meeting a housekeeper who looked like Mrs. Grundy and a butler with a pretty
young wife, would discharge the former and elevate the latter.

Kitty squirmed in her seat. Her initial coquettishness was
gone. Now she looked like a schoolgirl caught out of bounds.
The scheme to oust Mrs. Grundy struck him as cruel, but his
responsibility wasn't to insert himself in the staff dynamics. It
was to ferret out anything that might uncover the truth about
Bobby's death.

"Were you with Mr. Collins all night?"

"Yes."

"What happened to Bobby Archer?"

"I don't know," Kitty said. She shifted the worry stone from
hand to hand.

Lying again, Ben thought. *She knows, or she has a powerful
suspicion.*

"What's your instinct?"

They locked eyes for a moment. Perhaps Kitty believed he
could divine fact from falsehood. Or perhaps she wanted to
unburden herself. Either way, she began to speak, and he
thought she spoke truthfully.

"I said I didn't know Bobby. And I didn't—we weren't friends,
weren't acquaintances. But I knew his sort. He used to pinch my
bottom and make eyes at me when no one was looking. I don't
think he was coming to this house for any reason but one. And
he wasn't coming for me, or Polly, or Betsy. That leaves her ladyship. I can't swear to it because I never saw them together, but I

saw her with Charlie time and again. If she could carry on with him under his lordship's roof, why couldn't she do the same with Bobby?"

Ben, who'd come to the same conclusion, reached into his pocket and withdrew the blackened compact he'd rescued from John's wheelbarrow. He meant to ask Kitty if she recognized it, but he didn't have to.

"Her ladyship's Stratton. She said she lost it in Plymouth."

"You're certain?"

"Let me look at it." Kitty examined the compact. Turning it over, she wet his handkerchief with her tongue and scrubbed away some of the scorching. "There! Faint, but you can see it," she said.

He could: the engraved initials OMO.

"The second O is for Olivia," Kitty explained.

"Thank you." Slipping the compact back in his pocket, Ben decided to shake her up one last time, assuming that was possible.

"Did Lady Maggart kill Bobby and force some of the staff to help her cover it up?"

Instead of flinching, Kitty laughed. "Her ladyship? She can't even kill a rat. She shouts for me to do it. When she saw Phoebe dead in the kitchen, she was sick."

"Who then?"

"Mrs. Tippett knows how to use a knife. And no one ever accused her of being too gentle."

———

"They said I'd find you here," Lady Juliet told Ben, letting herself into Mrs. Grundy's sitting room before he could respond to her ceremonial knock. "What are you doing, Dr. Bones? If we don't set out in the next quarter hour, we'll reach Birdswing under cover of darkness yet again."

"I know. I'm just re-reading my interview notes while they're fresh in my mind." Ben closed his notebook and tucked it away. "I took them down after the fact, since you never turned up."

"I do apologize for the dereliction of duty. With whom did you speak, besides Helen Archer?"

"Lady Maggart, Mrs. Grundy, and Kitty, the maid who Boraxed the alleged blood stain," he said. "I still need to interview Mrs. Tippett, but she's in the midst of dinner preparations and chased me out of the kitchen. By the way—I don't suppose you smell that?"

"What?"

"Perfume." Ben hoped he didn't sound mad. He'd caught another unmistakable whiff of *Sous le Vent* toward the end of his interview with Kitty. Now the odor had all but vanished.

Lady Juliet sniffed. "Can't say that I do."

Time to change the subject. Rising, Ben indicated the plain manila envelope in her hands. "Are those the prints?"

"Yes. The rector hadn't started developing them yet, and he invited me into his darkroom to see the process. It's fascinating. There are four pans, you see. The first one is called the developer, and while that's a rather unimaginative appellation, I assure you, beholding the chemical reaction is a revelation...."

She continued describing it as they exited Fitchley Park by the tradesman's door, circling the house to his Austin. He enjoyed her enthusiasm about light-tight rooms and F-stops, and her boundless pleasure in learning new things.

"Now that we can't be overheard," he said once they were en route to Birdswing, "put me out of suspense. Do the photos show any detail we missed?"

"Not that I could tell. And I've examined them closely, as you might imagine. Father Rummage even taught me to enlarge them, which was great fun but not illuminating, from a detection standpoint. Something in your face tells me you did rather better."

"I think so." As he drove, he put her in the picture. It was a long discussion. First, Helen's self-inflicted wounds. Next, his encounter with the boot boy, John, and the contents of his wheelbarrow. Finally, the facts gleaned from his discussions with Lady Maggart, Mrs. Grundy, and Kitty, including her alibi for Mr. Collins and her belief that Lady Maggart and Bobby were having an affair.

"Ah, well, I suppose it would have been too poetic if the butler did it," Lady Juliet said. "So much for dining out on it forever. But it seems reasonable that if Odette summons servants to kill rats, she may have demanded someone take care of Bobby. I just hope to heaven it wasn't Mrs. Tippett."

"Why?"

"It would be breaking a confidence to expose the details," Lady Juliet said. "And it's not as if I know her personally. Let's leave it at this: I hope not. Can you return to Fitchley Park tomorrow?"

"No," Ben said, pleased to see Birdswing not far in the distance. "I have a full roster of patients tomorrow. I can't spend another day in Barking. Besides, I rather doubt Lady Maggart would be willing to have me back, particularly as I'm not a policeman."

"You could send our intrepid special constable to interview Mrs. Tippett," Lady Juliet said. "That would be appropriate, except for the fact I don't trust him to get it right."

"Precisely. I'll ring him tomorrow, if I can find a moment between patients. He needs to hear Kitty's accusation. And now that I think about it, Mrs. Tippett mentioned a missing kitchen knife. Which she also put down to rat-killing, I believe."

"I suppose it might be a euphemism for knocking off

Odette's lovers." Lady Juliet laughed. "But rats and large houses are inextricably bound. No doubt Fitchley Park has plenty of fat rats living like kings around the kitchen pipes. Belsham Manor, being newer and more stoutly built," she added, smiling, "tends to draw rats only in the granary and garden. In fact, it wouldn't surprise me at all if at this very moment, a preening, loquacious rat is pacing about my garden, smoking one of his ludicrous cigarillos Mother won't permit indoors."

"Hm?" Ben, who'd been wholly absorbed in the case, needed a moment to catch on. "Right. Ethan. I'd nearly put him out of my mind—a luxury you don't have, naturally. If you like, you're welcome to have dinner at Fenton House. It will mean another night away from your own bed, of course...."

"A small price to pay. But thank you, no. I can't abandon Mother to battle the vermin alone."

"I suppose not, though should it come to that, my money would be on Lady Victoria. You'll ring me tomorrow, won't you, around noon? Otherwise, my curiosity will eat me alive."

"Yes, of course. Unless I'm banged up for murder. In which case, don't bother trying to prove my innocence. If Odette turns out to be guilty, I only hope we aren't made to share a cell."

"Speaking of Lady Maggart, I told you what she said but not the circumstances." Lady Juliet was in a fine mood after her introduction to darkroom photography; Ben didn't want thoughts of Ethan Bolivar to spoil her evening any sooner than they had to.

"When I arrived, I was told Lady Maggart wasn't at home. But as I made a sweep through the family rooms, I happened into her bedroom."

"No!"

"Afraid so. She was in her dressing gown. By the time Mrs. Grundy interrupted, I was on my knees, practically under the bed."

"That can't be true."

"Oh, yes, it is." Pleased by her incredulous expression, he drew the story out as he drove her to Belsham Manor, exaggerating from time to time, simply because he liked to hear her laugh.

17

AN INVITATION

The next day, Ben's first patient, Mrs. Garrigan, was booked for nine o'clock. Habitually early, she outdid herself by turning up at eight, doggedly ringing the patient's bell until he abandoned his breakfast to let her in.

"Oh! Dr. Bones, you locked the door," she said disapprovingly, hurrying inside. "It's bitter cold out. I do hope being chilled to the bone doesn't hurt the baby."

That was the refrain Ben now heard several times a week: "I do hope it doesn't hurt the baby," with "it" being some facet of daily life. Mrs. Garrigan, only twenty, was seven months into her first pregnancy. Her husband had joined the Army ahead of conscription and was now in France with the majority of Britain's troops, waiting for the war to begin in earnest. This left Mrs. Garrigan home alone with unlimited time to obsess over her condition.

"Is that a napkin? Did I interrupt your breakfast?"

"Er—yes. As you may recall, I don't begin seeing patients for another hour. Is there some urgent problem?"

"Of course. I would never risk my baby by going out in this cold if there wasn't," she said. "You don't mind, do you?"

He did—it was his second truncated breakfast in two days—but he simply couldn't bring himself to say so when Mrs. Garrigan sounded so plaintive. A premature line had formed between her brows, and more would be etched around her mouth if it didn't stop making that O of uncertainty. So despite the fact he wanted his bacon and eggs, not to mention a second cup of coffee, he tucked the napkin away and shook his head.

"Must I disrobe?" Mrs. Garrigan cast a doubtful glance at the exam table.

"Not yet. Have a seat."

He sat behind the impressive black-lacquered desk he'd inherited from his predecessor, Dr. Egan. In his day, medicine had been one part sympathy, one part ancient wisdom, and one part reassurance, also known as quackery. His antiquated equipment, which Ben had also inherited, illustrated these maxims: cure the patient, cut it out of the patient, or confound the patient with tonics and elixirs until the situation resolved itself. Of all Dr. Egan's arsenal, Ben found the desk most beneficial, because it boosted his air of authority.

"Now. What seems to be the problem?"

"Dear me, I've forgotten my manners," Mrs. Garrigan said. "How are you, Doctor?"

"Fine, thank you. Now—"

"Only I know you motored to Barking twice in two days, so you must be exhausted. Isn't it a shame about Bobby Archer? And Helen! I don't know *what* to think," Mrs. Garrigan said in that way people do when they not only knew what to think, but had been thinking it emphatically. "I'm so proud our own Dr. Bones is assisting the Plymouth CID with their inquiries."

"I'm not—"

"As for Lady Juliet staying over the night before last," Mrs. Garrigan continued, "you should know, Mrs. Parry was quite vocal in your defense. All the ladies in Morton's agreed. Perhaps it looked irregular, but it was necessitated by the blackout. Just because things look irregular, or even scandalous, it doesn't mean they are. Now Lady Juliet's husband might say—"

"Mrs. Garrigan," Ben cut across her forcefully. "Please tell me you didn't turn up an hour early to bring me the latest gossip."

She lifted a hand to her throat. "Why, Dr. Bones. I would never."

"I'm glad to hear it. Let's crack on. What seems to be the problem?"

"Er." Her hands tightened on her handbag, positioned in front of her burgeoning belly. "I don't like to say."

Ben silently counted to ten. Lady Juliet was right; he needed to start attending church regularly. There, he could pray for patience as well as restraint.

"Mrs. Garrigan, I respect your modesty, but we've been through this. I'm not capable of helping you without at least hearing your complaint. Are you in pain?"

She shook her head.

"Do you feel unwell?"

"No."

"What, then?"

"I...." She squeezed the handbag again. "I'm turning colors."

"Really?" What he could see of her complexion looked normal. "Where?"

"I don't like to say."

"Right. Go behind, Mrs. Garrigan," he said, pointing to the changing screen. "Choose a gown from the peg and meet me at the examination table."

Despite her aversion to this necessity, Mrs. Garrigan presented herself as ordered, submitting to the exam with typical Cornish stoicism. For his part, he kept it brief, made no small talk, and allowed her to dress and return to the seat in front of his desk before issuing his verdict.

"What you're experiencing is perfectly normal," he said. Patients had a way of retaining less than half of what he told them, so he liked to start with the key point. "We all have pigment in our skin. In some parts of the world, people have more; we Brits tend to have less. As pregnancy progresses, extra pigment is produced, resulting in darkening of the skin in places."

"But the line...."

"It's always been there, even if you never noticed it," Ben said. "It starts just below your navel and travels down. We call it *linea alba*—a white line. During pregnancy it darkens, becoming *linea negra*—a dark line. The same darkening of other areas is normal, too."

"It's ugly. Like a scar. Will it go away?"

"Probably, after you give birth," Ben said. "Though even if it doesn't, you may be too in love with your baby to notice. One more thing: your blood pressure is still higher than I would like. Have you done as I asked?"

"I've cut back, Dr. Bones, really I have," Mrs. Garrigan said. "I stick with Players. They're sweet and mild. And I traded the hard stuff for Guinness. Like the advert says, 'Guinness for strength.'"

"Yes, well, adverts do offer a lot of medical advice. But I'll remind you, none of them are aimed at expectant mothers called Garrigan, who happen to have elevated blood pressure. I'll make you a bargain," Ben said. "Swear off the fags for a week. Then pop back for another check. If your reading hasn't improved, I'll write the cigarette ompany a letter of apology. As for those pints—no more than one a week."

"Thank you, Doctor," Mrs. Garrigan said sadly. "Not sure if I can live up to your orders, but I'll try. See you next week." Rising, she took a step toward the door and winced, clutching the chair for support.

"What is it?"

"These ruddy shoes. Aren't they the very thing? Too pretty for me to say no. I thought I could break them in, but they're breaking me in, and no mistake," she said, massaging her calves. "Never thought I'd go off heels so young."

"Stay off your feet and take it easy," Ben said soothingly, mind already back on his bacon and eggs. "You're in the home stretch now."

———

Mrs. Garrigan's concern over her skin discoloration proved the day's most medically significant complaint. Ben's other five patients, all of whom had booked in via Mrs. Cobblepot during the last twenty-four hours, were afflicted with the same disorder: curiosity.

Miss Munk, who complained of a headache, mentioned how astonished she'd been to note Lady Juliet's familiar Crossley 20/30 parked outside Fenton House Monday evening. "It was there all night," she informed him. "I even ventured into the street and touched it. Some are saying *she* was here all night."

Mrs. Keller, who complained of sleeplessness, blamed the blackout. Couldn't ARP Warden Gaston and his officers discharge their duty with greater consideration for the nerves of decent folk? "I know you must feel the same, Dr. Bones," she said. "Especially when Mr. Bolivar was ejected into the street and that officer shouted, 'Douse that light!'"

The vicar's wife, Mrs. Cotterill, complained of an infrequent cough, made worse by the fear Ben had been made to feel unwelcome at St. Mark's. The congregation would benefit from his weekly example, and her husband would gladly make time, should Ben request a private chat. "A young widower, new to Birdswing, is a natural target for gossip," she said. "My husband could offer pointers. Or act as a sounding board if you'd prefer to discuss something else. Like—the Archer case?"

Mrs. Parry, who complained of lower backache, admitted that paled beside her growing conviction she would be slaughtered in her bed. "Two murders in Birdswing this autumn! Now another in Barking? We're becoming the murder capital of the West Country," she said, sounding more delighted than terrified. "I do hope your association with Plymouth CID will make the village safer, Dr. Bones. Who knows what other killers lurk in our midst?"

His final patient was Mr. Jeffers, the butcher. Hopping onto the exam table with surprising agility, given his girth, he said, "Fine weather, don't you think? My old dad used to say, it's a waste of a frosty morning if you don't slaughter a hog. Ran a piggery near Truro, you see. Dead now. Heart attack at thirty-eight, if you can believe it. Worked too hard, I reckon. Always ate well, like me." He patted his vast midsection and laughed.

"Mrs. Cobblepot booked you special," Ben said. "Are you having chest pains or shortness of breath?"

"Oh, that." Mr. Jeffers flashed a gap-toothed smile beneath his ginger mustache. "Hope you didn't mind me leaning on Agatha to pencil me in. She's my favorite customer, truth be told. Can't let that get out. But only the finest cuts for her and never a thumb on the scale, no sir. You reap the benefits when you tuck in, don't you, Doctor? Nothing like a nice juicy joint. I do you a good turn, you do me a good turn, hey?"

"I don't understand." Ben's head hurt. It had started when he realized Miss Munk's complaint was fabricated, and now it throbbed ominously.

Mr. Jeffers's smile didn't waver. "My expertise isn't just in prime cuts and organ meat. I've read every Sherlock Holmes story. I've seen all the Charlie Chan pictures. I was trained to be a butcher but born to be a detective. I want in."

"What?"

"Bobby Archer was my mate growing up. We fell out over a bird, ages back, but I knew him well. As a result," the butcher said, voice dropping theatrically, "certain inside knowledge has come to me through secret means. I've developed an expert theory as to why there was no blood on the scene. I think Bobby was hung by his foot from a hook, hey? All his blood drained in a bucket, as with hogs?"

Ben knew Mr. Jeffers's "secret means" of getting inside information had to be Gaston. Like the rest of Birdswing, the man lived for gossip, and despite his warnings to others, his loose lips could sink a fleet.

"Mr. Jeffers, do you have a medical problem?"

"What? Never!" The butcher laughed. "Healthy as the fatted calf."

"Get out."

"Beg pardon?"

"Off my table. Out of my office. Now." Leaving Mr. Jeffers to grumble to an empty room, Ben retreated to the kitchen. He hoped Mrs. Cobblepot would take pity on him by putting the kettle on. As it turned out, she'd already poured two cups of tea: one for herself and one for her guest, Special Constable Gaston.

"Finally, the man himself. Agatha wouldn't open the biscuit tin till you turned up," Gaston said, turning to his sister. "Well?"

"Keep your hair on. Are you well, Dr. Bones?" Mrs. Cobblepot asked. "You look a wee bit cross."

"Not at all," Ben muttered.

"I'll fetch you a cup and saucer, then some biscuits," she said, and it was a measure of his bad mood that even the sound of her voice made his temples throb harder.

"What brings you here?" he forced himself to ask civilly as he sat beside Gaston.

"What do you think? To discuss the case. Agatha," the

special constable said gravely. "You're not wanted here while we talk official business. If you've nothing to do, there's a hole in my coat pocket that wants mending. Why don't you—*ow!*"

Mrs. Cobblepot, who despite her size effortlessly navigated the kitchen day in and day out, had taken a corner too narrowly, smacking her brother's head with the biscuit tin in the process.

"Did I do that? Oh, dear." She placed one shortbread biscuit on Gaston's plate and three on Ben's. "The rest are mine," she said, holding onto the tin. "If you have need of me, Doctor, I'll be in the sitting room. Doing nothing whatsoever except eating biscuits and enjoying the view."

"There's no joy in being a widower, is there?" Gaston said, rubbing his head. "Forever at the mercy of sisters and house-keepers. We're in the same boat, boy, tossed by evil winds. Womankind is devilish changeable. Except for my own dear Priscilla, God rest her soul." He bit into his biscuit.

"Did you come to discuss bachelor life or the Archer case?" Ben poured himself a cup of tea. Nothing tasted as good as that first sip of afternoon tea, except of course that first puff of a post-tea fag, and he was still off cigarettes.

"The case. You may have heard Lady Juliet mention a Yank detective called Dirk Diamond." Gaston said. "I've enrolled in his correspondence course. This war won't be won in a fort-night. In the meantime, crime in the West Country will explode. Mark my words. Every man you see between twenty and forty ought to be in uniform or have proof he's in a reserved occupation. If not, he's a coward, a defective, or a criminal."

"Which one was Bobby?"

"Hm? The first, I reckon." Gaston polished off the short-bread. "I'm not trying to shift blame onto Bobby for his own murder. I only mean to explain why I enrolled in Mr. Diamond's course. One of his rules is, 'When in doubt, act it out.' That's what I spent the better part of last night and this morning doing."

Taking another sip of tea, Ben braced himself for a torrent of idiocy.

"I put myself in Helen's shoes," Gaston said, leaning back in his chair as he expounded. "We know if she killed Bobby, she must have slipped out of her house while the twins were asleep in bed. Mind you, I wouldn't turn my back on them if they were pilloried, but that's me. Once Helen was out, she got to Barking by bicycle, if she took Clodgey Lane. Or on foot, if she cut through Pate's field and the woods, crossed the river, and followed Hummock Lane. So I took Mr. Diamond's advice and tried both routes myself."

"This afternoon?"

"No. Too easy in full daylight. I did it this morning, technically. Around 0400 for the first trip, 0700 for the second."

"You must have frozen solid." Ben regarded the old soldier with new respect.

"Mustn't give in to the cold, Dr. Bones. Nothing good ever came of giving in to the cold. Remember that when we're fighting Jerry in the streets." Gaston smiled fondly at the idea of physically beating back an invasion. Then he polished off the rest of his biscuit and continued.

"The first route, Clodgey Lane, wasn't as easy as those smug townie policemen might imagine," Gaston said. "First, Helen would have crossed the path of two ARP officers. Assuming she got lucky, and they were both off answering the call of nature, what followed would have been a long, dark ride."

"Did you cycle all the way to Fitchley Park?"

"Aye. At night, the gates are locked. So Helen would have needed to ditch the bicycle, find a scalable point on the wall, climb it, and go shank's mare another half mile."

"You really did all this before sunrise?" Ben asked.

"I'm not as old as all that," Gaston said proudly. "My father was a miner, and his father, too. I never worked a day in my life compared to Granddad. Even so," he said, helping himself to one of Ben's biscuits, "I couldn't very well act out the final bit— slipping into the house, choosing a weapon, finding Bobby, and killing him."

"It's too much."

"Far too much. Plymouth folk think of distance in terms of cars and buses. In their minds, an easy drive between Birdswing and Barking equals an easy trek, even off the beaten path."

"I certainly thought that way, but I'm not a police officer," Ben said. "No matter how busy or uninterested Plymouth CID may be, they must have worked that out by now. How can they justify keeping Helen locked up?"

"Never trust townies to see reason. At any rate, I took a wee refresher, forty winks, before I investigated the second route. By then the sun was up. Taking that route would have saved Helen an hour's travel time, but heaven knows it's tough. Without daylight, I couldn't have managed it. If I couldn't, that goes double for Helen.

"Last but not least, I checked with Helen's neighbors. I told you, I saw Helen scraping food into a bin. Mrs. Mansker saw her a bit earlier, chasing away your tomcat with a broom. Not exhausted from a long night of killing Bobby but sharp as a hornet's tail, as usual." He drained his teacup, setting it back in its saucer with a clatter.

"That's remarkable detective work," Ben said sincerely.

"Indeed it is. I enjoy being constable. But why would Helen confess to something she didn't do?"

Ben knew it was time to give voice to his suspicions. He only hoped he would be proven wrong, and swiftly. "I've been thinking about Caleb and Micah. What sort of relationship did they have with Bobby?"

"They loved him for being their old dad. And they hated him for betraying their mum," Gaston said. "Missed him every hour God sent and blamed themselves for him being gone. Bobby said motherhood ruined his pretty bride. That dropped the fault on the boys' shoulders, in their eyes."

"They're big lads. Strong for their age," said Ben, who had wrestled one down after the Bonfire Night debacle. "More underhanded than the average nine-year-old boy, which is saying something. Could they slip out of the house without Helen noticing?"

Gaston stared at him. "Could a fish swim?"

"So taking either route to Fitchley Park would have been easier for them than an adult?"

"Of course. But why do you—" He caught his breath. "No. You can't mean it. Never."

"The idea of children murdering anyone, much less their own father, is ghastly," Ben said. "But here's what we know. Bobby asked Helen for a divorce. The boys already blamed themselves for the separation, so I doubt they took the idea of him remarrying much better. Helen shut down her restaurant in midday to go to Barking. When you gave her the details of Bobby's murder, she let herself be arrested, and when the policemen interrogated her, she confessed. She'd do that, wouldn't she, to shield her boys?"

Gaston shut his eyes. "I dislike being constable. Maybe I'm not cut out for work like this."

Ben's telephone rang. A candlestick model made of black Bakelite, it occupied the phone cubby installed in the corridor between kitchen and office. Ben occasionally used it to ring his family or one of his colleagues at St. Barnabas's Hospital, but he rarely received calls, because most of the villagers lacked phones. That meant the caller was almost certainly Lady Juliet.

"Revolting!" she cried, forgoing "Hello" as usual. "Do you

know what that rat did? He got on his knees and begged me to take him back. I should have vomited on his head. I told him to get out if he wouldn't sign the papers. That I would never consent to see him or speak to him until we'd finalized the divorce. And do you know what he did then?"

"No." Ben's head still ached, but at least now he was smiling.

"He agreed, Ben. Can you believe it? He agreed!"

"Really? That's marvelous. I'm so happy for you, Juliet."

She gave a cry of joy so pure it made his heart leap. "I feel like a condemned prisoner granted a reprieve. He's returning to the manor tonight with his solicitor to sign the papers. That's all he asked—one last dinner with Mother and me as a farewell. After that, we won't see one another till the dissolution."

"A last dinner?" Ben repeated suspiciously.

"Ethan never pays for his own meals. He always finds a way, even if he has to crash a party for the *hors d'oeuvres* or get himself arrested for the bread and water. In light of which, his desire for French cooking and fine wine is hardly surprising. But the blackout makes it tricky. Before, I would have shooed him out by nine o'clock, and that would have been that. Now, having him for dinner means putting him up all night. Even with Mother present, the birds will sing."

"I suppose they will. Five snoops pretending to be patients wasted my afternoon."

"Mrs. Cobblepot is too soft-hearted. You need someone with a spine to handle your bookings. In the meantime, what I require is a buffer. Another guest, someone who'd appreciate *canard à l'orange*, *Côtes-du-Rhône*, a snifter of brandy, perhaps even a cigar. Of course, such an individual would have to endure three hours of Ethan, not to mention the sight and sound of him at breakfast the next day. It would be a sacrifice on that score. *But* said individual would also get to share in an occasion I've looked forward to for a very long time."

"You're inviting me?"

"Are you quite sure you're a detective, Dr. Bones?"

"It's only—your, er, soon-to-be-ex-husband and I didn't part on friendly terms. My presence could make the occasion a shade adversarial, as it were. Besides, won't the birds sing louder if you have two men in the house?"

"Three, if you count the lawyer. And that's the point. When it becomes a party, even a small party, the song is less compelling."

"Well. In that case, I can't possibly refuse. What should I bring?"

"Nothing but yourself," Lady Juliet said happily. "Be advised that Ethan will be tricked out in evening dress, because he imagines it makes him look dashing. Mother will wear a gown and look regal. As for me, I may appear in a kerchief and hip waders, to inspire Ethan to sign those papers with all due haste."

"Evening dress it is. Goodbye," said Ben, but Lady Juliet, predictably, had already rung off.

AFTER THE COMPARATIVE splendor of Fitchley Park, Belsham Manor was even more of an eyesore, despite a smoldering orange-red sunset as a backdrop. Lady Victoria kept no butler, only an ancient jack-of-all-trades called Robbie, still abed with rheumatism. She also had yet to replace her housekeeper, Mrs. Locke, who was missed by no one. So when Ben pulled up by the front steps, he expected to park the Austin there and show himself in. Instead, someone familiar hurried out to greet him.

"Good evening, Dr. Bones. I do hope you're well."

"I am, Bertha. Thank you. How do you find your new job?" he asked, smiling at the young woman's transformation. He remembered her as skinny, nervous, and spotty, but her skin had cleared up, and she'd put on a bit of much-needed weight.

They'd met under fraught circumstances—he'd lied to her face to catch a killer—and when the smoke cleared, Lady Juliet had demonstrated their joint gratitude by offering Bertha a place at Belsham Manor. Ben had assumed that meant a starched white cap and a feather duster, but instead, the young woman wore a sort of feminized chauffeur's uniform: navy skirt, smart jacket, and matching cap.

"Lady Juliet is very good to me," she said, smiling. "I'm in training as Old Robbie's assistant. May I park your car?"

"Of course." He tossed her the keys. "Not a scratch."

"Not to worry," Bertha said, getting behind the wheel. "I spent all morning learning how. Lady Juliet says I'm a natural!"

It was too late to rescind permission without crushing her confidence. Biting his tongue, Ben let her get on with it. As he watched, she drove to the mews at a measured pace, shifting gears smoothly. That was better than he'd performed on his first day as a motorist.

After he climbed the steps, another familiar young woman waited to usher him into the house. Dinah wore the usual maid-servant's black dress, but her cap was different. Its colors were reversed—black with a peep of white lace, instead of the other way round—and her welcoming smile looked pinned on.

"Hello, Dr. Bones."

"Hello, Dinah. How are you feeling?" He probably should have left it at "How are you?" but he couldn't help himself. Dinah, his very first patient in Birdswing, had concealed her illicit pregnancy right up to birth, which she'd endured in secret. Now that her son had been adopted by a loving couple in Plymouth, and the Lintons had refused to discharge her for immoral conduct, as most households would have, Dinah had resumed her place on staff. But a cloud of misery followed her, which he would have liked to lessen, if he only knew how.

"I'm pleased to welcome you to Belsham Manor," Dinah said

with less inflection than the average parrot. A whey-faced girl of eighteen, she looked physically strong again, with pink in her cheeks. "May I take your hat and coat?"

"Please." Handing them over, he tried another tack. "Is that a new cap?"

"Yes, sir. Lady Victoria says it means I'm acting housekeeper for the evening. The position rotates." An icy wind swept through vestibule, blowing Dinah's special cap askew.

"Oh! The door." She shut it hurriedly. "Keep forgetting that bit. Mr. Bolivar teased me something awful, and Mr. Duggin stared at me like I was simple."

"It takes time, adjusting to new roles." Ben glanced down the hall to be sure they weren't overheard before asking quietly, "How are you, really?"

She pinned the smile on again. "Good. And ever so grateful to you, sir. Thank you, sir."

"You know that's not what I—"

"Another arrival, Dinah?" Lady Victoria called from an inner room. "Do lead him in. The hall is positively arctic."

Dinah scurried toward her mistress's voice with Ben's coat still hugged to her chest. He didn't have the heart to suggest she hang it up, so he followed.

It was true that Belsham Manor's exterior was painful to look at; nothing short of a wrecking ball could cure the house's structural deformities. But the interior was as lovely as a strangely proportioned, irregularly laid-out house could be. Lady Victoria had worked miracles with everything at her disposal: carpets, wallpaper, paint, and furniture. The parlor was a fine example. Having seen it in daylight, Ben knew the room's shape was odd and the ceiling was too low, but it was beautifully lit by wall sconces and candelabra. On the hearth, a wood fire crackled invitingly.

"Dr. Bones, it's lovely to see you." Lady Victoria looked

younger than her years, particular in this forgiving light. Clearly, she'd been a great beauty once, given her high cheekbones, full lips, and dimpled chin. Her gown, black satin set off by a bolero jacket edged in white, revealed her trim figure, more ingénue than matron.

"Hello, Lady Victoria. Thank you for having me."

Turning, she gestured to the pair of men sitting by the fire. "Shall I make the introductions? This is—"

"Bones!" Ethan roared, surging out of his seat before Lady Victoria could finish. "Good to see you, old man."

18

"THIS GOLD MINE IS CLAIMED"

As foretold, Ethan was in his evening kit, an immaculately tailored, double-breasted suit that fashion columnists called "blacker than black" but was actually midnight blue. As he crossed the room, he looked like he'd stepped off the silver screen, one hand extended to Ben, the other holding a gin and tonic.

Ben's headache, which had limped away in late afternoon, lurched back on the scene, rested and ready for action. It made him wince as they shook, which Ethan clearly took as a sign of weakness.

"Sorry about that. I have a firm grip. Don't know my own strength," he said heartily, pounding Ben on the back like they were long-lost schoolmates. "Look at you. Tails, eh? A fine investment. As serviceable now as they were in your mother's day. But a white waistcoat with pearl buttons? You're a braver man than I. Somebody might ask me to strike up the band."

Ben looked down at his suit as if noticing it for the first time. "Sometimes the girl I walk out with remarks on my clothes. That sort of thing appeals to her, I suppose. But you may be the only man who's ever spoken two words to me on the subject."

Ethan's grin faltered. As a matter of fact, Ben had coveted Ethan's highly fashionable waistcoat, single-breasted with jet buttons, the instant he saw it. But a key part of his vanity was pretending he had none, particularly when faced with Lady Juliet's husband and his five-hundred-pound suit.

"You mistake me. I find other men's sartorial choices unspeakably dull," Ethan said, clearing his throat. "Whereas Lady Victoria's are endlessly appealing. Might I usurp you, my lady, and make the other introduction?"

"But of course."

"Dr. Bones, that po-faced devil nursing his G and T is my solicitor, John Duggin," Ethan said, gesturing toward the other man, who'd remained seated. "What do you have to say for yourself, Jack, my lad?"

Duggin, a nondescript man in a nondescript tuxedo, looked up from well-polished but equally utilitarian shoes. His face was the sort easily forgotten: no facial hair, no identifying marks. However, his stare was acute to the edge of impertinence. Ben felt like he was being x-rayed.

"How do you do," Duggin said.

"How do you do," Ben echoed. Was Duggin some sort of legal hatchet man, come to extort the maximum from Lady Juliet and her mother?

"Well. Now everyone's acquainted, which means the evening can really begin," Lady Victoria said. "I think I'll just pop upstairs to see how my daughter progresses. Do make yourselves at home, and pull the bell for Dinah the instant you have need of something."

After she exited, Ethan knocked back the remainder of his drink. "Just the lads now. As they say in Chicago, anything goes. I could use another," he continued, heading to the drinks trolley. "What about you, Bones? Fancy a G and T?"

"Yes, please." Since Ethan and his solicitor had claimed the brass-studded leather armchairs near the fire, Ben reluctantly took the sofa. It epitomized Lady Victoria's tastes: lemon and white stripes further feminized by chintz pillows edged in lace.

"I have a knack for this," Ethan said in that mellifluous voice. He poured liquor and twisted lime with a theatrical flourish, like a headliner playing to the box seats. "Mixing drinks is an art, not a science, and as Ju told me many times, mine is the soul of an artist. When I was twenty, I spent a summer in Paris. Glorious, living in a drafty old garret, drunk on the colors of life. What about you, Bones? Where were you at twenty?"

"Studying." Ben accepted the cut-crystal glass Ethan handed him. The drink was crisp, sweet, and thankfully double-strength.

"Studying?" Ethan tutted. "What about you, Jack? How did you spend your youth?"

Duggin looked up, expressionless. "Don't remember." He turned his attention back to his fingernails.

Ethan didn't seem offended by his solicitor's unwillingness to be drawn out. "Lovely to be home again." He settled into his armchair. "No matter where the tide takes me, Belsham Manor has a place in my heart. When Ju and I were newlyweds, we rarely emerged from the bedroom before noon. Those were halcyon days."

Ben said nothing. He wasn't sure Ethan was trying to engage him in conversation. Perhaps he just enjoyed hearing himself talk.

"But all good things must end, eh?" Ethan said, glancing toward the door Lady Victoria had closed behind her. "No disrespect to Ju's mummy. I hold her in the highest regard, but she fell prey to lies and half-truths, and once she turned against me, Ju was sure to follow."

Ethan paused, pointedly looking at Ben. He forced out a neutral sound that could be construed as interest.

"Oh, yes," Ethan said gravely. "The grandmother, you see. Beastly woman. Dredged up my youthful indiscretions and shamelessly exploited them. As for my alleged misdeeds after our nuptials—well. Jack here never married. But you're a widower, Bones, isn't that right?"

"Yes."

"As a former member of humanity's most populous club, you'll understand. I never claimed perfection. Who hasn't forgotten himself and chatted up a fetching bit of stuff? Conviviality is no sin." Ethan looked to Duggin for agreement, but the man seemed miles away.

"Alas, every time I crossed paths with a member of the fair sex, every time I dared have a bit of discreet fun, it was blown out of proportion and presented to Ju as further proof she'd married a cad. As if a man's philandering ever has anything to do with his wife."

A log popped loudly on the fire, attracting Duggin's interest in a way Ethan apparently could not. The clock on the mantel ticked, and Ben shifted on the sofa, which creaked.

"Are you men or mice?" Ethan boomed. If the parlor had better acoustics, his question would have carried all the way to the Sheared Sheep. "Duggin? Not a word of commiseration? Fine. What about you, Bones? What do you say?"

"Past is past."

"Quite right. *Jack*," Ethan said, loud enough to make the dour man look up. "Behold the mystery of the man before us. When I met him, he was entertaining my wife in the dark of night behind closed doors. Never so much as a sorry. Now he turns up here tonight, when any decent sort would have stayed away to give Ju and me a bit of privacy. Yet he doesn't push with both hands, does he? No. He comes dressed in rags and speaking in monosyllables. Aims to be underestimated, I think."

Ben set down his drink and stood up. "On your feet."

"No, no, no," Ethan laughed, still in his armchair. "I'm not criticizing you, Bonesy, my lad. I'm admiring your tactics. Take this bloody war. You've arranged it to your satisfaction. Most men have an appointment with destiny, but not you. You're snug in your reserved occupation. Safely out of London, too. All those kiddies and governesses pouring into the country to escape the threat of bombs. And then came Bones, hard on their heels."

"I don't see your uniform." Ben's face was hot. His heartbeat thudded in his ears.

"No. So surely we might have a civil discussion without fisticuffs?" Ethan grinned at Duggin. The lawyer had finally decided their exchange was more interesting than his manicure —though perhaps only just, if his stone face was any indication.

"I don't want to fight a man Ju considers worthy," Ethan said. "Nor can I fault you for being impressed with her worth. The entail's been kaput for a while, as you no doubt knew. As Ju's second husband, you'll be sitting pretty when she inherits Belsham Manor."

Mention of money threw cold water on Ben's ire. Accusing of him of avoiding the fate of other men his age touched a nerve. Accusing him of a mercenary plot against a friend made him smile.

"You've confused your motives for mine, Bolivar. I expect that's why you're finally willing to accept the divorce. You know it's your last chance to squeeze another penny out of Lady Juliet. But not to worry. Before long there's sure to be any number of lonely widows. One may keep you, if you play your cards right."

Ethan stood up. Duggin's expression didn't change, but he sat up straighter.

"Little man with a pretty face." Ethan glared down at Ben. "I'll never let Ju go. This gold mine is claimed. She may be tiresome as a toothache and homely as an old mule—"

Ben punched him in the solar plexus as hard as he could.

Ethan staggered, wheezing. Ben hit him again, square in the jaw. It was like hitting a brick wall. Pain rocketed through his knuckles all the way to his elbow, but the sight of Ethan on the rug, shielding his head to ward off more blows, more than made up for it.

"I think that's sufficient. You've made your point," Duggin said laconically. He hadn't risen during the altercation and showed no inclination to get up now that it was over.

"I bwit my tongth," Ethan moaned. Blood bubbled at the corner of his mouth.

Ben dared a glance at his hand. Had he broken a finger or fractured a knuckle? It looked all right, but every time his heart beat, it throbbed, both red hot and ice cold.

Ethan wiped his mouth and struggled to his knees. "You're a dark horse, Bonesy," he said from the floor. "Good God. Wee dogs have the worst bite."

"You've never seen a Doberman go at a man's throat," Duggin said.

The drumbeat of pain in his hand made Ben's eyes water. Before he could surreptitiously swipe them, Lady Juliet and Lady Victoria burst into the parlor. Their presence consigned him to suffering in silence, but for the occasional blink.

"Dr. Bones!" Lady Victoria cried. "What did he do to you?"

"I'm fine," Ben said, backing away before she could touch his hand.

"I'm the one on my knees," Ethan said.

"And you'll stay there if you know what's good for you." Lady Juliet loomed over him menacingly. "What's your role in all this?" she demanded of Duggin.

"Spectator. Hostage. Some combination of the two."

"What's wanted is a cooling off period," Lady Victoria said, latching onto her daughter and pulling her away from Ethan. "Mr. Duggin, I'm sorry to intrude upon your serenity, which is nothing short of remarkable, but would you help your client back into his chair? Thank you." She turned to Lady Juliet. "Darling, Dr. Bones could surely use a moment to collect himself. Why don't you accompany him to the library?"

THE LIBRARY WAS a part of Belsham Manor that Ben had never seen. Given Lady Juliet's love of books and reading, he expected a vast space with tall windows, richly carved wood panels, overstuffed armchairs, and green-shaded lamps. But that would have required her ancestor, Sir Thaddeus Linton, to have competently designed such a space. Instead, Belsham Manor's library turned out to be a windowless room. The walls were crammed with floor-to-ceiling shelves. Near the small hearth was a desk, love seat, and coffee table.

"We're not really tipplers, so there's no drinks trolley," Lady Juliet said as she ushered Ben inside. "However, Mother takes a little brandy now and then, so there's a decanter hidden behind *Silas Marner*, which may very well drive one to drink. Shall I pour you a glass?"

"Yes, please," he said, flexing his right hand. No fractures, no torn ligaments, but it would be sore for days to come.

She handed him a cut-crystal glass filled with amber liquid. "Sit down. How's your fist?"

"Better than my conscience."

"What do you mean?" She sat down beside him.

"If Ethan was looking for an excuse not to cooperate, I've given it to him, haven't I? He's probably storming off as I speak."

"You're forgetting the blackout. You also don't know him very well." Lady Juliet smiled. "Even if the road from the manor to the Sheared Sheep was lit, he wouldn't storm off. Not before he had his supper, brandy, cigar, and any little *objet d'art* he can palm when Mother isn't looking."

"I hope you're right. I got the feeling his solicitor will drive a hard bargain. Maybe too hard for you to accept."

Lady Juliet sighed. "I had the same thought. I'd be a lunatic not to. And I don't like Mr. Duggin's eyes. But the truth will emerge soon enough. Now. You simply must tell me—what did Ethan say to provoke you?"

"I don't know," Ben lied, wishing he'd formulated a response to this obvious question on the way to the library. "He spouted a lot of rubbish."

"Of course. Ethan's all talk. Perhaps literally." She smiled. "There's a good chance he has no skeleton and maintains his shape the way a balloon does—with hot air. But what did he say just before you punched him?"

"Oh. Er." Ben took a sip of brandy. "He insinuated I was a coward. That I took a post in the country because it was safer than London."

She made a disbelieving noise. "You wouldn't hit him for that."

He met her gaze. Her light brown eyes were warm, kind, and easily injured, despite all her polysyllabic rants to the contrary. Under no circumstances would he repeat what her husband had said about her.

"What's that you're wearing?" He suddenly became aware of her dress. It was fluttery-sleeved and emerald green, set off by a double strand of onyx beads that fell to her waist.

"This? It's what I wore to the fête," she said, referring to an occasion which had ended in disaster. "I'd planned to set it on fire, but Mother said no. I assumed she'd donated it to the less fortunate. Tonight, when I said I had nothing to wear, she brought it out and suggested I try it again—this time without the hat, gloves, earbobs, et cetera. She did away with the belt, too, and loaned me this necklace."

"Oh. Right. Wise woman, your mother," Ben said. Lady Juliet had never looked better, and it was a testament to the pain in his hand that it had taken him so long to notice.

"But I won't let you get away with changing the subject. What did Ethan say, verbatim, to make you strike him?"

"Called me a coward. I told you."

"I see." Rising, Lady Juliet made for the door. "Make yourself comfortable. I'll send Dinah to fetch you when we're called to dinner."

"Where are you going?"

"To hear the truth straight from the horse's arse."

19

DOING ONE'S BIT

Juliet found Ethan where she'd left him, sunk low in his fireside chair, legs splayed and arms spilling limply to either side. His tie was undone and a damp flannel had been laid across his brow. In the other leather armchair, Duggin appeared to be napping.

"How is Dr. Bones?" Lady Victoria asked from the sofa. Her tone was serene, but she'd put on her spectacles and brought out her embroidery, a sure sign of distress.

"Never better," she said. "Enjoying a pre-prandial refreshment as he peruses our literary potpourri."

Juliet's unintentionally alliterative reply caused Duggin to open his eyes. His faint, perhaps imaginary, flicker of amusement brought her rage to a boil.

"You. Begone. Now!"

"Juliet!" Lady Victoria cried.

"Forgive my rudeness, Mother, but surely a man who facilitates divorces becomes inured to abuse. I need a word with Mr. Bolivar."

"Your husband," Ethan said weakly. "I'm still your husband."

"I beg your pardon, Mr. Duggin," Lady Victoria said, rising. "Might I offer you a tour of Belsham Manor?"

For the first time, the dour man smiled. "Why not? Might come in use if I pass this way again."

Juliet waited until she heard the pair ascending the stairs. Then she snatched the damp flannel off Ethan's head and threw it into his lap.

As expected, he jumped out of the chair, brushing the flannel away from his trousers and inspecting them carefully for any blemish. He would have come out of a coma if that's what it took to rescue his crotch from a mortifying wet spot.

"What did you do to Dr. Bones?" There was no better time for Juliet to demand the truth than when Ethan was psychologically weakened by concern for his appearance.

"I tested him." Ethan turned toward the fire to dry the dampness. "And rather brilliantly, I might add. If you persist in this course, Ju darling, and actually divorce me, fortune-hunters will come out of the woodwork. I thought perhaps he was the first. So I felt about for weaknesses."

"Like what?"

"Anything I could think of. His height"—he glanced at her over his shoulder—"or lack thereof. His looks. His clothes. His courage. None of that had much effect, so I floated the notion he was a gold digger. I suggested he'd set his cap at becoming your second husband in pursuit of the estate."

"And that's when he hit you."

"No." Ethan adjusted his monogrammed gold cufflinks. "Though I think he was on point of ordering me out, or giving me a stern talking-to." He chuckled. "Finally, I said you were tiresome. Homely as an old shoe—or was it an old nag? No idea. The little blighter bruised my chest and loosened a tooth." Rubbing his jaw, Ethan turned away from the fire, smiling in a way she'd once found irresistible. "He didn't care to hear you insulted. If I'd said something worse, I think he might have beaten me black and blue. Which is all to the good. I'd never abandon you to a mercenary suitor."

His hypocrisy was too breathtaking to ridicule. Juliet folded her arms and sighed.

"Ju. Listen," Ethan said. "I came to win you back. I made terrible mistakes. It took exile in the wilderness for me to realize what I had in you. But I see I'm too late. And though it pains me, I can find no fault with Bones."

"You—you—" Juliet spluttered, unable to think of a bad enough word. "You've always been a fast talker, but this—this *mountain* of mendacity—takes the biscuit."

"Ju. Look at me. Please."

She did so, glaring, ready to send that loose tooth flying.

He reached into his inner coat pocket and took out a fountain pen. "Bring me the papers."

JULIET WOULD HAVE GONE to the library to collect Ben, but she was too excited by the prospect of Ethan signing to delay his action even a moment. Rushing into her bedroom, she opened her lockbox, seized the divorce petition, and raced back to the parlor. To her relief, Ethan was still there, pen in hand.

"You should know, I have various copies hidden away," she said, spreading the papers across the coffee table. "So melodramatic gestures, like ripping it to shreds or tossing it into the fire, will avail you nothing."

"You do think of everything." Chuckling, Ethan sat, held the first page at arms' length, and struggled to read it in the soft light. Then he sighed, brought out a pair of spectacles, and reluctantly put them on. "It's come to this. No sooner did I pass forty than the indignities began."

Ethan read the first section, the declaration that Juliet would retain the entirety of the Linton estate, both her small personal holdings and the larger one to be inherited from Lady Victoria.

He signed.

Ethan read the second section, the distribution of their assets acquired during marriage. They were few—two paintings, a sculpture, and some jewelry—and Juliet had directed he receive them all, to keep or sell as he saw fit.

He signed.

Ethan read the third section, the petition for the dissolution of their union. It was based on proof of adultery between him and Helen Parr, a secretary from Plymouth whom Juliet had briefly counted as a friend. The King's Proctor had already examined the evidence, provided by the private detective Grandmother Ellisson had hired. Juliet would have preferred to take those humiliating details to her grave, but divorce was an adversarial process. It was either prove adultery or prove abuse, and Ethan had never raised a hand to her. As it was, the King's Proctor might reopen the case to ensure there'd been no collusion between them. Husbands and wives who came together to manufacture the appearance of an affair were guilty of seeking a divorce based on mutual incompatibility, and that was against the law.

He lingered over the page, rolling his handsome gold-accented pen between thumb and forefinger.

"Helen," he murmured. "Nice girl. Bit flighty. Have you spoken to her lately?"

"No," Juliet said, calling on heretofore unimagined reserves of self-control to keep her answer to that one word.

"And we're back where we began," Lady Victoria said loudly from just outside the door. Then she swept in, smiling determinedly, with Duggin at her side.

Ethan looked up. "Hallo, Lady Victoria. Jack—you nearly missed the big moment."

Duggin shrugged. Drifting to Ethan's side, he merely stood there, reexamining his manicure.

"Never let it be said I didn't invite your solicitor to read the agreements," Juliet said nervously. Something was wrong, but she didn't know what.

"He's witnessing this momentous occasion. That's sufficient." And with that, Ethan put pen to paper, adding his sprawling signature to the decree.

"There we are," he said, capping the pen. "Done and dusted. Surely it's time for dinner. Someone dig up Bones. Ha! I'm so famished, I'm speaking in puns."

AFTER JULIET LOCKED the papers in the library safe and told Ben the news, stammering over the words in her jubilation, she sat down to dinner, which she experienced in a sort of happy delirium. She let Dinah, who was serving at table for the first time, give her a portion of each dish: *consommé de Volaille*, poached mackerel, *canard à l'Orange*, braised onions, and stuffed marrow. As the meal progressed, Juliet chewed, swallowed, and washed it down with *Côtes-du-Rhône*, tasting nothing but the prospect of her own freedom.

At last it was time for the pudding, Turkish quince. There was a wobbly moment when Dinah dripped syrup on the tablecloth, recognized her minor transgression, and nearly dropped the entire dish in horror. That shook Juliet out of her fog. Rising, she rescued the nervous girl by helping her serve. When she sat down again, she was back on planet Earth, truly aware of her fellow creatures for the first time since the signing.

Ben looked ill at ease. Perhaps he was tired. Or perhaps he'd simply grown weary of watching Ethan do what he did best, utilize his gift of gab. As the quince was doled out, tasted, and complimented, Ethan launched into a fresh story about dinner at an elegant Paris chateau. He claimed to have been so intimidated by the waiter, he ordered pureed beetroot for dessert.

"I don't believe that for a moment," Lady Victoria said warmly. "Your French is better than that."

"Alas, proof to the contrary arrived in a tureen large enough to serve six. The abominable waiter knew I'd got it wrong. I was far too cowed to object, so he had the cheek to curl his lip under his absurd pencil mustache and sneer at me. *Voilà*." Ethan imitated the waiter removing the lid with a flourish. "The other tables were riveted. I heard them whispering, what would this overdressed English buffoon do?"

"What did you do?" Juliet didn't actually care to know, as the entire story was almost certainly a charming fabrication. But her relief had transmuted into something like affection and a willingness to play the straight man.

"I tucked in with gusto. I did my best to convince my guests that pureed veg was all the rage in London. That stylish hosts were replacing Stilton and pears with turnips and peas. Needless to say, I convinced no one, but I kept my pride. Speaking of turnips," he said, looking pointedly at Duggin. "You're silent as veg. Can you offer any amusing anecdotes on the topic of fine dining, in gay Paree or elsewhere?"

Duggin looked up from his plate. It had been methodically cleaned, like every plate that preceded it. Either he didn't believe in waste, or he rarely ate so well. "Beg pardon?"

"An anecdote?" Ethan prompted.

"No, thank you." Duggin signaled Dinah to bring him a second helping of quince.

"How about you, Bonesy?" Ethan asked Ben. "I'll wager you have some stories to tell."

Ben seemed at a loss. Juliet sympathized. Ethan had that effect on people. A normal man couldn't take two punches, eat in the company of his supposed romantic rival, then jovially prod said rival to join the conversation. But Ethan liked being the center of attention more than he liked holding grudges. As long as there was one person left to impress or win over, his enthusiasm never flagged. He reminded her of champagne— sparkling, frothy, and likely to result in a blinding headache come morning.

"Stories?" Ben repeated warily. "I'll see what I can come up with. In the meantime, how's your jaw? And your solar plexus?"

"Agonizing," Ethan boomed happily. "I'll never speak out of turn to a physician again. You devils know how and where to attack. You'll notice I never took a swing at you. Why? I'm rubbish in a fight, that's why. Case in point...."

As Ethan embarked on a story about an investment scheme that proved fraudulent, Juliet viewed her estranged husband with new objectivity. He'd grown more distinguished since turning forty. The threads of silver at his temples lent him gravitas; the bit of extra weight suited him. She could appreciate all that without the slightest rekindling of emotion. Their marriage was well and truly dissolved. It might take weeks or months for the King's Proctor to affirm that truth, but for Juliet, the knot was untied at last.

She shifted her gaze to Ben. His attention was on Ethan, who was reenacting his escape out the second story window of a Mancunian hotel.

I'll be taking an awful risk, she told herself, but that was a lie. She'd taken an awful risk. The die was cast. If he told her that he thought of her quite as his own sister, if he stood up with Rose Jenkins and said "I do" before God and St. Mark's congregation, Juliet knew she would continue to love him, silently and without hope. She was all in. It felt terrible, and wonderful, and exhilarating, like a plunge into darkness that could end in only two ways: victory or death.

"... and then I was cornered," Ethan cried, breaking through her reverie. "Trapped like a rat with Scotland Yard—yes, none other—right outside my door. They had a warrant for my arrest on charges of fraud by representation. Fraud by failure to disclose information. *And* conspiracy to defraud. Do you think I was afraid?" He drained his wine glass. "Well. Let me remind you, I would never utter profanity in the presence of ladies," he said, favoring Lady Victoria with a wink, "but at that moment, should anyone have asked for bricks, I was producing them at an astonishing clip."

Everyone laughed, even Duggin. Ben said, "I'm surprised you aren't in prison."

"It was a very near thing. A *very* near thing. Fortunately, the men of the Yard are no fools. They saw in me a man with vast connections and rarefied gifts that could be put to use."

"As easy as that?" Juliet scoffed. "Come now. You specialize in tall tales, but this is too much. You must be quite a talented solicitor, Mr. Duggin."

Duggin cleared his throat. "I simply made the case his transgressions were small. Given the state of war, he should have a chance to do his bit."

"Ethan, surely you don't expect us to believe you joined up?"

"I did not enlist, my dove. Or should I say, my soon-to-be-exdove," Ethan said. "The worthies at the Yard proposed a special arrangement, the details of which are confidential. But even kiddies gathering scrap and ladies keeping themselves lovely may be said to be doing one's bit. Now I can make that claim as well."

JULIET EXPECTED the men to linger over brandy and cigars, but apparently the trio had had enough of each other's company. She and Lady Victoria had hardly sat down in the parlor before Ben popped in to say good night.

"It's a touch early, I know," he said. "But I'm having bad luck with sleep lately. Breakfast, too."

"We'll feed you well tomorrow, never fear. Thank you for coming," Juliet said warmly. "I do wish you could have witnessed the signing. Though I'll probably tell the story of that climactic event so often, you'll soon feel that you did."

"Please accept my thanks as well," Lady Victoria said. "I suppose this may go down as the worst dinner party of your life. Does your hand still hurt?"

"There's no point asking a man such a question," Juliet said. "You'll never get an honest answer."

"On the contrary," Ben said, flexing his fingers with obvious pain. "I was going to say you feel no pain, and consequently, neither do I."

She caught her breath. Fortunately, the moment passed without her blurting out anything humiliating.

After Ben went upstairs to his guest room, Juliet paced the parlor. She didn't know whether to pour sherry or ring for tea. Sherry rarely did anything for her, and tea might keep her awake.

"I'm having another sherry. I believe I've earned it," Lady Victoria said. She looked exhausted. Despite her determined efforts to carry on normally, she was still a woman living with heart failure, and acting as hostess could overtax her. "Did you believe Ethan's story about doing his bit?"

"No. Yes. I suppose it's possible," Juliet said. "He hasn't lost his looks. Perhaps the Army wants to use him on posters to get gullible young women to join the ATS."

"I'm afraid you're off the mark there, Ju, darling." Ethan entered the parlor with the eternally blank Duggin in tow.

"He's telling the truth. My name *is* John Duggin, but I am not a solicitor," he said, stepping forward. "Lady Victoria, I apologize for accepting your hospitality under false pretenses, but a certain amount of covert behavior is essential if we're to win this war."

"I don't understand." Lady Victoria looked from him to Juliet and back again. "If you're not a solicitor, what are you?"

"He's rather like a civil servant," Ethan replied. "One of those cloak-and-dagger types you hear about on the wireless."

Duggin looked displeased at the term "cloak-and-dagger." "It so happens I work from a rather unremarkable room near St. James's Park. What's more, I work for our side."

"Please believe me, the deception was never meant to stretch on," Ethan continued. "I would have put my cards on the table before dinner, but Ju took the step of bringing in Bonesy. The truth had to wait until he was out of the picture."

"Why?" Juliet demanded, struggling to contain her rising fear. "What do you have to say that can't be mentioned in front of him?"

"Most of what we have to say," Duggin said gravely. "It's a matter of national security. That means beyond a certain point, your participation is governed by the Official Secrets Act. You'll be asked to sign a paper, which amounts to an oath of loyalty to the King and Parliament. Repeating what we tell you to anyone else, anyone at all, renders you subject to prosecution. That leads to the noose."

"How dare you threaten me and my daughter in my own home?" Lady Victoria stood up. "I insist you leave. Both of you, this instant. Take your chances with the blackout. I won't have you under my roof."

"Jack meant no offense, Victoria," Ethan said. "Only these

chaps have no idea how to speak to those who are blameless without sounding threatening. Believe me, I learned the hard way."

"I assure you I have authority to warn of prosecution. I invite you to examine my credentials," Duggin said, reaching inside his suit jacket.

"Put that away. You're making my point for me." Ethan looked from Lady Victoria to Juliet. "Please. Hear us out. It's terribly important."

Juliet's heart dropped. The note of sincerity in his voice told her this wasn't one of Ethan's flights of fancy. This was something so important, a blank-faced man from London, from that maze of government buildings on Whitehall Road, had come all the way to Birdswing, population 1,022.

"But you signed the papers," she said weakly. "We're as good as divorced. Why should I care what arrangements you've made with the government?"

"Because when you hear them," Ethan said, not unkindly, "you may be persuaded to rip up the petition."

20

"LADIES HAVE SO FEW OPPORTUNITIES"

N o sooner had they arrived in the library than Duggin made the rounds, checking for ways inquisitive maids might overhear what was said. "It's early yet," he explained, "and the evening has been unusual enough to pique their curiosity."

Juliet folded her arms, still uncertain if he were really some kind of agent or spy. When he swung toward the room's west corner, she had her answer.

"What's that gap between bookshelves?"

"An entrance to the Master's Way," Ethan said. Never one to miss an opportunity to expound, he continued, "When Sir Thaddeus Linton built Belsham Manor—"

"Good Lord, Ethan, give it a rest," she cut across him. "It's a hidden door to a private passage."

"Put your hands under the middle shelf," Lady Victoria told Duggin. "Feel the latch? Slide it left. Now pull hard."

He obeyed. The hinged door swung inward, revealing a shadowed corridor. "Does the staff know about this?"

"Yes, of course," Ethan replied, clearly determined to explain something to someone. "It's meant for convenience, not skullduggery." Reaching inside the passage, he flipped the switch that turned on the lights. "Sir Thaddeus valued his privacy. This allowed him to pass easily from bedroom to dining room to library without interrupting the staff or being accosted by—"

"Sir Thaddeus kept a mistress," Juliet broke in. "This allowed her to move about without unduly embarrassing his wife."

"How many other entrances are there?" Duggin asked.

"Four," Lady Victoria said, taking a seat.

"Could someone enter the corridor and eavesdrop on us?"

"Unless we lock the other four doors, yes."

Duggin regarded Juliet expectantly until she sighed and crossed to the mantel. Opening a cloisonné box, she withdrew a large, old-fashioned key, carrying it with her into the Master's Way. As a little girl, she'd delighted in using this "secret passage," though it looked like any other hall, with the same wallpaper, carpet, and sconces. These days, it was merely a cut-through where skiving maids liked to hide. More than once, the smell of cigarette smoke had led to the exposure of a maid who'd decided to take an unauthorized break.

"Sorted," Juliet announced, returning to the library a few minutes later. The brief excursion had cleared her head; she felt more confident. This was simply more of Ethan's nonsense. Clearly, he was trying to access the Linton purse by appealing to their patriotism. He'd stoke goodwill by signing the divorce petition, then ply them with a sob story about wartime service. A request for money would surely follow.

"Gentlemen, I have no intention of ripping up those papers," she said, closing the hidden door and leaning against it. "Knowing that, you may proceed, preferably in a minimum of words. Mother is tired, and so am I."

"Won't you sit down?" Ethan asked.

"You're planning on speaking quickly, so I needn't," Juliet said sternly. She was prepared to stand until the end of time, barefoot on a bed of red hot coals, if it proved her resolve, but Lady Victoria shot her a worried glance.

"Fine. I'll sit." She settled behind the desk. "For heaven's sake, get on with it."

"The story I told over dinner, about being drawn unwittingly into a fraudulent scheme, was true. Apart from the more amusing details," Ethan began. "The escape out the hotel window was on the ground floor, involving a drop of perhaps three feet. I didn't actually clamber up a library's drainpipe...."

"Ethan," Juliet said warningly.

"... and none of this took part in Calais. I was in Penzance chartering a sunset trip to the Isles of Scilly. There I met an engaging young person who was charming to talk to, so I decided not to leave until dawn...."

Juliet closed her eyes, dropped her head, and pretended to snore.

"... but alas, my new friend was working for Scotland Yard. She maneuvered me into revealing certain personal details. I was arrested, transported to Truro, and left to sweat in a cell for three terrifying days."

"Of all your women, I like her best," Juliet said.

"I offered up many fervent prayers. Then, like an angel, there appeared—this man." Ethan pointed at Duggin. "And he said...."

Duggin frowned. "Forgive me. I said, 'Is it true your mother-in-law is a Nazi sympathizer?'"

Lady Victoria sucked in a breath. Juliet jumped to her feet, and Ethan lifted both hands in supplication. "There's no need to hit me again! I said no, never. I swear it, may I be struck down if I lie. I told Jack no in the strongest possible terms."

"He did," Duggin agreed. "My next question was, 'Then what is Lady Victoria Linton's true relationship with her eldest brother, the Earl of Calprin?'"

"I said, to my knowledge, she had none," Ethan said.

"Duggin told me the fate of my country might depend on my absolute honesty. Mind you, this was last year, when there was still hope the war could be averted. I hope you will forgive me, Victoria, but I told Jack everything I knew about the earl, and everything I suspected."

"I don't understand." Juliet turned to her mother, who was taking short, shallow breaths.

"What has Reginald been up to?" Lady Victoria asked in a tightly controlled voice.

"According to our sources," Duggin began, "the earl's ties to Germany have deepened. Did you know his daughter, Fiona, married Franz Von Koppenow? The earl used to visit her twice a year in Pomerania, till it became impossible."

"That doesn't make him a Nazi sympathizer," Juliet said.

"Perhaps not, but his financial ties to the *Vereinigte Stahlwerke A.G.* are no secret," Duggin said. "He still writes letters to the *Daily Mail,* contrasting Der Fuhrer's 'strength,' as he puts it, and Old Blighty's supposed weakness. These facts are a matter of public record." Reaching into his coat, Duggin withdrew two envelopes. "To go further, we must first discuss the Official Secrets Act and obtain your signatures."

Juliet listened in silence as he explained the government's oath of secrecy in simple, unemotional terms. Lady Victoria also said nothing, but she twisted her hands in her lap. They had no questions and chose to sign with no more than a glance between them. Juliet's hope that Ethan had simply devised a new con was dead. She felt like a woman trapped in a flooding room. There were no doors or windows; the water lapped against her chin, and still it rose.

"Thank you, Lady Victoria. Lady Juliet." Duggin tucked the envelopes away again. "Ordinarily, we take little interest in low crimes of the sort Bolivar usually commits...."

"I object to the word 'crimes,'" Ethan muttered. "Particularly 'low crimes.'"

"Oh, yes. Let's pause to inflate your ego regarding the grandeur of your career," Juliet snapped.

"But Bolivar turned up in our sights time and again," Duggin went on. "We observed him attending parties at the Duke of Cornwall hotel in Plymouth, which is always thick with fascists. We saw him have lunch with Oswald Moseley. And, er—pardon me, Lady Juliet—we tracked his evenings with a certain lady deeply connected to Lord Rothermere."

"I was only after her money," Ethan told Juliet.

"Shut it," she said, not looking his way.

"Moreover, we noted that Bolivar enjoyed a very cordial relationship with Lady Victoria's brother, the earl, not to mention several other well-placed people on the Continent," Duggin said. "Therefore, once Bolivar agreed to work for us, we asked him to resume his everyday life, with two new wrinkles. First, he would present himself as a convert to the pro-Hitler, anti-Semitic philosophy. Second, he would report back to us about what he heard, what he saw, and what he could gather when the opportunity presented itself. A peek into a man's desk, a glance at a lady's diary, intercepted notes, and so on. As it turns out," Duggin said with a half-smile, "he's far better at extracting secrets from the upper crust than he was at bilking money out of ordinary investors."

"The gentry is notoriously naïve," Juliet said.

"As you say." Duggin inclined his head. "Bolivar served his country with distinction until last month. Then, quite unexpectedly, his estranged wife nearly destroyed the operation."

"Me?" Juliet stared at him. "How?"

"You helped Dr. Bones uncover a pair of English traitors in Plymouth. While the matter was meant to be kept secret, parts of it leaked out. Now Lord Rothermere and his fine friends know

Bolivar's wife not only helped expose them but plans on giving evidence against them."

"Of course I plan on giving evidence," Juliet cried, the water rising higher. "You talk about serving our country. How can you fault me for doing my duty?"

"I've no doubt you take pride in doing your duty," Duggin said. "However, from the viewpoint of my friends, and indeed, the men at the very top, the completion of your duty is infinitesimal to Britain. Worse, it would be counterproductive. It would aid the enemy by removing a talented spy from the chessboard."

Juliet couldn't speak. Soon the water would be over her head. She wanted to stop the proceedings, hurry up to Ben's room, and ask him to join the conversation. But thanks to Duggin and the Official Secrets Act, she'd signed that right away.

"Yet all is not lost," Ethan said. "Men who live by their wits are accustomed to reverses. I secured a meeting with Harry—Lord Rothermere—and pled my case. I told him the Ellisson family was split on the issue. I said Reggie and I had the right of it, but my dear bride remains under the spell of her Jew-sympathizing mother. I said this difference in philosophy was, in fact, the secret reason for our estrangement. I promised Harry I'd prove my devotion by returning home and... well." He smiled hopefully. "Taking my wife in hand."

"What in the name of heaven does that mean?" Juliet asked.

"It means...." Ethan had the decency to look abashed. "It means I'll bring you into the fold. Or failing that, I'd exert my authority as your husband and forbid you from giving evidence."

Juliet and Lady Victoria exchanged shocked looks.

"It won't result in the guilty getting off, I assure you," Duggin said.

"Of course it will," Juliet cried. "I was the hostage! Mine was the life that was threatened. If I don't speak against them, I'll seem afraid to repeat the charges under oath. Like a hysterical woman. An attention-seeker."

"The trial is in camera. It's not a public spectacle with an audience awaiting your appearance. And forgive my candor, but the counsel for the defense has already painted you as such a person with some success," Duggin said. "They've used your situation—a wife living apart from her husband—and your long association with the guilty parties to paint a rather damning picture. They claim your allegations are merely the fever dreams of a woman scorned.

"However, the physical and circumstantial evidence is strong," he continued quickly, before she could erupt. "All that's needed to ensure their conviction is the testimony of a respectable citizen. We have that in Dr. Bones. The guilty will be condemned and they will hang. If you do as we ask, Lady Juliet, you will not subvert the course of justice, I assure you."

"But I'll be perceived as subverting the course of justice," she wailed, thinking only of Ben. "To change my mind... to withdraw as if I'm a liar who daren't show her face during a trial, even a secret trial... it would require the performance of a lifetime. And even then, I'm not sure anyone would believe it."

"Of course there will be personal difficulties," Duggin said. "You did bring up questions of ego and grandeur—"

"None of that, Jack," Ethan interrupted. "Lady Juliet deserves nothing but your deepest respect." To her, he said more gently, "Ju, darling. I understand how you feel. No, truly I do. Can you imagine what it's been like for me, pretending to side with the BUF? Acquaintances cut me. Friends pretend not to know me. I've never been so alone in my life, surrounded by people I despise. And there's no guarantee I'll stay alive to celebrate the war's end...."

Juliet let out a harsh laugh. Duggin regarded her stolidly, without a trace of humor.

"Do you expect me to believe that's true?" She looked from face to face. "That can't possibly be true."

"How many times have you wished to be a widow?" Ethan countered. "It may come to that. But I've made my choice. Twenty years in prison? I'd exit a broken man or sealed in a box. Better to go out doing what I do best—drinking, dancing, and listening when I seem to be talking."

"Let me see if I understand," Lady Victoria said. "For Ethan to continue spying for Britain, he needs Juliet to disavow her story about those—those *people*. Ethan will take credit for her reversal, restoring his relationship with the Nazi sympathizers."

"Yes. But your good name won't be sullied, your ladyship," Duggin said.

"I don't give a fig about my good name. I want to understand what you're asking of my daughter," Lady Victoria said. "Earlier, Ethan said something about Juliet ripping up the divorce decree."

Ethan and Duggin exchanged glances. Duggin said nothing. Ethan sighed.

"Please understand," he said with uncharacteristic humility. "My calling card, as it were, consists entirely of my connection by marriage to the earl, and to Ju, and to you, Lady Victoria. The truth about my family is less than exalted. My mum was a char-woman. My father was a self-made man and I won't speak a word against him. But he died in Pentonville. I can't expunge those facts. I can only obscure them. With regard to the gentry, I look the part and I speak the part. But without my marriage to you, Juliet, I'm no one."

Juliet shivered. The waters had closed over her head. "Ethan. Don't do this to me. Please."

Duggin cleared his throat. "Perhaps I can offer some

perspective. Although this concerns Dr. Bones, he was never told, and will not be told, because vital details of national security are only disclosed when it furthers the war effort. But at a party he overheard two words: chain home. Do you remember?"

Juliet nodded.

"Chain Home is a secret initiative. Its purpose is to detect and neutralize certain advantages enemy aircraft may have in attacking us," Duggin said. "England anticipates heavy casualties from German bombers. It's often said that the bomber always gets through. But the technology of Chain Home is unprecedented. It may save countless lives. By overhearing a chance remark and passing it on to the authorities, your friend Dr. Bones protected Chain Home. And Bolivar's work is every bit as consequential to our national survival. Perhaps more so."

No one spoke.

"Ladies have so few opportunities to do meaningful war work," Duggin continued. "Some fill in for men in factories. Others type memos or sew bunting or hold bake sales. If you choose to answer your country's call, Lady Juliet, you will aid England on an altogether different plain, by permitting Bolivar to continue his mission."

It took Juliet a moment to find her voice. "And if I say no?"

"The operation is rolled up," Duggin replied. "We discard Bolivar. He stands trial and goes to prison. Sir Oswald Mosely, Lord Rothermere, your uncle the earl—all will carry on with their treasonous activities. But your conscience, in the strictest sense, will be clear."

"You make it sound simpler than it is," Lady Victoria said. "She'll not only have to decline to give evidence. She'll have to pretend she's reconciled with Ethan. To lie to everyone she knows and loves." She paused as if someone might correct her. When no one did, she asked, "How long do you expect her to keep up such a charade?"

"How long will the war last?" Duggin asked. "How long will fascists at home seek to help bring down Britain from within?"

"Good grief, man. You needn't be so black about it all," Ethan said. "Look, Ju, no one wants a war. No one can even bring themselves to fire a shot, apparently. It could all be over by this time next year. Or I might say the wrong thing, or be caught snooping in the wrong room, and make you a widow in a month."

This time Juliet couldn't find her voice. She opened her mouth, but no sound came out.

"Leave us," Lady Victoria told the men. "You'll have her answer in the morning."

Duggin touched his coat pocket, where the two envelopes resided. "I must remind you of—"

"Come on, old man." Ethan slung an arm over the detective's shoulders and steered him toward the door. "The die is cast."

Juliet controlled herself until the door closed. Then she sank to the floor, buried her head in her mother's lap, and cried.

21

TWO GHOSTS

B en thought an early turn-in would do him good, but he had trouble falling asleep. Some of it he attributed to his hand, which still ached despite liniment and a dose of aspirin. The rest he put down to his guest room.

Clearly, Lady Juliet and Lady Victoria had wanted him to see Belsham Manor at its best. His window overlooked the garden, which was starkly lovely even in winter. The hearth's three-bar electric fire made the room toasty, and the heirloom furnishings seemed sumptuous enough for a palace. But the featherbed had an odd aroma—not revolting precisely, but unpleasant. Unfamiliar creaks and rattles kept drawing him back from the edge of slumber. In Birdswing, Ben was frequently asked how he could sleep in a haunted cottage, but he found it far easier than sleeping in Belsham Manor.

He was lying in bed with the duvet pushed aside, a bit too warm but also a bit too lazy to get up and turn down the electric fire, when he noticed the stars. Above him, a river of diamond pinpricks flowed through the night sky, trailing violet and silver toward a destination unknown. Part of him recognized that ribbon of brilliance, and knew he must someday rejoin the flow.

The idea wasn't troubling. It wasn't a reminder of life and death, but a reaffirmation of life and Life; the small realities that made up his days, and the great reality far beyond his ability to contemplate, at least from the beach at St. Agnes.

Or is this Port Isaac? Ben wondered, looking around.

On his Sunday rambles, he'd visited both, walking the cliffs wrapped in a wool coat. But it didn't feel like winter now. The damp sand was cool rather than cold; the sea was calm. Along the shore, where the shingle gave way to roots and leaves, a pair of tall gorse bushes swayed in the breeze. They beckoned, reminding him of something he'd discovered during waking life.

That's a wreckers' tunnel, he thought, remembering what a Port Isaac local had told him. *After they plundered a shipwreck, they had to get the spoils off the beach before the militia rode through. And they couldn't go home, because the soldiers would inspect every dwelling along the shore. So the tunnel led into the cellar of a pub or a church. A place they could hide the goods, and themselves, until the militia gave up and went away.*

Those tall gorse bushes had spikes, but he passed through them harmlessly, entering the tunnel. He expected walls of damp earth, studded with rocks and teeming with bugs. Instead, the passage was surprisingly ordinary, with white walls and a lino floor.

Am I inside Belsham Manor now?

The passage ended at steep stairs. Climbing them, he emerged in another place he recognized: All Saints, a Lambeth church he'd frequented during his rotation through St. Thomas Hospital. The congregation was singing "O Sorrow Deep."

Spying a blonde in a smart black frock, Ben slipped into the pew behind her. When the undertaker asked what Penny ought to be buried in, he'd picked that frock. It was a relic from their brief courtship, when he'd known how to love with abandon.

"Why are you haunting me?"

Penny didn't turn around. "There was no viewing," she said, somehow speaking even as she sang. "As for the funeral, it was a paltry affair. My brother didn't come. Neither did you."

"I couldn't stand. I was in too much pain to even sit in a wheelchair."

"Pity. Did you see what the lorry did to me?"

"No, but I heard the sound. As the wheels... well...."

"Passed over my head. Do you want to see?"

Suddenly he was beside her, looking upon the wreckage of her head and shoulders. The fresh injuries were precisely as he'd imagined. For many the sight would have been unbearable, but Ben knew the flesh was weak in life and weaker still in death. Only saints picked up their decapitated heads and restored them, or lay in their coffins like jewels upon velvet, immune to decay.

"It didn't hurt." Just like that, she was restored again, beautiful, never to age another day. "I didn't have time to be afraid. From a purely selfish standpoint, it was an easy end."

Relief washed over him. "I'm glad. Truly. I was afraid...."

"Afraid I suffered as much as you used to wish I'd suffer?"

"I didn't—" he began, then stopped. Maybe he had. Coping with her infidelities had required pushing his emotions down, substituting work for reflection and declaring certain thoughts unthinkable. Banished far beneath the sunlight and green grass of his conscious mind, his resentments had multiplied like grubs in wet earth.

"You're right." A weight lifted as he confessed. "Is that why I feel you watching me? Why I smell your perfume?"

Penny cupped his cheek. The stiff black lace of her gloves reminded him of the scratchy ones his grandmother had worn on Sundays. A stern woman, Grandmother Bones had always answered his questions truthfully. Even when he was very young, or when the truth was the last thing he wanted.

Penny asked, "How would you advise a patient who came to you with your symptoms?"

"I'd tell him it was guilt. Part of his bereavement. Something that would fade with time," Ben said. "And maybe guilt does explain why I feel you're judging me. Raging at me. For—for—"

"Living?" She kissed him lightly on the lips. "I forgive you."

Another weight fell away. Then he remembered. "What about the *Sous le Vent* I smelled in Fitchley Park? That was no figment of my imagination. It was real, I'm sure of it."

"If you're sure it was real, then it was. But you already knew that. Goodbye, Ben." Penny disappeared, taking the congregation with her. Beneath All Saints' vaulted ceiling, Ben was left standing alone, with the distinct suspicion he'd been alone all along.

BEN AWOKE. The dream fled the moment he remembered he was in Belsham Manor, and that unpleasant odor was the featherbed. Had he been dreaming of his old life in London?

Perhaps. For once the memory of those days wasn't tainted by recriminations. Maybe the cliché he'd spouted to Ethan —"Past is past"—applied to him, too. It was a comforting thought. After dwelling on it briefly, he rolled over, dropping into the bottomless black.

The hill was slick with frost. The ground was already inhospitable, dotted with holes, root tangles, and granite eruptions. He slipped every third step or so, head down, climbing through force of will alone.

At the top of the hill stood a tree which had grown in defiance of prevailing winds. Bent unnaturally, it reminded him of a woman in mid-dance, her head, shoulders, and arms swaying to a savage beat. Far beneath it, a forgotten chieftainess slept, her dreams bloody, her bones encircled by offerings both profound and mundane.

Topping the hill, he saw a woman standing beneath the windswept tree. Though no relic of pre-Roman Britain, her soul was trapped like the chieftainess's, bound to this world by a convergence of nature and human folly that few in the modern world now understood, or remembered how to undo.

"It's me," Ben said when Lucy seemed to look through him. "I've come to help you."

She didn't answer. Even as a gust of wind rattled the tree branches, her white cotton nightdress hung motionless, hair loose but still.

"Lucy!" He tried to shake her, but his hands passed through her. As they did, a horror swept over him, a fear from the deep place that man shares with beast. What had been a lovely young woman became a corpse, her face cherry red, her eyes turned white by hours of sightless staring. She stank of operating theater floors, of pus-soaked bandages, of overflowing bedpans. Ben recoiled.

"No!"

She was gone. Where she'd been there was nothing but a cloud of his own breath, hanging between him and the tree like a ghost's ghost. The absurdity of that idea made the scene turn on its head, like a kaleidoscope clicking to a new image. Night became day, replacing his terror with serenity.

The hill was spring green, the tree leafy, the sky painted in baby boy blue. Down at the heart of the hill, the chieftainess dreamt of golden wheat and a harvest that would never end. And down where the hill became a field, Lucy was alive and well, on a picnic with a young man.

Simply dressed in an everyday frock and cardigan, her wild curls contained by a chiffon scarf, she was far lovelier than her photo. Lovelier and angrier, judging by the fire in her dark eyes.

Snatching up her handbag from the blanket, she issued a curt goodbye to the man lounging beside the wicker hamper. But before she could walk ten steps, he was on his feet, catching her arm and spinning her around.

Hang on. Is that me? Ben wondered.

It wasn't. He and the man *did* share a similar build and coloring: brown hair highlighted with ginger, fair skin, blue eyes. But the man's face was rounder, forehead more prominent, lips pursed like a toddler denied his latest desire.

"Don't you walk away from me!"

"Get off!" she cried, trying to pull free of his grasp.

The man squeezed tighter. Energy rippled along Ben's scalp. His hair stood on end; the metal frame of his wristwatch buzzed. Although this had never happened to him in waking life, he knew what was coming with the certainty of dreams: a bolt from the blue.

Something boomed. Ben sat up in bed, heart pounding. Only when the knock was repeated, and someone at the door called "Sir?," did he once again recognize his surroundings. The bedside clock showed he'd overslept yet again, and breakfast was surely underway downstairs.

He washed up, shaved, and dressed in record time. He'd seen three aspects of Lucy—ghost, corpse, and living woman. Did that relate to the chieftainess? What about the lightning?

Head full of the dream, he went down to the solarium, which was pleasantly awash in winter sunlight. Five places had been set, but only Duggin was present. The resolutely blank man served himself in methodical fashion, lifting the lid of every silver chafing dish and extracting a helping from each: poached eggs, stewed tomatoes, beans, sausage, bacon, and potato cakes. Atop this he added two slices of toast, liberally buttered. Depositing this miniature mountain of food at his place, Duggin headed to the coffee carafe, where Ben was filling a cup.

"Good morning," Ben said.

Duggin said nothing. Perhaps he considered pleasantries rhetorical.

Dosing his coffee with milk and sugar, Ben couldn't resist interrupting the dour man's peace. "Do you know when the others will be down for breakfast?"

Duggin shrugged.

"You don't say much, do you?"

"Here's a piece of advice," Duggin said, tasting his coffee before adding milk. "Never take this sort of spread for granted. We may be eating our shoe leather before the end."

"Yes. Well. Thanks for that. They should get you on the wireless. You could be an inspirational speaker."

He chose a spot adjacent to Duggin so he could eat without making eye contact. Lady Victoria set a lovely table: crisp white linens, delicately-patterned china, and a centerpiece of fir, red berries, and cinnamon sticks. It seemed like something Lady Juliet might have concocted. Fleetingly, Ben wondered why she was so late to breakfast, but it was hard to focus on the real world as the dream of Lucy intruded like a spectral hangover.

If only the gas leak hadn't happened....

The sentiment had been rising in him for some time. Of course, indulging in such wishful thinking was the worst sort of foolishness. Even if he devised a way to reliably contact Lucy, to see her whenever he wished, there was no future down that road, only an unbridgeable gap. And yet the thought of her captivated him in a way Rose never could. He felt certain if Lucy hadn't died, if she were still alive and well and counted among his patients, he'd be courting her. And halfway to popping the question—assuming she'd have him, of course.

Who was that nasty bugger at the picnic?

Had he witnessed a true event? Dreamed up an unworthy suitor? Or was it some combination of the two?

"Bonesy!" Louder than life, Ethan burst into the solarium. "And Jack. Tucking in with both hands, no surprise there. What a glorious morning! I bestride the Earth like a colossus."

Ben barely managed a nod in return. Perhaps Duggin's stony disinterest was the inevitable result of listening to bombastic nonsense all day.

"Come now, Ju darling," Ethan called over his shoulder. "Mustn't keep our guests waiting. Connubial bliss is no excuse."

Lady Juliet entered at her mother's side. Lady Victoria wore a cashmere turtleneck, a tweed skirt, and a frozen smile. Ben didn't notice Lady Juliet's clothes, only her expression. She'd looked less desperate while held at gunpoint.

He stood up. "What is it? What's happened?"

"On your feet, man," Ethan rebuked Duggin. "Our hostesses have arrived."

Setting down his silverware, Duggin reluctantly arose, dabbing at his mouth.

"Thank you. I apologize for being so late to the table," Lady Juliet said. "Only we have wonderful news. The divorce is off. Ethan and I have reconciled."

22

JOLLY GOOD

1 DECEMBER 1939

For a moment, Ben thought he was dreaming again. "What?"

"Reconciled. Man and wife, till death us do part," Ethan declared, throwing an arm around Lady Juliet's shoulders and pulling her close. "I don't deny I was a dreadful husband. My Ju drove a hard bargain. Now I must walk the straight and narrow. I must become the man I pretended to be when she fell for me."

Lady Juliet wouldn't meet Ben's eyes, so he looked to her mother. "Lady Victoria, what's going on?"

She smiled at him like a mannequin. "Love prevailed. Isn't it marvelous?"

He was silent for so long, Duggin was moved to croak, "Congratulations."

Ben still couldn't force out a word. He stared at Lady Juliet until she finally met his gaze.

"Dr. Bones. I—I hope you'll be happy for me."

"Of course. It's good news. Jolly good," he heard himself say, like someone's daft old granddad.

"Look at her blush," Ethan said. "She's mortified because we lingered so long in bed. Don't worry, my sweet, there are no innocents in this room." He smiled at his wife in a proprietary way that made Ben want to hit him again. His hand throbbed, reminding him that despite its soreness, his fist was still available.

"Don't tease me," Juliet said, blushing still more furiously. "Shall we sit down to eat, so Dr. Bones and Mr. Duggin might resume their breakfast?"

"Yes, of course. Be a dear and fix my plate," Ethan said, dropping into the chair between Ben and Duggin. "After so little sleep, I'm useless."

Ben could only stare helplessly as Lady Juliet loaded a plate with bacon and sausage. How could this be happening?

"You're deep in thought, Bones, my lad," Ethan said.

"Er," Ben muttered. Juliet had never spoken or behaved in a manner that so much as hinted she'd consider reconciliation. Leaving aside Ethan's pattern of infidelity, he was duplicitous at best and an outright criminal at worst.

"*Deep* in thought," Ethan repeated. "Bonesy? Are you in there?"

Ben shook himself. "Yes. Well. It's just—I have patients booked. I really must say my goodbyes."

"Come now. You can spare a quarter hour with friends."

Pretending not to hear, Ben stood up and pushed his chair in. Lady Victoria looked dismayed. "Dr. Bones. Have we chased you away with poor hospitality? Please give us another chance. Ju, sweetheart, Dr. Bones is leaving. Help me convince him otherwise."

Lady Juliet continued loading her husband's plate. "If Dr. Bones has bookings, Mother, we mustn't stand in the way."

"You haven't chased me away, Lady Victoria," Ben said woodenly. "Thank you for everything. Dinner was superb. My room was quite comfortable. And the unexpected news was—jolly good," he put in, aggravated by the way all four of them were looking at him. "Jolly good. Yes. Thank you again. I'll see myself out."

He was halfway to the front door when he remembered he'd left his things in the guest room. By the time he hurried upstairs, gathered everything together, and returned to the ground floor, Lady Victoria was waiting for him.

"My dear Dr. Bones, I do apologize," she said in that warm tone that usually melted everyone, including him. "I feel like a miserable hostess."

"Nonsense," Ben said. For the first time since he'd known Lady Victoria, her courtesy struck him as grating. What sort of mother was she, anyway? One worth her salt would have put a stop to this. Locked her daughter in a tower, if necessary, till the madness passed.

"I realize Juliet's decision has perhaps startled you," she said, clearly oblivious to his blackening mood. "You've never heard her speak of Ethan, except in the most severe terms. But I assure you, they were once the happiest of—"

"Lady Victoria, please don't think me rude," he said through clenched teeth. "But I shouldn't keep my patients waiting. Goodbye."

On that dignified note, he strode out into the twenty-eight-degree morning, at which point it became clear he'd forgotten his hat and coat.

I'm making a fool of myself. He forced himself to go back inside, feign amusement, and bundle up, then stomped out to the mews to retrieve the Austin. Of course he was cross. He'd had no breakfast, only coffee, and for the third night in a row, his sleep had been interrupted by dreams of—what?

He groped for it but couldn't remember. Lady Juliet's surprise announcement had wiped it away, like a hand across a foggy pane of glass. And the glass wasn't a window, but a mirror, reflecting something he didn't expect.

BEN MANAGED to drive home without puncturing any tires or knocking any sheep over the rainbow. The real problem, he thought as he followed Old Crow Road back to the village proper, wasn't the marriage of Ethan to Lady Juliet, but the marriage of malice to incompetence. Thanks to Der Fuhrer, Prime Minister Neville Chamberlain, and a laundry list of government cockups, his country was at war. That war had dropped him smack dab in the middle of nowhere, with no men of his own age about. What he needed were some lads for a drink and a laugh, maybe a game of cricket on weekends, if his limp allowed him to play. Too much time in the company of a female, any female, upset the male equilibrium. What did he care if Lady Juliet had given Ethan a blank check to continue hurting her for the rest of her life? She didn't want his help. She hadn't even asked his opinion.

There must be a couple of blokes up for some mischief, he told himself as Fenton House came into view. At the same time, two blokes up for mischief came into view: Caleb and Micah Archer, perched on his roof.

"What the devil is this?" Ben demanded, out of the car and through the gate in record time. The twins regarded him placidly from their perch between chimneys on the roof's apex. "What are you doing?"

One twin saluted. "Sir! Monitoring the skies, sir."

"Sir," the other twin echoed. He lifted an outsized, antique pair of binoculars—or more specifically, he lifted his half. The other boy did the same, raising his right arm in perfect sync with his brother's left. Sunlight glinted on identical metal bracelets, and Ben understood. They were handcuffed together.

"Carry on," he said, entering the cottage and wondering what sort of explanation he was about to receive. It couldn't be any madder than what he'd already been served at Belsham Manor.

"Good morning," Special Constable Gaston called from the kitchen. Mrs. Cobblepot, who'd been sitting across from her brother sipping tea, jumped up.

"I didn't expect you home for breakfast. Let me pour you a cuppa."

"Why are the twins on the roof?" Ben asked as he took a seat.

"Because they blew up the constabulary and I couldn't find a pair of straitjackets," Gaston replied calmly. "Never fear, I'll have them off the roof directly. What happened to your hand?"

"Nothing," Ben said, flexing his fingers to prove it. "What's that smeared on your face?"

"Soot," Gaston said. "Reducing the natural shine of forehead, cheeks, and chin. Note I'm kitted out in drab colors. The crowning bit is this string vest I fashioned myself," he added proudly. "Special gear for a covert operation. The twins were out of bed and out of bounds last night. I intercepted them and conducted an interrogation."

"Well, don't keep me in suspense. Were the boys involved in Bobby's murder?"

"Do you imagine I'd be sat down passing the time of day if they were? The boys thought they had Agatha flummoxed, but she overheard them whispering about Pate's Field. When they passed through, I was there, squatting behind a patch of gorse."

"Were they headed for Barking?"

"Aye. Dressed in black. Carrying a shielded lantern they didn't light until they were well out of sight," Gaston said. "My junior wardens are vigilant, but no one would have seen them, unless they knew when and where to look. Besides, the boys are old hands. They've been making these expeditions to Barking for a month."

"Why?"

"Sir Thaddeus's gold."

From her place at the stove, Mrs. Cobblepot tutted. "When I taught school, the boys used to tease the younger ones with that story. They'd draw up maps and drop them where the wee ones would find them. Then the older boys would swear the younger ones to secrecy and deputize them to search for the gold, on the promise that whoever dug up the chest would share with everyone. Naturally, it was just a trick to get the smaller boys out of their hair. A bit of fun, watching them chase something that didn't exist. I'm surprised Caleb and Micah still believe the story. I took them for cleverer than that."

"Clever never stopped a man from believing what he wants to believe," Gaston said. "Or a boy. Caleb heard the story when he was seven, and he's been looking for the gold ever since. He's pigheaded, that one. Micah does as he's bid, even though he knows it's all a joke. He's heard the truth from Miss Jenkins, Father Cotterill, and the older kiddies. Caleb won't listen. They've been all over Birdswing, so Caleb thought it must be in Barking."

"Here's your tea, Dr. Bones," Mrs. Cobblepot said, putting a cup and saucer in front of him. "I haven't any biscuits, but there's a loaf of fruited bread in the oven. *Your favorite*," she sang.

"Thank you."

"Fruited bread, eh?" Gaston chuckled. "You'll be in skirts by spring if you don't spend more time with the lads down the pub."

Ben let that pass. It didn't matter that he'd just spent a quarter hour telling himself the same thing. Fruited bread warm from the oven was quite possibly his favorite snack. He wouldn't utter a word that might endanger his supply.

"Seems like treasure hunting is more of a summer pursuit," Ben said, getting them back on topic. "Why brave the cold and risk their necks in the dark?"

Gaston gave him that pitying look he always did when Ben missed some essential of country life. "Did Father Christmas visit you as a boy? Leave presents?"

"Three. A book, a shirt or trousers, and a toy."

"Good on you. Father Christmas has missed the Archer house five years running. Helen told the twins the jolly old elf only looks out for rich kiddies with a father at home."

Mrs. Cobblepot tutted again. "I understand her bitterness. I just wish she'd bite her tongue now and then."

Ben asked, "So they wanted gold to buy themselves Christmas presents?"

"They wanted gold to lure their father back to the house," Gaston said. "Micah told me. They planned to pay all their mum's debts, get her a new dress, and buy themselves an SS100 in British racing green. They reckoned *that* would bring Bobby home, which is what they wanted most."

Ben feigned sudden interest in his teacup. He'd been warned about his soft heart in medical school, told to blank it out, control himself, and resist sentiment. He rarely succeeded, at least not entirely, but the advice prevented him from indulging in public displays.

"The boys have fine taste in cars," he said. "The SS100 is a dream. Six-cylinder."

"No running boards," Gaston agreed. "I hear the inside is finished in sycamore."

"Listening to the pair of you talk, anyone would think you heartless," Mrs. Cobblepot said, removing the bread pan from the oven. "I burst into tears when Clarence told me. Children are always fanciful, but some of them have to get by on so little, even their wildest dreams are practical. Most would imagine their old dad returning because he missed them. They dreamed of bribing him to come back." She shook her head. "And now it's a reunion that can never be. I tried to console the boys, but they wouldn't have it. I wonder if they fully understand their father's dead."

"They understand. They're not daft," Gaston said. "Grief is private. You know that."

"I know nothing of the sort. A burden shared is a burden halved."

"Boys trying their best to be men will never be criticized by me," Gaston said. "But I was stern with them about tramping over hill and dale after sundown now that Helen's locked up. Caleb said something about using Sir Thaddeus's gold to hire a lawyer, and I said, enough's enough. I told them I was suckered by the story, every boy in Birdswing and Barking has been suckered by the story, and facing the truth is the first step to manhood."

"Do they realize their mum must have known they were going out at night?" Ben asked.

"Of course. It's been an ongoing battle. Them tunneling out, so to speak, and her plugging the holes too late," Gaston said. "They went out the front door, so she made them sleep in the attic. They went out the window and down the oak, so she had it chopped down."

"The drainpipe fell off the house with Caleb and Micah still clinging to it," Mrs. Cobblepot chimed in, shaking the bread free of its pan. "Helen put it back up wrapped in barbed wire and nailed their window shut for good measure. Yesterday I realized they'd loosened the window frame so the glass pops in and out."

"How did they get to the ground?" Ben asked, genuinely impressed by the boys' determination.

"The wee devils nicked a thirty-foot rope ladder," Gaston said. "I asked where from, and all they said was, 'We didn't steal it!'" He drained his teacup. "Never mind. It's a relief to know they didn't do in their old dad. I'm not sure Birdswing could bear the shock. Poor Helen must have realized they were slipping out to Barking and assumed it had to do with Bobby and his new bit of stuff."

"A shame," Mrs. Cobblepot said. "To be so sure her own sons were killers, she confessed to murder herself."

"I'm not sure Mrs. Archer's ever experienced much besides cruelty and selfishness behind closed doors," Ben said. "In her own way, though, she managed to behave unselfishly. What she did wasn't right, of course. If the twins had done it, she would have been letting two very dangerous boys walk free. Still, it was selfless, volunteering to take their punishment."

"Yes, well, with any luck, you'll be able to tell her so before long," Gaston said. "I've an appointment in Plymouth on Tuesday. I'll take the boys to see their mum and present my evidence to whichever overpaid imbecile is in charge. Till then, I'll keep them busy serving the greater good, even if that amounts to sitting on a roof, playing with my old field glasses."

"Here we are. Cinnamon and currant," said Mrs. Cobblepot, putting three slices of fruited bread before Ben. "I do hope it suits. Sugar is precious, so I tried a substitution."

Ben tasted a slice. "Oh, it suits, never fear. Is that rum I taste?"

Mrs. Cobblepot winked.

Gaston cleared his throat. "Am I not sitting here waiting, woman?"

"Aspersions were cast," she said airily. "Didn't you insinuate that fruited bread is effeminate? Far be it from me to unman you. Now, if you'll excuse me, woman's work is never done."

"Take some advice from an old widower," Gaston said to

Ben, pitching his voice so Mrs. Cobblepot would hear as she swept out of the kitchen. "Never remarry. Keep wooing spirit women. Easier than the real thing."

"I'm sorry?"

"Spirit women," Gaston said, gesturing in a way apparently meant to encompass Fenton House. "I'm not finding fault. Let the girl you're walking out with flit off to Plymouth. Make yourself a hermit in this cottage. Muck about with spirit boards and crystal balls. An imaginary woman is less trouble than an actual wife, am I right?"

Gaston waited, clearly expecting a laugh. When none came, he groaned.

"Fine. Sit there with your mouth hanging open. Let the flies in." He nicked a piece of cinnamon and currant bread. "I'll help you with that."

AFTER GASTON GOT the twins off the roof, promising to show them an even better location for watching for German planes, Ben tried to keep busy, so as not to stew in his own juices. He didn't like the idea of Helen Archer spending a single unnecessary moment believing her sons capable of murder, so he telephoned the Plymouth police. Unfortunately, under the conditions of her remand, no one was permitted to speak with her except in person and by appointment. The good news would have to wait until Gaston's visit on Tuesday.

With the twins and their mother eliminated as suspects, Ben took out his notebook and made a fresh list of those who might have killed Bobby. It would have been nice to turn to Lady Juliet for a sounding board, but he couldn't stomach the idea of ringing her. Better to keep his mind on murder.

LORD M.—CHANGEABLE, *irascible, may be dangerous*

    Lady M.—*almost certainly had an affair with Bobby*

    Mr. Collins—*helped cover up the murder after the fact*

    Mrs. Tippett—*callous enough to be involved, talkative, might let something slip, appears to be left-handed*

    Kitty—*left-handed, not entirely believable, expects Mr. C. to marry her*

HE ADDED A FEW OTHER NAMES, those who might have additional information or prove helpful.

MRS. GRUNDY—CLEARLY *loyal to Lord M., distrusts Mr. C. and probably Lady M.*

    John—*might remember more, but malleable, must be treated gently*

    Rev. Rummage—*spends so much time at Fitchley Park, he may have seen or heard something helpful*

A FEW SCENARIOS came to mind. First: Lady Maggart and Bobby had been having an affair. After surprising them in the act, Lord Maggart killed Bobby, perhaps in a confused or completely deluded state. Lady Maggart and the staff then acted to move the body, destroy evidence, and push the "lady in black" story to protect the dying baron from the humiliation of arrest and trial.

Second scenario: Kitty and Bobby had been having an affair. After surprising them in the act, Mr. Collins killed Bobby. Then he and his loyal staffers took action to conceal the truth, probably without Lady Maggart's knowledge. But why would Kitty or anyone else go along with such a demand? Would they care so much about protecting Fitchley Park's reputation, or was it simply out of fear of Mr. Collins?

There were other scenarios, of course. Kitty was left-handed and had referenced killing rats, but Ben had difficulty imagining the plump maid overpowering Bobby, even with the element of surprise. Mrs. Tippett's earthiness and jaded quality made her seem capable of anything, but would she have ever been alone with Bobby? John's passivity and desire to please *might* make him capable of murder, if sufficiently threatened into it, but the more Ben considered the notion, the more he discounted it. Even if John could go through with such a thing, he would probably collapse immediately after, confessing to anyone who would listen. He had an easier time imagining Kitty as the killer, or Lady Maggart herself.

That took Ben down an interesting road. What was it Lady Juliet said when she'd quoted *Hamlet*? Something about being a gifted natural actress? Perhaps that was true of Lady Maggart. He'd assumed her belief in the "lady in black" was genuine. Perhaps it was only a cover for various household aberrations, like footsteps, doors closing, and muted voices—all the things that went along with a secret affair.

Claiming to believe in the ghost also would have given Lady Maggart an alibi in Birdswing while her butler destroyed evidence at home. And they would have known it would be me charged with writing the death certificate. Perhaps they assumed the doctor who lives in a haunted house would sign off on a killer ghost without question.

That unflattering thought dropped him right back in the pot, stewing. With effort, he redirected his attention from his own stupidity to the idea of Lady Maggart as Bobby's killer. Perhaps Bobby had tried to discard her callously, as he'd discarded his wife, and Lady Maggart had snapped. Did she have the strength and grit to cut a man's throat and watch him bleed out? And did the other bits and bobs of evidence fit such a scenario?

That bloodstained rug, Ben thought. *The one John said Mr. Collins burned. If it was from her ladyship's room, that fits. But why burn her compact and other toiletries? Any blood spatter would have wiped off.*

Then there was Lucy's contribution to the investigation—moving his cane from wardrobe to nightstand. Lord Maggart possessed a pewter-tipped cane. And there had been a gaudy brass cane in Lady Maggart's bedroom, stuck in a vase with a couple of umbrellas.

Why were umbrellas in her bedroom? he wondered. *Why not downstairs, beside a door? Lady Juliet would know if it's a common affectation among the gentry. I could ask her.*

He pushed the idea away. Circumstantially, his theory was already solid, or at least plausible. Evidentially, he had nothing whatsoever.

As the physician who still had yet to finalize Bobby Archer's death certificate, Ben had a right to ring up Plymouth CID and inform them of his suspicions. But would they arrest Lady Maggart or even question her? Probably not until Helen was freed, if then. Like many Englishmen, Ben believed his country's system of laws second to none, but no one pretended its application was flawless. Ordinary flatfoots, as Dirk Diamond might say, would need strong evidence to accuse, or appear to accuse, a baroness, or their jobs would be forfeit.

Gaston, Ben decided. *I'll lay all this at his feet and see what he proposes to do about it. He eliminated the twins from suspicion competently enough. Maybe he's growing into his role.*

He sighed. The part of his nature that found puzzles irresistible didn't like that idea, but there was nothing else for it, except to see what Mrs. Cobblepot had cooked for lunch.

Around one o'clock, Ben decided to catch up on his paperwork: updating charts and writing letters. Most young men in Birdswing and Barking were anxious to join either the Army or the Royal Navy. Those who struggled to earn a living were enticed not by the pay, which was low, but what came with it: food, lodging, and plenty of respect when friends and family saw them in uniform. Most were patriots, determined to defend their island nation against threat of aerial gas-bombing and invasion. A few felt obligated to enlist because of social pressure, which even Ben, as a young man destined to spend the war out of uniform, occasionally felt. All pre-enlistees required a doctor's exam, certifying their fitness to serve. The exams were easy enough, but at the end, Ben had to type up letters—a duty that would drive him to take on a secretary, as soon as he could afford it.

With two fingers, it was slow going. Midway through the second letter, the typewriter's ribbon needed changing. As he searched for a replacement spool, he glanced out the front room's window and saw Mrs. Garrigan. She was heading for his office door.

I should get Mrs. Cobblepot to say I'm out on a call, Ben thought. *There's nothing wrong with her except a tendency toward neurosis.*

He tried to convince himself, but his conscience was having none of it. He had the right to be a little stern with her, perhaps. But he didn't have the right to dodge her, especially not during office hours.

"Hello, Mrs. Garrigan." He opened the door before she could ring the bell. "Come in."

"I'm sorry to bother you, Doctor," she began, as she always did. "I'm sure you're far too busy...."

"As a matter of fact, I'm not." Taking her coat, he hung it on a peg, then led her to the chair in front of his desk. "What's the trouble?"

"I didn't sleep well last night," Mrs. Garrigan said. "I had a terrible dream. My Felix was in his coffin."

"You dreamed your husband was dead?"

"Not dead. In his coffin. Dressed in his best. Handsome, smiling, joking with me," Mrs. Garrigan said earnestly. "But he wouldn't come out. Not even when I told him the baby was coming. And when it did come, it was only a doll."

"I understand," Ben said as patiently as he could. "Dreams can be frightening. But it's just the way our minds process our hopes and fears while we rest."

"But the doll," she insisted. "Only suppose—suppose it was a foretelling? Suppose it means the baby will be stillborn? I saw a stillborn baby once. It looked like a doll with a blue face. When I remembered that, I got lightheaded. I got out of bed and had a glass of milk. But I couldn't get back to sleep. My heart pounded, my head ached, and all I could see was that doll's queer face."

"Put it out of your mind. You're a healthy woman, and before long you'll have a healthy son or daughter."

"Thank you, Dr. Bones." Mrs. Garrigan's eyes shone. "I'm past grateful you came to our village. The mums down my way cross the lane to avoid me. One said she won't hear another word from me till the baby's born. If I say my heart races or my head hurts, they pull faces. But not you."

"I'm glad I could help," he said, thinking those mums were smarter than he was. "Let me fetch your coat."

Mrs. Garrigan stood up, tottering as he pulled her coat off the peg. "These ruddy shoes will be the death of me," she said. "I tried to stretch them with beans. Do you know that trick? You fill your shoes with dried beans and dribble in a bit of water. The beans take up the water and swell, plumping your shoes by morning."

"And then for supper, I suppose you must eat the beans, or ARP Warden Gaston will cite you for wasting food." Ben held out her coat, and she slipped into it. "Perhaps it's time to bin those shoes and chalk it up to experience."

"Cor, no. They're the only ones I've got. Have a good day, Doctor."

He held the door as she went down the steps and along the path. From behind, her right calf was so swollen, her legs looked mismatched.

"Um... hang on?"

Ben hurried to her side. She was so alarmed, he tried to address the issue without further adding to her distress.

"Forgive me. Only—one of your calves looks a bit larger than the other. Have you noticed?"

"I'd be blind not to." She laughed. "We women are used to suffering for our beauty. My feet throb and smell of beans besides!"

"The other day, when you came to see me," Ben said. "Was it as swollen then?"

"Oh, yes."

Ben suppressed a groan. When he'd examined her, he'd focused on the skin discoloration and the fetal heartbeat, ignoring the red flag under his nose. It didn't matter that Mrs. Garrigan had come in multiple times, fretting about cold weather, hot tea, and bad dreams. He was the one who'd gone to medical school, and he was the one who knew better than to let the patient's perceived issue dictate his exam.

"Would you mind terribly coming back inside for a moment?" he asked. "Coat off again, I'm afraid, and back in the chair. I just remembered. Did you mention your heart was racing last night?"

"Rat-a-tat-tat, like a drum. The face of that doll set it off. Monstrous dream! The day before, it beat like that while I did the wash. By the end, I felt half-delirious."

"Is that so?" he asked, getting his sphygmomanometer and stethoscope. "Headache, too?"

"Fiendish headache. My gran used to say, when your feet hurt, everything hurts."

"Of course," Ben said, working hard to sound casual. "Why don't I check your blood pressure, just to say I did? If you'll roll up your sleeve...."

He wrapped the cuff around her slender arm, inflating it by squeezing the attached rubber bulb, placed his stethoscope, and listened carefully. He would only get one chance at an accurate reading. If he asked to measure a second time, she would surely panic, driving the numbers up.

"How is it?" She didn't sound alarmed; on the contrary, she seemed to enjoy the extra attention.

The systolic was 200. The diastolic, 140.

"Jolly good," Ben said breezily. "Have you been following my advice?"

"As much as I can. Maybe a few extra pints to calm my nerves. Is there something I can do to get my leg back to normal size?"

"Yes, but it's a bit unusual," Ben said. "Do you ever travel by car?"

"Only once. To a funeral."

"Then you may not know that travel by car is quite relaxing. And relaxation is proven to reduce swelling," Ben lied, still in that carefree tone. "I don't have anyone booked for the afternoon. I don't suppose you'd let me try the treatment on you, as a sort of experiment? It's not a bad day for a drive. Bright and sunny, even if the trees are bare."

Most patients would have asked if he'd gone mental, but Mrs. Garrigan looked overjoyed. "Of course! I'm so tired of afternoons alone, scrubbing the same patch of lino."

"Wonderful." Ben scribbled a note for Mrs. Cobblepot, left it in the center of his big black desk, and walked Mrs. Garrigan out to his Austin Ten. She giggled as she accepted his arm, thinking it a chivalrous flourish; in truth, he wanted a hand on her in case she collapsed.

The drive felt endless. Ben kept her occupied with leading questions about Christmas in Birdswing. She was telling him about the time she was chosen to play Mary in the annual Christmas pageant, while her best mate was relegated to the role of a non-speaking sheep, when the two tall peaked roofs of St. Barnabas came into view.

"Oh. There's the hospital. Are those nuns on the veranda?"

"Yes, they run the place. We doctors come and go at their pleasure," Ben said. That wasn't literally true, of course, but it felt that way to him when he compared St. Barnabas, a tiny cottage hospital run by no-nonsense sisters, to London's St. Thomas, where nurses stood at attention for physicians and treated them with near-reverence. He parked just outside the front door.

"Do you have an errand to—" She stopped. "Oh, dear. My leg."

"Now you must be very brave, for the sake of your child as well as yourself," he said in a low, measured voice, looking directly into her eyes. "The condition is called deep vein thrombosis. That means there's a blood clot in your calf, in a proximal vein. It can't do much harm where it is, but we cannot allow it to shake loose and go to your lungs."

As he paused for breath, he fully expected Mrs. Garrigan to scream or cry. Instead, she kept still, listening.

"The doctors here can give you a new medicine called heparin. That, along with bedrest, is what you need to neutralize the clot. Heparin and bedrest *will* work," he said, not because he thought the drug was infallible, but because he wanted her to believe it was infallible, not only with her head but her whole heart. "You'll get the best of care around the clock. We won't stop till the danger has passed."

"I see," she whispered.

"Can you keep calm while I bring you in?"

She lifted her chin. "Of course. Whatever you say, Doctor."

He took her hand and squeezed it in both of his. "I'm so very proud of you. Just let me find a sister and a wheelchair."

BY SUNDOWN, Ben was still at St. Barnabas. Not because he was displeased with Mrs. Garrigan's care, but because he didn't want her to feel abandoned. With her husband in France, and her parents dead, she had no support system beyond those afore-mentioned neighbors, the fed-up mums. He wished they could see her now, cool and resolved with her life at stake. Some people were like that. They fretted endlessly over trifles, but when faced with danger, turned to steel.

Like Juliet, falling to pieces over a hat but standing firm when held at gunpoint, he thought, smiling. She was an astonishing woman. Then he remembered he was angry with her, or himself, or someone.

"Should I feel the medicine working?" Mrs. Garrigan asked Ben, who was stationed beside her bed. "Probably not. But my leg hurts less, and my feet are getting a proper rest."

"For now. But remember what Dr. Van Pelt said. St. Barnabas has a new approach to DVT," Ben said. "The dogma I was taught, leg splints and bedrest, is now obsolete. A nurse may get you up and walking as soon as tomorrow." He smiled at the thought. Drugs like heparin brought sweeping change, elimi-nating decades, even centuries, of accepted practice in a matter of months.

"Tell me the truth, Dr. Bones. Like you did in the car," she said, regarding him steadily. "Will I deliver this baby?"

"Yes."

"Will it be healthy?"

"I don't see why not."

She was silent. Then: "Will I get another clot someday?"

"Perhaps. But that's why St. Barnabas is here. And why I'm here."

"You saved my life. Thank you," Mrs. Garrigan said. "Thank you for listening to me."

Ben's eyes stung. For a moment, he was tempted to confess. Then he dropped his head, bit his lip, and accepted her gratitude with a spontaneous prayer.

I won't forget this. I'll do better in future. I promise.

23

THE PHANTOM

Dinner at St. Barnabas, although begged off the cook an hour after dinner, was better than most hospital meals. It was hot for one thing, and seasoned for another. The only meat was in the soup—boiled chicken—but it was filling. Along with the soup came mushy peas, boiled potatoes, and a roll, all quite decent. Only the pudding—literally tapioca pudding—looked like something out of a bricklayer's pail.

After dinner, he looked in on Mrs. Garrigan again. She was propped up on pillows, one hand resting on her belly.

"Hello, Dr. Bones. I hope they'll make you as comfortable as I am, since you're stuck here overnight."

"They will. It won't be the first time I've begged a cot from the charge sister."

"Dr. Bones? From Birdswing?" a young woman in a pink-striped pinafore asked. He nodded as she pushed her library cart to Mrs. Garrigan's bedside. The cart offered a modest collection of novels and magazines, all well-worn.

"Only look! *Picturegoer*," Mrs. Garrigan said happily. "Since my husband joined up, I've gone off dancing, but I go to the pictures every week."

Passing over the magazine, the volunteer glanced at Ben, dipped her head, and looked again amid a fluttering of black lashes. Her blonde hair was held back by a pair of tortoiseshell combs. He'd always liked blondes, especially her sort, with her slender neck and confident air.

"You'll enjoy that one," she told Mrs. Garrigan. "My friend donated it, but only after we'd read it to pieces."

As his patient started her dose of cinema gossip, Ben wished her a restful night, nodded at the pretty volunteer, and went downstairs. The charge sister was transparently annoyed by his request for a bed assignment. She consulted a ledger, rang another nurse, muttered about "some doctors," then marched off to survey the wards. Ben took a seat in the visitor's waiting room. His thoughts had only just returned to his list of Fitchley Park suspects when cart wheels squeaked across the linoleum.

"We meet again," the blonde volunteer said. "I'm Peggy Dean."

"I'm Ben." He gestured at the empty chair beside him. "I'm surprised you're here so late. Surely St. Barnabas doesn't require its volunteers to stay the night?"

"No. I could have ridden my bicycle home, but I left it too long," Peggy said. "My friend was meant to meet me around three for a bit of fun. By the time she rang to say it was off, it was too close to sunset for me to risk it. I decided to crack on until the wards were quiet, then kip for the night in a linen closet. Some coincidence we've both stuck overnight, eh?" She fluttered those curling black lashes again. "You're getting quite the reputation. Is it true you turned Mrs. Archer over to Scotland Yard?"

"No. Special Constable Gaston made arrangements with Plymouth CID. Mrs. Archer is my patient, and I consider myself her advocate, come what may."

Peggy looked around before leaning closer. Around her neck was a paper-thin heart, colored to look like gold, hanging on a junk chain. Only a very young woman could wear such a thing without looking undiscerning. Their dewy youth made it seem playful and fresh instead of worthless.

"I'm on Mrs. Archer's side, too," she whispered. "I think she'll be proved innocent."

"Is that so?"

Peggy nodded. "I live in Barking, but I know Mrs. Archer from her restaurant in Birdswing. Sometimes my sisters and I drop in for pie and a Schweppes. Sad old bird. I wouldn't swap places with her for a million pounds, stuck with those heathen boys while Bobby did as he pleased."

"'Bobby?'" Ben said, noting that Peggy used his Christian name. "Sounds like you knew him better than you knew his wife."

"Not by choice." She rolled her eyes. "He was in and out of the village all summer. Every time I walked the dog, there he was, winking or making a comment. When he wasn't in the pub, his lorry was on its way up to Fitchley Park. We used to joke about what he was delivering."

"We?"

"Oh. Betsy and me. She works at Fitchley Park, in the kitchen," Peggy said. "I told her Bobby was stinking up the pub again, pestering Old Mrs. Trentham, and Betsy said the man never sleeps, because he's visiting the park at all hours of the night."

"I see." Ben decided to find out how much more Peggy would volunteer. "I believe I've met Betsy, briefly. The cook, Mrs. Tippett, seems like a hard mistress."

"She's a beast. You know the sort. *Frustrated*," Peggy declared, glancing toward the charge desk as if to assure herself it was still empty. "She's the reason Betsy called off our get-together. Some matter of life and death involving the soup. Can you believe it? Let the old bat work in a hospital for a day or two, and she'll know about life and death."

"I wonder who Bobby was seeing at Fitchley Park," Ben said. "If it was a company lorry, I'm surprised he wasn't discharged for wasting petrol, what with the ration."

"Oh, I know all about that," Peggy said, toying with her necklace.

She didn't strike him as an entirely reputable source, but there was no harm in listening to what she had to say. "I'd like to hear it," he said in a low, just-between-us voice, holding her gaze till she giggled.

"Why, Dr. Bones! How can I say no when you look at me that way?" She shot another glance at the charge sister's empty desk. "Lady Maggart was feathering her nest. Bobby wasn't making deliveries in the furniture lorry. He was loading up heirlooms for auction."

"What?"

"It's clever, really," Peggy said, clearly enjoying his attention. "Lord Maggart's very ill. When he dies, Lady Maggart will be out in favor of whoever inherits. Perhaps a niece or nephew. Betsy said she heard Mrs. Tippett telling Kitty that when Lady Maggart goes, it will be with her clothes, her jewelry, and nothing else. So last year, her ladyship started selling off bits and bobs. Little sculptures, first edition books, and so on. Then she started selling off beds and chests and paintings, frames and all. Bobby whisked them away to an auctioneer and brought back replacements for the larger things. Betsy heard him say he knows a man who can make a new chair look a hundred years old with nothing but Borax and a wire brush."

Ben remembered the vast kitchen with its battered, mismatched implements, and the paltry decorations in every room but Lady Maggart's. Still, the brazenness of such theft was hard to believe.

"Surely Lord Maggart would have noticed?"

"His lordship doesn't know what day of the week it is," Peggy said. "Or if it's day or night, poor lamb. His long-lost heir will get the family portraits, the silver, and some imposters to fill out the solicitor's inventory."

"So everyone but Lord Maggart knew," Ben said. If Peggy's account were true, Lady Maggart and her staff had pulled off a conspiracy of unusual scope and duration. Which might embolden them to attempt something similar after a murder. Mr. Collins had already proven himself capable of offenses that could send him to prison, and Mrs. Tippett seemed jaded enough to at least turn a blind eye. The rest of the staff, like Kitty, Betsy, and John, would do as they were told, either to get along or in hopes of future gain. But that still left Mrs. Grundy, who'd grown up at Fitchley Park and would surely object to Lady Maggart's theft.

"It seems like someone would have tipped off the police. At least anonymously," Ben said. "What about the housekeeper?"

"The Phantom?" Peggy laughed.

Ben had a sudden image of Lon Chaney on the silver screen, unmasked by Mary Philbin. He'd seen the film several times in his mid-teens, when every boy he'd known had spent their pocket money on horror spectacles like *The Phantom of the Opera*, *The Cabinet of Dr. Caligari*, or *Nosferatu*.

"Have you had a look at her?" Peggy asked, glancing toward the charge sister's empty desk again. "Wouldn't she be at home banging on a pipe organ?"

"Yes, well. Beauty, skin deep, and so on," Ben muttered, wondering if that faux gold heart was the only one Peggy had. He wanted very much to add a cutting remark, but telling her off would get him no closer to finding out who killed Bobby and why. "Do you think Mrs. Grundy was in on Lady Maggart's scheme?"

"Cor!" Peggy giggled. "Never. She's in love with the old gent, and that keeps her busy. Nurses him through the night when he has one of his spells. Kitty told Betsy her ladyship invents things for Mrs. Grundy to do. Makes up errands. Even sends her into the village. The Phantom has been sighted in the Cow Hole rose garden, the pub, and St. Gwinnodock's."

In love with Lord Maggart? Ben thought, filing it away. As with everything Peggy said, it warranted verification, but struck him as plausible. They'd grown up together, perhaps shared secrets and become affectionate, at least on her side. It wasn't outrageous for a maid to dream of being raised up by her lord and master—popular literature was clogged with such fables.

"You said you thought Mrs. Archer would be proved innocent. Who do you think killed Bobby?" Ben asked.

"His lordship. Or the Phantom. Or the two of them together," Peggy said lightly, as if choosing horses to back at the races.

"Why Lord Maggart?"

"He's terribly confused. It makes him cross. He's always threatening to hit someone with his cane," Peggy said. "If Bobby was visiting her ladyship to do more than shift furniture, and the old gent came upon them, it would be a crime of passion. Mrs. Grundy would have helped him cover it up. Or she would have done it herself to avenge him," she added, as if the idea had just occurred to her.

"Have you ever known her to be violent?" Ben asked.

"No. But she's a thief. Not a clever one like Lady Maggart. I'd secure my future, too, if I was soon to be a widow with no children and nowhere to live. But the Phantom's different. She's a low thief," Peggy said scornfully. "Those *Picturegoer* magazines on my cart? They used to be Betsy's. She donated them to the hospital rather than let the Phantom confiscate them. She does searches and seizures, like the staff girls are her prisoners. Takes away everything she calls 'corrupting.' Novels, magazines, tubes of lipstick. I don't know how Betsy can bear it."

Ben bit his lip. Of course this girl with her high cheekbones and peaches-and-cream skin would cast Mrs. Grundy as a Hollywood monster. Then again—hadn't he glimpsed an issue of *Picturegoer* in the housekeeper's sitting room?

"Dr. Bones. There's an open bed in ward two. You may sleep there tonight." The sister in charge spoke so sharply, he stood to attention like a medical student. "Miss Dean. How disappointing to find you imposing on another physician's time and patience. I shall speak to the head of the Young Ladies' Auxiliary."

"Yes, sister." Peggy hurried off, head bowed. This left no chance for goodbyes, which suited Ben. Her casual cruelty about Mrs. Grundy had left a bad taste in his mouth.

His assigned bed was one of three in the Peace ward. In a quiet little cottage hospital like St. Barnabas, three to a ward was typical; to Ben, accustomed to what seemed like warehouses stacked with patients, two silent roommates was indistinguishable from none. Dressed in threadbare hospital-issue pajamas, he climbed into bed amid a host of familiar noises: cart wheels squeaking, sisters conferring, and the endless soft patter of footfalls on linoleum. Almost as soon as he closed his eyes, he fell asleep. It was the best sleep he'd had since leaving London.

24

HIS WISHES

3 DECEMBER 1939

D uggin hadn't been surprised by Juliet's decision to scrap the divorce. In fact, he'd been so confident Juliet would agree to assist with Ethan's spy work, he'd already conceived a plan of action to ensure their "reconciliation" appeared believable to the public at large.

First she would be disentangled from giving evidence at a certain trial. As it turned out, Juliet was a far less pivotal witness than she'd imagined, perhaps because of that preemptive character assassination Duggin had described. In fact, she didn't even have to go to Plymouth and explain herself to a judge, as she'd imagined. It was both convenient and galling to learn that Ethan could handle all the details himself, simply by virtue of being her husband.

Second, Duggin wanted Ethan to move back into Belsham Manor, at least on paper. Naturally, Ethan couldn't remain in Birdswing and spy for Britain. But having his personal possessions transferred back to the house, directing his mail to Birdswing, etc., would powerfully reinforce the illusion of restored influence over Juliet and Lady Victoria.

Third, Ethan would stay in Birdswing until after New Year's

Day. He was meant to have tamed the shrew, partly for his so-called friends and their vile cause, and partly for his own comfort. Now that he had regained access to the Linton fortune, he must be seen enjoying it.

Fourth, Duggin wanted them to be seen out and about as a happy couple. He even had the cheek to suggest possible activities, all of them abhorrent: taking in the pictures, dancing at the Palais, attending church, even taking a long holiday in Plymouth and booking the honeymoon suite at the Duke of Cornwall hotel, an action the BUF would surely consider friendly. Behind Duggin's blank face lurked the heart of a sadist, apparently. Juliet hadn't minced her words.

"Mr. Duggin. I will not accompany Ethan to the cinema," she'd said. "I will not dance with him at the Palais. We will not throw a Christmas party, and we will certainly not embark on a honeymoon pantomime for fascists. We *will* attend church together, during which I promise to pray for your soul as much as mine."

"I understand," Duggin had replied, completely undeterred by her defiance. "This is why we must manage the gossip as much as we can. Your staff will be cornered and questioned in your absence. It's no use asking them to recite a script. But if you keep up appearances, the desired narrative will take shape. Whispers are inevitable. It's imperative those whispers describe cordiality at home, meals taken together, and a shared bed."

"Hah!" Juliet had cried. "Try and make me."

"Darling, he speaks of appearances only. The master bedroom is quite large...." Ethan had begun.

She'd rounded on him, too. "*Darling.* Let me be clear. When staff or villagers are about, you may indulge in certain liberties, including the judicious use of endearments. But in private, you will not call me dear, darling, sweetheart, sugar, ducky, pigsney, or dear old thing. Nor will you refer to yourself as my hero, my white knight, or—most especially—my Romeo. As for the bedroom," she'd continued, scarcely pausing to draw breath, "there's a fine old tradition of respectable couples keeping in separate rooms. I happen to know Odette Maggart has a private boudoir with a lighted mirror from New York City. If she can lock out her husband at night, so can I."

Once Duggin and Ethan had been driven away, doubtless to dream up new ways to put the screws to her, Lady Victoria had asked, "What did the lighted mirror from New York City have to do with your argument, dear?"

"I don't know. Ben described it, and I thought it sounded rather wonderful. So in the heat of the moment, I threw it in."

Mentioning Ben proved unwise. It made tears threaten, and Juliet couldn't go to pieces every time she thought of him. How could she impersonate a cheerful wife if she always looked like she'd come from a funeral? Besides, excessive weeping was the first step on the road to becoming a ninny. And if she allowed herself to become a ninny, the subsequent responsibilities wouldn't be pleasant. She'd be required to shriek over a mouse, treat the arrival of dessert like a moral crisis, and wander about looking for ordinary things to declare offensive. It didn't bear imagining.

"Oh, Mother. I know I have to hold my head up and do this properly. I just don't know how," she'd confessed.

"I do," Lady Victoria had said. "You start by finding someone else with a problem, and try to help."

LADY VICTORIA'S PLAN, which initially struck Juliet as ludicrously pat, carried her through what otherwise would have been an excruciating week. That first day, after Ben departed without eating breakfast, she'd circled Birdswing on a number of ersatz errands, desperate to happen upon him and reassure herself they were still on speaking terms. Eventually, however, word came from Mrs. Cobblepot that he'd driven Mrs. Garrigan to St. Barnabas. Juliet decided her first act would be to pop in and visit the expectant mother.

She found Mrs. Garrigan in the cottage hospital's upper day room, where ambulatory patients were encouraged to take in the "good light" and "vitalizing view," as one of the sisters explained. Since they'd never been close, Juliet didn't know how she'd be received, but Mrs. Garrigan was overjoyed to see her.

This made Juliet feel a little guilty, since she'd gone mostly to cheer herself up. As she'd expected, they still had next to nothing in common, apart from gender and marital status. But then she learned Mrs. Garrigan loved to read but was afraid of the Birdswing lending library.

The fault lay with the librarian from her school days, Miss Ida Dratt, who'd been a one-woman scourge on children. She'd discouraged the boys and girls from touching the books, lest they leave dirty fingerprints, and read aloud to them only from *Pilgrim's Progress* or the Old Testament. Such animosity toward youngsters sprang, no doubt, from the childhood tragedy of being called Ida Dratt, but it no longer mattered; Miss Dratt had retired. The new librarian, Miss Verbena Harington, was kind to everyone and more than happy to encourage young readers or discuss literature—in an appropriately soft voice, of course.

"People speak well of Miss Harington," Mrs. Garrigan said. "It's nothing against her. Only as a girl, I made a firm rule to stay away from libraries."

That caused Juliet to launch into an impassioned defense of libraries in general and Birdswing's own library in particular. No one could withstand such a logical offensive; in the end, not only was Mrs. Garrigan convinced, but so were three other patients and a ward sister. Proud of herself, Juliet promised that on her next visit, she would bring a copy of *The Yearling* for Mrs. Garrigan to try, dismissing the expectant mother's fear that such a celebrated novel was meant for cleverer people.

"Anyone who's lived a country life will get on with it beautifully," Juliet assured her as she stood up to leave. "*Picturegoer* is all very well, but Woman cannot live by printed gossip alone. When I get back to the village, I'll tell everyone you're doing well, and I'll make sure Father Cotterill mentions you in our prayers, Sunday next."

Mother was right, Juliet thought, walking out of St. Barnabas with her head held high. Birdswing was full of people riding out their own crises, some minor, some grave. She couldn't cure Mrs. Garrigan, or promise her a healthy newborn, but she could lend her a book. It wasn't much, but it was better than sitting at home wishing for a shin to kick.

Other good deeds followed. On Sunday, she brought Old Robbie soup and visited with him for an hour. On Monday, she returned to the vicarage, the site of her dressing-down, and finally had her Christmas discussion with Father Cotterill. This time it went off without a hitch. Together, they sorted through St. Mark's mothballed decorations, posted an audition notice for daytime carolers, and made a list of children in need. Juliet committed to gathering clothes, getting them sorted by age and sex, and wrapping them in festive paper.

During their search for cheerful daylight activities, a Christmas bake-off came up. Of course, Mrs. Cobblepot would enter, which meant she would win. Foregone conclusions were discouraging, so Father Cotterill suggested she be asked to judge the competition instead.

"You're often at Fenton House," he told Juliet. "Next time you drop by, will you ask her to do us the honor?"

This was the moment Juliet both wanted and dreaded: legitimate business that would shunt her Ben's way. Wednesdays were usually busy for him, particularly in the afternoon, so she chose to arrive then, expecting to have Mrs. Cobblepot all to herself.

She'd forgotten the housekeeper's obligation to the Archer twins. School was still in session, but given the boys' parental situation, they'd been excused until further notice. Gaston had taken over their general management, but the indefatigable Mrs. Cobblepot was still expected to cook their meals and wash their clothes. So when Juliet arrived on Fenton House's doorstep, it was Ben who opened the door.

"Oh. Lady Juliet. It's good to see you."

"I don't mean to impose," she said, wondering if she ought to make an excuse and flee. "Do you have a patient waiting?"

"No. Things are quiet. I may visit Mrs. Smith in a bit. Down Pigmeadow Lane."

"I heard her rheumatism is kicking up."

"Yes, it is."

She regarded him steadily, wondering if she should manufacture another comment or wait for him to say something. The wind blew harder, making her shiver.

"Cold today," Ben said.

"Yes, indeed. I don't suppose I could, er... come inside?"

"What? Of course. Sorry!" Opening the door wide, Ben stepped back to let her in. "So. How are you?" he asked, clearing his throat. "How's your mother? How's Old Robbie?"

"Oh. Well. That is to say, I'm well," she began, wondering if she still had the right to plop down on the sofa without invitation, as she'd done so many times before. Probably not. She couldn't have felt more awkward if she'd burst into a stranger's front room and proceeded to quiz him on politics and religion.

"As for Mother, I hope the winter won't prove too stressful. I didn't like the sound of her breathing the other night."

"Call me at once if you think it necessary," Ben said.

"Yes, of course. As for Old Robbie, I think he's taken a turn for the better. One doesn't get to his age without being tough as old boots."

"Glad to hear it."

"Yes." Why did she keep saying yes? If she didn't come up with something better, Ben's next question might be about Ethan, which would only make things even more awkward.

"Caleb and Micah," she said, seizing on the twins in desperation. "I'm pleased to report that several times this week, I've caught them in the act of being good citizens. When I heard Gaston was taking over, I expected him to chain them to a cellar wall. Instead, he has them painting fences, weeding gardens, and standing guard. I asked Caleb if he didn't find it painfully boring, watching for enemy agents while Gaston sat in the pub drinking a pint. He told me, 'Pain builds character.' Can you believe it?"

Ben chuckled. "You're not the only one who underestimated Gaston's ability to handle those boys. I suppose it comes from rearing two of his own. Heaven help the German who chooses our village to infiltrate. Between Gaston and the twins, the surrender will be quick and unconditional."

"This morning at Morton's, I heard their visit with Helen went well," Juliet said. "Most children would probably be traumatized for life if brought to jail for a chat with their mum. I think the boys half enjoyed it. One can only hope they appreciated the idea of justice prevailing and evildoers put away, as opposed to the convenience of finding a few dozen soul mates gathered under one roof."

This time Ben laughed outright, which to Juliet felt like a monumental victory. "Sit down," he said, as if surprised to find her still standing. "I'll put the kettle on."

It was all she could do not to burst into song. "Have you made any progress with the case?" she called.

"No, but I need to try," Ben replied from the kitchen, over the sound of a running tap. "Did the Morton's crowd know Mrs. Archer recanted her confession?"

"Naturally."

"And that Plymouth CID still refused to release her?"

"That part went without saying. The murder took place in a great house," Juliet said. "Only think how it would look for them to release her and turn up empty pockets when the press comes calling. Until they find a new suspect, they'll keep her under lock and key for bearing false witness, or whatever the technical term is."

"She'll have to answer for that," Ben agreed, returning to the front room and sitting across from her. "Hopefully the judge won't be too hard on her, given she's a widow with two sons and a business to keep afloat. But to keep her behind bars just to make themselves look more competent is reprehensible. It defies all logic. When you work through a differential diagnosis, you collect the facts and strike out the diseases that don't fit."

"I'm sure that's true. But if you hit a snag in making a final diagnosis," Juliet said, "I doubt you'll open the next day's newspaper to find yourself described as incompetent and disinterested in public safety."

"Fair point." Ben sighed. "The coroner in Plymouth is a bit cross with me, by the way. He finished Bobby's post-mortem but can't clear the case from his docket until I write up my findings. I'm not willing to do so until I'm absolutely certain there's nothing more I can do to catch Bobby's killer."

"Did he say what the post-mortem found?"

"Death by exsanguination, second to a throat wound severing the jugular and carotid," Ben said matter-of-factly. "No surprises, like poison in the system or a hidden disease. Now that Mrs. Archer's recanted, I wonder if the detectives will return to Fitchley Park anytime soon? I mentioned the crime scene photos Father Rummage took, but they treated me like I was a ludicrous amateur. Quite possibly I am, but if they're back to square one, those pictures are the only record of the crime scene. Seems like as good a place to start as any."

"Oh! The photos." Juliet stared at him. "I only just realized we never looked them over together. Perhaps they contain a smoking gun, as Dirk Diamond likes to say."

"I doubt it. You said they were unremarkable."

"To me, yes. But I should still bring them round for your opinion, when I'm in the village next. Two heads are better than one." If Juliet had felt like singing before, she now felt an aria coming on. Possibly a light opera.

"When you're in the village next?" Ben look surprised. "I know things have been—disrupted, so to speak, due to your, er, happy news. But tomorrow is the day we give evidence. I thought we'd take the train to Plymouth together."

Juliet didn't know how to answer. Rather, she knew what she was meant to say. Duggin had been very firm on that point. Though treason proceedings were kept from the public, word of her change in stance would still reach those who had ears to hear. It always did. But knowing her duty didn't make doing it any easier.

"I won't be giving evidence," she said quietly.

"What?"

"It shan't affect the verdict. The defense council has already constructed an opposing narrative to render my testimony unreliable," she said. "They'll say I was in love with—you know. That I was jealous and hysterical, and now I'm out for revenge."

"How do you know what the defense will say?" He sounded gobsmacked.

Juliet cringed. She'd done exactly what Duggin had warned against—inserted privileged details that couldn't be explained.

"Well, it's obvious, isn't it? You don't have to be Dr. Carl Jung to work out what the defense's position will be," she said, hoping the celebrated doctor would forgive her for dropping his good name into her web of lies. "Why should I go and be insulted when your evidence will be more than sufficient to convict them?"

"You've been champing at the bit to have your say," Ben snapped, a flush rising from under his collar. "Two weeks ago, you were practicing a monologue about English patriotism in the mirror. I threatened to inject you with a sedative."

"Don't let's quarrel over it," she pleaded. "I changed my mind. Isn't that a woman's prerogative? And just because I won't give evidence, it doesn't mean the outcome is endangered. I'm certain of it."

Ben stared at her. "Your husband," he said at last, in a tone he'd never used with her. "He objected, didn't he?"

"Yes."

"Why?"

"He—he doesn't approve."

"*Why?*"

"He thinks the courts are unfair. That some people are being persecuted for their political views," Juliet said. Those were the phrases Duggin had supplied. "I don't agree. Of course I don't agree. But at the end of the day, Ethan is my husband, and I must accede to his wishes."

Ben's flush turned scarlet. He stood up. "I just remembered. I said I'd visit Mrs. Smith a quarter-hour ago. She'll be wondering. I'd better go."

"But—tea. What about tea?" Juliet asked. On cue, the kettle started to whistle.

"Help yourself. If Ethan doesn't object," Ben said contemptuously. Then he yanked his hat and coat off the rack and strode out, leaving her sitting alone in his front room.

25

THE ESPECIAL GENIUS OF MONSIEUR BAPTISTE

4 DECEMBER 1939

I n the winter, Victoria Linton liked to rise early. Some mornings she sat in front of her electric fire reading; other mornings she went down to the kitchen, where bread for lunch and dinner was already baking, and shared a pot of coffee with the cook. Since the illness that had killed her husband and weakened her heart, she found cold-weather forays into the village proper more tiring than she cared to admit. Fortunately, her cook—a lifelong friend named Ruth—was a lively conversationalist more than capable of passing along the latest. As chairwoman of the Council and Birdswing's chief citizen, Victoria considered it her duty to know what went on. Strictly the facts, with a minimum of editorializing. Of course Juliet was always brimming with news, but her version of events was usually filtered through the concern *du jour*. For a week after her involvement in a young girl's rescue, Juliet had been unable to relate anything about current events without connecting it to Dr. Bones and his piercing blue eyes.

After lunch and bit of embroidery, Victoria sometimes grew drowsy. Sometime around two, she often returned to her bed for a nap. It allowed her to replenish her strength and gave her the stamina to stay up late with Juliet, who liked a long conversation after listening to a favorite wireless program like *It's That Man Again*.

She was on her way upstairs when she heard raised voices. As usual, it was Juliet and Ethan. Duggin's instructions for them to "keep up appearances" at home—to behave like lovebirds in view or earshot of the staff—had clearly fallen on deaf ears.

"I only said—"

"I don't care. I'm going to bed, and I'm locking the door," Juliet shouted. "What a curse it is, never to have a moment to oneself!"

Victoria found Ethan standing beside the staircase, hand resting on the lintel. He was wearing one of his ensembles she secretly thought of as "The Master Rides to Hound," which meant a woolen jumper, knee-patch breeches, and black riding boots topped with bands of russet leather. He looked like a berk, but an upper crust berk, his jacket mended in spots, his boots down-at-heel. Only the aristocracy would dare to wear clothes until they fell to rags; the *bourgeoisie* would die of shame.

"What happened, Ethan?"

"I'll be deuced if I know. I think I said hello."

"It had to be more than that."

"It wasn't," he said, and she believed him. Ethan was an accomplished liar, but mostly about the big things—his family history, his bank account, etc. Lying about a remark he'd made two minutes ago wasn't grand enough to be worth his while. "I'm concerned about her demeanor."

"She's been weepy lately, which is understandable, given the circumstances."

"Not weepy. Gutted," he said with conviction. "If I knock on her door, it'll be curtains. I don't suppose you could go up and have a look?"

"Of course." Victoria started up the stairs and then paused, looking back at him over her shoulder. "Congratulations on keeping in character. One who didn't know any better would imagine you genuinely care."

Ethan smiled wryly, looked at his feet, and for once had the decency to say nothing.

———

"Go AWAY," Juliet called through the door when Victoria knocked. "'When beggars die, there are no comets seen.'"

"Yes, well, I'm not sure what *Julius Caesar* has to do with it, but some believe a quote from Shakespeare is always appropriate," Victoria said. "Please let me in. I'll fret endlessly until you do."

She waited. After a moment, the lock rattled and the door opened.

Juliet was not weeping, which was a relief. Still, Ethan had hit the mark. Gutted was right.

"Thank you, dear," she said as she entered. "What's happened between you and Dr. Bones?"

"How do you know it's him?"

"I begin to be psychic in my old age. Also, I didn't like how he left it, the morning after the dinner party."

"He's lost all respect for me." Juliet heaved herself onto her four-poster, which had been in the Linton family for many years. It was sturdy enough to withstand such a blow, which would have flattened ordinary beds. That was fortunate, as she'd acquired the habit of throwing herself down during her melodramatic teenage years and now continued it into her semimelodramatic adulthood.

"I told him I wouldn't give evidence. He asked why, so of course I said Ethan. Now he thinks I'm a ninny."

"I doubt that very much. He's probably just bewildered by

what seems like a hundred-and-eighty degree change of direction," Victoria said. "You've been on fire to enter that courtroom and say your piece ever since the arrest. To suddenly announce, 'Never mind,' would strike anyone as bizarre. Particularly a close friend."

"Friend," Juliet repeated bitterly. She lay on her back staring up at the four-poster's canopy. "Not anymore. Ethan's destroyed everything I ever wanted, including my connection to the only person worth talking to in this godforsaken place."

"Small wonder you feel like a dying beggar," Victoria said, fighting a smile. "But I must say you're bearing up beautifully. I expected to find you sobbing inconsolably."

"I've issued a moratorium on sobbing. It doesn't do any good."

"Sometimes it does. Bottling up sadness is like borrowing money with interest. In the end, the bill still comes due, only larger. Do you know what I think?"

"I should have gone to Clarion Academy and learned how to catch a respectable husband?" Juliet asked with still greater bitterness, if such a thing was possible.

"I think you need a change. I've embarked on a secret project," Victoria said. "It began a few weeks ago. To be honest, I haven't covered my tracks very well, and I've kept expecting you to confront me. But unless you'd care to confess now, I think it's possible I've succeeded in keeping you in the dark."

"Dark is exactly right. Dark as the grave." Juliet sat up suddenly. "Wait. Does it have to do with secondhand clothes for the poor? If it does, I had an inkling. I just chose to ignore it, because I'm unforgivably self-absorbed."

"It has to do with the coming clothes ration," Victoria said. "I know you haven't taken much interest, but I've thought about it a great deal. Tell me, darling. Do you trust me?"

"What? Of course I trust you."

"I mean deep down. Where the sole meets the soil. Do you believe I have nothing but your happiness at heart?"

Juliet blinked at her. "You know I do."

"Then allow me to reveal what I've been up to. And do try to keep an open mind."

MONSIEUR BAPTISTE ARRIVED the next day with his retinue: one apprentice, two assistants, and three chests that looked like props from a magician's act. The slender Frenchman was of indeterminate age, with dyed black hair, powdered cheeks, and a drawn-in beauty mark at the corner of his mouth. His heeled shoes, mint green, recalled an age when French aristocrats had worn long curled wigs and twice the lace of their female counterparts. In his sumptuous studio, these qualities seemed precisely right. In Belsham Manor, in midmorning's full light, he looked like an elf who'd gotten lost on the way to the fairy pool.

"The train was no good. A journey of horror," he said by way of introduction. Victoria glanced at Juliet for reaction. English was Monsieur Baptiste's second or third language, but he'd mastered the dialect her daughter spoke: hyperbole.

"Horror? I'm sorry to hear that," Juliet said. "I usually find the train from Plymouth quite relaxing. I'm Juliet Linton, by the way. Linton-Bolivar, as it were."

"You think I don't know who you are? Your soul has cried out to me over many miles," Monsieur Baptiste replied so smoothly, Victoria suspected he said it to every new client. "Nothing wounds me more than to see a stupendous woman dressed in sackcloth and ashes. Except a train that does not serve the vintage I desire. And has the nerve to offer me coffee instead with the excuse it is breakfast time."

"Stupendous? Well. I appreciate that," Juliet said, sounding as if she might fling a vase at his head. "But I assure you, my clothes are practical, comfortable, and the furthest thing from sackcloth and ashes."

"So you say." Monsieur Baptiste lifted one shoulder, the quintessential French expression of indifference. "Is there someone who can direct my staff to Mademoiselle's boudoir? They must unpack the trunks before we begin."

"Dinah." Victoria signaled the girl, who looked slightly more interested than usual. Victoria, who had caught her messing about with one of her frocks, had asked the maid if she was drawn to fashion, but Dinah had been too mortified to say.

"Yes, milady." She started upstairs. Monsieur Baptiste's retinue took up their chests and followed.

"It will take them some time. You will offer me a drop of red, I pray?" the fashion designer asked Victoria. "It needn't be French. Italian will suffice."

She suspected his affectations were entirely calculated, but with artistic types it was impossible to be sure. During her previous consultations with Monsieur Baptiste, he'd sipped wine throughout their exploration of sketches, fabric swatches, and the direction wartime fashion was likely to take. Why should the fitting process be any different?

They retired to the parlor to open a bottle of Bordeaux. Unsurprisingly, the uncorking was followed by the appearance of Ethan, who had been warned to make himself scarce.

"Why, isn't this festive," he declared.

"Get out," Juliet said.

"Ju, dear. You know I have a knack for these things."

Monsieur Baptiste, who'd been swirling the wine in his glass, turned in his chair. "A knack? Is that what you said, sir?"

Ethan nodded immodestly.

"This may be," the designer said in a tone of deep skepticism. "But whatever gifts you may possess, they are nothing to the especial genius of Monsieur Baptiste. Begone."

It took all of Victoria's self-control not to burst out laughing as Ethan was forced to retreat, denied both Bordeaux and a chance to play style connoisseur.

Monsieur Baptiste tasted the wine. Permitting himself a small shudder of discontent, he turned to address Juliet. "*Mon chéri.* A woman of your magnificence is like an elephant. Perhaps a rhinoceros. You have seen this marvelous beast? A rhinoceros does not obey commands, even from one such as Monsieur Baptiste. It will trample the poor man before he can finish this sour swill."

Victoria, who had spent twenty-odd years watching her daughter's verbal eccentricities confound other people, did her best to commit Juliet's expression to memory. She might never see such perplexity on her face again.

"I'm... a rhinoceros?" Juliet repeated.

"Yes, of course. If I try to order you about, you will crush me," Monsieur Baptiste said, taking another sip. "So I will not say 'Juliet, do this' or 'Juliet, do that.' I know you distrust fashion. How could you not? None of it was conceived with you in mind. Until today." He smiled. "So instead of killing this poor man choking on his wine, will you allow me to prove myself? I have but one mission in life. The draping of stupendous women."

Juliet shot Victoria a glance. For a moment, she feared all was lost.

Then her daughter took a deep breath and said, "Very well. But if you make me look foolish, I won't wear a stitch of it."

"But of course." Rising, Monsieur Baptiste picked up not only his glass, but the bottle of Bordeaux. "Today I am Father Christmas. Let us go upstairs and see what gifts my tiny reindeer have brought."

As a mother, it would have been the easiest thing in the world for Victoria to shoehorn Juliet into a gown, zip the zippers, button the buttons, and parade her before Monsieur Baptiste for inspection. As a tactician with a long-term goal, however, she knew the perils of taking the easiest route. Therefore, when the fitting began, she took a seat, accepted a cup of tea from Bertha, and allowed events to unfold with pretended neutrality.

"I dislike changing screens," Monsieur Baptiste declared the moment they entered Juliet's bedroom. "Take that away and bring me a mirror. Full-length."

"Where will I change," Juliet asked in a strangled voice, "without a changing screen?"

"The next room over. The moon. I don't care," the designer said, refilling his wine glass. "My apprentice will give you a frock to try. That one"—he pointed at Dinah—"will help you into it. The rhinoceros must have a monkey or the fine fabrics will tear."

"I've embraced my new identity as a rhinoceros," Juliet said. "But I really must draw the line at referring to Dinah or anyone else as a monkey. In English, the parallel is insulting."

"Is insulting in French, too." Monsieur Baptiste issued another one-shoulder shrug.

"I don't mind," Dinah said in a loud voice. "I'm happy to help."

Monsieur Baptiste and his retinue looked startled. So did Juliet. Victoria, who'd prearranged Dinah's selection and declaration of assent, sipped her tea. High time the girl did something besides dust poorly, serve awkwardly, and brood about the son she'd put up for adoption.

The first dress, a scarlet gown made of silk, was an ambitious choice, but Juliet, being afraid of women's clothing, mistook its simplicity for ease of wear. She and Dinah disappeared into the adjacent room for so long, Victoria began to fear one or both had gone out a window. Then Dinah opened the door, and Juliet slunk in.

"I bloody well know how I look. Ridiculous," she spat. Her cheeks were almost as red as the dress. "My hair's wrong. It's always wrong. And I haven't any stockings or shoes."

Monsieur Baptiste clapped his hands. An assistant hurried forth bearing a shoe box. Juliet scowled.

"Whatever glass slipper you have in there, I'm sure I couldn't cram a toe in."

"Glass slipper. Hah! Do you think I don't know a stupendous foot requires a stupendous shoe?" Monsieur Baptiste retorted, leaving out the fact Victoria had told him the correct size. "Put on the shoes, stand before the mirror, and we shall see."

Juliet did as she was bid. Then Monsieur Baptiste took over, pinning, tutting, and spot-checking her limbs with measuring tape.

"Now it needs only a few minor adjustments, which will take me less than a week. Well. It will take them less than a week," he corrected, nodding at his retinue. "How fortunate you have no breasts. The fabric hangs just so."

Victoria was tempted to issue a rebuttal. Her daughter certainly did have breasts, they were simply the teacup sort, or a bit less. But why argue when the Frenchman's view of the big picture was correct? In the scarlet gown, she cut a flawless silhouette.

"But my *hair*," Juliet wailed. "And I thought the dress would look prettier."

"Darling, don't fret about your hair," Victoria said, joining her daughter in front of the mirror. "I'll discuss the possibilities with you after the fitting. As for the dress, it isn't meant to be pretty. A dress with a fancy pattern or elaborate frills would wear *you*. Every time you entered a room, people would see the dress first and you second. But in this dress—look."

Heaving a sigh, Juliet glared at herself in the full-length mirror.

"I see a graceful neck. A trim torso. Not an iota of surplus flesh to spoil the line," Victoria said. "Strong arms. Long legs. In other words, I see you first and the dress second. Which is the entire point."

After that, the fitting began to flow like water. Many of Monsieur Baptiste's offerings were rejected. Many more were accepted and pinned up for final alterations. Throughout the process, the designer kept up a running commentary, enlivened by a second bottle of the Bordeaux he so disliked.

"The secret is in the details. Folds and gathers," he said. "Ruched waists and cascading ruffles. A matching wrap for that one, yes?"

"Yes," Juliet and Dinah said in unison.

"And maybe a brooch," Dinah added. Instantly she looked worried that she might have overstepped herself, so Victoria smiled reassuringly.

Definitely an interest in fashion, she thought.

"The crisscross is evergreen," Monsieur Baptiste declared as Juliet modeled the final dress. "Ration or no ration, it will always be in style. And see how it wraps? A tree trunk would have a waist in this dress. More shoes!" He clapped his hands again.

"I explained that you're far too busy to tolerate uncomfortable shoes," Victoria told Juliet as the assistants brought forth more offerings. "People call those bar shoes, but I prefer the American term: Mary Janes. And no, they're not the usual choice with a frock these days. But every woman must cultivate an individual style. It's no use buying perfect shoes you'll never wear. Imperfect flats, worn with *élan*, are a far better choice."

After the dresses came skirts, blouses, and variations on a certain sartorial item that made Juliet squeal.

"Trousers! I hardly dared hope."

"Wide-leg," Monsieur Baptiste said proudly, as if he'd invented the style. "Do you know this shameless woman? Katharine Hepburn? In my trousers, you will be even more shameless."

"I should hope so," Juliet said, hurrying out of the room with Dinah to try them on. She returned in less than five minutes wearing her favorite pair. "Look, Mother. They fit like a dream. But I still have grave reservations about my hair."

"This is why God invented hats," Monsieur Baptiste said. Two bottles of wine had affected him the way two cups of water affected Victoria, which was to say, not at all, apart from a sudden need for the W.C.

"My body rejects the poison. Now I must inspect your facilities. Let us hope they are not too English. You will direct me," he told Bertha. To an assistant, he said, "The cloches. Why aren't you presenting them? Did I not say 'hat?'"

"Mother," Juliet said, frowning as the assistant came toward her with a plain, camel-colored felt hat. "Even I know those are out of style. You wouldn't be caught dead in one. It looks like a bucket."

"Sit down, darling. Dinah," Victoria said, "please brush out my daughter's hair and show her how a cloche is to be worn."

Style had indeed left the humble cloche behind. Currently, the trend was a homburg, shako, or some derivation of the sailor. Most had ribbons or feathers or lace net, and all were meant to be pinned askew. Victoria had faith in many things, but she believed Juliet would be willing to go to such a daily effort as much as she believed in the Tooth Fairy.

Dinah did as much with Juliet's limp brown hair as a brush

could do. Then she placed the cloche on her head, stepped back, examined Juliet critically, and said, "No."

"What?"

"It's too small. And it doesn't suit the shape of her ladyship's face," Dinah said. She gave Victoria a furtive look. "If I'm not speaking out of turn, milady."

"Not at all." Victoria tried to hide her astonishment, lest Dinah mistake it for censure. "By all means, try the others."

"It won't work," Juliet said. "I'm cursed when it comes to hats."

"Tosh. Be quiet. This is all to your benefit," Victoria said.

Visibly emboldened, Dinah picked through the hats, tried a few on her subject, and settled on one with minimal trimming. "French blue," she said, stepping back to admire her choice.

"Is it meant to be pulled down so far?" Juliet reached for the brim.

"Don't touch that. Look in the mirror first," Victoria said.

"Good heavens. That isn't too terrible." Juliet smiled at herself. "It does cover a multitude of sins. Even on my most windswept days, I could pop this on and conceal the worst. But isn't it hopelessly old-fashioned?"

"My darling, you've worn whatever you pleased since you were old enough to choose your own clothes," Victoria said. "If you turned into a slave to fashion now, it would break my heart. And as I said—every woman must cultivate her own individual style."

At the end of the fitting, Monsieur Baptiste looked on happily as his retinue packed things up. "Especial genius," he declared and grinned, apparently finding his own praise the highest possible compliment. "Give me five days to complete the work. Five days, *mon chéri*, and the world will appreciate your magnificence as I do."

"Mother, this isn't a change of wardrobe, it's a trousseau,"

Juliet told Victoria after the designer and his staff had gone. "You must have paid a fortune for Monsieur Baptiste's expertise. Not to mention the fabric. And at Christmastime, too. How on earth did you manage it?"

"I didn't start after this business with Ethan. I began after the fête," Victoria said, referring to a day she knew Juliet would've preferred to forget. "Ordinarily I would have been content to let you manage your own wardrobe. But the ration will begin soon, and when it does, we won't be permitted to place large orders or buy out the shops. Having the means to pay won't matter. It'll be down to a voucher or a lottery. If I was going to buy in quantity, it was either now or wait out the war." Uncertain how to interpret her daughter's expression, she continued, "I know that rubbish about the silk purse and the sow's ear wounded you. And when I promised never to force my fashion choices on you, I meant it, truly. But times have changed, and I broke my word. Do you forgive me?"

"Forgive you?" Juliet threw herself into Victoria's arms. "I've never been more grateful to you in the whole of my life."

No mother heard a statement like that as often as she deserved, so rather than move on to a discussion of hair and makeup, Victoria basked in the moment. It would all come together eventually. Or it wouldn't, depending on whether or not her daughter was willing to learn such feminine arts. Maybe Dinah could help with that. There was still such a thing as a lady's maid, though the position was vanishing fast.

And who can say? Victoria thought. *Perhaps curls and hairpins and rouge are unnecessary. Perhaps a certain young man who couldn't stop saying "Jolly good" has already begun seeing Ju in a new light.*

26

THE FURNITURE SCHEME

12 DECEMBER 1939

"Done and dusted!" Gaston announced when Ben, napkin in hand, opened his front door. The special constable pushed past him as if invited, striding into the kitchen where his sister had just sat down to breakfast. "Helen's out of the hoosegow!"

"The what?" Ben said.

"Hoosegow, my boy," Gaston said, grinning. "One of Dirk Diamond's words. The poky. The clink. Splendid American terms for jail."

Ben thought perhaps "the clink" originated closer to home, but that was hardly the point. "Great news. Do you mean to say Plymouth CID now accepts her confession as false?"

"Naturally." Gaston put on his "knowing" look, again bringing to mind a discombobulated fish. "They've arrested the true villain, after all."

"Oh!" Mrs. Cobblepot leapt up. For a large woman, she was remarkably nimble, especially when energized by gossip. "Sit yourself down, Clarence. Would you like biscuits with your tea?"

"I would indeed." Seating himself at the kitchen table, he told Ben magnanimously, "Allow me to put you in the picture."

Ben returned to his place. It was no use asking Gaston to
skip to the point. For him, the point was unspooling the events
at a leisurely pace and bringing his listeners to the brink of
anticipation or exasperation—either appeared to suit him
equally well.

"From the beginning, I knew something unwholesome was
afoot in Fitchley Park...."

Ben, who'd been buttering his toast, went back to it. If they
were retracing their investigative steps to the day of the murder,
and all the nonexistent forebodings and inklings Gaston would
now pretend he'd had, it might be lunchtime before the guilty
party was revealed. Mrs. Cobblepot, also inured to her brother's
narrative style, went about pouring tea. By the time she was
back in her chair, he was coming round to the point at last.

"... an aura of conspiracy, as I believe I told Dr. Bones,"
Gaston said. "Who else could compel the staff to assist in
covering up a murder than the butler?"

"Mr. Collins?" To Ben, it sounded reasonable enough. "I knew
he had a hand in matters. But I stopped thinking of him as a prime
suspect after someone accounted for his whereabouts during the
murder. I suppose she was lying," he said, recalling Kitty had
started their interview by deducting five years from her age. "Her
credibility did leave something wanting. Why did Collins do it?"

"Don't try and make me get ahead of myself." Gaston sipped
his tea. "Nothing good ever came of getting ahead of one's self."
In an apparent effort to prove this, he took a deep breath and
cleared his throat unhurriedly before going on. "It's actually a
story of theft gone wrong."

"Do you mean Lady Maggart's theft? The way she was
selecting family heirlooms for auction and replacing them on
the cheap?" Ben asked.

The special constable gave a startled *chuff*. "What? How did you know about the furniture? Have you been holding out on me?"

"Not at all. I heard a rumor, that's all. But I've been too busy with patients and, er, other things to follow up." Ben felt a touch embarrassed. Those other things had, of course, been his highly unsatisfactory conversation with Lady Juliet and a subsequent trip to the Sheared Sheep. All in all, the pub was a friendlier place these days, and a night away from the wireless and his charts should have been pleasant. In reality, he'd been too angry with Lady Juliet over her bizarre capitulation to Ethan to do what he came to do—make a friend. Instead, he'd done a slow burn over two pints and left without saying much of anything to anybody.

"Tell us," Mrs. Cobblepot pleaded. "I don't even know who Mr. Collins is, and I'm on tenterhooks. Tell us!"

"He's the butler, as I said, and quite vain," Gaston replied. "I thought he was part of the domestic gentility, as it were—one of those blokes whose dad was a valet, and his dad before him, and so on and so forth, straight back to the Plantagenets. But when the detectives put the handcuffs on him, he bawled bloody murder like a stevedore shorted his wages." He took another sip of tea. "Haven't heard swearing like that since I was in the trenches."

"How did his sister handle his arrest?" Ben asked.

"Mrs. Tippett was shocked, of course. Would have fallen to her knees when they led him out, I think, if not for the rector. He comforted her. Led her back to St. Gwinnodock's to pray."

"Sounds like she's softened on the God-botherer. So she wasn't named as part of the conspiracy?"

"No. Her and her brother didn't get on well enough for him to include her, apparently." Gaston reached for the teapot to refill his cup, became aware of his own sister's threatening stare, and gave in. "Right. Here's the bare bones, if you must have them.

"It was all to do with auctioning baronial heirlooms and replacing them with imposters. But it wasn't Lady Maggart's idea," Gaston said, gaze flicking to Ben. "Mr. Collins cooked up the scheme with Bobby. Turns out the lorry Bobby drove belonged to a company connected to dodgy antiques dealers. They knew Lord Maggart was too ill to have much of an idea what was happening. They banished him to the ground floor. Told him he was too weak for the stairs, even though he can manage them fine. It's his head that soft, not his limbs.

"At any rate," Gaston continued, "Mr. Collins told Lady Maggart he'd cut her in if she turned a blind eye. She denies it, of course. She says she thought the items were being sent off for appraisal and cleaning, then returned in due course. As if anyone sends out a four-poster for cleaning." He chuckled. "The staff was in the dark, too. Mr. Collins put it about that the heir to Fitchley Park, Lord Maggart's cousin, wanted to take early possession of certain items. He said Lady Maggart was insulted by the process, as she was entitled to the house and all it contained for as long as her husband lived. So the staff pretended not to notice the disappearing items or the occasional inferior copy that came back.

"Then Bobby did what low criminals do. He let greed over-take him," Gaston said, probably appropriating Dirk Diamond's wisdom again. "He told Mr. Collins that since he was doing most of the work and taking most of the risk, they should split the profit eighty-twenty rather than fifty-fifty."

"Sounds like the sort of renegotiation that ends in a cut throat," Ben said. He was so engrossed, he'd neglected his toast and tea, both of which had gone cold. "Did you happen to notice if Mr. Collins is left-handed?"

"He opens doors with his right," Gaston said. "Otherwise, I

couldn't say. But I can say Mr. Collins is a hot-tempered man. He took a knife from the kitchen and killed Bobby in a fit of passion. Then he set about covering his tracks."

"Seems like it would have been easier to get rid of the body than to strip it naked and put it in a disused room," Ben said.

"Aye. But according to my sources," Gaston said, clearly meaning Private Dick Academy, "it's a typical failing of the criminal class to commit murder without any thought for what comes next. Most killers act on impulse, never troubling to plan what they'll do after the deed itself, so concealment is carried out in a state of terror."

"I suppose so." Ben thought of the boot boy's wheelbarrow. If they'd loaded up clothes for burning in the woods, why not a body? "You said Mr. Collins went back to his roots, so to speak, raging against the detectives when they took him into custody. How much did he confess before he turned belligerent?"

"None of it." Gaston seemed surprised by Ben's question. "I could hear him howling about his innocence from the back of the car as they took him away."

"Then how did this all come about, Clarence?" Mrs. Cobblepot said. "How did the police reckon the butler did it? Besides that phrase, I mean."

He wagged a finger at her. "You pushed me to get ahead of myself. Didn't I tell you nothing good ever comes of that?" To punish her, he picked up the teapot and poured that second cup with exaggerated slowness.

"Now," he said after taking a sip. "As I mentioned at the beginning, a conspiracy was afoot. But a chain is only as strong as its weakest link. Mr. Collins ordered Kitty and John—the boot boy—to help him. John is delicate and simple. He went to the Cow Hole and told Mrs. Richwine he needed to report a murder. Bobby's murder. Poor lad said he couldn't bear the weight of it another day."

Ben winced. "Really? I met him, you know. He seemed rather desperately shy. I can't imagine him keeping mum for so many days and then striking out to the village to confess."

"You know the mind of a murderer, do you?" Gaston asked. "You can fathom what it's like to be intimidated, and take part in the cover-up, and endure the simmering guilt till it boils over?" He shook his head. "The wee daft lad cracked, and I'm glad of it, because it's caught out Mr. Collins and set Helen free. I just hope he doesn't have too bad a time of it."

"Who? Collins?"

"No. I hope he has a very bad time of it, indeed. *John*," Gaston replied, as if Ben were the simple one. "He's behind bars in Plymouth, as well as Collins. Kitty, too. With any luck, the courts will deal gently with them. But the poor lad, being feeble-minded, will have a hard row to hoe."

"I imagine he will." It was probably too much for Ben to hope the guards would be gentle with a young man like John. More likely, they would deal gingerly with the intimidating detainees and terrorize the meek ones.

"I should ring them and schedule a visit. Since John lives in Barking, I'm not out of bounds to consider him a patient. Perhaps if someone in authority knows they'll have to answer for John's welfare, they won't behave too badly."

"Good idea," Mrs. Cobblepot said. "But what about Lady Maggart? Will she be arrested?"

"She's under house arrest," Gaston said. "I'm not sure what comes next. She'll be made to answer for the value of the items sold, I reckon. Can't imagine Lord Maggart's heir will overlook a missing chunk of inheritance. But why are you so po-faced, Dr. Bones? Are you fretting because you didn't get to play Sherlock Holmes?"

"Not in the least. I need to keep up with my actual duties," he replied, thinking of Mrs. Garrigan, who was making a rapid recovery. "So the Bobby Archer case is closed, and the butler did it. Remarkable. Lady Juliet will be overjoyed."

"You should be the one to tell her," Mrs. Cobblepot said, rising to busy herself at the sink. "Ring her up."

"Or go by the manor," Gaston suggested. "Look in on Old Robbie. Ask after Lady Victoria's heart, er, thingy. Plenty of reasons not to avoid the place. Nothing good ever came from avoiding a place."

Ben lifted both eyebrows, but neither of them saw it. Back turned, Mrs. Cobblepot scrubbed a convenient patch of filth. Gaston's gaze wandered along the floor and up a wall in a successful effort not to look Ben in the eye.

He cleared his throat. Though his irritation with Lady Juliet persisted, and threatened to grow stronger if he allowed himself to brood on it, a few days' space had done him good.

"I suppose I've seemed a bit cross with her," he said. "But I was just, er, caught up in taking care of my patients. And going to Plymouth, if you'll recall. To do that thing we should all have been more discreet about."

During Ben's appearance in court, he'd been cautioned against discussing the trial and scolded as Birdswing's representative for what the judge had called "an unpatriotic display of curiosity and gossip." It would have been no good to explain about the birds singing and all that. Therefore, Ben had taken his lumps with good grace, promising to discourage his fellow villagers from speaking openly of the trial until the war was over.

"I'm glad to hear you weren't actually cross," Mrs. Cobblepot said, still scrubbing industriously. "But in my experience, a perceived falling out can be every bit as painful as the genuine article."

"It's like I told the lads," Gaston said, gaze still halfway up a wall and holding. "Choose your words carefully, or your words will choose you."

That made no sense whatsoever, as far as Ben was concerned, but he had no intention of pursuing Gaston's mangled meaning down the rabbit hole. "Thank you both for your advice," he said, standing. "I know it's kindly meant. I also know that for a number of years, I've conducted my own affairs with some success, on balance. Now, if you'll excuse me, I'm off."

"Where to?" Mrs. Cobblepot sounded startled.

"Belsham Manor."

27
___

AN OPEN DOOR

Ben had set off with the idea of simply telling Lady Juliet about Mr. Collins's arrest. That would break the ice, and then he could revert to his usual posture of interjecting sardonic remarks as she reacted. It felt like an absurdly long time since he'd heard her bemoan a failure, crow over a victory, or insult the village of Barking, and this would allow her to do all three.

But as he drove from Birdswing proper to Belsham Manor, he remembered that Ethan would probably be knocking about. The Sheared Sheep wouldn't open for another few hours, after all. The man was quite likely to question why Ben hadn't simply picked up the phone, perhaps followed by some insinuation about the best man winning, et cetera. Ben's hand had only just stopped aching, and he didn't want to injure it again.

He'll try to paint me as jealous, which is outrageous, he thought. *It's the principle of the matter. A woman like Lady Juliet shouldn't allow a bounder to dictate terms to her. Marriage doesn't enter into it, not when justice is at stake. When we said our vows, Penny and I left out the bit about "obey." I thought women went off that old chestnut around the time of Jack the Ripper.*

As he reached the manor, a plausible excuse for his visit finally occurred to him. Old Robbie was finally on the mend, so that wouldn't wash, and if he turned up out of nowhere to quiz Lady Victoria about her heart trouble, she'd think him mad. But those photos of the Bobby Archer crime scene were still in Lady Juliet's possession. Surely it was his duty as a good citizen to collect the pictures, review them, and turn them in to the authorities.

Bertha answered his knock at the door. Once again, she wore her feminized chauffeur uniform.

"Hallo, Bertha. Still at your apprenticeship, eh?"

"Yes, sir." She took his hat and coat. "Well, not today, as it happens, but I like to wear this. Quite flash. Does your leg trouble you?" she added, meaning his cane.

"No more than usual. December is hard on the joints, that's all. I can show myself in. I know the way." Giving her a pleasant nod, Ben headed for the parlor. He hoped to find Lady Juliet alone and Ethan elsewhere. Instead, he found Lady Victoria sitting by the window. The book on her lap was closed, and she was staring into space.

"Sorry. Terribly rude of me to blunder in," he said, feeling a fool.

"Dr. Bones! It's lovely to see you." Lady Victoria's smile was too brilliant to be feigned. "And never mind the apologies, you're always welcome. To what do we owe the honor?"

"Lady Juliet has some photos taken by Father Rummage on the day of Bobby's murder," Ben said. "She was kind enough to develop them and look them over. I've come to collect them at last."

"Of course." Rising, Lady Victoria put aside her book and reading glasses. "Only Juliet is engaged at the moment. I'm not sure how long she'll be...."

Ben felt the fool all over again. He'd walked out on their last conversation, avoided her for days, and finally deigned to turn up in his own good time, with an excuse that didn't involve the word "sorry." How egocentric, assuming Lady Juliet would rush out to see him. Perhaps she was enjoying a late breakfast with Ethan. Or a champagne brunch. In bed.

"She'll be delighted to see you," Lady Victoria continued. As always, she sounded gracious, but Ben thought he detected some sort of hesitation. "I realize you're a busy man, but you've come all this way, and there's the petrol to consider, isn't there? Let me ring for tea. We can discuss the new du Maurier, if you've read it. She isn't a native Cornishwoman, but she's viewed as something of a favorite daughter, all the same."

"Ah. Well. That's very kind." Ben cleared his throat. "But I shouldn't like putting you to any trouble. Perhaps when Lady Juliet's in the village next, she could leave the photos with Mrs. Cobblepot?"

"That would be no trouble. Only—" Lady Victoria twisted her hands. "Do you know? I think she left them in the dining room. Can you believe it? She had them in a manila envelope, very neatly labeled with the word 'confidential' written in black ink, and she left them on the table. I can't think why. Perhaps she meant to pop by Fenton House with them later. Shall we go collect them?"

Ben stared at her. It didn't trouble him that she was obviously lying. Polite people lied all the time, including him. His recent effort to keep Mrs. Garrigan calm on the way to St. Barnabas had only solidified his belief that while the truth may set you free, a good lie could save your life. No, what troubled him was the lie's nakedness and her apparent desperation for him to believe it.

"I can fetch them myself," he said, wondering if that's what he was meant to say next.

"No, no, we'll walk together. It seems like ages since we've spoken." Lady Victoria took his arm and slipped hers in it, as if they might stroll down a moonlit beach. "They say on the wireless that bacon, butter, and sugar will be rationed first. Thank goodness Mr. Morton started his scheme in October. We've all grown accustomed to buying what we're permitted according to his ledger. Do you suppose the Ministry of Food will force every community to use ration books? I don't see why we should, when we have a perfectly good system already in place. Why, ARP Warden Gaston could simply ask your neighbor, Mrs. Parry, to submit a weekly report on who served what for dinner. She *does* know these things...."

And so Lady Victoria went on, without pause and completely out of character, until they reached the dining room. Ben wasn't at all surprised to find it spotless, with no trace of a manila envelope labeled "confidential."

"Oh, dear. I think the maids have already been through," she said, circling the table as if double-checking for something that clearly wasn't there. "Perhaps someone returned it to Juliet's bedroom. I'll look there next. Is the door behind you closed?"

Ben looked behind him and was surprised to see no door, only a wall decorated with the usual chair rail. "What do you mean?"

"The door to the back passage. Surely Juliet's mentioned it."

"Er, Lady Victoria. I feel as if things have taken a turn for the, well, atypical. Did you bring me to this room for something other than the photos?"

"I'll take that as a no," she said cheerfully. "For me, the door is quite visible when the curtains are closed and the wall sconces are doused. Look at the floor."

Ben looked at his feet, expecting to see nothing but feet, and wondering how to go about delicately asking Lady Victoria if he might check her vital signs. Instead, he saw a faint sliver of light emanating from beneath a door-sized section of the wall.

"Sir Thaddeus's staff called it the Master's Way. A secret passage, if you like," Lady Victoria said. "He claimed to want one because the oldest homes in these parts had them, in the days of Cromwell. Cavaliers fleeing Roundheads would take refuge with sympathizers, who hid them in secret chambers, just as wreckers used to hide out under pubs and churches."

Ben suffered a rare moment of *déjà vu*. Then he remembered a snippet from a dream, a flash of white walls and a lino floor.

"Someone left the light on inside," Lady Victoria said. "Perhaps it isn't open, *per se*, and merely looked open to me because of the light spillage. That's what Juliet would call it, now that she's planning a dark room. The pastime requires a light-tight room, as she's told me a hundred times. Press in the middle of the chair rail. No, harder—there!"

The mechanism clicked, and the cunningly disguised door opened inward, revealing a hall that was nothing like the stark passage in Ben's dream. This looked like any other part of the house, with wallpaper, sconces, and a polished floor.

"Remarkable." He turned back to Lady Victoria. "Thank you for showing it to me. But—"

"You can travel unseen from here to the library," she cut across him. "You need only put your palm against the left wall and follow it. Mind the stairs, they're steep. You'll see the door to the library not long past the stairs, but don't try to enter. Juliet and Ethan are inside."

"Oh. Um...."

"Now, if you'll excuse me, Dr. Bones, I'll leave you here while I search for the envelope. I expect I'll be gone a quarter-hour or more. I should warn you against taking the back passage. From the other side of the door, you could hear everything Juliet and Ethan are saying to one another quite easily. Heaven knows what sort of questions *that* might clear up. If you put your palm against the left wall," she repeated, holding his gaze, "and follow it up the stairs." Smiling, she turned and exited, leaving him alone.

When faced with an ethical dilemma, Ben had a tendency to internally litigate the matter. To draw up a list of pros, cons, alternatives, worst case scenarios, and so on. Often, he did this even when his gut had already told him which choice to make. Had the circumstances been different—had it been Dinah who showed him the door, for example, or Bertha who'd mentioned a chance to shamelessly eavesdrop—he would have been so torn, the window of opportunity might well have closed before he decided. But Lady Victoria was the one who'd all but told him to go and listen at the library door. A chance to finally understand what the devil was going on was too good to squander.

The passage was rather low, which made him feel taller, and the stairs were as steep as Lady Victoria warned. In a minute or so, he knew the library was close, because he could hear Lady Juliet shouting. Or, if not precisely shouting, speaking in a loud and forceful manner.

"... out of the question. I can't abandon Mother. She's not a well woman."

Ethan's voice was pitched lower. His tone was quite different when he had an audience of one, and that one knew him well. "Only the good die young, which means Victoria will outlive us both. I know it's been hell for you, playing the lovestruck little wifey. But there isn't a soul you care about in London. All you'd have to do is appear at my side once or twice and refrain from calling me names."

"You have no idea how hellish it's been," Lady Juliet said. "Now I know why the government skips prison and caning and goes right to hanging. If the penalty wasn't absolute, no one could go a week without breaking their oath."

Ethan's reply was muffled. Ben, too instantly engrossed to

give a fig about ethics, was reduced to putting his ear against the door. In terms of self-respect, it wasn't an action he'd look back on with pride, but it allowed him to pick up the remainder of Ethan's words.

"... for two weeks hardly constitutes abandonment. Besides, you're tackling this rift all wrong, if you want my opinion. The way to make a man regret his behavior isn't to mope about, hoping for an apology. It's to get on with your life. Have a roaring good time without him."

"I don't want your opinion," Lady Juliet said. "I only mentioned the rift, as you put it, to prove how well I've acted my part. I realize falsehood is entirely natural for you. I, however, find it excruciating. I'd never make a spy."

Ethan replied, but Ben didn't register the words. He was too busy assuring himself that he'd actually heard everything he'd heard. Much of what came next made little sense, concerning people he didn't know and vague references to the Ellisson side of Juliet's family. But after a quarter-hour of listening in, he knew two things for sure. Juliet's reconciliation with Ethan was entirely for show, and it had been arranged by the blank-faced Mr. Duggin, who was apparently some sort of handler for Ethan's spy career.

"Yes, Mother?" Juliet called suddenly, startling Ben.

Lady Victoria's reply was inaudible, coming as it did from the other side of the library's primary door.

"Yes, of course. Please don't let him leave," Lady Juliet said. "I'll collect the photos and be down directly."

"Well, I'll be boiled," Ethan said. "Perhaps your moping worked better than I thought."

"This is business. I'm quite sure he's come only on business."

"I doubt it," Ethan said. "Break a leg!"

Back in the dining room, Ben tried to sit down and wait for Lady Victoria, but kept jumping up and pacing around the table. During the treason trial, the Official Secrets Act had been referenced several times. The penalty for disclosure was execution. He was caught between delight that Lady Juliet, who craved usefulness like a flower craved the sun, had been given such a responsibility, and dismay that she couldn't talk about it. Swearing her to silence seemed crueler than asking her to feign wedded bliss with her strapping great mooncalf of a husband.

"Dr. Bones," Lady Victoria said, entering. "You must forgive me. I couldn't locate the photos. However, Juliet is on her way downstairs with them now. Oh, dear. That will never do."

Reaching inside the hidden passage, she switched off the lights and closed the door. Now that Ben knew where to look, he saw the tell-tale breaks in the chair rail, and a ridge where the wallpaper had been imperfectly matched. So often it was like that with secrets; once revealed, the truth seemed too obvious to have ever been missed.

"A maid must have left that open," Lady Victoria said. "It's just a poky hall leading nowhere. One of Belsham Manor's eccentricities. I trust you didn't enter. I certainly didn't invite you to do so."

"No," Ben agreed, cottoning on at last. "I seem to recall you telling me to sit and wait. You wouldn't condone trespassing."

"No, indeed." She gave him one of her radiant smiles. "It really is wonderful you chose this morning to drop by. And—oh. Here's Juliet."

"Good afternoon, Dr. Bones," Lady Juliet said as her mother withdrew. "Cold today."

"Bitter cold," Ben agreed automatically. "Bright, though."

"Oh, yes. Unseasonably cold but wonderfully bright." She offered a hesitant smile. "I wondered what you've been up to. We've left the séance lie, haven't we?"

"We did. Recent experience suggests I might profit from a sharper focus on the mortal coil," he said, returning her smile. "Patients and Army letters and so forth. I'm not sure what happened in the attic, or if any of that was supernatural. I only know that Lucy wanted me to carry my cane." He rapped its tip on the floor. "Beyond that, I think life will go smoother if I wait for her to contact me. Will you be riding?" he asked, noting her grass-stained jodhpurs and extraordinarily tall boots. Riding boots usually finished below the knee and had spurs; the ones she wore looked rubberized and came up to mid-thigh. Hip waders, he thought they were called.

"Riding? No. These are a stopgap," she said, looking down as if only just realizing what she had on. "My best boots are out for repair. Mother is determined to provide fabric to any woman who plans on sewing new clothes for her family next year. I said I would love to help, which she interpreted quite broadly, as it turns out. Today I opened my wardrobe and could have shot a cannon through it. Hence the jodhpurs, which have rips in the knees. Hence the tall boots, for warmth. Because this morning, when I asked Bertha to fetch my coat, I discovered Epona was wearing it."

"Your horse?"

"Yes. You know Mother and her sewing. It's eternal, like the tide. I did notice her at work on my erstwhile coat. It's quite woolly, you know, so I couldn't have missed it. She took my silence as assent, but the truth is, I thought she was mending a tear. When in fact she was snipping off the sleeves and turning it into a horse blanket."

Ben couldn't think of a better use for the horrible coat, but saying so would only add insult to injury. By the same token, something was happening with her hair. Instead of scraped back in a bun, it was loose and fuzzy, as if recently attacked by a

potato brush. He valued their friendship too much to
inquire why.

"As it's far too cold to spend the winter coatless," Juliet said,
"Mother and I are off to Plymouth in the next hour. She's dragging me to the shops, and I've promised to behave. In return, I'm
permitted some fine dining afterward, and a quiet night in a
hotel room. Just the three of us. Me, Mother, and Edith
Wharton."

"What about Ethan?" Ben asked.

"He's better left at home. Even if the hotel lacks a casino,
there's sure to be a game of cards he ought to avoid." She cleared
her throat. "Not that I begrudge my husband a bit of fun. He's
the one who's decided to give games of chance a miss. And I
support him in that, wholeheartedly."

Ben nodded. Astonishing how frankly fake those happy-wife
sentences sounded, now that he knew the truth. Or now that he
evaluated them without... what?

Not jealousy. Dislike of Ethan, perhaps. But not jealousy.

"I don't want to delay your trip to the station," Ben said,
wondering if she meant to wear her hip waders on the train. "I
only want to look over the photos, then give them to Gaston. He
tells me the case is closed. Mr. Collins did it."

"The butler!" Juliet cried. "How marvelous. Remember how
he manhandled me? Scurrilous varlet." Opening the envelope,
she spread the photos on the dining room table for Ben's inspection. "Why did he kill Bobby? Is he quite unhinged? He cast an
evil eye at me over that possible blood stain. Perhaps he would
have tried to murder me, too?"

It was on Ben's lips to explain about the theft scheme when
he noticed something in a photo. It was one of a series Father
Rummage had taken of Bobby on the bed, body contorted by
cadaveric spasm.

"What's that?" he asked, tapping the picture.

"Hm? Probably an artifact."

"Meaning?"

"A part of the photo accidentally created by the photographer. From a dusty lens, a finger shadow, that sort of thing."

"Dust would leave a black mark, wouldn't it? And that isn't a shadow," Ben said. "It's a line on the floor. See? Like a crack of light. I know that's a wall, but I've had secret passages on my mind lately. I've even been dreaming about them. You don't suppose....?"

"Ridiculous. I happen to know a thing or two about secret passages as well as amateur photography, and I can assure you —" She broke off, picking up the photo and studying it more carefully. "Great Scott. I suppose it could be. Parts of Fitchley Park are very old."

"Someone on staff mentioned strange doings since the days of the Cavaliers," Ben added, remembering suddenly.

"Does a secret passage figure into it? Now that the murderer has been unmasked?"

"I don't know," Ben said, gathering up the photos and envelope. "Enjoy your day out in Plymouth. We'll talk about it when you get back."

ST. GWINNODOCK'S tower was in sight when Ben realized he'd torn off to Barking without taking two obvious steps. He hadn't taken the trouble to hunt down Gaston, and he hadn't formulated a good reason for turning up at Fitchley Park unannounced. Throughout the drive, his thoughts had bounced back and forth like a squash ball, from Juliet's sham reconciliation to Ethan's spy career to the secret passage and back again. The passage, if there was one, didn't call Mr. Collins's guilt into question; on the contrary, evidence of such a thing would explain how Bobby had died in one place and been quietly conveyed to another.

But Lady Maggart might not appreciate further exploration on the topic, he thought. *She's already under house arrest for her complicity in the theft. If she knew about the passage, and she must have, failure to disclose it might result in more questions. Perhaps additional charges.*

He felt sure Mrs. Grundy would permit him entrance, so long as her mistress wasn't about. Having lived in Fitchley Park all her life, she would know as much about the house's secrets as Lord and Lady Maggart.

Didn't Lady Juliet say there was a pub in Barking? When it wasn't serving as the post office?

Realizing that a pint and a quiet moment would be just the thing, Ben parked on the street and wandered among the cottages until he found the Trentham house. As Lady Juliet had said, both operations were run out of Old Mrs. Trentham's front room, and fortunately for him, today it was lager on offer, not stamps. The front room offered few concessions to its dual purpose, other than extra chairs and a service counter. Behind the counter sat a wall-eyed woman and a tearful girl.

"Wotcha," a patron whispered as Ben walked in. All were male and in the vicinity of seventy except for one female, who looked like a man and might have been fifty.

"No crème de menthe here," she said, guffawing like a man.

"Shut it, Myra." The wall-eyed woman sounded more than capable of taking on even the rowdiest patron. "This must be Dr. Bones from Birdswing."

"Birdswinger," someone muttered.

"Barkers do it better," another said, and everyone roared.

"I am Dr. Bones," Ben agreed. "Ex-Londoner, aspiring Birdswinger, and Barking fancier, if you please. I hope to scare up some patients here. But not just now." To the woman he said, "Pint, please. Your choice."

"My choice is the only choice. We have one keg on tap today. I'm Hannah Trentham, by the way. That's my youngest, Shelagh." She prodded the tearful girl, who seemed poised between regaining her composure and a fresh bout of weeping. "Glass, love."

The girl, who was unusually pretty in a wide-eyed gamine sort of way, took a glass from the rack and began polishing it with delicate strokes.

"Other fish in the sea, and here's proof," Mrs. Trentham said. Her left eye was on her daughter; her right seemed be looking at Ben but probably saw nothing at all. "Shelagh reckons her heart's broken. Seventeen and it's all over. Tragic." Taking the clean glass from her daughter, she put it under the tap. "As if my little lady couldn't do better than *that*. Shelagh's got a certain something, Doctor. Not just beauty, though she has that in spades. A genteel nature, that's what I call it. If I could scrape together the pennies, I'd send her to one of those finishing schools on the Continent. Not that she needs it. Even weeps like a duchess."

Shelagh sighed and dabbed at her eyes. "Bobby said I was a proper lady."

"Bobby said all sorts of things, and I'll not miss the sound of his voice," Mrs. Trentham replied. As she handed Ben his pint, her right eye fixed on him and her left eye slid toward the wall, going temporarily sightless. It was a recognized phenomenon, but Ben would have needed his books to identify it.

"Folks put about you're a widower," Mrs. Trentham said.

He nodded absently, studying Shelagh.

"I'll just check on Granddad," Mrs. Trentham announced, and disappeared into the house.

"Shelagh. I'm sorry for your loss," Ben said. "I suppose news of Mr. Collins's arrest reopened the wound."

"Oh, yes," she said, clearly starved for sympathy. "I don't know why he killed Bobby. I've known Mr. Collins all my life. He could be cross with people but never violent."

"Had you fixed a date?"

Shelagh shook her head. "We hoped for spring, but it was no use planning. Not till his divorce went through."

Here's Bobby's intended second wife, Ben thought. *Not Lady Maggart or Kitty. Out of all his women, Shelagh's the one Bobby wanted so much, he finally asked Helen for a divorce. If he had a lover at Fitchley Park, I wonder what she made of it? Of finding out she was good enough to sleep with but not good enough to marry?*

"Hey! You haven't touched your pint," Shelagh said as Ben tossed a coin on the counter.

"Sorry. Something just occurred to me," Ben said, hurrying toward the door.

"Birdswingers," someone whispered as he left.

28

INSIDE THE CAVALIER ROOM

A maid he'd never seen admitted him into Fitchley Park. She was older than Lady Maggart's usual range of preference, with crooked teeth and a prominent mole on her forehead. After taking his hat and coat, she directed him to the great room. There he found not Lord or Lady Maggart but Mrs. Grundy, sitting in her master's chair.

"Thank you, Louisa," she told the maid. Something about her comfortable position before the fire reminded Ben of Lady Maggart in her boudoir. Mrs. Grundy wore her usual black uniform rather than a dressing gown, but she had the same book—*Rebecca*—on her lap. That surprised Ben, as Lady Maggart didn't strike him as the sort who would share, particularly with someone she regarded as a social inferior.

"I see you've taken on new staff."

"Yes, indeed, Dr. Bones," Mrs. Grundy said, rising. "And of my own choosing, for the first time since her ladyship was a bride. Lord Maggart has full confidence in my abilities." A smile softened her exaggerated features. "As for Louisa," she said, without apparent regard for whether the new maid or anyone else might hear, "Beauty is only skin deep, but a willingness to serve goes straight to the marrow. Poor Louisa has had difficulty finding a place. Too homely. Bad figure. That mole. Most employers would rather have a pretty idiot. But I'm sure she'll be a credit to Fitchley Park."

"I hope so," Ben said. "Where is Lady Maggart?"

"She's not at home. Which is to say, upstairs," Mrs. Grundy replied. "Perhaps you've heard of our troubles and come to offer condolences?"

"In part. How is she? I imagine the arrest of Mr. Collins and the others must have come as a terrible shock."

"Not really," Mrs. Grundy said calmly. "The fact he murdered Mr. Archer made an impact, insofar as no one likes the idea of a killer close at hand. It's put her ghost nonsense into perspective. Otherwise the arrests haven't touched her ladyship at all. She's too busy contemplating the possibility of her own incarceration."

"Yes, well. Speaking of that." Ben cleared his throat. "I understand she's not at liberty to leave the premises."

"Under an order of house arrest, they call it. A pair of London solicitors will come next week to try and sort it out. I hope it can be resolved without further sullying the reputation of this house."

"Of course. Getting back to her ladyship—may I ask a rather indelicate question? I danced around it before. Now I'd like to be direct."

"Fire away." Mrs. Grundy looked straight at him, head high. She no longer hunched her shoulders or stared at the floor to lessen the impact of her face.

"Was Lady Maggart having an affair with Bobby?"

He expected a crisp assent. Instead, Mrs. Grundy didn't answer.

"I suppose it's possible you wouldn't have absolute proof," he said. "I'm not asking you to give evidence against her. I only want your opinion."

"I think they must have been having an affair," she said slowly. "If you've eliminated Kitty and Betsy and the other maids, who else could it have been?"

Ben thought perhaps he'd offended her by asking about sex. Peggy, the volunteer at St. Barnabas, had said something about the housekeeper's distaste for gossip magazines and cosmetics. How much more distasteful had it been for her, working for Lord Maggart while his wife brought a lover into the house?

"And how is his lordship?" he asked.

"His days and nights are muddled. Night terrors again," Mrs. Grundy said. "And no, they weren't brought on by the loss of Mr. Collins. Lord Maggart has suffered violent delusions since the war. They're the reason he was sent to Craiglockhart."

"I thought he injured his hand," Ben said, remembering the baron's missing finger.

"No. It was the dreams."

"And he still has them?"

"They're never spoken of beyond these walls, but they started when he was a soldier. He sleepwalks. Roams the house searching for Germans, trying to prove his battle-courage."

"That could be dangerous."

"It is. The last time we permitted him to sleepwalk, he seemed to think his cane was a bayonet. Used it to frighten Mrs. Tippett. That frayed her loyalty, as you can imagine. It seems her brother's arrest smashed it completely."

"What do you mean?"

"After the police took Mr. Collins into custody, Mrs. Tippett went off to pray, or some such, and never returned. Abandoned her post entirely. But there's a silver lining," Mrs. Grundy said, smiling again. "As it happens, I have another friend. Those who knew me in childhood still think of me as human, instead of a monster. She's in the kitchen now, trying her hand at dinner. If it's deemed acceptable, I will have replaced Kitty and Mrs. Tippett in less than forty-eight hours. Proof of my ability to look after Fitchley Park."

"Would it be possible for me to see Lord Maggart? I'll do my best not to overexcite him."

"I suppose," Mrs. Grundy said. "He's confined to quarters, as I like to call it."

"What?"

"I told you, Dr. Bones. We can't allow his lordship to roam the house, not when he's revisiting the war in his mind, or someone may be seriously hurt."

"That dog you told me about. The Pomeranian found dead in the kitchen," Ben said. "He killed it, didn't he?"

"Of course."

"You sound quite certain. Why didn't you tell me before?"

"Because my loyalty is to Fitchley Park," Mrs. Grundy said serenely. "I could never divulge such a thing to an outsider. Not when it might have been used against us. We've been maligned enough as it is." As Ben digested this, she continued, "Now. Follow me, if you please, and I'll escort you to Lord Maggart."

THE DOOR to Lord Maggart's ground floor bedroom was locked. Mrs. Grundy located the correct key, fitting it to the lock with her left hand.

"I didn't realize you were left-handed."

"I'm not. Not as such," Mrs. Grundy said, switching the key to her right hand before slipping it back in her pocket. "I tried to write with my left as a girl, but the governess answered with the rod. I've used my right hand ever since. Except when I'm particularly engrossed in thought, or performing an important task."

Seeming poised to enter the room alongside Ben, she added, "Remember. You promised not to upset him."

"Of course. Do you think I might speak with Lord Maggart alone?" Ben asked. "If you're present, he may deny his symptoms. Out of a desire to appear strong, you see."

Mrs. Grundy's eyes narrowed. "I'll accompany you to make sure he's lucid. If he is, I'll absent myself."

Unlocking the door, she led him into a converted parlor without windows. Poorly ventilated, it stank of disinfectant, mentholated rub, and old urine. Apparently, when confined to quarters, the baron wasn't allowed to exit for any reason, including the W.C.

"There's an overflowing chamber pot nearby," Ben said.

"Is there? When confronted with such matters, I don't miss the ability to smell," Mrs. Grundy said. "Good afternoon, Dudley."

"Lord Maggart, if you please." He was in bed but not asleep. Rather, he sat on top of the covers, back against the headboard and arms folded across his chest. He had on striped pajamas, carpet slippers, a great coat, and a fur-trimmed hat.

"*Lord Maggart.* Forgive the lapse." To Ben, she stage-whispered, "I use his Christian name when we're alone."

"Alone?" the baron snapped. "What do you call the undertaker standing beside you? Another so-called delusion?"

"Do forgive me," she repeated, using that sing-song tone generally reserved for fussy children and the mentally infirm. "You must be overheated in your hat and coat. Are you going somewhere, my lord?"

"Yes. I'm getting out. You're all mad." He shot Ben a look of naked appeal. "Get me out, lad. Say I'm dead, stash me in a coffin, just get me out. Jasper never killed anyone. Ask lemon sherbet there. Maybe she'll tell the truth if you beat it out of her."

"Lemon sherbet?" Ben repeated.

"A pet name," Mrs. Grundy said.

"The hell it is!" Lord Maggart leapt out of bed. Much as he had with the non-ghost in the attic, Ben reacted automatically, interposing himself between the baron and his housekeeper. This time he didn't fall over, thanks to his cane.

"Mrs. Grundy, I really must insist. His lordship and I will do better without you."

"The whole world would do better without you." Lord Maggart trembled from head to toe. "Fetch my swordstick, lad. I'll do what I should have done years ago!"

"Are you quite sure you want me to leave you alone with him?" Mrs. Grundy asked.

"Yes," Ben said in near-unison with Lord Maggart, who threw in a few curses.

"Very well. Good luck, Dr. Bones. Perhaps he'll allow you to treat him for his delusions. A month in hospital would do him good." She shut the door, and the key scraped in the lock.

"Bloody monster," Lord Maggart muttered. "Didn't think she'd lock you in. Or slander you that way. She thinks I'll turn on you if she calls you a white coat."

"Yes, well... what was that about a swordstick?" Ben looked around. Whether he came clean to the baron or not, if there was a deadly weapon at hand, he wanted some idea of its location.

"An heirloom. Relic from my grandfather's day," Lord Maggart said, slipping out of his great coat and beating the pockets as if it might be inside. "Back when men wore horsehair wigs and high heels to court, they carried poncy canes, too. A swordstick was a clandestine weapon. Pretty enough to look at, but if a man got into a tight spot in a pub or back alley, he removed the handle and hey, presto—a blade."

He tossed the coat over the back of a chair and started pulling open drawers on the writing desk. "Anyhow, it's not in this room. I've checked. Doesn't matter how she tries to confuse me. Waking me up at three o'clock in the morning and telling me it's dinner time. Coming in at midnight to ask if I wanted breakfast. When I complain, she says I've had my time muddled since the war. A lie," he declared, looking up from the drawer he was rifling. The whites of his eyes were yellower than Ben remembered. "My confession will be the death of me."

"What confession?"

"About why I was sent to Craiglockhart," Lord Maggart said, pulling a drawer all the way out and dumping its contents atop the desk. His actions seemed quite mad, and Ben was keenly aware of the locked door, but he wasn't afraid, only fascinated.

"I was in the Duke of Cornwall's Light Infantry," Lord Maggart said. "Father saw to that. I wasn't born a coward, but I was a sensitive boy, and he knew it. The DCLI was good for me. But my battalion was retrained as Pioneers before going to France. Our job was to dig and mend the trenches. We made them watertight as could be, then strung barbed wire barricades. It doesn't sound flash, but it was important. Our careless work could kill dozens of Tommies. Our good work could save them. Ah! Here we are." From the heap of desk-detritus, he plucked a hairpin, twisted out of shape.

"This will do for a rake, but I need something flat for a torque-key. What do you have in that case?" Lord Maggart asked, frowning at Ben's doctor's bag as if truly seeing it for the first time.

"Do you mean to pick the lock?" Ben wondered if the poor man were completely delusional.

"Only if you can find me a small, flat bit of metal."

Ben opened the bag and looked over his tools of the trade, all of which seemed enormous beside the twisted hairpin. "Tongue depressor?" he asked doubtfully, holding up the metal item.

"Just how big do you reckon the lock is, lad?"

"Right." Ben opened a little case with his precious fine instruments, paid for out of his own pocket, and intended to collect crime scene samples. He hadn't told anyone about the purchase; Lady Juliet and Gaston had their silly correspondence course, and he had his ludicrous instruments for chemical analysis.

"Sorry. I don't see how any of this could—"

"Well done. That little bugger should do the trick." Lord Maggart plucked the most expensive item, a collection spatula, from the kit. "But what was I saying? Ah, yes, the war. It turned ever more grim."

He went to the door and knelt awkwardly, bending one knee slowly, then the other. "Then came the biggest attack of the war, along the Somme. The loss of life was so great, my battalion was tapped for other work. Sent in with stretchers onto battlefields where the fighting was done. Finding the wounded, loading them up, and bearing them back to the aid stations. Can't see worth a toss, but this is all about listening for clicks," he added, working his makeshift tools into the keyhole.

"But the battlefields, lad. They made Hieronymus Bosch look like Brighton Beach Pavilion. The dead were bad enough. But the grown men calling for their mothers. Praying aloud, and dying all the same, dying just as we got them in sight of the white tents...." He broke off. "There's the first pin. Hah! She doesn't reckon I can still do this. Arrogant cow. Learned when I was eight, and the beastly governess used to lock us in the school room. I got us out, and Nan applauded. Now she's the governess, isn't she?

"The point is," Lord Maggart went on, straining to get his ear closer to the lock, "the battlefields took their toll on me. Then my unit was charged with repairing trenches instead of digging them. This couldn't be managed in daylight. We had to catch forty winks while the sun was up and work under cover of darkness. Think of it. As our fellow soldiers went over the top, we lay huddled in our funk-holes, trying to sleep within earshot of hell. I lay there, listening to men screaming as they were bayonetted. At night, we rose like ghosts from a barrow, doing our work in dead silence. Ah! There's the second pin.

"It was during the repair detail that I cut my hand," he continued. "I didn't dare show my face in the white tents over such a little thing. That was a mistake. Before long, I was feverish. We kept on, laboring by night and sleeping by day, and I fell into nightmares. It was as if I never slept or I never woke. I don't remember what happened, only what they told me. There now!" Triumphantly, he turned the knob, and the door opened. "Saves you trying to break it down. A half-crippled man with a cane... I didn't like your chances."

Ben was too grateful to the baron, and too transfixed by his story, to take offense. "What happened?"

"Hm? Oh. I was in the funk-hole, wrapped in a blanket. They say I started to shake. To mutter about Germans. Then to shout and finally to scream." Lord Maggart's voice trembled, even after twenty years. "What could they do with a lunatic endangering so many lives but gag and bind me, and carry me out on a stretcher. Next thing I knew, I was at Craiglockhart, under MacHardy's thumb. When I came home, no one wanted to hear anything about it. Certainly not Odette. So in a moment of weakness, I unburdened myself to *her*. Nan. As kiddies, we were pals. I never realized how much she hated me for our difference in status. Not till she tricked me into putting on my evening dress and walking about like a madman. Then I knew it was all deliberate."

Ben gave Lord Maggart a hand up, straining to get the man back on his feet.

"Well done. But there's more. Now I begin to think I'm not

really sick." Lord Maggart's eyes bulged, making him look mad as a hatter. "My food tastes of chemicals. I complained, and she told Odette I thought mustard gas was in my dinner. But I know I detected something bitter. Like ground-up pills."

It could be true, Ben realized. There was a host of common medicines, including sulfa, that were poisonous if misused. Many would cause severe pancreas or liver dysfunction, as signaled by jaundice.

"Lord Maggart, is there a secret passage in Fitchley Park? A secret room?"

"What?" The baron looked startled. "Yes, yes, of course. Two concealed passages. They each lead to a cell called the Cavalier Room. Talk about a funk-hole! Of course, as kiddies, Nan and I thought it was brilliant. We hid inside and eavesdropped on the adults, and made knocking sounds. Nearly had dear Mummy believing in the woman in black, until we were caught and soundly thrashed for our sins."

"Show me how to get inside."

"IF YOU'RE GOING IN, perhaps I should come along. There's been talk of murders in Barking," Lord Maggart said. The uncertainty in his tone suggested he wasn't fully informed about Bobby's death, or if he was, he'd forgotten the details.

Ben hesitated. Was he actually putting his trust in a man who didn't know what transpired in his own house? Then again, the baron had picked that door lock quite ably, hadn't he? Perhaps Mrs. Grundy really had been poisoning him. If so, maybe she hadn't dosed him lately, or maybe Lord Maggart had regained some lucidity by eating as little of his poisoned food as possible.

"In the old days, it was hidden by something less obvious, I shouldn't wonder," Lord Maggart said, guiding Ben into a parlor that contained a floor-length portrait of a Cavalier. Ben recognized him by his regalia: cape, extravagant lace collar, and big black hat.

"The painting's on hinges. Go on, lad."

Ben swung back the portrait to reveal a wooden door. It opened onto what looked like a glorified hole in the wall.

"I tried showing it off to Odette when we were newlyweds. She thought it was cramped and dark, and likely to have spiders. Now she's probably forgotten it exists."

"Does it connect to the servant's quarters below stairs?"

"Not this one. This is the original, to hide the Royalists. It goes straight from here to the Cavalier Room. The second passage was added during one of the park's renovations. It goes from the Cavalier Room to the master bedroom and down below stairs. As you can guess, it was created for less patriotic and more, er, earthy uses."

"And the master bedroom is now Lady Maggart's bedroom," Ben murmured. "I think Mrs. Grundy has been playing the woman in black. There was a ruckus with her ladyship's vanity in the middle of the night, wasn't there? Cosmetics pitched about and smashed. Did Lady Maggart have a bottle of *Sous le Vent*?"

"What the devil is that?"

"Never mind. I'm going in for a look around," Ben said. "I'd prefer it if you'd wait for me on this end. Shout down the passage, should anything go amiss. I don't suppose the corridor was fitted for electric light?"

Lord Maggart shook his head. "As kiddies, we brought lanterns."

Ben stuck his head into the passage as far as he dared. Faintly, he could make out a bend in the distance, which meant there was a source of light somewhere along the line.

"Mind this for me, would you?" Ben held out his cane to Lord Maggart.

"Carry it with you. The floor is anything but even."

"Right. Here goes." Taking a deep breath, Ben ducked his head and stepped into the secret passage.

As his eyes adjusted, Ben used his cane to probe the floor. It was smooth but not level, continually rising with ramps and sudden shallow steps. At first, the low ceiling forced him to hunch, but after he turned the second corner, it soared from five feet to at least eight, allowing him to lift his head. Faint light emanated from somewhere in the distance, possibly the Cavalier Room. He couldn't see well enough to thoroughly check for blood, but between his dark-adapted vision and his cane, he managed to move forward with confidence.

All I need is one shred of proof. Something that will force the police to come to Fitchley Park this afternoon or first thing in the morning. Once I find it, I'll take Lord Maggart with me back to Fenton House. Lady Maggart, too. Bugger the order of house arrest. Both their lives are in danger.

Up he went, tripping on a loose floorboard in spite of his cane. The walls smelled of rising damp. Somewhere near the heart of the original dwelling, mold was spreading, black and stinking, like cancer.

The light grew stronger. Now Ben could see the walls, gray with neglect and riddled with holes. Then the passage opened into the room where Royalists had hidden, sometimes for days on end, while the Parliamentarians conducted their house-to-house searches. Two lanterns hung on opposing pegs, bathing the room in yellow light.

Ben had expected something like a prison cell. Instead, he

found a lady's boudoir, or a rough approximation of one. There was a brass bed made up with a pink coverlet. A nightstand. An antique vanity, its mirror missing but otherwise very fine. Two Turkish rugs, both heirlooms, if Ben were any judge. And on another peg hung a heavy mantle with a full hood, the sort every respectable Victorian woman put on before she left the house. Even from several feet away, Ben could smell the French perfume emanating from its thick black velvet.

Piled on the vanity was a collection of items that must have been stolen, either from Lady Maggart or the maids. Cinema magazines, tubes of lipstick, pots of rouge. It seemed that while Mrs. Grundy liked to shame girls like Betsy or terrorize Lady Maggart in the middle of the night, she kept a stash of her own feminine treasures, hidden where no one could mock her for using them.

"... don't need to explain yourself, I swear it," a woman said, her voice echoing slightly.

The sound drew Ben's gaze to the mouth of the second passage, which looked far newer and had been properly finished. Its floor was lino; its walls were white—or would have been, if not for two giant brown-red stains that marred the paint and been allowed to dry.

"Oh, but I want you to understand," Mrs. Grundy replied. "I want *him* to understand. I could have ended his life a thousand times over the years. But it's his lot to waste away in agony and yours to be shut in down here."

"No, no, you have it wrong," Lady Maggart said. She spoke in the overly-bright voice of one who believed her next few sentences would determine if she lived or died. "Bobby was nothing to me. A bit of misappropriated furniture doesn't trouble me at all. Of course you feel owed. I could arrange an annuity. You could retire to—oh!"

Lady Maggart, dressed in the same confectionary peach wrap

and fur-trimmed slippers Ben remembered from their bedroom encounter, quailed as she saw the blood stains. Her knees buckled.

She would have fallen, if not for Mrs. Grundy just behind her. Seizing Lady Maggart by her well-coiffed blonde hair, the housekeeper hauled her upright with the strength of one who'd worked long and hard her entire life.

"Yes, that's Bobby's. I mopped the floor but couldn't bring myself to scrub the walls. Feel that?" she asked. Her captive squealed as if poked in the ribs. "That's the blade I used to do it."

"Help," Lady Maggart wailed. Mouth twisted and eyes darting, she spied Ben and shrieked, "Help me! *Help me!*"

"Doctor." Mrs. Grundy released her grip on the baroness, who collapsed to the floor in heap. "Don't tell me you broke down that door."

Cautiously, Ben took a step closer, studying the gaudy weapon in her hand. The Baroque cane's concealing handle was off, revealing a long, serrated knife. Its bottom half, decorated with scrolls and flourishes and tiny jewels, looked like the one he'd glimpsed in Lady Maggart's bedroom.

"So that's the swordstick?"

"Yes. I'd heard you were a detective," Mrs. Grundy said scornfully. "I hoped if I gave you a nudge, you'd conclude that one killed Bobby." She pointed at Lady Maggart, who sat sobbing. "So I put the swordstick in an umbrella stand, and the stand just inside her master bedroom. I presumed a *detective* would recognize the absurdity of umbrellas in such a place. That he'd notice a jewel-encrusted antique, remove its top, and see the murder weapon inside. I even left Bobby's blood on the blade." She pointed it at Ben. "I should have known you were too thick for anything but a signed confession."

"Why are you doing this?" Ben didn't care, but he had to say something, anything, to give him time to think. If he rushed at her, weaponless, she might stab him before he wrestled the swordstick away. Or she might turn and finish off Lady Maggart, whom she clearly hated.

"Why? Because they deserve it. You all deserve it," Mrs. Grundy growled, and launched herself at him.

The collision sent Ben staggering back onto the bed. The small of his back connected with a brass bed knob, knocking the wind out of him. His diaphragm spasmed. He would have doubled over in pain, but Mrs. Grundy thrust the knife at his eyes and instinct took over. Arm shooting up reflexively, he used his cane to knock the swordstick away.

It flew through the air, clattering to the floor not far away. He hoped she'd dive for it. Instead, she jerked the cane out of his grip and cracked him over the head so hard, he saw stars.

Something thumped hard against the floorboards. It was his knees. But this time he felt no pain, only unreality. The Cavalier Room tilted on an invisible axis.

Concussion? he thought, aware that something far more important was happening but unsure what he ought to do about it. *Should I test myself for signs of concussion?*

A scream pierced his confusion. *The swordstick. She's got her hands on it,* Ben decided.

He tried to regain his footing and couldn't. The room stopped turning, but his body was still muddled. It seemed to be receiving his brain's instructions via carrier pigeon instead of spinal nerves.

"Stay still, lad," a man said. It was the baron, still in his striped pajamas and a single carpet slipper. "The vile wench rang your bell. Give yourself a moment. Odette, for the love of God. If you're not hurt, stop that noise."

Lady Maggart, who'd been sobbing loudly, quieted a bit.

"Lord Maggart?" Ben shook himself. His head responded

with a thud, and his stomach lurched, but he steeled himself and the nausea passed. "I thought...."

"I'd wait by the painting for Nan or one of her minions to recapture me? Hah! I still know the corridor. Only stubbed my toe twice."

Blinking, Ben managed to focus on the swordstick in the baron's hand. The serrated knife points were still bloody, but now the stains weren't brown. They were red and dripping.

"Funny thing." Lord Maggart stared at the blade. "I always thought if I brought myself to wield one of these, I'd feel brave. Like a man. But I feel just the same. Useless."

"Useless?" Ben tried to chuckle, but it made his head hurt. "Not quite the word I'd choose. Did you get to the swordstick first?"

"No, she did. But I took it away from her. Tried plunging it into her heart. Got her thigh instead." He shrugged. "Slightly important artery in the thigh, isn't there?"

"Slightly," Ben agreed. Sitting up, he saw that Mrs. Grundy had fallen nearby. She lay sprawled on her back, dazed but conscious, fresh blood spreading rapidly across her skirt.

"Help me with her," he commanded Lord Maggart. "I need a look at that wound."

When Ben bared her legs, Mrs. Grundy moaned and batted at him, but Lord Maggart caught her hands and held them tight. A quick assessment revealed that the femoral artery probably wasn't nicked. Still, the wound was quite deep. Without a tourniquet, Mrs. Grundy would bleed out long before she could be arrested.

"Didn't I tell you to stop that infernal racket?" Lord Maggart asked his wife, who continued to sob steadily, like a little girl on a crying jag. "You haven't a scratch. It's over. Go and ring for help. Birdswing, Barking, I don't give a fig. Dress yourself and wait by the door for rescuers to turn up."

"Before you go," Ben said. "Your dressing gown. May I have the sash?"

"What?" Lady Maggart wiped her eyes and stared at Ben.

"The sash, woman. Give it over," Lord Maggart snapped.

Seeming grateful for clear direction, she handed the sash to Ben. "Very well. But that horrible creature. She attacked me. Threatened me. I daren't go away and ring anyone, Dudley. I'm frightened. Petrified."

"Poppycock. Do you want it to be daybreak before she's arrested?" Lord Maggart asked. "Go on. Be frightened later. The fear will keep, I promise."

After she'd gone, he watched Ben apply the tourniquet. When he'd finished, and took Mrs. Grundy's wrist to check her pulse, Lord Maggart said, "You *are* a bloody white coat, aren't you?"

Ben glanced up. He was glad not to find a swordstick poised to jab him. He was still too muzzy to defend himself. "I'm afraid so."

"More fool me, thinking I'd found an ally. Now I know you're not to be trusted."

"On the contrary," Ben said, releasing Mrs. Grundy's wrist. Her heartbeat was reasonably strong, but the wound was serious, and shock was setting in. "You should trust me to the exclusion of everyone else."

Lord Maggart frowned. "Why?"

"Because you just saved my life. It's a debt I can never repay, unless I save yours. What do you have to lose by letting me try?"

29

BEHIND THE MASK

Because the Cow Hole's cell lacked the usual barred door, Special Constable Gaston had insisted Mrs. Grundy lie in bed, one wrist handcuffed to its iron frame, until Plymouth CID collected her the next day. Ben didn't think she was capable of walking, much less attacking anyone, but Gaston's refusal to underestimate the woman was probably wise. Sweet old Mrs. Richwine, overwhelmed by the list of the charges against Mrs. Grundy, had gone home in tears. That clearly suited Gaston. He took over guard duty, armed with a long gun borrowed from Lord Maggart.

The Cow Hole had a more sinister aura, now that it contained a prisoner worthy of its medieval history. Ben would have preferred to take up Lady Maggart's invitation to stay the night at Fitchley Park, but given Gaston's age, he felt duty-bound to offer his assistance. Besides, as galling as it was, Mrs. Grundy was his patient. He was responsible for her life until she was taken into custody, beginning the process which would almost certainly end in her death.

"As it's too late for me to go home, shall I help guard her?" he asked Gaston. "We could take shifts."

"Kind of you to offer, but no need." Gaston looked fully ener-
gized, his eyes snapping with good humor. "See that chair?
Perfect for me to doze in. Only need a few winks." Glancing at
Mrs. Grundy, motionless on the bed, he added in a louder voice,
"In the Great War, I learned to sleep with a gun in my hands.
And to wake up shooting."

Mrs. Grundy chuckled. She'd said very little since the stab-
bing, enduring Ben's ministrations with gritted teeth. During her
conveyance to the Cow Hole, she'd slipped in and out of
consciousness, often laughing softly to herself. He wasn't sure
why. Perhaps she was reacting to blood loss and the local anes-
thetic he'd administered before stitching the wound. Or perhaps
she'd taken a hard turn into that dark territory she'd long
intended for Lord Maggart.

"Gives me the creeps, she does," Gaston whispered. "Is she
starkers?"

"I don't know. Can I speak to her alone?"

"I suppose. The old man in the next cottage but one offered
me a hot cuppa," Gaston said. "I could take him up on that. Be
back in a quarter hour."

He exited, allowing a blast of cold air into the Cow Hole as
Ben approached the bed. The roundhouse had no electricity or
gaslight, only paraffin lanterns. They cast shadows that distorted
her face, making her seem less than human. But that was
too easy.

Her eyes opened. "All alone, Doctor. You arranged that
rather neatly. Here I am, at your mercy."

"Can you blame me for wanting to understand?"

She chuckled again. "Bloody Odette said the same thing.
Everyone wants to understand but only when they've exhausted
every other option."

"I've worked out some of it on my own," he said. "Did you
enlist help to transfer Bobby from the Cavalier Room to the

bedroom below stairs? Mr. Collins, perhaps, or Kitty? I suppose you could have convinced them to go along with you, if you played on their loyalty to Fitchley Park or Lord Maggart. You worked so hard to make him appear incompetent. The bit with the dead dog was a stroke of genius. You killed it yourself, didn't you? Then made sure everyone thought he did it. After that, it was easier for them to believe he'd taken a human life."

Mrs. Grundy didn't answer.

"Were you poisoning his food? You said he deserved a slow death. To waste away."

Silence.

"That black cloak you wore stank of perfume. I know you came into Lady Maggart's room and flung her cosmetics about. Broke a bottle of *Sous le Vent* and never realized it. So when you used the passage wearing the mantle, I smelled French perfume. Why do you hate her?"

Mrs. Grundy said nothing. Pulling up a chair, Ben sat beside the bed and tried to see her as a patient rather than a murderess. But it was hard to feel a connection when her actions were so appalling.

"Lord Maggart called you 'lemon sherbet.' He saw you with the sweeties, didn't he? A sack of them to turn John's head. Steady his nerves while you taught him what to say to get Mr. Collins arrested. Poor lad. It was cruel of you, using him so."

"You scold me for using the boot boy," Mrs. Grundy said, "but not for killing Bobby? For trying to kill you?"

Ben sighed. His head still ached; he rubbed his temple beneath the goose egg she'd given him.

"I'm a grown man. I understand that life is unfair. But John will always be a child."

"Do you think I don't know that? I've known him since the day he was born," she said. "Perhaps I dealt unkindly with him. But did God deal kindly with me? At least John was born defective. He didn't start out clever, then watch helplessly as his wits faded. He'll never realize that God chooses winners and losers. Understanding that fact is the root of all suffering."

Ben struggled to form an answer.

Mrs. Grundy laughed. "How handsome you look as you think up a high-minded rebuke," she said. "The furrow of your brow. The pout of your lips. If you'd developed Paget's disease of the bone at seventeen, if you'd been turned from beautiful to grotesque, no doubt you'd forgive everyone who snickered or looked away."

"I don't think so," Ben said. "But I don't think I'd kill anyone, either. When did you start playing the lady in black?"

"I don't know. Years ago. The passages were how I kept informed. Knew the truth about what people thought of me," Mrs. Grundy said. "One day Odette told Charlie my face would curdle milk. He said, maybe some of her cosmetics would help. They had a good laugh at that. Until that moment, I thought Charlie was my friend.

"But they payed for that laugh, didn't they?" she continued. "Charlie was found out and sacked, thanks to me dropping hints to Dudley. Odette cried herself to sleep every night. Then the lady in black paid her a midnight visit. Destroyed her vanity and made off with a few choice bits. I kept them in the Cavalier Room until Bobby bled on them."

"I'm surprised you didn't just wipe it off," Ben said, hearing the censure in his voice despite his best efforts not to judge. "But Mr. Collins threw them into the fire along with Bobby's clothes and the rug."

"Yes. Good of the pompous old arse, wasn't it? I was in a state. That's why I didn't just wipe the blood off, Dr. Bones.," Mrs. Grundy said. "I was too elated to think straight. I bundled all the incriminating bits in a rug and buried it in the garden. Not very deep, given the hard frosts, so Collins found it later. He decided to destroy it himself. I suppose he assumed Odette was guilty, and he was protecting the Park."

"Did you hate him and Kitty, too?" Ben asked. "Is that why you offered them up to Plymouth CID? So you could swan around a great house pretending to rule it while torturing the Maggarts?"

She tried to sit up, but the handcuff stopped her. If it hadn't, the deep gash in her leg would have done so. She paled as her movement jarred the wound but bit her lip rather than cry out.

"All right. No more thrashing about. Let me have a look." Ben lifted her skirt to check the dressing.

"Does it give you a thrill?"

"What? Seeing you've reopened it?" A fresh bloodstain marred the wrapped white gauze. Applying pressure to it, he continued, "Once I get it stopped, I'll put on a fresh dressing. You'll have to travel to Plymouth by ambulance. Don't let the detectives force you to move about too much. I did my best, but you won't be out of the woods until the wound is repaired by proper surgery."

"How heroic of you to save me, so the Crown may kill me in due course," Mrs. Grundy said. Reaching up with her unfettered hand, she clasped his wrist. Startled, Ben took it for a moment of vulnerability. Then she tried to pull his hand off the wound and down to someplace else. He jerked away.

"What are you *doing*?"

"So it truly doesn't give you a thrill. Me on my back with my skirt up," Mrs. Grundy said bitterly. "Even though the disease hardly affects me below the neck. Bobby knew that. Before this happened to my face, before he wed, he walked out with me, you know."

More of the pieces fell into place. "The furniture scheme came first, didn't it?" Ben asked. "Lady Maggart arranged something with Bobby's employer, then stepped back to let you oversee it. You and Bobby were thrown together by the scheme and started an affair. Did you expect him to divorce Helen for you?"

"Of course. Even though it started in the gutter," Mrs. Grundy said. "I wanted what every woman wants, and Bobby— Bobby was Bobby. I think the first time he was just having a laugh—me past forty, ugly, and a virgin. But I surprised him. Afterward, he came back once a week, and not for a laugh."

"But he didn't take you seriously," Ben said. "Not like Shelagh Trentham. He fell in love with her, so he asked Helen for a divorce. Is that why you killed him?"

"Yes. I only wish I could have done it more than once. I dream about that rush of blood, you know. I dream about it and wake up smiling. He was so offhand as he told me. He said, 'It's all over, Nan, but you knew it had to end. I'm divorcing Helen and marrying the youngest Trentham girl. Hannah will open a proper pub soon. A share in it will be the making of me.'"

The glint in her eyes was repulsive. Perhaps self-pity had driven her mad. Or the world's assumptions had convinced her to claim the role of monster.

A monster called Nan.

"When you first questioned me, I was a little afraid," she admitted. "I thought, because you were a physician, you'd see behind the mask. But you went right past me, didn't you? You suspected Lady Maggart and Kitty. Betsy and Mrs. Tippett, too, for all I know. But not me. All you saw was the mask."

Ben drew in a breath to call her a liar. Then he shut his mouth, opened his black bag, and applied a new dressing.

30

INTO THE STRATOSPHERE

17 DECEMBER 1939

F itchley Park was decked with boughs of holly, heavy with red berries. Spruce garlands perfumed the hall, and ribbon-tied bundles of mistletoe hung from the doorways. As the gathering was billed as a brunch, beginning around ten o'clock and meant to finish by three, Ben wasn't obligated to trot out his evening dress for the second time in a month. Like most of Lady Maggart's male guests, he wore his Sunday suit. Some of the women, like Old Mrs. Trentham, felt comfortable enough to mingle in a housedress accessorized with hand-knitted accessories. Others, like Mrs. Tippett, had made a special effort with dress and hair. Rarely more than a few steps from Father Rummage's side, she looked completely transformed, her newfound glow of happiness exceeded only by his.

"It's good to see you again," Ben told the erstwhile cook. "After everything that happened, I half-feared Mrs. Grundy had done something to you."

"I think she would have, had I loitered about to wait and see," Mrs. Tippett said. "There was a mad gleam in her eye at the end. Stephen told me I was welcome to stay at the rectory until I felt safe to return to the park. Of course, thanks to you, it only took a day, and yet...." She glanced at the beaming little man beside her. "Now it's all changed. I pop in every day at noon to check the new cook's progress. She'll be a Beaton devotee by the new year, mark me. By then, Stephen's replacement will have arrived at St. Gwinnodock's."

"That's right," Ben said, smiling at Father Rummage. "I see you're still in the dog collar."

"Yes." For once, the priest issued no nervous laugh. "My sabbatical officially begins shortly after Epiphany."

"And the wedding?"

"Sunday next," Father Rummage said. "I do hope you'll come and wish us joy."

"Try and stop me."

Ben paid his respects to Lady Maggart, who was discussing the WI's plans for 1940 with a knot of interested ladies. She was still under house arrest for the furniture scheme, but everyone pretended not to know, and according to the latest birdsong, the charges would soon go away. Lord Maggart had lied and told Scotland Yard he'd approved the liquidation. No one knew if this signaled a renewed bond between baron and baroness, but it had rescued Fitchley Park from further infamy, which Lord Maggart no doubt saw as his paramount duty.

Ben drifted toward the punchbowl. Betsy, on ladle duty, gave him a timid nod. Kitty, out of her maid's uniform and dressed in festive red, held out a cup for Betsy to fill, then pressed it into his hands.

"There he is! The man who rescued me from a life behind bars!"

"Hallo, Kitty. You look well," Ben said politely. "I hope your experience in Plymouth wasn't too harrowing."

"Cor. Harrowing is exactly right," she said. "Those wenches in uniform are bone-cruel. I cried myself to sleep, hoping some man would hear and take pity. But no one did. I think those wenches would have killed me in the end, if you hadn't sorted things out."

"I was lucky, that's all. But I heard you've left Fitchley Park. Someone even said you mean to leave Barking."

"While I'm young," Kitty agreed vehemently. "I could have died in this house. Can you imagine? After a life of nothing but scrubbing floors and boiling unmentionables. I've had it with village life. Time to see what Plymouth has on offer."

"What about your engagement to Mr. Collins?" Ben asked. The butler was back at his former post, none the worse for his own ordeal, except for his hair. Apparently lice had been prevalent in the men's lockup, forcing him to shave his once-luxuriant locks down to a quarter inch. The pink of his scalp shone as he made the rounds, but the guests tried not to stare.

"Him? Pull the other one," Kitty said. "I told him, 'Jasper, it's now or never. Take me away from Barking or let's shake hands and go our separate ways.' I should have known he'd never pick me over his lordship."

"Speaking of his lordship, he's ever so much better," Betsy put in meekly. "That's good news, isn't it?"

Kitty ignored that. "I still have the worry stone. I ought to fling it at Jasper's shiny bald head."

Excusing himself, Ben went to greet Lord Maggart, already less jaundiced and half a stone heavier. Mrs. Grundy's food tampering had shortened his life, and would no doubt contribute to its premature end, but he no longer had the look of a man at death's door. He might live another year, or five, or ten. It depended on what a full exam at St. Barnabas turned up, a prospect he had yet to agree to, but was considering. Given where they'd started, Ben was content to let his patient wait until after Christmas before pushing.

The punch was laced heavily with rum. Pleasantly surprised, Ben was contemplating a second cup when he saw Rose Jenkins. She lingered in the doorway, head positioned under a certain bunch of poisonous greenery.

Her back was to him. Maybe she was searching for someone else; maybe she was letting herself be seen. Either way, she was the prettiest woman in the room. Her red hair shone; her frock showed off her petite figure to full advantage.

Ben turned away. He didn't try to justify the decision to himself. He just did.

To the left of the mantel was a door he remembered from his search of Fitchley Park. It led to an old-fashioned smoking room. He decided to venture inside.

It was a pleasant space with walnut-paneled walls, Turkish carpets, and lots of red leather studded with brass. Altogether it would have been ludicrously masculine, if not for vase upon vase of fresh-cut flowers. Someone had cleared out a hothouse to stage the room for a champagne reception. In a bucket stand, a bottle of *Veuve Amiot* was already chilling in ice.

Ben decided to take refuge inside. Lady Juliet's Crossley wasn't among the cars parked out front, which meant Mr. and Mrs. Bolivar had yet to make their entrance. He didn't fancy being forced to hang about pretending happiness as they did. Ethan was sure to be insufferable, and the prospect of seeing Lady Juliet in person felt tricky. They'd spoken by telephone, of course—the rumor that Mrs. Grundy had tried to kill him had shot through Birdswing like pink eye through a pump room. Thanks to Lady Victoria and her open door, Ben felt certain the two of them could rekindle their friendship. But not at a party, with that strapping great mooncalf lurking about.

Besides, I don't want to fall back into the same pattern. Maybe I should ask Rose to the cinema. Or wise up and take a look about. There's sure to be a few women here I haven't met. Perhaps a blonde.

That hospital volunteer, Peggy—she was pretty enough to ask out to lunch someday. Clearly, he'd judged her far too harshly for speaking ill of Mrs. Grundy. Perhaps he owed her a second look.

Blondes on his mind, he headed for the sitting area facing the window. Two overstuffed armchairs overlooked the east lawn, which offered leafless trees and the odd patch of green. As if conjured by his thoughts, a woman with honey-blonde hair sat in a chair, head tilted as if dozing. Her smart bob, enlivened by finger waves, emphasized an elegant neck and glittering teardrop earrings. Was this Peggy? Or had he stumbled across a new possibility?

She yawned, putting aside a book and sitting up straighter. Not dozing, then.

This is exactly what I need, he thought. *To chat up a woman who makes me feel like a man.*

His suit was pressed, his shave was close, and his hair approached Mr. Collins's pre-arrest perfection. He liked his chances.

"A party's all very well, but I needed a break from the conspicuous gaiety," he announced, strolling forth to introduce himself. "It seems you did—"

He broke off. The next word, "too," had gone out of his head, possibly never to return. "I... er...."

"Dr. Bones. Sorry I was hiding in here. You know me and parties. I always escape to read for a bit if I can manage. Besides... I was a little shy of seeing you again."

The voice confirmed that he was looking at Lady Juliet. It was uncanny. He didn't know what to say, but he had to say something.

"You look stunning," he mumbled. "I can't believe it."

She raised both eyebrows.

"Sorry. That is to say...." He stopped, took a deep breath, and tried again. "When did you become a blonde?"

"Round about the time Lord Maggart saved your life, I think," Lady Juliet said, crossing her legs at the ankles. She sounded composed, but color was rising in her cheeks. For the first time since they'd met, she was made up. The cosmetics were so skillfully applied, the change seemed almost like a flattering trick of the light: complexion more even, lips redder, eyelashes jet-black.

"It suits you." He stuck his hands in his pockets, pulled them out, and tried to remember what he usually did with them. The aura of casual interest he'd perfected with Rose had deserted him.

"So does the, er...." His hands waved about absurdly, indicating the sapphire blue dress. It celebrated her proportions instead of trying to conceal them, emphasizing her broad shoulders and that unexpectedly graceful neck. He wondered what it would be like to lift her hair and brush his lips along a soft, hidden curl.

"What is it? Have I got it wrong?" Lady Juliet sounded worried. "Is it the fête all over again?"

"No, no. It's just—my detection skills must be failing. I missed the Crossley parked out front."

"That's because it's parked out back. Ethan and I brought these flowers," she said, indicating the extravagant blooms. "It was easiest to take them through the tradesman's entrance. We brought the champagne, too. For a toast in your honor."

"Oh. I see. Well. I'm glad you and Lady Maggart called a truce. But I'm not sure I deserve all this. I didn't realize what Mrs. Grundy was about until it was nearly too late."

"Odette's alive because of you. You're the hero of the hour. Act like it," Lady Juliet said, sounding more like her old self now that she was telling him what to do. "I heard you went to Plymouth to give evidence. I do hope it went well."

"It did," Ben said. "Justice will be done."

"And it's already been done in Mrs. Grundy's case. Self-inflicted," Lady Juliet said. "Unless you think it was an accident. How her wound reopened in the night."

"No. I warned her. She must have flexed her leg when Gaston wasn't looking. Then lay there, bleeding to death, in total silence." Ben sighed. "Maybe it's for the best. It spares Lord and Lady Maggart from further scrutiny. It will also keep the details of her affair with Bobby from getting back to the twins. Still, I can't help feeling like the world failed her. She accused me of romanticizing her because of her deformity. Perhaps I did. In which case, my empathy was wasted."

"I used to worry about that when a charitable scheme flopped. As if my goodwill had been squandered by the undeserving," Lady Juliet said. "But now I've come to believe kindness is never wasted. Genuine interest in another person always opens a door, if only within ourselves."

"You really are one of a kind," Ben said. "And I was an arse when I left you alone at Fenton House. Forgive me."

Tears sprang to her eyes. She blinked awkwardly. "I don't know what to do. I'm not used to mascara. They warned me quite severely not to rub my face."

"Let me." Gently, he swept away a tear as it fell. "There. Good as new."

"Ju! His Lordship found it," a familiar hearty voice intruded. "A saber to open the champagne. Good thing the merry murderess didn't use it to cut throats, or we wouldn't—oh-ho! Bonesy! This room was meant to be off-limits. You've cracked the case on our little tribute."

Reluctantly, Ben turned. Ethan Bolivar was wearing another "blacker-than-black" suit. Its glossy midnight blue undertones would perfectly complement Lady Juliet's dress when they stood side-by-side. But instead of barging in between them, Ethan remained where he was, fingering the ceremonial sword. The gold tassel hanging from the D-guard caught a ray of sunlight and gleamed.

"You're going to open a bottle with a sword?" Ben asked.

"With a sword and with style. Sabrage is a vanishing art," Ethan said. "French in origin. Napoleonic, I think. The ladies love it."

"I don't know how you discover these things," Lady Juliet said.

"I only just said. The ladies love it." Ethan slashed playfully at the air. "Arise, my darling. Your ensemble isn't seen at its best when seated."

"I don't mean to be rude. Darling." She tacked on the endearment with such woodenness that it would have made Ben laugh, had he not been obligated to feign belief. "But could Dr. Bones and I have a moment alone?"

"Oh. Yes. Certainly." Ethan slashed at the air again. "I'll just make the rounds in the other room. Show off the saber and all that."

"I'm sorry," Lady Juliet murmured as Ethan exited. "He won't be around forever. Business will call him away before long. No doubt you think me mad. It's only... the truth is ...."

Ben couldn't let her break her oath. "Ethan's right," he interrupted. "You really must stand up. Let me see you in those heels." He nodded at her black patent-leather pumps.

"These? Mother insisted, but they're devilish hard to walk in. Besides, they make me so tall, I feel as if there's a beanstalk I ought to climb."

"Nonsense. Stand up."

She did. In heels, her legs were elongated and nothing less

than spectacular. She was also three inches taller, forcing him to lift his chin to take her all in.

"See? They propel me into the stratosphere," Lady Juliet said.

"Yes." He smiled. "And there's no one I'd rather look up to."

— THE
END

31

FROM THE AUTHOR

I hope you've enjoyed book two of this series, the *Dr. Benjamin Bones Mysteries*. If the ending left you wanting more (and I hope it did!) please have a look at *Dr. Bones and the Christmas Wish*. It takes place a few days after the conclusion of this book, and will answer at least one burning question, I promise.

I had so much fun writing *Dr. Bones and the Christmas Wish*, I decided to write another novella, *Dr. Bones and the Lost Love Letter*. Look for it in February 2017.

For those who've enjoyed my Lord & Lady Hetheridge mystery series, I want to assure you it will absolutely continue, hopefully as long as I continue! I'm already at work on book #5, *Blue Blooded*.

So thank you for reading *Divorce Can Be Deadly*, and if you enjoyed it, please consider leaving a brief review. Reviews are the lifeblood of my mysteries, and honest reviews make all the difference in a book that's noticed and a book that goes unread.

Cheers!

Emma Jameson

32
ACKNOWLEDGEMENTS

The author would like to thank her expert early readers, Kate Aaron and J. David Peterson, for their help with countless small details. It is a truth universally acknowledged that no matter how many history books you read, or how many times you turn to Google, there's no substitute for a conversation with an expert. In the event that errors, like bombers, still got through, those errors belong to me alone.

The author would also like to thank the following priceless early readers, most of whom are published authors: Shéa MacLeod, Karin Cox, Alisa Tangredi, Tara West, and Mary Ellen Wofford. Cheers!

MORE BY EMMA JAMESON

- Ice Blue (Lord & Lady Hetheridge Book 1)
- Blue Murder (Lord & Lady Hetheridge Book 2)
- Something Blue (Lord & Lady Hetheridge Book 3)
- Black & Blue (Lord & Lady Hetheridge Book 4)
- Coming Soon: Blue Blooded (Lord & Lady Hetheridge Book 5)

Made in the USA
Columbia, SC
15 April 2020